W9-ASW-798

Too Wilde to Tame

Too Wilde to Tame

JANELLE DENISON

BERKLEY SENSATION, NEW YORK

THE BERKLEY PUBLISHING GROUP
Published by the Penguin Group
Penguin Group (USA) Inc.
375 Hudson Street, New York, New York 10014, USA
Penguin Group (Canada), 90 Eglinton Avenue East, Suite 700, Toronto, Ontario M4P 2Y3, Canada
(a division of Pearson Penguin Canada Inc.)
Penguin Books Ltd., 80 Strand, London WC2R 0RL, England
Penguin Group Ireland, 25 St. Stephen's Green, Dublin 2, Ireland (a division of Penguin Books Ltd.)
Penguin Group (Australia), 250 Camberwell Road, Camberwell, Victoria 3124, Australia
(a division of Pearson Australia Group Pty. Ltd.)
Penguin Books India Pvt. Ltd., 11 Community Centre, Panchsheel Park, New Delhi—110 017, India
Penguin Group (NZ), Cnr. Airborne and Rosedale Roads, Albany, Auckland 1310, New Zealand
(a division of Pearson New Zealand Ltd.)
Penguin Books (South Africa) (Pty.) Ltd., 24 Sturdee Avenue, Rosebank, Johannesburg 2196,
South Africa

Penguin Books Ltd., Registered Offices: 80 Strand, London WC2R 0RL, England

TOO WILDE TO TAME

A Berkley Sensation Book / published by arrangement with the author

Cover art by Gregg Gulbronson.
Cover design by Lesley Worrell.
Interior text design by Stacy Irwin.

For information address: The Berkley Publishing Group,
a division of Penguin Group (USA) Inc., 375 Hudson Street, New York, New York 10014.

ISBN: 0-7394-5914-7

BERKLEY® SENSATION
Berkley Sensation Books are published by The Berkley Publishing Group,
a division of Penguin Group (USA) Inc.,
375 Hudson Street, New York, New York 10014.

PRINTED IN THE UNITED STATES OF AMERICA

To my Plotmonkey Pals: Carly Phillips, Julie Leto, and Leslie Kelly. I treasure our circle of friendship and our yearly plotting trips. I couldn't have pulled this one off without you guys! Happy 40th Birthday to us all!

To Carly Phillips, for blessing my life with your unconditional friendship. You are my soul-sister in every way!

A special thank you to Jenny Bent, agent extraordinaire! Thank you for believing in me, my writing, and for taking my career to new heights. I wouldn't be here without you.

As always, to my husband, Don, for putting up with me during insane deadlines (which is all the time!). I love you more each day.

Dear Readers,

For all of you who have been anxiously awaiting Cameron Sinclair and Mia Wilde's story—here it is! Out of all the Wilde stories I've written, this one has been the most anticipated—and my personal favorite to date. When I first created the Wilde family, I knew that Mia's story would be something special, especially since she was the only girl and the baby of the family. When Mia and Cameron made their first appearance together in *Wilde Thing,* there was no denying who she was meant to be with. From the get-go, the chemistry between these two was smoldering hot, and in *Too Wilde to Tame,* all it took was one unbelievably hot kiss to send these two over the edge and into a fiery, passionate relationship that takes them both by surprise.

As I was writing *Too Wilde to Tame* I discovered that there was so much more to Mia than her outrageous personality and smart mouth. I learned that she'd been deeply and emotionally affected by her mother's death, and as Cameron and I gradually began to peel away the layers of that sexy facade she hid behind, we both revealed a woman who was hiding a wealth of insecurities. It took a special man like Cameron to understand and accept who Mia really was, and finally be the one to embrace that wild spirit of hers.

For those of you who might be reading about the Wilde family for the first time, I hope you enjoy this story enough to want to read about the rest of the Wilde gang. So far, there are six stories (with more to come!), and those books can still be found at your favorite on-line book source or at your local bookstore.

Once you finish *Too Wilde to Tame,* I'm certain you're going to want to know if Joel Wilde is going to get his own story. Yes, he is! I have a bodyguard-type story in mind for him that is going to be hot, hot, hot! His story will spin off into my Elite series and will feature five new sexy heroes who served in the Marines together and who are now all working for the same security specialist firm.

For now, enjoy Mia and Cameron's story, and be sure to visit my website at www.janelledenison.com to read more about the Wilde series, check out my upcoming releases, and enter my monthly giveaway contest.

Happy Reading!

Janelle Denison
www.janelledenison.com

Too Wilde to Tame

One

CAMERON Sinclair took a long, satisfying pull on his ice-cold bottle of beer as he surveyed the newest hot spot to open in downtown Chicago. The Electric Blue was definitely *the* happening place, and Cam could easily see why. It wasn't your normal laid-back bar atmosphere, but rather the place combined the frenzied excitement of a nightclub with all the shocking yet riveting antics worthy of a roadhouse saloon—where customers were having Screaming Orgasms, demanding Blow Jobs, and enjoying Slippery Nipples. The drinks, that is, he thought in amusement.

The place certainly didn't lack for entertainment. And as a people-watcher by profession, Cam was definitely stimulated and intrigued by the ambiance, the customers, and the décor. A huge oak bar with shiny brass trim covered the length of one long wall. Behind it, three bartenders were filling the constant barrage of drink orders while juggling bottles of liquor in the air and grooving to the beat of the rock 'n' roll music the DJ was playing.

Cameron was sitting on a barstool up on a higher level across the room, which overlooked the main bar area and afforded him, and his good friend Rick, the best view in the house. In front of where they were sitting extended a thick, sturdy, two-foot-wide platform with floor-to-ceiling brass poles on either end, which, according to Rick, the waiters and waitresses used as their own personal dance floor to rile up the crowd whenever one of the bartenders rang a loud, obnoxious cowbell every half hour.

The dance floor, also on the same higher level, was fully packed with gyrating bodies and scantily clad women, and a banner across the back wall proclaimed tonight "Wet T-shirt Night." That was the main reason why Rick had coaxed him into joining him for a beer at The Electric Blue. His friend believed Cameron was spending way too much time at work and not enough time having fun and enjoying the opposite sex.

Okay, so it had been a while since Cameron had been out with a woman on a casual, no-strings basis. Longer still since he'd been in a committed relationship. His heavy caseload and erratic hours as a P.I. were mainly responsible for his lack of female companionship, and after the busy week he'd had at work, Cameron decided what he needed was exactly what Rick had suggested. A fun, entertaining evening—and The Electric Blue promised to deliver all that, and more.

Cameron took another drink of his beer, feeling his body unwind and his mind open to the possibilities of what the night might hold.

"Well, well, well," a familiar, sultry female voice drawled from behind him, followed by the sensual trail of fingertips along his shoulders as she came to stand in front of him. "What's a nice, straight-laced guy like you doing in a place like this?"

Cam recognized the soft, taunting voice before he saw the face that went with it, and every muscle in his body grew taut with immediate awareness.

Mia Wilde—an infuriatingly smart-mouthed woman who had the ability to frustrate the hell out of him with her bold and brash ways, as well as tempt him beyond reason with her innate sensuality. Despite all the reasons why this certain female was all wrong for him—and there were many—*she* was the main reason why no other woman had appealed to him in a very long time.

Maintaining a bland expression, Cam slowly, leisurely glanced up the length of her figure, taking in her sexy bare legs and smooth, supple-looking thighs that never failed to make him entertain sinful, erotic thoughts. Her curvaceous hip was cocked sassily to the side, and she was wearing a short leopard print mini-skirt that was barely street legal, along with a tight black top with "Too Wild to Tame" emblazoned in sparkling rhinestones across her ample chest.

He almost laughed out loud. The flashy slogan was very appropriate, not because of the similarity to Mia's last name but because this particular woman was unpredictable, headstrong, and aggressive enough to make any sane man dismiss the notion of ever trying to subdue that assertive nature of hers.

Him included. He liked his women modest, manageable, and undemanding. And Mia was anything but those things. She was a woman who didn't know the meaning of demure and refused to conform to anyone's rules but her own. She liked being in control and was used to getting her way, especially when it came to men. One come-hither smile, one crook of her finger, and the male gender turned into whipped little puppies who were eager to please while hoping for more of her attention.

And Cam knew, beyond that sexy, confident facade Mia presented in front of him, deep inside it irked the hell out of her that he was immune to her sensual charms. Or at least that's what he'd spent the past two years pretending. No way would he ever give her the satisfaction, or the leverage, of knowing she affected him on a sexual level—and that only made her all the more determined to prove that he *did* have the hots for her.

It was an ongoing battle between them, a push-pull kind of magnetism that always generated a whole lot of heat and lust whenever their paths happen to cross. Which was much too often lately for his peace of mind and sanity.

Finally, his lazy gaze reached her face, and he had to admit it was one of great beauty. Silky, tousled shoulder-length black hair framed her exquisite features and added to her exotic look. Her complexion was smooth and creamy, and she possessed the kind of lush, Angelina Jolie mouth that inspired all kinds of provocative, X-rated fantasies. Those full lips were painted a soft, shimmering peach hue, and when he reached her gaze, her smoky silver eyes glimmered impudently, prompting him to remember the question she'd just asked, along with the fact that she'd pretty much accused him of being stuffy and boring.

No big surprise there.

He leaned back in his seat and regarded her with mild interest. "So what, exactly, do you consider this place?"

"Hip. Fun. Trendy." She took a sip of her drink, which looked like a frothy piña colada, and then her glossy lips curled up in one of those slow, cheeky smiles of hers. "You know, the exact opposite of your uptight personality," she said as she glided a finger along the collar of his knit shirt and down the buttoned V neck.

Beside him, Rick chuckled at her reply, and Cam shot his friend a withering glare. "Don't encourage her," he muttered.

As soon as Cameron addressed his friend, Mia turned her gaze toward Rick, curiosity lighting up her eyes. "Who's your friend, sugar?"

Rick, as much of a bachelor as Cameron was, looked eager to make Mia's acquaintance. Too eager, Cam thought in annoyance, but made the introduction anyway. "This is Mia Wilde. Mia, this is a friend of mine, Rick."

Rick's brows rose in surprise. "Any relation to your business partner?" he asked Cameron, obviously recognizing her last name.

"Yes, I'm Steve Wilde's cousin," she said before Cameron had the chance to explain. Completely ignoring Cam, she extended her slender hand toward Rick, who didn't refuse the opportunity to touch her. "It's a pleasure to meet you."

She poured on the flirtatious charm, and that easily she ensnared herself yet another besotted admirer. Rick grinned at her, completely captivated. "Ummm, likewise."

Their handshake lingered longer than necessary, and despite Cam's resolve to keep his involvement with Mia on a casual, amicable level because of his business partnership with her cousin Steve, he felt the unfamiliar stirring of envy rising to the surface. And that wasn't a good sign, considering he didn't give a damn who Mia set her sights on.

Or so he sternly reminded himself.

His fingers tightened around his bottle of beer. "So, who are you here with?" he asked abruptly, recognizing his own ploy to interrupt the warm, cozy moment between Mia and Rick.

"I came with my roommate Gina and her new boyfriend, Ray, and another friend, Carrie." She pointed to a table across the way where her three friends were sitting and then tipped her head toward Cameron and cast him a sly, knowing look. "Were you wondering if I came here with a date?"

"Does it look like I care?" He tipped his beer to his lips and took a long drink.

She leaned in close, her lashes falling half-mast over her beguiling gray eyes. "Oh, you care, sugar," she said in a low, husky tone that was as intimate as a caress. "You don't want to, but you do."

He watched her lips move as she spoke and inhaled the sweet, fruity scent of her drink on her breath. His gut clenched with a smoldering heat and desire, giving too much credence to her words.

With effort, he managed a cool, indifferent response. "Don't flatter yourself, sweetheart."

Mocking laughter lit up her gaze. "And you just keep trying to fool yourself into believing otherwise." Straightening, she set her glass on the table and redirected her attention back to Rick. "So, would you like to dance?"

Rick replied with an enthusiastic "Sure" at the same time Cameron said, "We're not here to dance."

Too late, he realized just how ridiculous he sounded—especially considering they were in a bar with a DJ and dance floor. But dammit, he didn't want her dancing with Rick.

He swore beneath his breath.

"Obviously *you're* not here to have a good time, but Rick *is,*" Mia said, taking the opportunity to point out just how stuffy she thought Cameron really was. She held out her hand toward his friend and gave him a dazzling smile no red-blooded man could resist. "I'm looking for a dance partner. You interested?"

Rick jumped up and grabbed Mia's hand, nearly knocking over his barstool in his haste to accept her offer. "I'm not about to refuse a lady."

Cameron snorted at the term *lady,* but his attempt at sarcasm was lost in the wake of their departure. Annoyed at Mia's calculated attempt to provoke him, which had worked too well, he watched as the two of them made their way through the throng of people in the bar and up to the crowded dance floor.

The loud, upbeat music combined with the pulsing colored lights flashing above the dance stage encouraged a person to shed inhibitions and move to the suggestive rhythm—and Mia didn't hesitate to do exactly that. Despite all the other women bumping and grinding up on the stage in tight, skimpy outfits, his gaze never strayed from Mia—and every once in a while he caught her glancing his way as well, as if to make certain he was watching her have a good time with his friend.

Every one of her movements were damn sexy and arousing, and he couldn't help but notice he wasn't the only guy in the place who was drawn to her. She was naturally sensual, her body loose and unrestrained as she rolled and swayed her hips in time to the music. Then she turned, raised her hands above her head in sheer abandonment, and shimmied her curvaceous backside against the front of Rick's jeans. Rick made a grab for Mia's hips to pull her closer, and she laughed and easily slipped away in a lithe move that was as playful as it was teasing.

Cam clenched his jaw, along with his fist, shocked by the uncharacteristic and too-possessive urge he had to plant his knuckles against Rick's jaw for being way too intimate with Mia—even if *she'd* been the one to encourage his friend to be a little touchy-feely in her attempt to incite some kind of reaction out of Cam.

Typical Mia. She never missed an opportunity to taunt, tease, and provoke him in her never-ending quest to see just how far she could push him before he finally snapped and gave in to the heat and attraction simmering between them.

It wasn't going to happen, he vowed. He'd spent the past two years resisting her, and no way would she ever find out just how much she aroused him, and just how badly he wanted her. Doing so would undoubtedly be his biggest downfall and her greatest triumph.

Forcing his fingers to relax, he drained the last of his beer, which did nothing to ease the burn of frustration churning in his belly.

"Would you like to dance?"

Startled by the question because he hadn't been aware anyone had approached him, Cam glanced at the woman who'd issued the invitation. He instantly recognized the pretty redhead as Carrie, the friend Mia had pointed out earlier as one of the women she'd come to the bar with.

Her expression was hopeful and expectant, and he hated to be the one to deliver a rejection, but he wasn't in the mood to join Mia and Rick on the dance floor. "I'm sorry, but I'm not much of a dancer," he said with a friendly smile, trying to let her down as gently as possible.

She looked at Mia, then back at him, something akin to resentment flaring in the depths of her hazel eyes. "Sure, I understand."

She turned around and walked away. Cam frowned, finding her sudden change in attitude totally bizarre, considering she was a friend of Mia's, but Cam didn't have time to contemplate the woman's behavior for long. One of the bartenders rang a loud cowbell, and more bedlam broke loose in the bar.

The DJ put on "Legs" by ZZ Top, and the crowd went wild. Their ecstatic cheers and whistles seemed to reverberate off the walls as the cocktail waitresses and waiters jumped onto the surface of the bar and platforms and gave their audience quite a dance performance. The guys threw in some outrageous bump and grinds for the female customers, while the girls strutted their stuff in their low-riding jeans and their cleavage- and midriff-flaunting bar shirts.

Above Cam, one of the cocktail waitresses tried to grab his attention with a provocative dance move. Any other time he would have appreciated the girl's flirtations and rewarded it with a wink and a grin, but not tonight. He was too obsessed with a woman who had him completely tied up in knots.

Once the song was over he ordered another beer and was grateful to see Rick and Mia finally leave the dance floor. Mia said something to his friend, and they parted ways. Rick made his way back to the table with a goofy, infatuated grin on his face, while she headed toward the bar where she bought herself another one of those frothy, froufrou drinks. Then she met up with Carrie, the woman he'd turned down earlier, who was talking to a young guy who barely looked old enough to drink the beer he held in his hand.

As soon as Mia arrived, the guy's attention shifted from Carrie to Mia. Once again Cam watched her friend's posture stiffen and her expression change because of Mia's uninvited appearance, along with the fact that the guy Carrie had been talking to now barely acknowledged her. Though Mia spoke to both of them, it was clear to Cameron that she was oblivious to the underlying jealousy Carrie seemingly harbored against her.

"God, she's hot," Rick said as he settled into the seat next to Cam and finished off the rest of the beer left in his bottle.

"She's a royal pain in my ass," Cam muttered irritably. Not to mention she gave him a serious ache in other parts of his male anatomy.

"Then you wouldn't mind if I hooked up with her, right?"

Without thinking of what his actions might imply, Cameron shot Rick an ominous look that said way too much about his feelings toward Mia.

Rick immediately held up his hands in supplication and grinned knowingly. "Hey, say no more. But if I don't hook up with her, you've got to see that at least a dozen other guys in this place will."

The waitress came by with his second beer, and Cameron drained half of it in one drink. "I don't give a damn what Mia does, or with whom."

Rick laughed heartily at that. "You're a piss-poor liar, Sinclair. It's pretty obvious that she makes you hot, bothered, and very tense. You clench that beer bottle any tighter in your fist, and it's going to shatter," he said, pointing out just how on edge Mia had made him. After a moment, he asked, "What's the deal with you two, anyway?"

Wasn't that a loaded question, Cam thought. And where did he start in his explanation?

"I've known Mia since she was a teenager because of my friendship with her cousin, Steve, and his brothers, but it's only been in the past few years that she's—"

"Gotten under your skin?" Rick said with a smirk.

There was no use denying the truth. Not to his good friend who obviously knew better and had no qualms calling him on his pretense to feign otherwise. "Yeah."

"So why not just go for it?"

Such a simple solution for such a complicated situation. "Because she's so *not* my type. She's wild, brazen, and unpredictable." Having grown up with three older sisters and a mother who were stable, focused, and more on the refined side, now that he was in his thirties he'd come to appreciate and look for those sophisticated and dependable qualities in a woman.

And then there was the issue of Mia's brothers and cousins, who'd be none too happy if they found out he'd slept with their sister and the baby of the family. The Wilde men tended to be a protective group when it came to one of their own, Mia especially, and despite her continual efforts to rebuff their paternal instincts, Cam wasn't about to chance their wrath or screw up his working relationship with Steve because he couldn't keep his hands off Mia.

Cam shook his head and stated the other important fact. "I'm sure I'm nothing more than a conquest to her, like every other man before me."

Rick considered that for a moment and then shrugged. "I don't see how that's a bad thing."

Rick was a quintessential ladies' man who wasn't looking to settle down anytime soon. "Of course *you* wouldn't, but personally, I have no desire to be a notch in her bedpost." And Cam was certain she had many. "Besides, one-night stands just don't do it for me anymore."

He'd lost that urge a while ago, when he'd come to realize that sex for sex's sake left him feeling empty and craving something deeper that had so far been elusive to him. He supposed a part of that decision had evolved after witnessing just how happy and content his partner Steve was with his wife, Liz, and their new baby boy. He'd watched Steve go from being a confirmed bachelor to devoted husband and a doting, hands-on father, and the transformation was an amazing, inspiring sight to see.

Now, these days when Cam slept with a woman, it was important to him that there was something more substantial to back up the physical release. Like an emotional connection and some kind of commitment that made the romantic affair more meaningful and worthwhile. And from what he'd seen with Mia over the years, she lacked the ability to sustain a long-term relationship with any of the guys she'd dated.

One of the bartenders announced the wet T-shirt contest and encouraged the women in the place to enter, luring them in with a cash prize of a hundred bucks. The customers cheered enthusiastically, and Cameron paid no attention to the frenzy as the DJ put on the song "Do Ya Think I'm Sexy" by Rod Stewart to rile up the crowd and contestants.

A headache started throbbing in his temples, and he'd just decided it was time to leave and go home when he heard a loud, raucous sound that made him, and Rick, glance toward the dance floor. What Cam next laid eyes on hit him like a solid punch to the stomach.

There was Mia, a willing and sexy participant of the contest, along with a dozen other adventurous women. All the ladies had changed into the bar's white T-shirts that were cropped to expose their stomachs and were deliberately a size too small so the soft cotton molded to their breasts. That was nothing compared to how the fabric adhered to their curves as the waiters poured a pitcherful of water over each contestant's chest.

And it was obviously *very* cold water at that.

Rick gaped right along with him. "Holy . . ."

"Shit," Cameron bit out succinctly.

"You can say that again," Rick said humorously.

Cameron almost did, except his mouth had suddenly gone dry as dust. He stared at Mia and the way she looked in clinging, wet cotton, certain she'd had too much to drink and wasn't thinking with a clear head. Yes, she was bold and outrageous, but he'd never known her to be an exhibitionist. Alcohol *had* to be clouding her judgment tonight. There was no other lucid explanation for this scandalous display of hers.

Most of the women were completely bare beneath their now see-through T-shirts, but a few of them had opted to keep their bras on. And thank God Mia was one of those women, Cam thought gratefully, because he was certain he would have had a heart attack if she'd gone *au naturel* in front of all these strangers.

Still, that thin, damp material molded to her full, shapely breasts and tight nipples like a second skin, and it was apparent that her bra was sheer, lacy, and unpadded. That provocative peek at her sexy lingerie left enough to the male imagination, yet also made her look far more alluring and seductive than the other girls who'd dared to go braless.

Desire flowed hot and molten through Cam's veins, along with an unholy amount of lust. Both of those physical reactions were becoming way too frequent when it came to Mia—and they were unwanted as hell.

When all the women were soaked, it was up to each contestant to draw as much energy and excitement from the crowd to ultimately win the contest. A group of frat boys had surged toward the stage and were spurring on Mia with catcalls and whistles as she worked to earn her share of attention—of which she had plenty. Her hips swayed to the beat of the music, and she caressed her hand across her bare, wet, sleek stomach, sending the young bucks into another round of enthusiastic cheers.

Jealousy twisted like a sharp knife in Cameron's belly, and he was fairly certain that was exactly the response from him Mia was hoping for. Still, somehow he managed to remain outwardly composed as he continued to watch her too-arousing performance.

Her skirt had inched up higher on her legs, exposing way too much of those smooth, toned thighs of hers, but she didn't seem to notice . . . or care. Her lustrous hair swung around her shoulders as she tossed her head back and laughed, her eyes sparkling seductively as her gaze latched onto him and she gave him a slow, bewitching smile that spoke volumes.

Gut instinct told him she didn't give a damn if she won. This performance was all for him, and him alone. She was deliberately tempting him. Teasing him. Daring him to let go and have *fun,* with her.

Under normal circumstances, he would have walked away from this latest antic of hers and chalked it up to another battle of the sexes between them. But this time, he couldn't do it.

Cam knew without a doubt that if it was one of his sisters up there on that stage in a wet, see-through T-shirt and too-short skirt, and one of his friends was in the audience, he'd want them to be sure she got the hell out of there and home safely. As it was, there was too much potential of some stranger taking advantage of her inebriated state. Being a P.I. and having investigated too many sexual assault cases, he was well aware of the possible dangers this kind of atmosphere bred—especially when half the men in the place had their eye on a certain woman and that hot little body of hers.

Then there was the issue of Mia's brothers. If it ever got back to one of her siblings that he'd left their baby sister in this bar in her condition, or if something happened to her because he'd decided to leave, he knew *his* ass would be on the line. And her brothers and cousins aside, he couldn't live with himself if he abandoned her.

A raw expletive escaped him. God, she was pure trouble. The bane of his existence. And this situation proved it.

She wanted a reaction out of him? Well, she was about to get one, he decided.

Two

UP on the dance floor, Mia continued to work the crowd with a shimmy and a shake, but her gaze remained locked on Cameron, who was currently pushing his way through the throng of unruly patrons and toward the stage. His normally sensual lips were stretched into a grim line, and his green eyes blazed with a simmering anger. That very fine body of his was wired with determination and an underlying impatience that didn't bode well for her.

And still, none of those negative vibes he was giving off detracted from just how devastatingly gorgeous the man was. And sexy. And so incredibly hot. Cameron Sinclair was all male, from his thick tousled dark blonde hair, to those wide shoulders of his, to his lean hips and strong-looking thighs . . . and certainly everything in between.

And she'd wanted him for a very long time.

Unfortunately, Cameron Sinclair had remained elusive to her. He'd presented quite a challenge over the years and most especially lately, but that's exactly what she liked about him and what attracted her so strongly.

He was so far removed from all the other guys she'd dated, most of whom she'd easily managed to wrap around her finger in no time flat. And once that happened, the thrill of the chase always diminished, her interest in them waned, and she'd end the brief affair. It was a cycle she was well familiar with and one she used to protect her heart and emotions.

But Cam wasn't one to bend to her will. At least not without a whole lot of provocation—like her impulsive decision to enter the wet T-shirt contest, all as a harmless, fun ploy to make Cameron squirm. Except tonight, it appeared she'd finally managed to crack that staunch control of his. And she couldn't wait to see how this situation between them played out.

As he neared the steps to the dance floor, his darkened gaze shifted back to her. A rush of adrenaline shot through her veins, and a heady mixture of awareness and delicious anticipation curled low in her belly. Going with the wicked urge to ruffle his feathers just a bit more, she lifted her hands to her hair and made sure he was watching as she slowly wet her bottom lip with her tongue and rolled her hips in a sinuous dance move that was as seductive as it was suggestive.

There was no mistaking the desire that flared to life in his striking eyes, and she reveled in that small victory. Cam might have spent months skirting the electric chemistry between them, but she'd seen enough proof lately to confirm that he was far from immune to her and their attraction.

Now it was just a matter of finally doing something about all that potent sexual tension that had them both so on edge around one another.

Reaching the dance floor, he crossed the stage to her, ignoring the way the other participants tried to entice him into joining them in the wet T-shirt contest. His gaze never wavered from Mia's, except to briefly skim over the front of her damp top in a heated caress. In response, her nipples tightened into tingling, sensitive points against her lacy bra. It amazed her how Cameron didn't even have to physically touch her to coax a sensual reaction out of her body. He was the only man she'd ever known who possessed that impressive talent.

He halted directly in front of her so the customers in the bar no longer had a clear view of her or their exchange. "Show's over, sweetheart," he announced, his direct, blunt approach leaving no room for argument.

She stopped dancing, amused by this macho, take-charge side to Cameron. Normally all she saw was the uptight and gruff attitude, and while she supposed that curt tone intimidated some people, she took it as an invitation to be just as daring.

"Says who?" she challenged.

"Me." With that, he grasped her wrist, started down the stairs, and tugged her along behind him—amidst whoops and ribald remarks from the male patrons cheering him on.

Unwilling to be a passive female to his caveman routine, she pulled back and finagled her arm from his grasp. "I'm not ready to leave yet." She turned and headed down the corridor leading to the restrooms.

Behind her, she heard him curse at her defiant maneuver and she bit back a smile. She so loved getting the best of Cameron whenever the opportunity presented itself, especially because it didn't happen often.

Halfway down the hallway, he caught up to her. In a quick, lithe move, he had her back pressed up against the wall with his strong, muscular arms braced on either side of her shoulders so this time she couldn't escape him—at least not easily. Raw frustration etched his expression as he stared down at her, his entire body taut as he tried to keep a firm rein on the temper she knew was simmering right below the surface.

"Dammit, Mia," he said through gritted teeth. "You've obviously had too much to drink and you're not thinking straight. I'm not about to leave you here in your condition. Your brothers would be furious with me if I didn't at least be sure you got home safely."

Ahhh, now she understood where all his high-handedness was coming from. He obviously believed she was intoxicated, and for some ridiculous reason he was driven to save her from herself. Well, she wasn't impressed with his chivalry. In fact, his do-good deed only chafed at her more rebellious side and made her want to buck this charitable gesture of his.

Anger nipped at her own emotions, and she inhaled a deep, calming breath. God, why was it that every man in her life thought it was his duty to keep her safe and sheltered and protected like a weak female? They treated her as though she couldn't take care of herself on her own. Especially her brothers and cousins, and now, it seemed Cameron had also developed the urge to join the ranks by assuming the worst of her condition and making sure she had a chaperone home.

His grand and honorable intention was the very last thing she wanted from him.

She ought to set him straight and tell him she was far from drunk—not even close after two lightweight piña coladas that contained more fruit juice than alcohol—but what was the fun in that, she decided. However, on a brighter, more appealing note, if stuffy, uptight Cameron Sinclair continued to believe she was tipsy, she might be able to get away with all sorts of outrageous and wicked mischief.

And that was certainly *her* idea of fun.

That thought improved her mood immensely, because she'd love nothing more than putting one over on this man. If he had the inclination to rescue what he perceived as a damsel in distress, who was she to argue? She'd give him exactly that—a helpless woman in need of saving—until she decided it was time to end the farce and prove to him that she'd been completely lucid the entire time.

The look on his face when he realized the joke was on him was bound to be priceless and worth a good laugh.

With that in mind, she let her body relax and glanced up at him from beneath heavy-lidded lashes. "My mind is functioning just fine, sugar," she refuted in a slow, convincing drawl with the slightest bit of a slur. "See what I mean about you not being able to handle fun?"

The frown creasing his brows deepened into a scowl. "Watching you parade half-naked in a bar full of randy men isn't exactly my idea of fun."

Hmmm, such censure in his tone. That was the thing about Cameron—despite being attracted to her, she knew he disapproved of the way she lived her life, along with her assertive and uninhibited personality. Now, she decided being *drunk* gave her even more license to be brazen, to touch him without guilt, to enjoy their attraction and find out exactly what kind of temptation Cameron couldn't resist.

She tipped her head, letting her disheveled hair fall around her face, and stared in fascination at his mouth, which had been the source of many of her late-night fantasies. She wondered what it would take to see those lips smile at her in one of those slow, sexy grins she knew he was capable of. She wondered how his seductive mouth would feel pressed against her own in a deep, hot kiss, or skimming along her neck, her breasts . . .

She swallowed, her throat suddenly tight, and gave into the urge to place her hands on his chest. She'd thought a lot about his incredibly honed body and what it looked like naked. She figured this was probably the closest she'd ever get to finding out—by *feel*.

As soon as she touched him, his muscles flexed beneath her palms and his breathing hitched. She felt the heat of him through his shirt, along with the way his heartbeat accelerated.

She held back a secret female smile. Oh, he was far, far from immune to her. Just as she was certain he'd been far from indifferent to her dancing up on that stage a while ago.

She decided to call him on it.

"Awww, come on, sugar," she said in a breathy voice as

her fingers brushed over his nipples, which were as hard as her own. "Watching me in that wet T-shirt didn't turn you on, not even a little bit?"

"Nope." He sounded *very* sure of himself.

She didn't believe his adamant denial. Not for a second. "You're such a liar, Cameron," she said and set out to prove it. With her gaze holding his, she skimmed a hand down his torso, past the waistband of his jeans and lower . . . until she held the most masculine part of him in her hand. He released a hiss of breath, and satisfaction curled through her when she found him already aroused, the firm length of him impressive in size.

He was definitely more than a handful. Desire curled low and deep in her belly at the heady thought of that aggressive male flesh filling her in all the different ways she'd imagined and fantasized about over the past few months.

Satisfied with the evidence she'd discovered, she let a sultry smile emerge. "Unless this is a very thick sock stuffed in your pants, I'd have to say you *are* a little bit turned on."

A strangled sound erupted from his throat, and he yanked her hand away, as if her touch had the ability to burn. His fingers circled her wrist, and his thumb pressed against the rapid pulse beating there. "That smart mouth of yours is going to get you into big trouble one day, sweetheart."

"Promises, promises," she taunted softly, which earned her a warning look from him that did nothing to quell her shameless approach. "Actually, it's nice to see I can get a rise out of you after all."

The double entendre wasn't lost on him, and for a moment it looked as though he was going to say something in response to her comment. Then he shook his head as if to clear it, causing the dim lights in the hall to cast intriguing golden highlights through his soft-looking strands of hair.

"Give me your car keys."

She blinked at him, thrown by his abrupt request. "I didn't drive. I came with Carrie."

"Even better." He ignored the two young college girls who turned down the hallway, whispering and giggling as they passed them on their way to the women's room. "Where's your purse?"

"I didn't bring one." She had her money, apartment key, and lipstick in the small pouch clipped to the waistband of her skirt.

"Good. One less thing to worry about. " He tightened his grip on her arm. "Let's go," he said and started back down the corridor toward the bar area, with her in tow.

The wet T-shirt contest was over, but the place seemed even more packed than before and twice as rowdy. The music was loud, and Mia actually had a difficult time keeping up with Cameron as he made his way through the crowd. He stopped at the table her roommate, Gina, had claimed earlier, and Carrie was there, sitting alone and nursing a drink.

"Mia won't be needing a ride back to her place," Cameron said to her. "I'll be sure she gets home safely."

Carrie shrugged indifferently as she swirled her straw through her drink. "Okay."

Mia wasn't in the habit of leaving nightclubs with strangers, and she felt compelled to explain who Cameron was so Carrie didn't think she was about to indulge in a one-night stand with someone she didn't know.

Keeping up the pretense of being intoxicated, she leaned into Cameron and patted him on the chest in a placating way. "He's a friend of the family and seems to have this need to play my white knight tonight." She rolled her eyes at that notion.

Carrie's stare was distant, her demeanor standoffish. "Lucky you."

The sarcasm lacing Carrie's tone took Mia off guard. Her friend had been acting oddly toward her all evening, but before Mia could ask Carrie what was wrong, Cameron was pulling her along again, seemingly eager to get out of the place. With his fingers still locked around her wrist, she had no choice but to follow as he wended his way through the mass of people filling the establishment.

"Mia!"

Hearing someone shout her name, she craned her neck around and saw Gina trying to make her way toward them, a worried look on her face. No doubt her roommate was wondering where she was going . . . and with whom.

"I'm fine, promise." She mouthed the words to Gina because she knew her voice wouldn't reach her over the loud music and gave her an "okay" sign, but her friend seemed insistent on reaching her . . . until her boyfriend, Ray, grabbed her arm and jerked her back.

The physical command was rough enough to make Gina wince in pain. Ray said something to her friend, his expression harsh, and Gina seemed to shrink back from him.

Mia had come to the conclusion very quickly that Ray was extremely dominating and possessive when it came to Gina, which contradicted Ray's own roving eye and womanizing ways. But the few times Mia had tried to talk to Gina about Ray and how he treated her, her friend promptly dismissed her concerns and assured her she was just fine. Mia was left with no choice but to believe her friend knew what was best and could take care of herself.

What Mia didn't have the heart to tell Gina was the fact that Ray had even made a major move on *her*. She'd immediately made it very clear to Ray she wouldn't tolerate his hands-on approach or his licentious behavior. He'd instantly backed off, insisting it was all a joke, but she hadn't even been slightly amused by the lustful look in his eyes as he'd raked her body over with his gaze.

The entire incident had left a bad taste in her mouth when it came to Ray. She didn't like the man, or trust him—around herself or Gina. But her roommate wasn't willing to hear the truth about her boyfriend and made excuses for his conduct, so Mia knew there was nothing much she could do. Ultimately, it was up to Gina to face the truth and realize what a jerk Ray truly was.

Mia just hoped Gina didn't get hurt in the meantime—emotionally or physically.

Because she was paying more attention to Gina than to where she was going and was just blindly following Cameron's pull on her arm, Mia bumped hard into someone, who turned and glared at her for not watching where she was going. The impact made Mia lose her balance, and she wobbled on her heels to keep from ending up sprawled on the floor. Cameron, obviously realizing what had happened, came to an abrupt stop, and Mia collided into his hard, unyielding body and then bounced right off—sending her stumbling all over again.

She was beginning to feel like one of those steel balls in a pinball game, ricocheting from one obstacle to another. A bit dazed from the jostling, she swayed dizzily into Cameron, and luckily he caught her in his arms. She clung to him like the helpless female he was under the impression she was tonight.

He frowned down at her, and the muscle that ticked in his cheek was a good indication his tolerance level with her was quickly evaporating. "Since you don't seem capable of walking out of here on your own without making a scene, I guess I'm going to have to take over from here."

Before she realized his intent, he bent low and hefted her over his shoulder like a sack of grain. Shock rendered her momentarily speechless as he locked an arm around her thighs and made his way toward the exit. She was grateful he had the good sense to hold down the hem of her short skirt, or else she would have been mooning the crowd.

Any other time she would have protested, *loudly,* to his arrogant, sexist display, but considering her decision to have fun at Cameron's expense, she just settled in for the free ride, which included an outstanding view of his backside.

Cameron passed the bouncers at the front entrance with a quick explanation of the situation. They were obviously thankful for his interference so they didn't have to deal with an intoxicated customer themselves.

As he crossed through the parking lot, she took advantage of her position and admired Cameron's very attractive *ass*ets. With bold, shameless daring, she caressed her hands over his firm buttocks, gave them an affectionate squeeze, and sighed in adoration.

"Ummm, you have a really nice ass, sugar," she drawled.

His fingers tightened on her bare thigh, making her very aware of just how intimate his touch was on her body. "Knock off the touchy-feely stuff before I smack yours," he growled as he unlocked the passenger door of his car with his free hand.

"Ooohh," she cooed breathlessly. "Don't tell me you're into kinky stuff like spanking. Because I've been a very, very naughty girl . . ."

With a sudden, jarring jolt, she found herself back on her feet again and staring into the heated depths of his gaze. "I'm not going to touch that one," he said, though he definitely looked tempted. Instead, he opened the door to his metallic blue Porsche Boxster and motioned for her to get inside. "Get in the car."

Without argument, she slid into the low-slung vehicle and was instantly enveloped in the soft, luxurious leather seat. Cameron quickly and efficiently buckled her in, keeping any contact with her to a minimum, and then headed around to the driver's side.

When he was settled behind the wheel and the key was in the ignition, he cast her a speculative glance tinged with wry humor. "I'm beginning to think you ought to drink more often."

Amused by his comment and curious to hear his reasoning, she rested her head against the back of her seat and lifted a lazy brow his way. "And why's that?"

"Because it actually makes you more agreeable and manageable than I've ever seen you before." For the first time that night he actually *smiled,* and it was such an amazing and sexy sight to witness. "Normally, you would have fought me the entire way out of the bar."

Manageable. She nearly laughed at that description, because it was a word she would never associate with her personality. Being meek and mild wasn't a part of her nature—intoxicated or not—but she'd let him think that for now because he seemed to be enjoying her more *docile* side. He'd discover soon enough that it was all an act.

And just so he didn't think she was becoming completely complacent, she decided to throw a major wrench in *his* plans. "So . . . what makes you think I'm going to stay at home once you drop me off?"

He was silent for a moment as he contemplated the possibility. "You've got a point," he finally conceded. "I'm not willing to take that chance, so you can crash at my place tonight, where I can keep an eye on you."

Seemingly satisfied with the way he'd solved that particular problem, he turned the key in the ignition. The high-dollar sports car came to life with a low, rumbling purr that sent delicious vibrations rippling along Mia's spine.

Closing her eyes, she let out a soft sigh and thought about the intriguing opportunity that had just presented itself—not to mention all the provocative, seductive ways this night might end.

For months they'd evaded the lust and desire building between them, and she was beyond ready to let their escalating attraction take its natural course. Even if that meant being the one to lead Cameron down the path to temptation.

She smiled to herself as Cameron navigated the Porsche toward his place. Oh, yeah, the *real* fun was just about to begin.

* * *

TWENTY minutes later, Cameron pulled into the driveway leading to his house, which was located at the end of a cul-de-sac in a well-kept neighborhood just outside Chicago. He pressed the remote for the garage door, and once it rolled opened, he parked his Porsche inside and cut the engine.

He glanced over at Mia, who'd remained uncharacteristically quiet on the drive over. There could be only one reason for that, because it wasn't often that Mia was silent by choice: she must have given in to drunken exhaustion and had fallen asleep. Her eyes were closed, her breathing deep and even, and she looked very relaxed against the soft leather seat, though he could only imagine how uncomfortable and cold she must be in the damp T-shirt she was still wearing.

It was so odd seeing Mia this way—so calm and compliant. He was still amazed she hadn't put up a fight when he'd carried her out of The Electric Blue, which was so unlike her. He was used to dealing with a feisty, impetuous woman—like when she'd pressed her hand against his cock in the bar's back hallway.

He swallowed back a groan. Just remembering how she'd brazenly stroked and squeezed his shaft through the tight denim confining his erection made him hard all over again. Such a predictable and unwelcome response when it came to Mia, yet he couldn't stop wanting her, no matter how hard he tried. There was no blocking the lust that kicked up his adrenaline whenever she was near. No shutting out the recurring fantasy he had of burying himself deep inside her soft, lush body and hearing his name on her lips when she came.

He shook his head hard to dispel that erotic image. God, this woman was going to be the death of him, he was certain. No doubt he was going to expire from the excruciating, all-consuming sexual tension driving him slowly insane.

She stirred against the seat and then her lashes slowly drifted open, revealing her smoky gray eyes that looked soft and dreamy. "Hi," she said, a slight rasp to her voice.

"Hi, yourself." He searched her face, wondering if she

was still feeling tipsy, or worse, woozy from the drive. "Are you doing okay?"

A slight, knowing smile hitched up the corner of her mouth. "I'm not going to get sick all over your fancy car if that's what you're worried about."

She obviously knew him better than he would have given her credit for. "I'll admit, the thought did cross my mind."

"My stomach is fine." She shivered delicately and rubbed her bare arms with her hands. "I'm just a little cold from this wet top."

Yes, definitely cold, he agreed, and dragged his gaze away from her full breasts and the twin points pressing so enticingly against her shirt. "I'll give you something warm and dry to sleep in. Can you make it into the house on your own?"

She pressed the back of her hand to her forehead, suddenly looking distressed. "I don't know. I'm feeling so . . . light-headed," she murmured and then cast him a forlorn glance. "But if I have a big, strong man like you to lean on, I could probably manage."

He couldn't tell if she was exaggerating or not, but he wasn't about to take any chances. So he got out of the car, went around to the passenger side, and helped her out. With one of his arms tucked around her back and her arm draped over his shoulder, he navigated the way into the house and down the hallway with her swaying on her high-heeled shoes by his side.

He still couldn't believe she'd entered that wet T-shirt contest and spoke without really thinking. "If your brothers had any idea what you've been up to tonight . . ." As soon as he felt her stiffen beside him, he let the rest of his comment trail off, sensing he'd hit some kind of nerve.

"They'd *what*?" she demanded.

Oh, yeah, he'd definitely broached a sensitive subject with her. The defensive note to her voice was unmistakable, and as he turned the corner and escorted her into the guest bedroom, he chose his words carefully. "They certainly wouldn't have applauded your efforts during the wet T-shirt contest, and I'm sure they would have limited your alcohol intake."

Abruptly, she pushed away from him, surprisingly steady on her feet. Standing beside the bed, she braced her hands on her hips. "Between my brothers and cousins, and now *you,* you'd think I'm some kind of helpless female in need of constant protection."

"Your actions tonight, not to mention your drinking, was pretty damn irresponsible. If I hadn't been there, who knows what might have happened." He sliced a hand in the air between them. "Don't you think those guys out in the crowd wouldn't have tried taking advantage of you and what you were offering up on that stage? Mix in the fact that your inhibitions are dulled from alcohol—"

She cut off his statement with a sound of disgust. "I am so *not* drunk."

He snorted in disbelief. "Sure. Whatever you say."

"Watch closely, sugar." To prove her point, she stood on one high-heeled shoe, closed her eyes, dropped her head back, and touched the tip of her nose with her finger without so much as a waver—a difficult feat for most people with all their wits about them.

Once that was done, she straightened and met his gaze, silent laughter glimmering in the depth of her eyes. "See? I had one and a half drinks. And they were piña coladas at that. It's not like I consumed hard liquor cocktails. I wasn't the slightest bit tipsy at any point tonight."

The truth was like a slap in the face. Cameron stared at her, stunned that she'd deliberately duped him. Then again, it was so like Mia to scam him and enjoy every moment of it. No wonder she'd been so damn obliging.

What he didn't understand, though, was her reasoning behind this elaborate ruse she'd concocted. "Then what's with this act of yours?"

Her chin lifted a fraction, showing a hint of her stubborn personality. "You automatically believed the worst, so

I figured why not give you exactly what you expected?"

He clamped his jaw tight. She'd got him there. He *had* assumed the worst about her condition right from the beginning, but what was he supposed to think when she'd deliberately given him that impression?

He narrowed his gaze, scrutinizing her more closely. "So you entered that contest sober?"

"Yep." She crossed her arms over her chest, which plumped the upper swells of her breasts and added to her already eye-catching cleavage. "If you want the truth, I entered that wet T-shirt contest because I wanted to see you squirm a little bit."

He lifted a brow in a challenging manner. "What makes you think that would make me uncomfortable?"

"I'm not talking about uncomfortable, as in making you embarrassed," she said sweetly, which contradicted the sinful, taunting light in her eyes. "I'm talking about making you restless, as in hot and hard. And we already proved back at The Electric Blue that I have that effect on you."

His entire body tightened at the recollection, and renewed awareness sliced through him, sharp and intense. He struggled to keep a tight rein on his desire and knew it was tenuous at best. "Give it up, Mia. We're so not going there." Because to do so would undoubtedly lead them down a path of no return this time around.

"Why not?" She shook her hair away from her face and strolled toward him, hips swaying gracefully, seductively. "Do I intimidate you? Or perhaps I'm too much for you to handle?"

She was back to doing what she did best—goading him. He clenched his hands into fists at his sides, refusing to rise to her bait.

Stopping in front of him, mere inches away, she slid her hands up along his shoulders and around his neck, searing him with the exquisite feel of her breasts brushing against his chest. "Or maybe, just maybe, you're afraid of letting go, losing that precious control of yours, and liking it?"

She'd just pegged his deepest fears when it came to her, that a sober, clear-headed Mia was much more dangerous to his body and senses than an inebriated one. She knew exactly what she was doing, knew the risks she was taking, and was ready and willing to accept the consequences of her direct and calculated actions. Cameron suddenly realized he was in big, big trouble.

It was a potent combination he was hard-pressed to resist.

"Come on, sugar," she whispered against the corner of his mouth, teasing him with the promise of everything he'd denied himself for much too long. "I know you have it in you, and I know you want me as much as I want you." She nipped at his bottom lip and then soothed the slight sting with the soft caress of her tongue. "Maybe it's time we did something about this attraction of ours . . ."

His entire body shuddered, and a little voice in his head urged him to go for it, to take full advantage of what she was offering so freely and get her out of his mind, his constant thoughts, and nightly fantasies.

Finally bedding her would strip away the mysterious allure she presented, get her out of his system, and end this insanity that threatened to consume him. And that thought held a whole lot of appeal since this woman had been tying him up in knots for months now.

"Yeah, maybe we should," he agreed gruffly and then took her mouth with his before his good common sense had the chance to talk him out of what they were about to do.

Three

ONE minute Cameron was contemplating having sex with Mia, and the next he had her pushed up against the nearest wall with his mouth on hers like a man starved for the taste of her. And that's exactly how he felt . . . ravenous, greedy, demanding.

There was nothing gentle or sweet about this first, long overdue kiss, or the way the deep stroke of their tongues dueled for supremacy. She clenched her fingers in his hair and returned the sensual assault with abandon and equal hunger—not that he'd expect anything less from this woman who'd worn a shirt proclaiming she was too wild to tame.

Her heady, feminine scent seemed to be everywhere and infused every breath he managed to inhale. He could feel her breasts, warm and yielding, against his chest, and he had the overwhelming urge to touch her everywhere at once, to drown every one of his five senses with her essence and sensuality.

Keeping his mouth on hers, he slid his hands around to her ass and pulled her closer, fitting the hard ridge of his cock between her thighs. The soft, needy sound she made in the back of her throat, combined with the provocative way she rolled her hips against his, had his blood roaring in his ears and pure, unadulterated lust surging through his body.

That easily, she'd pushed him to this madness. And now that he'd let go, he'd lost the ability to slow down or stop. He *couldn't* stop, not even if his life depended on it. And at the moment, his life depended on kissing her, touching her, and feeling her hot and wet around him.

But Mia seemed to have other ideas, and true to her nature she took charge, becoming the aggressor. Breaking their kiss, she skimmed his shirt up and over his head, tossed it to the floor, and then pushed him toward the bed. He fell back onto the mattress, and she gave him only a handful of seconds to move upward before she crawled on top of him, hiked up the hem of her leopard print mini-skirt, and straddled his waist like the pagan she was. She stripped off her own damp top, leaving her clad in a see-through lace bra that was sexy as hell.

His fierce erection was nestled against her bottom, and he groaned when she leaned over him, braced her hands on either side of his head, and rocked sinuously against his thick, aching shaft. An inviting, wholly female smile played at the corners of mouth, and she closed her eyes, tossed her head back, and moaned her own enjoyment as she arched into him all over again.

Watching Mia in the throes of pleasure was an incredibly arousing sight, but Cameron wasn't about to let her be the only dominant one in this sexual encounter—as she no doubt expected to be. Reaching up, he dragged her bra straps down her arms and peeled away the flimsy fabric covering those twin mounds of flesh. Her breasts spilled out, full and firm and crowned with dark pink aureoles. He cupped the heavy, delicious weight of her breasts in his palms and scraped his thumbs across her rigid nipples, reveling in the soft warmth of her bare skin, the catch of her breath in the back of her throat, and how amazingly responsive she was to his touch.

He wanted to take her in his mouth. Wanted to circle her nipples with his tongue and suck on her breasts until she pleaded for him to stop. Oh, yeah, he'd enjoy hearing Mia beg for mercy for a change. He would love watching her ultimate surrender to *him*.

Before he could make that gratifying image a reality, she stole back the reins of control once again, distracting him with the soft press of her lips to his chest and the hot, damp trek of her lush mouth skimming its way down to his stomach as she moved lower and then lower still. Her slender, nimble fingers followed, stroking along his taut abs until she reached the waistband of his jeans.

She nuzzled his belly, and he felt a distinct tug as she deftly unfastened the top button on his pants. Then he heard the growl of his zipper as she drew it down over his huge, rock-hard erection. Before he could inhale his next ragged breath, she'd released his cock from the confines of his briefs and had her fingers wrapped tight around the straining length.

His entire body shuddered, and he clenched his fists into the bedcovers, realizing just how much power this woman actually had over him. Especially when she held him in the palm of her hand the way he'd fantasized for what had seemed like a lifetime.

He glanced down to where she was kneeling between his thighs and found her looking up at him with a come-hither smile on her lips and a sly, seductive *I've got you right where I want you* twinkle in her quicksilver eyes. The woman was a minx, and he realized she was keeping score on who had the upper hand. He was extremely pleased it was her at the moment.

She stroked his shaft, teasing him with light caresses and tormenting him with the promise of more. He closed his eyes and grit his teeth as she skimmed her thumb up over the tip of his penis and spread the slick drop of pre-come over the sensitive head. And if that wasn't enough for him to bear, he nearly died when she took every single hard inch of him into the silky, wet heat of her mouth. He groaned at the delicious friction she created with her lips and tongue and fingers as she slid up and down his throbbing shaft. She added suction, and his body tensed as he fought against the overwhelming urge to come.

Not like this.

He needed to get inside of her, *now,* and it was that urgent, desperate thought that drove him to reach for Mia and pull her back up. In a quick, lithe move, he had her flat on her back. Her eyes widened in startled surprise, and before her shock had a chance to dissipate, he shoved her skirt up and removed her wispy, barely there, G-string panties. Then he slipped off both of her high-heeled shoes so there was no chance she'd accidentally injure him with the sharp spikes when he wrapped her legs high around his waist.

Pushing her knees apart, he spread her wide and swept his hands down her smooth, supple thighs. His thumbs grazed the neatly trimmed thatch of dark hair on her mound; slid along her slick, glistening folds of her sex; and dipped into the moist, giving entrance of her body. She sucked in a sharp gasp as his fingers filled her and moaned loud and low when his thumb rubbed against her clit.

He was satisfied to discover that she was already incredibly wet and aroused. Unable to wait a moment longer to fuck her, he moved up and over her body and felt the head of his cock glide along her sex as he pinned her beneath him. Their eyes met and held, hers filled with dark desire, and he watched as she gasped and arched into him when he abruptly thrust into her, a seemingly endless journey as he drove himself to the hilt. She was snug around him, like slick, wet satin gripping his shaft, and the intensely erotic sensation made his head spin.

Her bare breasts were crushed against his chest, her knees bracketed his hips, and the urge to possess her in the most elemental way possible overwhelmed him. Tangling his fingers in Mia's soft, thick hair, he held her head in his hands and slanted his mouth across hers in a hot, deep, tongue-tangling kiss.

Then he began to move.

Her hands slid to his shoulders, and her fingers dug into his muscles as he surged into her, again and again, tearing a moan from the back of her throat. His strokes became faster, longer, ruthlessly demanding, and a whole lot primal. With each thrust he felt himself grow harder, thicker, until lust and need collided into white-hot heat and an all-consuming pleasure that threatened to engulf him.

Lost in the rush of sensation, lost in *her,* he wrenched his mouth from hers, tossed his head back in pure ecstasy, and arched into her one last time, high and hard and infinitely deep. A guttural growl tore from his chest, and his entire body shuddered as he came, harder and stronger than he could ever remember.

His scorching release seemed to go on and on, wringing him dry and leaving him weak and devastated, until he could do nothing else except collapse on top of Mia. He buried his face against her neck, and as he gradually recovered and his mind cleared, he became intimately aware of the woman beneath him—especially the fact that her body wasn't nearly as slack and relaxed as his own. Although he'd just experienced the most explosive orgasm of his life, Mia had not.

Swearing beneath his breath, he moved off her so he was laying by her side and no longer crushing her with his weight. Normally, he enjoyed foreplay. Loved every aspect of it, actually. Making a woman come was just as exciting and pleasurable to him as his own release. Except tonight, with Mia, he hadn't even given her the opportunity to reach her own orgasm. Hadn't even taken the time to make it good for *her*. He'd been so hot for her, so eager to finally end the sexual tension that had been building for months between them, that he hadn't been able to think beyond his own satisfaction.

Disgusted with himself, he zipped up his jeans and reluctantly glanced over at Mia, expecting to find her glaring at him for being such an insensitive, selfish cad—which was no less than he deserved. Instead, what he saw made him feel as though someone had just sucker punched him in the stomach.

She was lying next to him on her back, just the way he'd left her, with her head turned slightly away from him, eyes closed. If he didn't know better, he would have thought she was sleeping, but he instinctively knew she was giving herself a few private moments to recover from what had just happened between them. Her face was flushed, her breathing still choppy, and she'd draped one arm over her exposed breasts in a belated show of modesty—which was very telling considering she was half-dressed, with her bra bunched beneath her breasts and her skirt hiked around her hips.

It struck him as a pose of self-preservation, a way to protect herself—without even realizing she was doing so.

Finally, her lashes fluttered open and she slowly glanced his way. Her gaze was guarded and her expression was tentative, even a bit uncertain. She looked so damn vulnerable, and that was a term he never would have equated to this woman beside him. No, the sassy, impudent Mia he was familiar with would have shattered the silence with a smart-ass remark and brushed off the encounter as just another casual, one-night-stand affair.

But this Mia staring at him . . . oh, Lord, she had the ability to cripple his emotions and make him care. At the moment he had the strong urge to reach out and touch her, gently this time. To smooth away the silky strands of hair that had fallen across her soft cheek. To lean down and kiss her slowly, leisurely, and make love to her with only *her* needs in mind this time.

That thought reminded him once again of what a self-absorbed lover he'd been, fueling the need to make amends for being so thoughtless with her.

"Mia . . . I'm sorry," he said, his tone low and rough, though the words alone seemed inadequate.

She stiffened, her gaze suddenly flaring with rebellion. Abruptly, she sat up and tugged the hem of her skirt down her thighs and readjusted her bra so her breasts were covered again. That quickly, her entire demeanor shifted and changed. Gone was that glimpse of insecurity he'd witnessed, and in its place was a spark of defiance that put a wall between them and shut him out.

"You don't owe me an apology, or anything else for that matter," she said, her tone infused with a thread of sarcasm he immediately recognized as a defense tactic. "I'm a big girl, and what we just did was completely consensual."

She thought he was apologizing because he was feeling guilty about what just happened. Oddly enough, he had no regrets—and that was something he refused to analyze too closely at the moment, although he knew he'd eventually have to face that issue at some point. She'd also made it very clear in her comment that she wasn't the type of woman to develop expectations about them, or him, just because they'd slept together.

Now *this* was the Mia he'd come to know. He found it ironic that he was beginning to realize that her stubborn, too-confident attitude was an act of some kind—a possible way to protect herself and emotions when a situation became too intimate or personal.

As it just had with them.

Exhaling a deep, frustrating breath, he stood up, went to his dresser, and pulled out a clean T-shirt, which he handed to Mia so she didn't have to put her wet top back on. She slipped the shirt over her head and let it fall to her thighs, dwarfing her petite frame. He was just damn grateful it covered her adequately so he didn't have to look at her bare skin and lush curves, which had the potential to distract him from the conversation they needed to have.

She glanced up at him in silent thanks, and as soon as she met his gaze and he had her attention, he spoke what was on his mind. "I'm not apologizing because we had sex," he said, wanting to be sure she understood his stand on that score.

Her expression turned wary and confused. "Then what are you sorry for?"

There was no sugar-coating what he had to say, so he didn't even try. "I didn't exactly give you the chance to come."

Her brows rose in surprise and then the corner of her kiss-swollen mouth quirked in amusement. "I'll spare you your male pride," she said as she stepped around him to the other side of the bed. "I'm not one of those orgasmic kind of women, so don't let it keep you up tonight worrying and wondering. The fact that I didn't have an orgasm wasn't something you did or didn't do."

Stunned by her admission, he turned to stare at her as she picked up The Electric Blue T-shirt she'd worn earlier. "You mean to tell me you've never had an orgasm?"

"Oh, I've had plenty of orgasms, sugar," she drawled, resorting back to the sassy woman he was all too familiar with. "Just not with a guy or during sex."

That made him think of how she *did* achieve sexual satisfaction—all on her own. It wasn't difficult to imagine Mia pleasuring herself, with intimate caresses, the slow, sweeping strokes of her fingers and her soft, sweet moans. In fact, that particular fantasy dancing in his mind was downright erotic and made him hard all over again.

He shook his head, still trying to comprehend the fact that all her sexual encounters had lacked one crucial element. "I can't believe you've never climaxed during sex."

Her shoulders lifted in a nonchalant shrug as she slipped on her skimpy panties, as if she'd come to accept the way things were for her. "It just doesn't happen for me that way, and I'm not into faking an orgasm for the sake of a guy's ego, so don't give it a whole lot of thought."

How could he not? He wanted to be that guy who gave her an amazing sexual experience, complete with an earth-shattering orgasm while he was buried deep, deep inside her. He wanted to be the one who took the time to make it so good for her, she'd never settle for less than the ultimate pleasure her body was capable of feeling—pure, unadulterated ecstacy. And if he was lucky, she'd scream his name when she came.

Oh, yeah. Now that was a fantasy he'd love to make a reality. Except he was certain his erotic daydream would never come to fruition, considering he had no intention of repeating what had happened between them tonight. To do so would be emotional suicide for him, not to mention all the other complications of having an affair with Mia. Mostly, having to explain to her brothers or cousin and his business partner, Steve, that he was having a hot, but temporary, affair with her.

That announcement would certainly go over like a lead balloon, and he'd probably end up castrated by the protective bunch for daring to touch Mia—the *baby* of the family. It didn't matter that she'd instigated tonight's sexual encounter—they'd expect him to show some restraint, to be the strong one, to resist the temptation Mia had been tossing his way for months. And if that control happened to slip, as it had tonight, they'd expect more out of him than a one-night stand with Mia. Except he didn't see a future with Mia and himself, not when she was so completely opposite of the kind of woman he was looking to spend his life with.

She was reckless, defiant, and trouble just waiting to happen. However, what Cameron couldn't erase from his mind was that unguarded, unplanned glimpse of a more vulnerable side to Mia he'd seen earlier. But he understood this woman well enough to know that she'd never admit to such a weakness.

He watched as she sat down on the edge of the bed to put her shoes back on, and an important thought struck him, one he couldn't dismiss. "Mia . . . there's something else we need to talk about."

She glanced at him hesitantly, and he couldn't blame her for being cautious after the discussion they'd just had about orgasms.

He pushed his hands into his front jeans pockets, calling himself a hundred kinds of fools for being so careless, but he'd completely lost his head with her and hadn't given a single thought to using a condom. No, that had been the very last thing on his mind. "We didn't use any protection."

She looked away and finished sliding her foot into her heeled shoe. "I appreciate the concern, but we're fine. I'm on the pill."

"Great." He was definitely relieved. The last thing he needed was to worry for the next few weeks about the possibility of Mia being pregnant. He couldn't imagine her settling down into domestic bliss and devoting her time to a husband and a baby, and he was certain such a fate would put a major crimp in her carefree lifestyle. That was obviously why she took her own precautions.

She stood and approached him. Her gaze met his steadily, her features giving nothing away as to what she was really thinking or feeling. "Since we've pretty much established that I'm not drunk, there's no reason for me to stay here and you can take me home."

With that, she walked out of the bedroom, head held high, leaving him to follow behind.

EARLY the next morning, Mia sat at the small drafting table she'd set up in the corner of her bedroom in the apartment she shared with Gina and absently sketched out a design for a new stained-glass project. After last night's escapade with Cameron, she'd woken up feeling tired, emotionally and physically, but mentally inspired, and she always followed her muse when it beckoned.

Besides, other than grocery shopping, she had nothing planned for the day, or the weekend for that matter, which gave her the perfect opportunity to develop the image in her mind on paper, then begin the creation process with stained glass.

During the week, she worked a normal nine-to-five grind as a secretary at the tile company her oldest brother, Scott, along with her other brother, Alex, now operated for their father. Her job at Nolan and Sons provided a steady and reliable paycheck, but *this* was her dream, and had been for years now.

She longed to set the artist within her completely free and make a name for herself with her unique, custom-made stained-glass designs. And if she was completely honest with the inner child still locked inside her, she ached to use this talent of hers to validate herself as more than just the baby of the Wilde family and to support herself on her own, without having to rely on her brothers or the family business for her income.

Unfortunately, everyone treated her stained-glass art strictly as a hobby and brushed it off as something she did in her spare time or out of boredom. She had to admit they'd never discouraged her artistic flair, but neither had they done anything to cultivate her confidence in marketing her work.

Her family, her father especially, had been relieved when she'd gone off to college. But instead of the business degree everyone had been expecting her to bring home, she'd stunned them all by graduating with a degree in 3D glasswork. Her father and stepmother wrote it off as yet another act of rebellion, one of many since her mother's death when she was five. But to Mia, that degree had been her proudest achievement—an accomplishment that was hers and hers alone and something no one could ever take away from her.

She sighed to herself, wishing all those college courses and techniques she'd learned had been put to better use than making gifts and holiday presents for friends. Foolishly, she'd harbored grand illusions of expanding the family business to incorporate her stained-glass designs in some of the bigger projects and restoration work Nolan and Sons took on, but Scott had shot down the idea. Gently, of course, and in a very placating manner, but the sting of that particular rejection still hurt.

Scott felt there just wasn't a big enough market for her custom stained-glass artwork, which included an array of abstract designs, mosaics, impressions, floral patterns, and Celtic reproductions. She'd made some gorgeous, one-of-a-kind pieces over the years, but obviously none of them had been good enough to elevate her status in the family business.

A small, private smile tugged at the corners of her mouth as she gazed down at her current drawing. Little did anyone know, but her stained-glass designs had recently evolved to include some very daring and head-turning pieces. Her family would be stunned speechless to learn she created *erotic* stained-glass art. At first glance, her patterns looked like vibrant abstracts, but upon closer inspection, the composite of colors meshed into a loving, committed couple entwined in intimate and sometimes shocking positions.

The images were highly seductive and shamelessly provocative, a bit of fantasy mixed with an inviting bit of reality. The erotic pictures depicted love and lust, desire and ecstasy. And each one she created held a piece of her soul and tapped into wistful longings and dreams of finding a love so rare and true.

Her pencil scratched across the thin paper as she continued to bring her vision to life. The process was usually accompanied by a spark of excitement as the images developed, and this time was no different. Except as the embracing couple took shape and form, her enthusiasm took a decidedly sensual and personal turn . . . because the man and woman making love in her drawing became Cameron and herself.

Her heart tripped in her chest, and the rest of her body followed suit. The tips of her breasts tingled, and the muscles in her belly tightened as she gazed at the way the woman held onto the man, with her legs wrapped securely around his waist. One of the man's hands clutched at her hip, and the other was buried in her tousled hair as they arched into one another in the throes of passion.

She'd managed to avoid thinking about last night's incredibly hot tryst with Cameron, so it shouldn't have come as a surprise to her that everything she'd suppressed manifested itself in her most recent design. Now, the memories proved much too strong and came rushing back in that moment, flooding her mind with vivid details and forcing her to recall every pleasurable, thrilling, and emotional sensation of having Cameron buried deep inside her body and the way he'd ultimately lost that staunch restraint of his with her.

It was the emotional part she had trouble dealing with, because she'd never, ever expected to feel so connected to Cameron in anything more than a physical way. Sex with him had been exceptional, hotter and better than she'd ever imagined, but it was what happened in the aftermath of their encounter that shook Mia to her very core.

She'd definitely anticipated that he'd regret his actions because he was a man who didn't lose control easily. When he'd offered up an apology, she'd countered it with a sarcastic reply to buffer her own vulnerable state . . . until he'd explained that he wasn't sorry for what they did, but that he felt bad because he hadn't given her the chance to come.

She laughed and shook her head at the absurdity of the situation. Her pleasure, or lack thereof, wasn't a conversation she'd had with any guy, mainly because none had ever given a second thought to whether or not she climaxed during foreplay or sex. But Cameron . . . he had to go and muddle things by caring about something that never should have caused him any concern or even a second thought. Add to that the glimmer of tenderness she'd seen in his gaze, and was it any wonder her heart was feeling a bit torn and confused?

The closing of the front door startled Mia out of her thoughts and told her Gina was finally home after spending the night out—most likely at Ray's—a common occurrence on the weekends. Mia closed her sketch pad, and less than a minute later her friend knocked softly on Mia's half-closed bedroom door and poked her head inside. Finding Mia already awake, she tentatively entered.

"Hey there," Gina murmured, a slight smile tipping up one corner of her mouth.

Mia couldn't help but notice that the other side of Gina's bottom lip was swollen, and as her roommate came to a stop at her drafting table, she could clearly see that her lip had actually been split open about half an inch. Gina had tried to cover the gash with a colored gloss, but the bruise forming around the wound was too obvious for Mia to ignore.

Immediate anger welled up inside Mia, because she highly suspected Ray was the culprit for that laceration. But she also knew from experience that should she express that simmering outrage, Gina would totally shut her out. So she inhaled a calming breath and decided to tread carefully in addressing the issue.

"Gina, what happened to your lip?" she asked, her concerned toned masking her true feelings.

Her friend averted her gaze and shrugged, as she did whenever Mia asked one of these kinds of direct questions. "I opened Ray's car door too fast last night after we left The Electric Blue, and the corner accidentally hit my lip and split it open." She gingerly touched the swollen spot and laughed, but the sound was forced. "You know me. I can be so graceless sometimes."

Mia had to give Gina credit for being so innovative with her excuse, but she didn't believe her explanation for a second. Not when bruises and other marks on her body were appearing with alarming frequency.

Ray could be extremely charming when he wanted to be, but having been on the receiving end of his aggression, Mia knew he also had a darker side to his personality. She could easily see him crossing the line to abusive, but she had no real, solid proof and Gina wasn't offering up anything concrete, either.

Mia tipped her head and regarded her friend speculatively. "You know, you've gotten awfully clumsy since you started dating Ray." She managed to keep her tone light and even a bit teasing, but there was no mistaking the significance of her words.

Her comment made Gina stiffen, and those defensive walls of hers quickly went up. "Fine," she said curtly. "The truth is, things got a little out of control last night during sex."

If there was one thing Mia understood, it was "out-of-control" sex, because that's exactly what she'd experienced with Cameron last night. But for as wild and primitive as things had gotten, he'd never once hurt her, and he certainly hadn't left any bruises on her body. Their encounter had been driven by lust and passion . . . whereas she got the uneasy feeling that wasn't exactly the case between Gina and Ray.

"He didn't mean to split open my lip," Gina went on in her attempt to justify her boyfriend's actions. "And he apologized afterward for being so rough. It was an accident."

It didn't escape Mia's attention that Gina didn't say *how* Ray had cut her lip, and judging by her friend's uptight disposition, Mia didn't think she was going to find out, either.

"I'm not trying to make you upset," Mia said gently as she stared into Gina's soulful blue eyes. "I care about you, and I just want to be sure everything's okay."

As soon as Mia backed off, Gina's posture relaxed. "I'm fine," she insisted.

Reaching for Gina's hand, Mia gave it an affectionate squeeze. "Just *please* be more careful, okay?" Again, she infused a deeper meaning to her words, and all Mia could do was hope her friend heeded her advice. Then, she pasted on a smile and changed the subject, because she didn't want any further argument to come between them. "Have you had any breakfast this morning?"

"Just coffee." Gina adjusted her purse on her shoulder and offered another half-smile. "I wasn't hungry earlier."

"Well, you need to eat, and so do I." Mia stood and

stretched the kinks from her shoulders and lower back from sitting at the drafting table for the past hour. "Let's go see what we've got left in the kitchen."

A few minutes later, after scouring the cupboards and refrigerator and coming up with one foil package containing two frosted strawberry Pop-Tarts for them to split, Gina declared, "We *so* need to go grocery shopping."

Mia laughed in agreement as she grabbed the last two bottles of water from the fridge and handed one to Gina. "I know. Let's go shopping together, and maybe we can catch a movie today, too."

Enthusiasm lit up Gina's pretty features. "Yeah, I'd like that."

"Then consider it a date," Mia said, and bit into her Pop-Tart. Yes, she'd planned on working on her new stained-glass project, but that could wait. She didn't get much girl-time with Gina these days, not since Ray had come into the picture, and she'd take whatever time with her friend she could get.

"Speaking of dates . . ." Gina opened her purse and pulled out a familiar piece of clothing. "You left something behind at The Electric Blue."

Mia stared at the Too Wild to Tame top she'd worn last night—before her stint in the wet T-shirt contest. "Ummm, I guess I did."

Gina draped it over the back of the chair Mia was sitting in. "I asked the manager for it after you left with *your* date."

Mia rolled her eyes at that but refrained from issuing a reply to her friend's comment.

Unfortunately, Gina had no problem prying. "So that was the *infamous* Cameron Sinclair, huh?"

"Yes." Mia finished off her Pop-Tart and washed it down with a drink of water. "I take it Carrie told you who he was?" Gina knew of Cameron's existence but had never seen him before last night.

Gina nodded as she picked at the edges of her breakfast

pastry. "Yep. God, Mia, you didn't tell me he's so . . . *everything*."

Unable to help herself, Mia laughed. "So *everything*?" she repeated, amused by Gina's choice of word to describe Cameron.

"Hot. Gorgeous. Sexy." Gina sighed appreciatively. "The full package."

The man *definitely* had a full package, and then some, Mia thought, remembering how the hard, thick length of him had felt in her hands and stroking deep within her. Heat rose to her cheeks, and she doused the rush of warmth with a long, cool drink of water.

Luckily, Gina didn't seem to notice her reaction. "So where did he drag you off to?" she asked.

"His place. He thought I was drunk, and he was trying to keep me from causing a scandal that would get back to my brothers."

"And?" Gina prompted, wide-eyed and curious.

"And what?" Mia replied casually, not wanting to encourage any further discussion on the matter.

Gina puffed out an exasperated breath of air. "And what happened at his place?"

Mia wasn't emotionally ready to discuss her intimate night with Cameron with anyone, maybe not ever. What had transpired between them was personal and private, and because it wasn't going to happen again, there was no point in making an issue of her one-night stand with Cameron.

"Nothing happened," Mia said and dismissed the pang of guilt she felt for not confiding in Gina when just minutes ago she'd wanted that same trust from her friend. She justified that this situation was different, that her relationship in no way threatened her physical state. Her heart, she feared, was another matter altogether. "Once I set him straight on the fact that I wasn't drunk, he brought me back home. End of story."

Gina was staring at her too intently, as if she suspected there were at least a few more chapters to that story, and Mia quickly changed the subject before her friend could say anything else.

"By the way, what was up with Carrie last night?" Mia asked. She and Gina had met Carrie at the gym about six months ago, and they'd all become friends—mostly Carrie's doing, as she'd been the one to pursue the friendship. They hung out together occasionally, but lately Carrie had been acting strange and distant, and last night her attitude had not only been cool, but even a bit abrasive.

A confused look passed across Gina's features. "What do you mean?"

"She snapped at me a few times for no real reason I could figure out." She shrugged. "She just seemed on edge, and it didn't take much to set her off."

"Sounds like a classic case of PMS to me," Gina said and laughed.

Mia thought about Gina's explanation for Carrie's odd behavior, and she supposed it was completely plausible. "Yeah, I guess so."

Gina stood and walked over to the kitchen sink, a light spring in her step Mia hadn't seen in a long while. "So can we go see a chick-flick today? I've been dying to see that new Richard Gere movie."

The enthusiasm in Gina's voice made Mia smile. Besides, who could resist gazing for two hours at one the best-looking actors in the business? "Richard Gere it is."

She had a feeling the distraction would do them *both* good.

Four

FIRST thing Monday mornings Cameron met with his partner, Steve, to discuss the week's agenda and divide up the new investigative cases that needed to be handled. They were retained by quite a few large corporations, so there were more than a dozen background checks and evaluations to perform on new employees. A new law firm had hired them to locate and interview a key witness for one of their cases, and a woman had contracted them to help her find out who had committed identity theft against her because the police weren't getting anywhere with the complaint she'd filed.

There were deadbeat dads to locate, a sexual harassment claim to investigate, domestic cases to sort through, four new requests to find a long-lost friend or loved one, and surveillance to set up on a forty-eight-year-old construction worker who'd filed an insurance claim for a back injury but apparently wasn't disabled at all.

As always, the cases seemed endless, and halfway through the meeting, as Cameron was reading through a file on a skip trace, his thoughts drifted and eventually images of Mia filled his mind. No big surprise there. He hadn't been able to get her out of his head since Friday night, and in fact, he had spent the entire weekend dissecting Mia's dual personalities—the shameless, brazen spitfire he'd believed she was, and the uncertain, contradictory woman he'd glimpsed in an unguarded moment after their fast, heated encounter.

He'd made a career of analyzing people and their actions. After spending too many hours reflecting on Mia's behavior, he'd come to the conclusion that there was so much more to her than he'd originally assumed and what she obviously wanted him and everyone else to believe—because he'd been privy to the emotional depth she tried to hide beneath her scandalous attitude and impetuous personality. He'd seen a vulnerability he never thought her capable of because of the strong, rebellious facade she wore around her like an impenetrable cloak.

It was all an act, he'd come to realize, and a damn good one at that because he'd fallen for it—hook, line, and sinker. And obviously, so had every one else, her brothers and cousins included. They all accepted her as the *Wilde child* of the family, and her reckless and outrageous conduct had become an expected thing—whether they approved of her antics or not.

But there was one question that kept tumbling through Cameron's mind, one he didn't have an answer for but had kept him up the past two nights trying to figure out. Who was the *real* Mia, and what kind of emotional secrets were lurking behind that come-hither smile and those smart-ass remarks she tossed his way to keep him at a distance.

And why the hell did he even care?

Shit. He was so in over his head where Mia was concerned, like a drowning man with no lifesaver in sight who kept getting sucked in deeper and deeper. He'd spent what seemed like forever resisting her, sparring with her, lusting for her until it all had collided in a frenzy of demanding, carnal sex. And what Cameron had come to realize in the aftermath of that culmination had nearly sent him reeling. Somewhere along the way he'd started developing feelings for Mia. Beyond the smoldering desire and aggravation she inspired, his subconscience had taken an emotional turn, and he wasn't at all happy with that particular revelation.

Their attraction was no longer a teasing, seductive game between them they were both skirting. They'd leapt over personal and intimate boundaries that never, ever should have been crossed. He wasn't the type of guy who sought out one-night stands, and he hated that his time with Mia had been reduced to something so cheap. But there was no future for the two of them together, and they both knew it.

He'd be crazy to get mixed up with her beyond their one night together. They couldn't be more opposite—he colored inside the lines, and Mia did not. She bucked convention, and he was a man who lived by the rules. And she was completely opposite of what he wanted and needed in his life. Someone solid. Grounded. Not a woman who loved the thrill of being impulsive and lived to drive him insane. Her defiant and rash decisions went against his grain, especially when he'd seen in his line of work where that kind of behavior could lead.

Unfortunately, none of those strong and valid arguments made him stop wanting her. Just the opposite, actually. It was as though one taste of her had left him ravenous for the whole entire feast. He wanted to eat her up and use his tongue to lick and savor every single inch of her body. Especially her breasts, the soft curve of her belly, and between her thighs . . .

"Yo, Cam. You still with me?"

Startled out of his thoughts, Cameron jerked in his seat and shook off the erotic images dancing in his head. He glanced up at Steve from across the conference room table and was reminded of yet another reason why he'd do well to keep his distance from Mia. Any further involvement with her could only lead to trouble for him, and he wasn't about to risk his friendship and business with Steve for another tumble with Mia. No matter how much the provocative thought tempted him.

"Sorry 'bout that," he muttered and tried to remember what they'd been discussing before his mind had taken a sharp detour down a road better left untraveled.

"What's up with you anyway?" Steve asked as he leaned back in his chair and regarded Cameron in that speculative way of his. "All morning you've seem distracted, like something's on your mind. Rough weekend?"

Cameron scrubbed a hand along his jaw and released a frustrated sigh. "Yeah, you could say that."

A dark brow arched over one of Steve's blue eyes. "Does it involve a woman, by chance?"

Cameron looked away and realized too late that by breaking eye contact with Steve he'd just answered his question with a resounding *yes*. "I'd rather not talk about it."

"Well I'll be damned." A huge grin curved up the corners of Steve's mouth, and his eyes glinted with amusement. "Judging by that miserable look on your face, I'm betting some woman has finally tied you up in knots, and it's about time. You've been playing the field for much too long, and you need to settle down."

Cameron rolled his eyes at that, because it was a comment Steve made much too frequently. "Just because you're deliriously, happily married, doesn't mean everyone else needs to be as well. Some of us are just fine being bachelors."

"Until the right woman comes along," Steve conceded, speaking of his own experience with his wife, Liz, and how he'd resisted any kind of commitment after his divorce until she'd come into his life. "Personally, I always thought you and Mia would hook up, but I guess I was wrong. Then again, the two of you are like mixing oil and water, and you're probably better off with someone who didn't aggravate the hell out of you at every turn with her reckless, provoking ways." Steve followed that with a smirk.

Growing increasingly uncomfortable with the direction

of their conversation, Cameron shifted in his chair. The last thing he wanted to do was discuss Mia with Steve and the way they "mixed." Not like oil and water, but rather like kerosene and a flame. Once they touched, they'd ignited an intense and fiery passion that had burned hotter than anything he ever could have imagined.

Quickly putting the mental breaks on that recollection, Cameron redirected his focus. "Has Mia always been like that?" He kept his tone light and casual, but he was more curious than ever to learn as much as he could about Mia, the girl she'd been as a child, and what had happened along the way to create the woman she'd become. He figured Steve might just have the answers he was searching for.

Confusion etched across Steve's expression. "Has she always been like what?"

Cameron shrugged. "You know . . . reckless. Wild. A daring, headstrong, pain in the ass."

Steve's deep, humorous laughter filled the conference room. "Yeah, ever since I can remember." He thought for a moment and then seemed to grow more serious. "Actually, she was pretty mellow as a child. Until her mother died, anyway."

Intrigued, Cameron pushed on a bit further. "What happened?"

"I was about fourteen when my Aunt Cynthia died, and Mia was five at the time," Steve said, recalling the past. "She didn't handle losing her mom very well and started acting out in small ways at first, which was probably a normal thing. But as she grew older, and the more her brothers tried to shelter and protect her because she was the baby of the family, the more she'd rebel. So, yes, it does seem like she's always been that way."

Cameron nodded, unable to imagine losing a parent at such a young age. Obviously, the loss of her mother had been a huge, defining moment in Mia's life that had forever changed the young, innocent little girl she'd been. He didn't have specific details and knew if he pushed for more information Steve was going to get suspicious and wonder what was up with his interest in Mia. So he kept his questions to himself. Besides, the bits and pieces Cameron had just learned about Mia's childhood was enough to tell him that she most likely had unresolved emotional issues from the past that were going to end up taking her down a path of destruction if she didn't learn to curb her daring and brazen behavior.

Figuring it was time they finished their meeting so they could get to work for the day, Cameron shifted their discussion back to business and off of Mia. "So what else is on the week's schedule?"

"Just one more thing. Here, I saved the best case for last," Steve said wryly and pushed a file folder across the table toward Cameron. "And I do believe it's your turn to handle the next infidelity surveillance."

Cameron groaned as he took the file and opened it to peruse the contract and the notes the client had written on the application. He hated these kinds of extramarital affair cases, as did Steve, thus the reason they took turns investigating them when they came through the office.

Having grown up with two parents who were still in love after forty plus years of marriage, Cameron believed strongly in the power of monogamy. If you weren't happy in a relationship and couldn't work out the problems, it was time to move on. Having an affair solved nothing and usually ended up hurting too many people once the infidelity was out in the open.

In this current case, the husband suspected his wife of cheating on him. Judging by the comments and notes the man had written on the application, all the key signs were there: his wife working more overtime than usual, receiving hang-up calls at home when he picked up the phone, his wife insisting it was all his imagination.

Yep, they were all classic, textbook ploys a significant

other commonly used to deceive and manipulate the other person. And Mr. Shelton was most likely being duped by his not-so-loving wife. He was asking for surveillance, written reports on his wife's activities and who she spent any time with outside of the office, and pictures to use as evidence.

Closing the file on the Shelton case, Cameron blew out a long breath. "Damn, it's going to be one hell of a busy week."

"Speaking of busy," Steve said, a wry note to his voice. "I think we're both feeling overwhelmed by all the business that's come our way lately, wouldn't you agree?"

"Definitely," Cameron said, nodding. "The extra work is great because we've busted our asses to get the company to this point, but I have to tell you, I'm exhausted by the end of the day." And even at that he was taking cases home with him to work on in the evenings.

"Me, too." Steve picked up a pen from the table and rolled it between his fingers. "I've been thinking, maybe it's time to hire someone new to help us out."

It had been him and Steve for so long, the thought of a third person seemed intrusive. However, there was no denying they were swamped with cases and the two of them were only capable of handling so much. "That's not a bad idea."

"We've got to do something. I'd really like to have more quality time to spend with Liz and Cody," Steve said of his wife and son. "I can hardly believe we'll be celebrating his first birthday in a few weeks. Time flies when you get old."

Cameron chuckled. "Yes, you are an old man. And I agree you should spend more time with Liz and Cody."

"And you need more of a social life, and time to pursue things with whatever woman was giving you grief this weekend," Steve added with a grin. "So as we're in agreement, I'll put the word out that we're looking for someone experienced in the investigative field, and we'll see what happens from there."

"Sounds good," Cameron said.

Standing, Cameron gathered his case files, wondering

what Steve would do if he knew the woman who'd given him the best kind of grief he'd had in a while was his cousin, Mia.

Cameron was pretty sure he knew the answer to that. Most likely, *he'd* be looking for a new partner.

AS soon as Mia walked into her apartment Wednesday evening after a long day at work, she set her purse and the day's mail on the kitchen counter and then kicked off her heels. Out of habit, she glanced at the message center on the wall next to the phone and found a note from Gina stating that she was staying at Ray's for the night.

Mia tried to ignore the all-too-frequent sickening feeling in her belly that accompanied the thought of Gina being alone with Ray. Gina was an adult, Mia reasoned, and even though she worried about her roommate and the man she was currently involved with, she couldn't protect Gina if she wasn't willing to admit there was a problem in her relationship with Ray.

Retrieving a cold bottle of water from the refrigerator, Mia twisted off the cap and took a long drink to quench her thirst. Considering her own lack of a love life, which did *not* include her spontaneous night with Cameron, it looked like she had a quiet night of solitude ahead of her. She should have been happy about that, but she enjoyed Gina's company and had grown used to having someone else in the apartment at night, even if she was in her own room working on a stained-glass design.

Being alone was her own fault, she knew. She hadn't had a real relationship with a guy in nearly two years. But like every relationship she'd attempted before, that one had lasted a scarce three months before she'd started to feel restless and stifled and had broken things off. It was a familiar pattern that made her face the fact that she just didn't do relationships. At least not well.

Which was too bad, she thought as she made herself a

chicken Caesar salad for dinner, because she'd really enjoyed being with Cameron the other night—their banter, her teasing, and the way Cameron had ultimately lost control with her. But it wasn't as though he'd asked to see her again when he'd dropped her off at her apartment. No, she'd gotten the distinct impression that she was the kind of woman he'd have a hot, illicit affair with but not a long-term relationship. It appeared that their fling was a one-time deal to finally get her out of his system—even if she did secretly wish for more.

Finished making her salad, she took the plate and her water to the kitchen counter and sorted through her mail, figuring that was about as exciting as her evening was going to get. She took a bite of chicken as she separated the bills from junk mail and catalogs. At the bottom of a pile she came across a regular-size envelope addressed to her, but there was no indication of who the sender was because there wasn't a return address. The envelope was bulkier than normal, indicating there was something more than just a letter inside.

Curiosity piqued, she set her fork down on her plate and opened the envelope. She pulled out the folded piece of paper, opened it, and the contents spilled onto the counter. There was nothing written on the white stationery, and when Mia glanced down to see what had fallen out, her heart nearly stopped in her chest.

There were five photos of *her,* and while the pictures were grainy, there was no mistaking that all of them had been taken at The Electric Blue last Friday night. She knew this because two of the photographs were of her with Cameron. The other three showed her with one man she'd flirted with at the bar before Cameron had arrived, and two other guys who'd asked her to dance and she'd taken up on the invitation.

But it wasn't the pictures themselves that devastated and shocked her. It was what someone had written in bold red ink across each photo. *Whore. Tramp. Slut.*

Prickles of unease skittered down her spine when she thought of someone watching her so intently with the sole purpose of taking pictures of her. The photos might have been taken in a public place, but she still felt as though someone had invaded her privacy.

She double-checked the envelope and piece of paper but came up with nothing. There was no note or any clue as to who had sent the photos or why they felt the need to malign her with such spiteful verbiage.

There was a wealth of anger and hate behind those words, and Mia's first instinct was to take them to work with her tomorrow and drop each one through the paper shredder and pretend she'd never received the offending photographs. But her more practical side told her this could be serious. Whoever had followed her to The Electric Blue and taken those pictures had done so for a reason. And one of those reasons had been to scare her. Though she hated to admit it, even to herself, the person's tactics had worked, because the fear making her heart pound hard and fast in her chest was very real.

She'd like to believe this was a one-time thing, but what if it wasn't? If whoever had followed her to The Electric Blue was deranged enough to take pictures of her out in public and send the copies to her with slurs written all over them, what would stop them from possibly approaching her when she was alone and defenseless? She had no idea what this person was capable of, and she wasn't about to underestimate the situation. Someone needed to know what was going on, just in case something happened to her.

She thought about calling her brother Joel, who was a security specialist, and immediately dismissed the idea. Same with her cousin, Steve, even though he was a private investigator. Both could help her and possibly figure out who had sent her the photos, but she knew all too well what their involvement would cost her. Not only her privacy, but her entire life would be scrutinized and turned upside down more than it already was. And of course Joel and Steve would tell Scott and Alex what was going on, and between all of them, they'd smother her with their overly protective ways and undoubtedly drive her insane.

No, contacting her brother or cousin definitely wasn't an option. Not if she could help it. As she tucked the pictures back into the envelope, she considered her other choices, but the only other person who came to mind who could possibly be of any help to her was Cameron. *If* she could even convince him to help her without letting her family in on the fact that someone was stalking her. And *if* he'd even want to get involved with her, even on a business level, after their night together.

The only way to find out was to ask him, she supposed. And because she wasn't about to stop by his office during the day and risk Steve seeing her with him, she'd have to meet with him privately at his house. The sooner, the better. Like tonight.

So much for a quiet night alone, she thought as she headed to her bedroom to change out of her skirt and blouse and into something more comfortable. It appeared she'd just gotten more excitement than she'd bargained for.

Five

CAMERON finished up the last twenty reps on the bench press in his home gym, sat up, and reached for the towel he'd left nearby. Drenched from his hard, hour-long workout, he swiped the towel across his face and along his neck, then stood and made his way to the shower in his master bedroom. He turned on the water, stripped off his damp shirt and shorts, and stepped into the spacious glass cubicle. The cool water felt great on his heated skin, as did the hard, pulsating spray beating against his pumped-up muscles.

After being presented with the newest extramarital case that past Monday, Cameron hadn't expected to have much free time in the evenings. At least not at home. But so far, the Shelton case hadn't required any nightly surveillance because Mrs. Shelton hadn't been working any overtime this week and had gone straight home after work. She seemed to be on her best behavior, and from what Cameron could conclude, even her lunch hours had been spent running legitimate errands. Alone and on her own.

If Cameron didn't know better, he'd say Mr. Shelton was being paranoid about his wife's whereabouts and activities. Unfortunately, Cam knew that a few days without any contact with a potential boyfriend didn't mean Mrs. Shelton was in the free and clear. Most likely, the opportunity to meet up with her lover hadn't been convenient for either of them, for whatever reason. So Cam had to just sit tight and wait for the two lovers to make their move and then exploit the opportunity when it presented itself. He was very familiar with the process and just how long it could take to gather enough solid, accurate evidence to present to a client.

With his hair scrubbed clean with shampoo, he soaped up his body and thought of all the other cases he'd brought home with him to work on. Most required some kind of Internet research, and because he spent a lot of daylight hours outside the office investigating other cases, handling interviews, and tracing leads, his evenings were filled with getting caught up on paperwork and what he and Steve fondly referred to as grunt work. It was boring, monotonous work, but it had to be done. And that was a great reason for them to hire another investigator, or even an assistant who could help them do the tedious work that would free him and Steve up for other more important things.

Finished with his shower, Cameron turned off the water and stepped out of the stall just as the doorbell rang. Swearing at the visitor's timing, he quickly dried off his body and ran the towel through his wet hair as he headed back into his bedroom to put on some pants.

The doorbell pealed again, followed by a brisk knock. As quick as he could manage, Cameron pulled on a pair of Levis, sans briefs, and buttoned them up as he jogged down the stairs to the entryway. Once there, he opened the door to find the person walking away and already halfway down the sidewalk.

He wasn't expecting company, but he'd recognize the sway of those curvaceous hips anywhere, as well as that sexy, heart-shaped ass that looked as though it had been poured into a snug pair of jeans.

"Mia?" His obvious surprise reflected in his tone.

She turned around quickly, causing her shoulder-length black hair to swirl around her shoulders like a cloud of silk. "Hi," she said, her voice catching on a sweet, breathless hitch. "You're home. I rang the doorbell and knocked a couple times, but when there was no answer—"

"I was in the shower," he explained.

"Oh." She started back toward the porch. "Sorry for the interruption," she murmured, but there was nothing contrite about the way her eyes took in his wet, tousled hair and then gradually dropped to his bare chest, which was still damp from his shower.

In that brazen, unapologetic way of hers, her eyes followed the light sprinkling of hair covering his pecs, all the way down his abdomen, past his navel, to the waistband of his jeans. She licked her bottom lip, prompting him to recall how soft and warm that tongue of hers had been when she'd taken his hard cock deep inside her mouth.

His lower body stirred accordingly to that provocative thought, and he bit back the groan that automatically rose to the surface. No doubt about it, this woman was going to be the death of him, and he wondered if she'd come by for the sole purpose of torturing him with what he wanted so badly. *Her*. Hot and melting beneath him. Again. It was clear to him that even after sleeping with her, Mia Wilde was far from being out of his system. He was beginning to wonder if she ever would be.

She stopped in front of him, close enough to touch, tempting him to reach out and run his fingers through her hair, pull her close, and kiss her senseless. Instead, he leaned casually against the doorjamb and crossed his arms over his chest.

"So, what brings you by?" he asked in a lazy drawl.

Her full breasts rose and fell as she inhaled a deep breath, and something akin to distress flashed in her gaze. The brief glimpse was quickly masked by that tough facade of hers. "Something's happened, and I need your help."

He raised a brow, both intrigued and concerned by her statement. He couldn't begin to imagine what had happened for Mia to admit she needed help, let alone come to him of all people for it. But whatever had transpired, it seemed serious, and he wasn't about to turn her away without hearing what she had to say first.

"Come on in." He stood aside so she could enter the house and then shut the door after her and led the way into his kitchen.

He opened the refrigerator and grabbed himself a cold beer, thinking he could probably use something stronger to deal with Mia, but he wanted his wits about him tonight. "Would you like something to drink? I have water, soda, or beer."

She shook her head. "Nothing for me, thanks."

Twisting the cap off the bottle, he tossed the metal disc into the trash and took a seat on one of the kitchen counter bar stools across from where she was standing. Distance was the key with this woman, he decided, because any kind of close proximity was dangerous as hell to his libido. Except the counter cut off his view of her at the waist, drawing his attention to her low-cut, snug-fitting, lace-trimmed camisole top and the way the soft pink cotton material molded to her voluptuous breasts.

Oh, hell.

Forcing his mind to concentrate on the situation at hand and not on Mia's very luscious body, he guzzled a long drink of his beer as he lifted his gaze back up where it belonged and took in her expression. He could immediately tell by the crease of her brows that she was upset about something, even though she was trying hard not to let it show.

It was such a novelty to him to see yet another side to her persona, to realize that Mia was a woman with real feelings and emotions, and even had a few chinks in that headstrong personality of hers. He wondered what really lurked beneath all that bravado of hers and then decided he was probably better off not knowing.

"So what's up?" he asked, turning the conversation toward business and the reason for her impromptu visit.

She met his gaze, not as the sultry seductress he'd come to know, but as a woman seriously in need of help. "I received something very disturbing in the mail today."

That immediately piqued his interest as well as his P.I. instincts. "What, exactly, did you receive?"

"Pictures. Of me. They were taken last Friday night at The Electric Blue," she explained calmly. "But it's not the pictures that bother me so much as what someone wrote on them."

Cameron was more curious than ever. "Do you have the pictures with you?"

She nodded. "I figured you'd want to see them, so I brought everything for you to look at." Opening her purse, she pulled out an envelope and then handed it to him from across the countertop.

Setting his beer aside, he checked out the envelope, front and back. He noticed that Mia's name and address had been typed out and there was no return address, though the postmark indicated the envelope had been mailed from Chicago. He withdrew the contents, unfolded the plain piece of paper, and checked out the enclosed photos and the offensive slurs someone had written across each one.

On one hand, he was stunned by the degradation behind the pictures and insulting words. On the other, he'd always known Mia's reckless behavior had the potential of courting this kind of trouble. But that didn't mean she deserved to be the target of such a sick and deranged joke.

"Not very flattering, is it?" she asked, striving for a humorous approach to the pictures that showed her wilder side with four different men—him included.

She was trying to be light and breezy about the photographs someone had taken of her without her knowledge, but there was nothing remotely amusing about her predicament. Someone obviously had some kind of grudge against Mia, and they were intent on exploiting and scaring her.

He arranged the pictures on the counter so he could compare each one and met her gaze. "Do you have any idea who might do something like this?"

A wry grin canted the corner of her mouth. "If I did, I wouldn't be here."

"Good point," he murmured. Mia never would have dropped by his house to see him on a personal, intimate level. No, their very brief affair was done and over with, and other than a business-related issue, there was no real reason for them to spend time together.

"I have no idea who sent the pictures, or why," she went on, her tone frustrated as she waved a hand toward the photos. "There wasn't a note in the envelope, or anything else to indicate what the person wanted."

He rubbed his hand along his unshaven jaw as he studied the prints again. The images weren't crisp and clear, indicating that they'd either been taken with a camera phone, a disposable camera, or by an amateur. "Well, they don't appear to be professional shots."

"I thought the same thing myself." Mia bit on the corner of her lip and then met his gaze. "I thought of something when I first saw the pictures."

"And what was that?" he prompted.

"I saw my neighbor there Friday night hanging out with a few of his guy friends," she explained. "I always thought Will was a nice enough guy, and I've never felt uncomfortable around him or threatened in any way, but I suppose he could have taken these photos."

He frowned, not quite following the conclusion she'd drawn. "What makes you think your neighbor might be responsible for the pictures?"

"I've seen him taking pictures around the apartment building with one of those big, bulky cameras," she said, gesturing with her hands. "You know, the kind with the big lense that looks way too complicated for a novice to use."

Abrupt laughter escaped him. "I highly doubt a camera of that caliber would take such grainy pictures." And he should know, because he and Steve used a professional Canon when a client requested photos of their investigation.

Her shoulder lifted in a half-shrug, giving her breasts a sweet, eye-catching bounce. "Maybe's he's just learning."

"Maybe." Cameron wasn't about to dismiss any possibility. "But why would he take pictures of you with other guys and write these words on them? Has he asked you out before and you turned him down?" It was the most plausible motive he could come up with.

"No." She absently tucked back a strand of silky black hair brushing along her cheek. "We've talked a few times, but there's never been any kind of attraction between us."

Cameron didn't want to analyze why her answer relieved him so much. He didn't want to give a damn about her social life with other men, and he definitely didn't want to think about another man touching or kissing her the way he had last Friday night. But after having tasted what it was like to be with her so intimately, he was beginning to care too much.

"I'm just going on the fact that he has this camera and I've seen him use it when I've been around," she continued, completely unaware of the direction Cameron's thoughts had wandered. "His apartment balcony is across from mine, and he's got a perfect view of my place. And a few weekends ago when I was laying out by the pool I saw him standing out on his balcony with his camera. As soon as he realized I was watching him, he hurried back inside his apartment. At the time, I didn't think much of it, but now I can't help but wonder."

Mia's concerns were believable, and warranted. "Well, he's certainly worth checking out." Cameron reached for the pad of paper and a pen he always left by the phone on the counter, prepared to take notes to pass on to Steve, who would most likely handle the case. "What's Will's last name?"

She blinked at him in surprise. "I don't know. We were on a first-name basis only."

"Not a problem. I'll find out." Not only the man's last name, but Cameron planned to make sure Steve did a thorough background check on the guy as well. "Let's talk about who else you remember seeing at The Electric Blue Friday night. What about the girlfriend who drove you to the place?"

Mia came around the counter and sat on the bar stool next to his. Much too close for comfort, Cameron thought.

"You mean Carrie Jansen, the woman we spoke to as we were leaving the bar?"

"Yeah, her." Ignoring the awareness kicking up the beat of his pulse, he jotted down the woman's name for future reference. "She seemed a bit on edge that night."

She tipped her head, her expression curious. "How would you know?"

He tapped the end of his pen against the pad of paper. "Because I was watching her."

Mia's spine stiffened, and her curiosity shifted not-so-subtly to indignation. "You were?"

He nodded, barely able to suppress a grin at Mia's reaction. "Actually, she asked me to dance."

A fascinating flash of jealousy passed across her features, an emotion that pleased him way too much, because he'd like to believe that on some level that show of envy meant *she* cared. Maybe even more than she, herself, realized. He found that bit of knowledge both exciting and disconcerting.

A few long seconds ticked by before he finally let her off the hook. "I turned her down, and she didn't seem too happy about that." But amazingly, Mia appeared *very* relieved. "Does Carrie have any reason to slander you this way?" he asked, because the woman's actions that evening had him questioning just how good a friend she was to Mia.

She glanced back at the photos and visibly shuddered at the images and words staring back at her. "She's been moody lately, but I can't think of anything I've done to make her stoop to this level."

Cameron wasn't so sure, but he let the issue slide for the time being. "All right. Who else?"

She thought for a quick moment. "Other than my roommate, Gina, and her boyfriend, Ray, there was no one else there I knew personally. Just casual acquaintances I've seen at The Electric Blue on other nights."

"I don't much care for your roommate's boyfriend." His statement was as blunt as it was honest.

"You don't even know him," she said, laughing lightly.

"I don't have to know a person to see what a bonafide jerk he is," he said, a thread of disgust lacing his tone. "I saw the way he treated Gina. The guy's possessive as hell, and I'm betting he's got a temper to match."

"You're very perceptive," she murmured, seemingly impressed with his accurate assessment of the guy.

A slow, easygoing grin eased up the corners of his mouth. "It's my job, sweetheart."

Mia wasn't sure what affected her more, the devastatingly sexy smile on Cameron's face, or the deep, husky endearment that had slipped from his too-sensual lips. Both caused a warm, tingling rush of sensation to settle low. Then, because he still hadn't put on a shirt, there was all that naked male flesh tempting her to reach out and caress. The man had a body to die for, and she would have loved to spend hours worshiping all that lean muscle and sinew in the most reverent, thorough way.

Back to business, Cameron's expression turned serious and focused once more. "What's Ray's last name?"

Sighing, she attempted to dismiss her arousing thoughts so she, too, could concentrate on their conversation. "Wilkins."

He wrote that down on his notepad, underlined the name

a few times for emphasis, and then glanced back up at her. "What do you know about Ray?"

"Actually, you pegged him pretty well. He's very controlling when it comes to Gina, and I've seen him handle her a bit too roughly a few times."

A fierce frown pulled at his dark blond brows. "Then what the hell is Gina doing with him?"

"I honestly don't know." She recalled Gina's split lip and the exchange they'd had a few days ago, as well as her friend's reluctance to listen to what she had to say. "I've tried to talk to her about Ray and the way he treats her, but she always has an excuse or she cuts the conversation short."

"Sounds like a classic case of battered woman's syndrome."

Surprised by his knowledge, she asked, "And you know this how?"

His wide shoulders lifted in a shrug, making the muscles across his chest shift and ripple with the movement. "Those psych classes I took in college come in handy sometimes, not to mention that I've dealt with all kinds of abuse cases in my line of work. Gina's obviously being emotionally and mentally manipulated by Ray, and maybe even physically abused, as well." As he spoke, he wrote the words *possible abusive tendencies* beneath Ray's name. "He might have even threatened to really hurt her if she leaves him, and she's scared enough to stay in the relationship and not tell anyone what's going on."

Mia hated the thought of her friend being in such a dark place and knew she needed to tell Cameron about her own run-ins with Ray for him to do his job and help her find out who was behind the pictures. And maybe, in the process, he could do a check on Ray to see what secrets lurked in his past.

"He's made a couple passes at me," she said.

That snagged Cameron's full attention. "What happened?"

"He's grabbed my butt, which he claimed was an accident, and he's made a few lewd suggestions that he's tried to couch as a joke, none of which I found the least bit funny." If anything, she'd been not only offended, but revolted by his behavior. "I also don't care for the way I've seen him look at me, either. It gives me the creeps."

The hand resting on the counter curled into a tight fist, and Cameron's expression darkened. "If he touches you again, you let me know," he said gruffly.

"Why, so you can go beat him up?" she joked and batted her lashes playfully at him.

"It would be my pleasure to kick his ass *and* emasculate him so he'd think twice before touching any woman ever again," he said in a deep, menacing growl.

She rolled her eyes at his he-man approach. "You're beginning to sound like my brothers and cousins."

He shot her a hot, smoldering look that spoke volumes and told her that there was nothing siblinglike to the attraction still simmering between them. "Speaking of which, I'm going to hand these notes over to your cousin Steve so he can follow up on these leads."

Her amusement fled, immediately replaced by a heavy weight of dread. *"No."*

He looked taken aback by her adamant tone. "I think your cousin should know about this."

"If I wanted Steve to know about this situation, I would have gone directly to him," she said in a firm, precise tone that brooked no argument. "I came to you for help *specifically* because I don't want any of my cousins or brothers involved." This was an issue she wasn't about to budge on, no matter what it took to convince Cameron to take on the case.

But at the moment, he appeared completely unswayed. "Why wouldn't you want your family to know about this?"

She exhaled a frustrated breath. "Because once you tell Steve about the pictures, he'll tell my brothers what's going on, and before you know it I'll be under watch 24/7; they'll be pressuring me to move back home where they feel it's *safe*. Joel would probably assign one of his guys at his security firm to be my constant shadow, too. Being smothered by my brothers and cousins is *not* an option for me, and that's *exactly* what will happen if they get involved."

"All our cases are handled confidentially," he said, attempting to reassure her.

Her laughter held a cynical edge. "Not when it comes to my family. You know as well as I do there is no way Steve would keep something like this to himself."

He leaned back on his barstool and crossed his arms over his chest. This time, he didn't argue her valid point. "If you want the truth, because of our . . ."

He seemed to struggle for the right phrasing, and she supplied it for him. "Affair?"

"Okay, affair," he said, accepting her choice of word to describe what had happened between them that past Friday night. "Because of our involvement, I don't think I'm the right person to handle this case. Conflict of interest and all that."

Bullshit, she wanted to say but didn't. She'd never been a potty mouth, and she wasn't about to start now. She also hated to resort to scheming tactics, but she was desperate to persuade him. "Fine, I'll handle this myself," she said abruptly and scooped up the pictures still spread out on the counter. "Forget I ever came by, and I'd appreciate you keeping this to yourself."

He grasped her wrist before she could shove the photos back into the envelope. Her pulse thrummed erratically beneath the press of his warm thumb, and she lifted her gaze to his. Heat and desire arched between them, and she watched him struggle to keep his reaction to her in check.

"Mia, don't be stupid," he bit out in annoyance. "You can't go off on your own with the possibility of someone stalking you."

"I *prefer* not to."

He groaned, knowing exactly what she was insinuating. "You always have to make things difficult, don't you?"

She flashed him a sassy grin. "You should be flattered that I came to you for help."

He lifted a brow at her attempt to manipulate him. "Flattered enough to agree to help you, you mean?"

"It's all semantics, sugar." She shrugged and started to withdraw her hand from his grasp. "But the bottom line is, you're not interested."

He tightened his grip, and her heart skipped a wild beat. "No, that's the problem," he said in a rough, gravely tone of voice. "I'm way too interested . . . in *you*."

The honest emotion in his beautiful green eyes startled her. Many men had sweet-talked her in an attempt to get under her skirt, but never with the kind of intensity and need she'd just witnessed in Cameron's gaze. It was thrilling to know he wanted her that much, because the feeling was definitely mutual.

She licked her suddenly dry lips. "And that's a problem, why?"

"Because I don't think you and I are a good match. Outside of the bedroom, anyway." His thumb brushed gently, seductively over that sensitive spot on her wrist as if to soothe away the sting of his words. "I want you, Mia, and being inside of you that one time was nothing short of amazing, but the truth is, you're all wrong for me, in so many ways, and I just don't think you and I working together is such a great idea."

She couldn't deny that his comment hurt, though she had to admit it didn't come as a huge surprise. She'd always known she wasn't Cameron's type—outside of the bedroom, anyway. She was good enough for him to have sex with, but not good enough for him to consider a relationship with. At least he was being open and honest with her and taking her feelings into consideration, because that was the nice, do-right kind of guy he was.

But for as much as his comment made her heart feel a little battered and bruised, she wasn't looking for a long-term relationship, either. Especially considering her own lousy track record with men. So she supposed on some level they wanted the same thing, which made for a perfect arrangement, in her way of thinking.

"What's the matter, sugar?" she taunted, drawing strength from her ability to push her true feelings deep down inside, which was a helluva lot easier than dealing with them outright. "Afraid it will happen again?"

"The thing is, if I'm near you for any length of time and the opportunity presents itself, I *know* it'll happen again."

With that bit of honesty out in the open between them, he tugged gently on her arm, pulling her off her chair and toward him, until she stood between his widespread thighs. He rested his big hands on her waist to hold her in place, and her lower body quickened when she felt the hard, thick length of him pressing against her jeans zipper. Face-to-face, their eyes locked, and she was mesmerized by the carnal desire she saw glittering in his gaze and absolutely breathless with anticipation of what he intended to do.

"I can't stop thinking about last Friday and how much I want to be with you again," he said as he slipped his hands upward, beneath the hem of her camisole top. His warm, slightly callused thumbs stroked along her belly, and her nipples tightened into hard points. "Except this time, I'd make it right."

She'd deliberately goaded Cameron to protect her emotions and to show him she was unaffected by his remark about the two of them not being a good match. But what she hadn't expected was for Cameron to turn the tables on her and draw her into a web of sensuality so powerful, she felt helpless to resist him. And why should she curb her desires when she wanted him so badly?

With that arousing thought tumbling through her head, she placed her hands on his forearms, loving the feel of his hair-roughened skin, toned muscles, and the heat radiating off him. Undeniably curious, she asked, "What do you mean, 'make it right'?"

"I'd take it real slow this time," he explained as he dragged his hands back out from under her top.

She almost whimpered at the loss of his touch, until he filled both of his palms with her heavy, aching breasts and squeezed them through the thin material of her camisole top and sheer bra.

His gaze melded with hers, so hot she felt singed by his sizzling stare. "I'd give more attention to these lovely mounds of flesh and take each one into my mouth so I can finally know how you taste. I'd suck on your nipples for a good long time before moving on."

She bit her bottom lip and swallowed back a moan as he closed his thumb and index finger around those stiff, sensitive tips and gave a firm, tantalizing tug on each one, which she felt all the way down to her core. She might have been able to hold back her verbal response to his seduction, but her body automatically arched into his skillful hands.

The slight, sinful smile that curved his mouth told her he knew how hot and restless he was making her, and he was enjoying every minute of having the upper hand. "When I finally have my fill of your breasts, I'd kiss your belly and dip my tongue into your navel," he went on as his fingers skimmed downward, mimicking his words. "And then, when you were writhing beneath me and begging for more, I'd go down on you and use my tongue to make you come, no matter how long it took."

This time, she did moan, long and loud, as he slid his long fingers between her jean-clad thighs and pressed his thumb hard against her cleft.

Her helpless sound of wanting seemed to please him, though the rogue wasn't done tormenting her just yet. "I'd spend hours kissing you here . . . long, slow, soft kisses. Deep, tongue-swirling kisses. Hard, sucking kisses against your clit, until you finally screamed with the pleasure of it."

She was melting, her sex tingling where his fingers were

rubbing against her swollen flesh, and she suspected that if anyone could make her have an orgasm that way, it would be Cameron.

It was all she could do to keep herself from crawling up onto his lap and straddling his waist for a more direct, illicit contact. Instead, she grasped his bare shoulders with her hands before her legs gave out on her and she dropped her head closer to his. "And then what?" she dared to ask, even as her breath came in short, anxious pants.

Lifting his free hand up to her face, he gently brushed the backs of his knuckles against her flushed cheek before threading his fingers through her hair and curling them around the nape of her neck. He drew her head down to his, and the last thing she caught was the lust simmering in his eyes before she felt his lips graze along her jaw, all the way up to her ear.

He pressed his cheek against hers, the electric scrape of his evening stubble on her soft skin an erotic sensation that heightened the sexual tension rising between them. She closed her eyes and leaned more fully into his hard, lean body, anxiously awaiting what he'd say next.

He certainly didn't disappoint her. "And then, when you were wet and soft and ready for me, I'd slide deep, deep inside of you," he murmured, his breath warm and damp against her ear. "I'd fuck you slowly, make it last so I can savor everything about how you feel, inside and out . . . how hot and tight you are, the way you moan when I thrust high and hard, and the way your soft breasts and hard nipples feel rubbing against my chest. Then there's the friction of our bodies straining together, and finally, how exquisite you feel gripping my cock as I come."

She shivered, and with his fingers tangled through the hair at the back of her neck, he gently tugged her head back so their gazes met once more and their lips were mere inches apart. There was something strangely exciting about being at this man's mercy, as she currently was. God, she wanted him, with a fierce, powerful kind of need she'd never experienced before.

With her own mouth poised so close to his, she issued a challenge to get exactly what she desired. "So what's stopping you from doing all that?" *Certainly not her.*

"At the moment, not a damn thing," he said gruffly, and took her mouth with his own.

Six

WHEN it came to his kiss, Cameron made good on his promise to go slow and take his time, giving Mia a small sampling of what kind of ecstasy he was capable of giving her with his mouth. And his hands.

At the moment his palms were sliding down her spine in a provocative caress that made her arch toward him like a cat craving more of his petting and attention. He traced the indentation of her waist with his fingers, the curve of her hips, and when he reached her bottom, he cupped her buttocks in his hands and pulled her lower body flush to his. His thick erection pressed against the crux of her thighs, right where he belonged, making her wish they were both naked so she could feel that hard, sleek length sliding along her weeping sex.

The connection of their mouths gradually deepened, but only because he allowed it. Their tongues touched, slid together, and mated in slow, sweeping strokes. He ate at her mouth like a succulent piece of fruit, alternating licking and sucking with mind-blowing precision. He made her weak with wanting. Excited with anticipation. And anxious to feel him pushing deep inside her again.

A woman could die from so much lust and sexual tension surging through her all at once. At least, that's how she felt at the moment.

Moaning deep in her throat, she rolled her hips against his, seeking more pressure. More friction. More *everything*. She wanted to be taken, right here, right now. On his lap, up on the counter, or even on the floor. Fast or slow, she didn't care, so long as he appeased the growing ache spreading like wildfire through her veins. She was on the brink of going mad, and it was all his doing.

But instead of following through on the rest of the erotic fantasy he'd just shared with her, he ended the kiss and leaned back in his chair, though his hands remained touching her, lingering on her hips. She couldn't read his expression and had no idea what he was thinking or feeling at the moment, though it was obvious by the huge bulge straining against the fly of his jeans that he was still plenty aroused.

Mia's insides clenched with disappointment that he'd brought everything to an abrupt stop, especially when she'd been more than willing to go all the way, but she was hopeful she'd at least managed to sway him to take on her case. "So does this mean you'll help me out?" she asked, striving for a playful, teasing tone.

A half-grin tipped up the corner of his mouth. "Why do I feel totally and completely manipulated into saying yes?"

He was going to make her work for this, she realized, and she was certainly willing to play the game his way to get what she wanted. "*You're* the one who started all that sex talk, not me." Not that she was complaining, though her body was certainly protesting the way he'd revved her up, only to leave her strung tighter than a bow. But they'd get back to that problem in a few minutes, just as soon as she secured his help.

He crossed his arms over his chest, which only made him look more devastatingly male. More masculine. More sexy. "Yeah, well, talk is cheap."

She laughed. His way of talking had been anything but cheap. "And actions speak louder than words," she quipped right back. "Did it ever occur to you that maybe I want the same thing as you?"

His gaze narrowed, though she could tell he was toying with her. Maybe even testing her. "Why? You got what you wanted from me last Friday night."

And of course he believed she was a woman who only indulged in one-night stands. And she couldn't blame Cameron for his way of thinking, considering that's the impression she'd always given *him*—that she was carefree and frivolous and only out for a good time, nothing more.

She pushed away the unexpected hurt and focused on seducing Cam instead. "Maybe I want more than one night," she said as she trailed her fingers up his hard, muscular thigh, which tensed beneath her touch. "Maybe I want to see if you're really up to the challenge of making me come with a guy. Specifically, with *you*."

His eyes flashed with heat and lust. "Okay, you've definitely got my attention."

She couldn't contain her triumphant grin. "You want me. I want you." She shrugged as if the end results were obvious. "The way I see it, this can be a win-win situation the whole way around, for both of us."

"A temporary affair while I help you figure out who sent the pictures, while leaving your brothers and cousins out of the equation?"

"It works for me."

But despite her grand plan, Mia was well aware that she'd have to protect her heart in the process, because she was beginning to fear that this man had the ability to affect her on a much deeper level than any guy she'd dated before. And a broken heart at the end of their affair wasn't something she wanted, or needed, because there was no doubt in her mind they would go their separate ways. No matter how good the sex between them might be, she could never be what Cameron wanted in his life—someone demure and sweet and accommodating. Everything about what he wanted in a woman went against who she was, and she wasn't about to change for any man. And especially not that drastically.

"So what do you say, sugar?" she asked in a cajoling tone of voice. "Do we have a deal?"

He stared at her for a long moment, seemingly weighing the pros and cons of accepting her *deal*. "I'd say you drive a hard bargain."

"*Hard* being the operative word?" She grinned shamelessly at him.

He chuckled and shook his head. "You're something else, you know that?" Then he grew serious once more. "I'll agree to help you out, with a few conditions."

She should have known he'd set down rules. The man was a straight shooter and did everything by the book. "Which are?"

"When it comes to the case, you do as I say and don't do any kind of investigating on your own or without me knowing about it," he said succinctly.

She didn't care for his terms, which were too restrictive for her tastes, but she had no choice but to comply. "Fine."

"And if you do anything stupid that jeopardizes your safety, you can guarantee Steve is going to find out what's going on."

That wasn't a condition to their deal or even an idle threat, but a firm, unnegotiable statement she knew Cameron would back up in a heartbeat if she went against his wishes.

He lifted a brow when she remained uncharacteristically quiet. "Agreed?" he prompted.

"Agreed," she said begrudgingly.

He did a poor job of smothering the smile trying to make an appearance. "With that settled, I'm thinking the two of us should hit The Electric Blue on Friday night."

"Together? As a couple?" she asked with feigned shock that he'd be seen with her out in public.

"Together, but separate. I'm certainly not letting you go there by yourself when someone could be stalking you," he replied, not committing to anything in terms of their relationship. "I'll be there watching everyone and how they interact with you, but I think it would be best if it looks like you're single and on your own."

"So you want me to do what I normally do when I go to The Electric Blue? Mingle. Dance. That sort of thing?"

"Yeah, except no entering the wet T-shirt contest," he said with a frown.

She caressed her hand along his cheek and ran her thumb along the groove turning down the corner of his mouth. "That was all for *you,* sugar. That was my first time entering a contest like that."

"And your last," he muttered beneath his breath.

She lifted a brow, surprised to hear the possessive tone to his voice. To think he might be even a tad bit jealous sent a tiny thrill racing through her. "Be careful, or else I'll start to think I matter to you."

She was teasing him, but her traitorous heart skipped a beat when she realized he wasn't the least bit amused. His serious, piercing, protective look said more than words ever could—that maybe, possibly, she was beginning to matter too much. And she wasn't quite sure what to make of that.

Then he glanced away, severing the profound moment. "I figure with you and I arriving separately, this will be the best way for me to keep an eye on Carrie and Ray, and maybe even your neighbor, Will, too," he said, back to business. "Because we're essentially trying to set up the culprit into doing something to draw attention to himself, you might want to mention to your friend Carrie and your roommate

Gina that you'll be at The Electric Blue on Friday. We'll see who shows up and what happens."

She nodded. "That's easy enough to do."

"Great." He picked up the photos of her that were still on the counter and tucked them back into the envelope. "I'll keep these for now, and any others you might happen to get."

She shuddered to think there might be more. "I really hope this is a one-time joke, even as sick and deranged as it is."

"Me, too," he said, though he didn't sound at all convinced this was the end to her predicament. "Come on, I'll walk you out to your car."

He stood, and she quickly placed her hand on his chest to bring him to an abrupt halt. She couldn't believe he'd arouse her to the point of unraveling with his carnally whispered words and bone-melting kiss and was then just going to send her on her way instead of following through on his seduction.

"You can't leave me like this," she blurted out.

He looked genuinely confused. "Like what?"

How could he be so dense when she was still so incredibly turned on from his detailed outline of what he'd like to do to her. "Like I'm right on the verge of . . . *something*." Something that felt so very close to an explosive, breathless orgasm.

A crooked grin canted his mouth. "It's called foreplay, sweetheart."

"It's called cruel and unusual *punishment*." She couldn't resist poking him in the chest with her finger for extra emphasis.

He grabbed her wrist before she could jab him again, humor glimmering in the depths of his gorgeous green eyes. "It's torture of the sweetest kind."

She jutted her chin out stubbornly. "Well, there's a cure for what ails me if you won't finish what you started."

"Oh, I plan to finish you off," he murmured wickedly and brought her fingers to his lips so he could nibble on the tips. "But not tonight. And in the meantime, don't you dare take the edge off all this sexual tension I worked so hard to build up. *I* want to be the one to make you come, not some battery-operated device."

She opened her mouth to issue a smart-ass retort but lost her voice when his soft, wet tongue slid down between two fingers and flicked at the sensitive webbing connecting the two. She squirmed as if he'd just licked her intimately. "Oh, God, I can't wait that long."

"Yes, you can." He placed an infinitely sweet kiss in the center of her palm, a direct contrast to the ripples of heat and awareness arcing between the two of them. "You might be calling the shots about me being the one to handle your case, but I'm the one in charge of how and when you come."

Her jaw nearly dropped open. "That's ludicrous!"

"Yeah, probably so," he agreed unrepentantly. "But you'll do as I ask."

Every one of her instincts rallied at her to object to his assertive and cocky attitude, as well as his arrogance in taking control of how and when she achieved her own sexual gratification. If it was anyone else, she'd tell them to take a hike. But much to her chagrin, she found herself swallowing back a scathing reply and once again playing the game his way.

Because, as she'd discovered last Friday night, Cameron Sinclair and his sexual expertise were worth waiting for.

CAMERON'S surveillance on Trish Shelton was turning out to be a complete bust, not to mention it was putting a major crimp in his Friday evening plans to meet up with Mia at The Electric Blue.

After a solid five days with no action, Trish had placed a last-minute call to her husband claiming she'd forgotten about a dinner meeting she had with a client. It was definitely cause for suspicion, and Doug Shelton had immediately called Cameron to let him know his wife's plans had abruptly changed.

Seeing it as a prime opportunity to catch the woman in action, so to speak, and put an end to the case, Cameron had grabbed the keys to the company's unmarked Ford Excursion, which was fully stocked with surveillance equipment, and had followed Trish from her office to a nearby restaurant where she was supposed to meet up with her "client."

After parking across the street, Cameron had entered the restaurant, scanned the dining area for Trish, and was lucky enough to find a seat at the bar that afforded him a view of her table. He nursed a bottle of beer and waited for a man to arrive to contradict what she'd told her husband. He was sorely disappointed when a woman showed up instead, shook Trish's hand in a professional manner, and sat down to discuss what appeared to be business over dinner.

So much for wrapping up this case, Cameron thought irritably. Once he'd finished his beer, he'd headed back out to the truck to wait for Trish to leave the restaurant so he could take a few pictures of her with the other woman, to show to Doug Shelton that his wife's business dinner had been completely legitimate.

He could have just taken off for the night when the other woman had arrived and written up a report for his client, but Cameron prided himself on being thorough in his surveillance and his investigations. Especially because there was no telling where Trish might be heading once her current business was concluded for the evening.

So in the meantime, he made some calls on his cell phone that he needed to return and set up the camera with the zoom lense so he could capture the evidence on film when the opportunity arose. Time slowly dragged on, and he grew restless and eager to be on his way.

Finally, Trish and the other woman walked out of the restaurant together, enabling Cameron to get the shots he needed. The two ladies went their separate ways, and he tailed Trish from a discreet distance all the way to her house, while placing a call to Doug Shelton to give him a quick update. Once

Cameron was assured she was home for the night, he turned around and made his way back into the city.

By then it was nearly eight P.M., a good hour later than when he'd promised Mia he'd be at The Electric Blue. He'd called her earlier to let her know he'd be running late, but he didn't like the thought of Mia being alone at the bar, where someone was possibly watching her and waiting for an opportunity to do something more nefarious than just taking a photograph of her. And he definitely didn't like the thought of other guys hitting on her, dancing with her, or touching her in any way whatsoever.

He stepped on the gas and increased the speed of the Excursion, wishing he was in his power-charged Porsche instead. God, he was getting so sucked in by Mia, and even though she'd managed to manipulate him into helping her, he had to admit he'd agreed for purely selfish reasons, too. Having sex with her again was certainly an incentive, but the woman intrigued him on too many levels to count, and the two mixed together proved to be a dangerous combination not only to his unruly libido, but emotionally as well.

Beyond the scorching heat and attraction the two of them generated, he was drawn to her and all the different facets of her personality: the good qualities, her vulnerable side, and even her way of goading and annoying him. He'd always enjoyed unraveling mysteries, and Mia was one big giant puzzle he was determined to solve. It was all a matter of peeling away the different facades she hid behind and discovering the real woman beneath. Having her and all that fire, energy, and passion in his bed was merely a bonus he had every intention of enjoying to the fullest.

And hopefully, once he figured out her allure, he could get her out of his head and system and move on. Just another case closed.

The ringing of his cell phone pulled him from his thoughts of Mia. He glanced at the hands-free unit display, saw that the call was from his mother, and hit the connect button.

"Hi, Mom."

"Hi, Cameron," she said, her soft, cultured tone filling the cab of the vehicle. "How have you been?"

He winced, knowing his mother's question held a deeper meaning, but she was too polite to outright say he'd been remiss in calling or stopping by lately. "I've been good, Mom." And then he wondered if maybe something was wrong. "Are you and Dad okay?"

"We're fine, honey, though your father has mentioned he sure has missed having a golf outing with his son the past few months."

Another sting of guilt he couldn't avoid. "Yeah, I know. Work's been crazy. I'll have to set aside a Sunday morning for a game."

"Your father would absolutely love spending the time with you," she said, and he could hear the satisfied smile in her voice. "But I didn't call you for that. Your sister, Claudia, is turning forty next week, and I'm having her birthday dinner at the house next Sunday for her and the family. I want to be sure you keep the evening free."

Claudia was the oldest of his three sisters, and as each kid had left home and started lives of their own, his mother had made it a ritual to have birthday dinners for each one of them to be sure there were at least a few family gatherings that brought them together throughout the year. Over the years, their birthday dinners had grown in size, because each one of his sisters was married with children of her own.

"I wouldn't miss it, Mom," he promised and made a mental note to add the date to his PDA so there was no way he could forget, since his schedule had been so hectic the past few weeks.

"I also wanted to let you know, you're welcome to bring a friend."

His mother's subtle comment made Cameron smirk. "So I can bring Rick, then?" He knew damn well that's not what she meant, but he hadn't been able to resist contradicting her just to see how she'd respond.

"Well, I was hoping you'd bring a friend of the female gender. You know, someone you might be dating?"

Cam turned into The Electric Blue's parking lot as images of Mia immediately filled his mind, with her innate sensuality, wild ways, and smart mouth. She was so different from any woman he'd ever brought home to meet his family, and it had been a long time since he'd even done that. He could only imagine what Mia would say or do to shock his refined mother and equally straitlaced sisters and found himself smiling at the thought.

Finding an open space a few slots away from Mia's flashy red Celica, he parked the truck and turned off the engine. "Sorry, Mom, but I'm not dating anyone right now."

Her disappointed sigh drifted through the intercom. "And that's such a shame, too."

Cameron rolled his eyes, having heard the "you need to settle down like your sisters have" lecture many times before. He would, when the right woman finally came along.

"I hate to cut you short, Mom, but I need to go," he said before she could launch into her speech. "I promise to be there next Sunday for Claude's dinner."

After a quick good-bye he ended the call, clipped the cell phone onto the waistband of his jeans, and got out of the truck. A minute later he was entering The Electric Blue, and it was just as loud and jam-packed as it had been the previous Friday night. At the moment, the waiters and waitresses were dancing up on the bar and tabletops, which had the riled-up crowd whistling and cheering them on. He half expected to find Mia up there doing a few shimmies and shakes of her own, but much to his relief, she wasn't part of the evening's entertainment.

His gaze scanned the establishment, and just when he caught sight of Mia standing at the bar with a group of men, he felt a large hand clamp down firmly on his shoulder. He turned around with his fists clenched tight, instinctively in defense mode, until he came face to face with Mia's brother Joel, who was flanked by two of his business partners and Marine buddies, Kevin and Ben. As security specialists, all three were big, muscular, intimidating-looking guys—the kind women looked twice at and men didn't mess with.

Cameron had never considered the possibility of running into anyone from Mia's family here. Her three cousins were married, along with her brothers Scott and Alex, and they were no longer into the bar scene. But Joel was a consummate playboy who enjoyed having a good time, especially when there were single women involved, and The Electric Blue certainly provided that.

He swore beneath his breath. This was a scenario he hadn't anticipated, and now he had to tread carefully because not only had Cameron promised Mia he wouldn't apprise her brothers about her situation, but there was no way in hell he wanted anyone in her family to find out about their relationship. He didn't need the grief, the headache, or any of the Wilde brood beating the crap out of him for having a hot and heavy, no-strings-attached fling with Mia.

It seemed like an hour had passed between them, when in fact it had only been a handful of seconds. "Joel!" he said, unable to keep his genuine shock and surprise from his tone.

"Hey, Cam!" Joel replied in an enthusiastic voice loud enough to be heard above the music and noise. "You hang out here?"

"I've been here a few times," he said evasively and gestured toward the waitresses dancing up on the bar for the customers, and for better tips. "The place is quite lively and entertaining."

"So we heard." Joel grinned up at one of the women who blew him a kiss while gyrating her hips to the seductive beat of the music. "We thought we'd check it out for ourselves, and it appears we aren't going to be disappointed. Want to grab a beer with us?"

Despite having other plans, which had included finding an inconspicuous place to sit alone and keep an eye on Mia, Cameron knew he couldn't turn down Joel's invitation without him wondering why . . . and eventually pinpointing the reason as Mia once Joel discovered his sister was there. Besides, sitting with the trio didn't mean Cam had to reveal his true reasons for being there, and he could still keep an inconspicuous eye on Mia.

"A beer sounds great," he finally said.

It took some time on such a crowded, busy night, but they eventually managed to claim a table up on the second level as a small group vacated it. It was a perfect spot for Cameron, because it gave him a decent view of the bar and dance area. And that's all he cared about.

As he sat down, his gaze found Mia once again. She was still talking to the same group of guys at the bar. Just as a waitress came up to their table to take their order, he watched as Mia tucked her hair behind her left ear, a signal they'd decided upon earlier to let him know she was speaking to her neighbor, Will, if he happened to show up.

He studied the guy, who was more of a pretty boy than a man's man, with short hair that looked like it actually had blond highlights woven through the strands—and not the kind from the sun, but the artificial kind from a salon. At a distance, his features appeared more effeminate than masculine, and he looked barely old enough to drink—as did his three friends.

Just as Mia had told him, there were definitely no sparks between her and Will. They were conversing like old friends, when most of the other men at the bar were openly eyeing Mia with appreciative interest. There was something different about Will other than his appearance, but for the moment Cameron couldn't quite put his finger on what was bothering him.

Mia smoothed her hair back once again as she laughed at something one of the other guys said. Most likely, she hadn't seen him arrive. Under normal circumstances, he would have called her on her cell phone to let her know he was at The Electric Blue and where he was sitting, but meeting up with Joel had nixed that idea. He figured in time she'd locate him, and he couldn't help but wonder how she'd act once she discovered her brother Joel was there.

Cameron waited for the waitress to finish taking their drink orders and move on to the next table before striking up a conversation. "So how's business been?"

"It's been great," Joel said as he leaned back in his seat. "Getting busier by the week."

"I hear ya," Cam replied with a shake of his head. "Steve and I are swamped. We've been interviewing potential assistants, but we haven't found anyone we both like yet." He glanced at Kevin and Ben once more. "Where's Jon?" he asked of their other friend and partner.

"He's on an assignment that took him to California for the next week." Abruptly, Joel stopped speaking, and his body tensed as he stared just beyond Cameron's shoulder.

Cameron was very familiar with that intense kind of look. Certain that Joel had finally spied Mia, Cameron's own personal radar went on alert. "Everything okay?"

"That waitress looks familiar," Joel said with a confused frown. "Like I've seen her before."

Cameron, along with Ben and Kevin, glanced in the same direction to appease their own curiosity. The woman who had caught Joel's attention wasn't the waitress who had taken their order. This one was curvy and very pretty, with shoulder-length brown hair and an alluring smile. As attractive as she was, she seemed much too reserved and sweet compared to the more outgoing women Joel normally chose to date.

"Yeah, you've seen her before," Ben said with a snicker. "In your dreams, man."

"I'm being serious," Joel said, a frustrated edge to his tone. "But I'll be damned if I can place *where* I've seen her."

Kevin slapped Joel on the back. "I'm sure she's just

another face in the long string of women you've seduced with that Wilde charm of yours, then left behind."

Joel's scowl deepened as he combed his fingers through his pitch black hair. "I've never slept with her. *That* I would have remembered," he said adamantly.

As if the woman had sensed Joel's stare, she turned from the table she was clearing and looked his way. Their gazes seemed to connect, and something intangible passed between them for the briefest of seconds before their waitress arrived with their beers and the other woman headed back to the bar area.

It was the oddest, most bizarre thing Cameron had ever witnessed, as if the two *did* know one another but had never met in person before.

For the next half hour, while Joel watched the woman who'd captured his attention and Cameron kept up a steady stream of conversation with Ben and Kevin, who were also flirting with the women around them, Cameron managed to keep a close watch on Mia. She left Will with his friends at the bar to mingle with other people, and Cameron noticed that her neighbor didn't appear interested in the other women who came up to him, and neither did he accept any invitations to dance.

Interestingly enough, Mia's girlfriend Carrie was nowhere to be seen, and he figured she'd had other plans for the night, which helped narrow down Cameron's list of potential suspects. He'd caught sight of Ray and Gina a while ago, but now as Mia made her way through the crowd to her roommate, Ray wasn't by Gina's side as he normally was, which led Cameron to believe he was off getting drinks at the bar or had gone to the restroom.

About ten minutes later Ray reappeared, fresh drinks in hand. Mia talked to the two of them for a bit longer and then moved through the crowd once again. She headed in Cameron's direction, a sultry smile on her glossy lips.

As she climbed the stairs to the second level, Joel finally

spotted her. "Jeezus," he muttered in annoyance. "What the hell is Mia doing here?"

Cameron wanted to laugh at Joel's brotherly reaction, not to mention his double standards where his sister was concerned. Instead, he kept his amusement to himself.

Kevin, however, had no problem stating the obvious. "I suppose she's here for the same reason you are."

Joel didn't care for that insinuation and shot his friend a dark look. "Don't be a smart-ass."

"Well, she sure does *look* like she's here to have a good time," Ben chimed in.

Cameron had to agree. From a distance, he'd only been able to see glimpses of what she was wearing. But now, up close, his mouth went dry as the full effect of her outfit hit him. Her beige, halter-top-style mini-dress bared a hellavu lot of skin and cleavage and left no room for her to wear a bra. The stretchy fabric molded to her perfect breasts, as well as the rest of her curves, all the way down to her mid-thigh. A belt designed of chunky gold links draped low on her hips with the end piece bouncing loosely against her thigh as she walked. If the image of using that strand of belt as a leash wasn't enough to make Cameron hard as stone, her shoes most certainly did the trick.

She was wearing the hottest, sexiest, most arousing pair of dress boots he'd ever seen on a woman. Made of supple beige leather, they reached just below her knee, and it wasn't just the spiked heel that had his temperature, and other parts of his anatomy, rising. No, it was the way they laced up the side of her leg and showed glimpses of skin between the criss-crossing of ties, prompting erotic images of her being a bit of a dominatrix in the bedroom—which suited Mia's personality very well.

He groaned and shoved those images right out of his head as she came to a stop at the side of the table between himself and Kevin. She slid her hip to one side, the one nearest *him,* and the chain on her belt jingled temptingly.

"Hi there, boys," she greeted them with a sexy smile that encompassed them all. "Fancy running into the four of you here."

Ben grinned at her, and it was obvious to Cameron that the other man could be *very* interested in Mia, given the chance and Joel's approval. "We were just saying the same thing about you, Mia."

She shrugged, and Cameron hoped to God he was the only one who noticed how her firm breasts bounced oh-so-provocatively with the gesture. Unfortunately, Ben and Kevin were all male, and their gazes strayed accordingly.

"It's a fun place," she said, fingering the end of her chain belt. "And where's there's fun, I'm there."

Joel crossed his arms over his massive chest. "You shouldn't be here alone," he said gruffly.

"Don't go and get your feathers all ruffled, Joel," she said and rolled her eyes at her brother's protective statement. "Gina is here, too, so I'm not alone."

"Would you like to sit down and have a drink with us?" Kevin offered, eager to accommodate Mia. "We can pull up another chair for you, if you'd like."

"No, thanks," she said, dashing the other man's hopes, only to raise them all over again with her next comment. "Actually, I came up here looking for a dance partner. Anyone here interested?"

Cameron kept quiet, while both Kevin and Ben glanced at Joel as if to gauge his reaction should they accept Mia's invitation. Luckily for them, Joel was once again distracted by the waitress who'd ensnared his attention earlier.

"Hell, why not," Kevin said and stood before Ben could beat him to the punch. "I came here to have a good time, so let's do it."

"That's certainly my motto." Mia laughed, a sultry, husky sound that tied Cameron's insides into a heated knot of desire.

As Mia led the way to the dance floor and Kevin followed

behind, Cameron blew out a harsh breath. He knew her flirtations with Kevin and Ben were all an act, knew she was trying to pretend all was normal and Cameron didn't have carnal knowledge of her body—and they hadn't agreed to a brief affair. But it was still difficult to watch her go off with another man and move that lithe, centerfold body of hers all for Kevin's viewing pleasure.

Cameron kept both Ray and Will in his sights, while keeping an eye on Mia as well. She was having a great time with Kevin, and if that wasn't torture enough, when the two of them returned to the table after enjoying a few songs, Ben was quick to offer himself up as her next dance partner, and Mia was happy to oblige. She looked so damn sexy up on the dance floor, with her dark tousled hair, flushed face, and that seductive, body-hugging dress. And those sexy boots . . . Cameron had no doubts they'd star in some very erotic fantasies for a long time to come.

"You know, if you don't like anyone else dancing with her, then you ought to speak up."

This came from Kevin, and Cameron couldn't believe he'd allowed himself to be so transparent around men who were trained to be just as perceptive as he was. Still, he tried to brush it off. "I'm not interested in dancing with Mia."

From across the table, Joel gave an inelegant snort. "Sure you're not," he drawled, then explained to Kevin, "Cameron and Mia have this love-hate thing going on between them."

"I don't hate her." Far from it, Cameron thought. Mia inspired many emotions from him, but none that even came remotely close to disliking her.

"Okay, *hate* is a strong word," Joel conceded as he rubbed his fingers along the condensation gathering on his bottle of beer. "You want her, but you don't want her. She annoys the hell out of you, and you still want her. Bottom line is, you want her."

That pretty well summed up his feelings for Mia, not that he was going to admit it out loud and give Joel the satisfaction of knowing how badly his sister affected him. "Don't worry, it's not going to happen," he reassured Joel, the lie slipping too easily from his lips.

Joel studied him for a long moment, and Cameron tried not to squirm under the scrutiny of his stare.

Finally, Joel spoke. "That's probably for the best, considering the two of you would end up strangling one another within a few days of being together."

Cameron could think of a dozen other things he'd rather do to Mia with his hands and fingers, rather than wrapping them around her pretty neck. Still, for Joel's benefit, he played along. "Yeah, you're probably right."

Much to Cameron's relief, Kevin and Mia came back to the table, which put an end to his awkward conversation with Joel. Ben sat in his chair, and Mia sidled up to Cameron.

"Whew," she said, breathing hard from the workout she'd gotten while dancing with two different men back to back. "I sure am hot . . . and thirsty."

Before anyone could offer to get her a drink, she picked up his bottle of beer and lifted it to her mouth. Cameron watched in fascination as her lips closed over the tip and her tongue dipped inside the opening. Then she tilted the bottle back and moaned deep in her throat as she finished off the last little bit of cold liquid left inside.

Cameron nearly groaned right along with her as images filled his mind of her soft warm mouth sucking on him in the same erotic way—which he knew had been her intent all along. To deliberately arouse him when he couldn't do a damn thing about it, the minx.

With a soft sigh of satisfaction, she set the empty bottle down on the table and met his gaze. Her lashes fell half-mast, and she slowly licked the excess moisture from her lips. "Mmmm, that tasted good."

His blood rushed hot and molten through his veins. God, she was so brazen and bold!

She smiled at him, a heady, come-hither curve of her lips

that told him she wasn't done teasing him just yet. "So how about you, sugar?" she asked as she leaned in close and skimmed the tips of her fingers along his tensed jaw. "Care to take your chances with me?"

She meant out on the dance floor, but there was a wealth of meaning and innuendo behind her words. It took every bit of strength Cameron possessed to pretend indifference to her, when all he could think about was wiping the table clear in one clean swipe of his arm and taking her right then and there, with those fuck-me lace-up boots wrapped tight against his hips.

"I'll pass," he managed, just barely, in a bland tone of voice.

A disappointed sigh escaped her parted lips. "I guess I'll just have to find someone who will."

She turned to go, and something within Cameron snapped—mainly, his normal ability to keep a tight rein on his emotions. He understood that for Mia this was all a performance for her brother and his friends, even if she was enjoying herself a tad too much at his expense. But he'd had enough of her dancing with other men, and he wasn't about to watch her with yet another guy while he sat on the sidelines and stewed about it.

Abruptly, he stood up and started after Mia, with Kevin and Ben encouraging him on. Cameron glanced back at the trio and found Joel watching him quietly with an unsettling kind of speculation that made Cameron feel uneasy.

Dismissing the feeling for the time being, he caught up to Mia before she could find herself another dance partner, grabbed her hand, and led the way. Once they were up on the stage, he merged the two of them into the middle of the crowded dance floor, away from the prying eyes of Mia's brother, and then whirled around to face the woman who tempted him beyond reason. She was only a foot away, but he wanted her closer.

Much closer.

Wrapping the end of her chain belt around his fist, he pulled her to him until their bodies were touching intimately. Awareness sparked in her smoky gaze, as did a glimmer of heat he recognized as a direct challenge. She wanted this, and she was silently daring him to be bad, to throw every bit of caution to the wind and give in to some reckless, shameless kind of fun. With her.

He let a wolfish grin emerge, and her eyes widened with a bit of surprise and excitement. Grasping her hips in his hands, he wedged his leg between hers so the hem of her dress was hiked up and she was riding his thigh. From there, their eyes met and held as they moved to the beat of the music in a way that mimicked the act of hot, grinding, down-and-dirty sex. Cameron grew thick and hard as each seductive move was countered by another, in ways that would have gotten them arrested for public obscenity if anyone could have seen what they were doing.

Fortunately, they were surrounded by a crush of people who weren't paying any attention to them or their dirty dancing. They didn't care that his hands were on Mia's ass, and they couldn't see the slow, provocative way she arched and rubbed against his erection again and again.

It was the most erotic form of foreplay Cameron ever had the pleasure of indulging in, and he planned to get even with Mia tonight, when they were alone. He had a score to settle with her—for tempting and teasing him earlier in front of her brother and his friends, and for driving him to the brink of sexual frustration now.

The song ended, and he and Mia agreed to part ways for a while. Cameron was grateful for the cooling-off period, because after that encounter, he had no idea how he was going to survive the evening.

But somehow, he managed. Before long Gina and Ray left for the night, followed by Mia's neighbor Will and his friends. Soon after that, Joel, Kevin, and Ben decided to head off to Nick's Sports Bar, which was their normal hangout.

Once Cameron was certain that Joel and his buddies were long gone, he made his way across the room to Mia and lowered his mouth to her ear.

"Let's get the hell out of here."

"Your place or mine?" She grinned up at him, her face still flushed from their dancing.

That all depended on a key factor. "Is Gina going to be home tonight?"

She shook her head. "No. She'll be at Ray's."

Perfect. "Your place, then." Because what he had in mind for Mia, he wanted her to be completely comfortable and relaxed, and being in her element would accomplish that.

"I'm parked two cars away from yours," he told her, wanting to be careful about the way they left The Electric Blue, just in case *they* were being watched. "I'll walk out first, and you follow about a minute after me so I can keep an eye on you."

She nodded in agreement. He headed out of the bar and crossed the parking lot to their vehicles. As Mia's Celica came into his sights, a sick feeling of dread twisted through him, followed by a jolt of outrage at what someone had done to Mia's car. He swore a string of expletives as he tried to figure out a way to spare Mia from having to see this latest attack.

Unfortunately, he didn't think fast enough. Her audible gasp of shock had Cameron spinning around, and his stomach cramped when he saw her face. Mia's eyes were huge, her complexion drained of color, and her expression was etched with disbelief and horror as she stared at her vandalized car.

"Oh, my God!" she wailed.

Seven

SLUT. *Tramp. Bitch. Whore.*

A distinct chill slithered through Mia. The vile, cruel words someone had written all over her car's windows in a thick, white paste swam before her eyes. Her legs felt weak, as though they were going to give out on her if she tried to take a step in any direction. She folded her arms around her middle, but it was Cameron's strength that held her upright as he wrapped his arms around her in a secure embrace.

"You're trembling," he said gruffly and rubbed his big hands up and down her bare back in an attempt to soothe her.

Closing her eyes, she leaned into him and buried her face against his neck, wishing she could make all this ugliness go away. She inhaled the scent of his cologne and the warmth of his skin, taking comfort in the fact that Cameron was there and she didn't have to deal with this latest assault alone.

She wasn't used to relying on anyone for anything and had spent years striving to prove to her family that she was an independent woman who didn't need protecting or sheltering.

Yet here she was, clinging to Cameron like a damsel in distress. Geez, she was so pathetic.

Inhaling a deep, calming breath, she pulled back, and he gradually let her go. "Sorry about that," she said, hating that he'd seen her in such a vulnerable state.

"You're entitled to be upset," he said as he swept a hand angrily toward her car. "This is bullshit."

She couldn't bring herself to look at her car again, or the offensive phrases mocking her. "I can't believe someone would do such a thing."

He exhaled a disgusted breath and shoved his fingers through his hair. "I'm sorry, Mia."

She heard the apologetic tone of his voice and was stunned that he'd feel responsible for what had happened. "Cameron, this isn't your fault."

His expression was a glowering mask of barely suppressed fury. "I'm just pissed that I didn't come out here in time to catch the creep who did this to you."

Actually, that person was very lucky Cameron hadn't caught them in the act. Judging by the fierce look in his eyes, there was no doubt in Mia's mind he would have beat the living daylights out of them.

She shivered again and wondered if the culprit was watching them now, taking a sick delight in shaking her up so badly. That possibility sent a frisson of unease rippling along her spine. "Well, it's done and over with, and I want to go home."

"I have some rags in the truck," he said, his gaze gentling with understanding. Let me try to get this mess cleaned up as much as possible before we go."

She waited while Cameron did his best to wipe away the vulgar words and clean her windows of the white gunk, which he suspected was toothpaste. Her car would definitely have to be washed thoroughly, but she appreciated not having those words emblazoned on her windows for everyone to see on the drive home.

Once they reached her apartment building, she parked

her Celica in her carport and because Gina wouldn't be home until the next day, Cameron went ahead and took her spot. Together they walked to her place. As she entered the apartment, she turned on the living room light and tossed her purse and car keys on the table.

Cameron came up to her, touched the tips of his long, warm fingers beneath her chin, and brought her gaze to his. His stunning eyes, she noticed, were bright with concern.

"Are you going to be okay?" he asked.

She refused to admit just how upset she really was, and even a little frightened by the intensity of an unknown person's wrath against her.

"Yeah, I'm fine." She summoned a smile and caressed her hand along his jaw. The slight stubble abraded her palm in a very arousing way, and that's what she focused on . . . her desire for Cameron. "I'm glad you're here."

"Me, too," he murmured.

The undisguised emotion in his eyes made her heart skip a beat, mainly because it was a rarity for her to see such genuine caring from a man when it came to her—outside her family, of course. She and Cameron had been at opposition for so long, and now that they'd given into their desire for one another, she was coming to realize just how much this man threatened her own heart and emotions.

But allowing herself to need or rely on someone on an emotional level was something she'd avoided since she was a little girl. And she wasn't about to start now, with Cameron.

Pushing those unsettling thoughts aside, she slid her arms around his neck and sifted her fingers though his hair. Lifting her mouth to his, she kissed him, and he was quick to respond. She savored the heat of his lips on hers, the slow, lazy sweep of his tongue as their connection deepened, and the feel of his hands sliding along her shoulders. Hands that were big and strong yet achingly gentle as they glided down her back and then drew her close against a body that was hot and hard and already aroused.

Desperately craving the distraction of something intensely physical to forget about what had happened earlier, she attempted to move things along at a faster, more urgent pace. Except Cameron wasn't giving in to any of her aggressive moves, and she couldn't contain the soft sound of frustration that rumbled up from her chest.

"Slow down, sweetheart," he whispered against her lips, though she could hear a hint of laughter in his tone. "We've got all night, and there's more where that kiss came from."

She pulled back, just enough to slide her hand between their bodies and cup his thickened shaft in her palm. "I want more," she said huskily as she stroked the heated length of him. "A whole lot more."

He groaned, circled her wrist with his fingers, and pulled her hand away. She couldn't help but feel confused and even a little bit rejected by his actions, though she wasn't about to let her hurt show. Instead, she rebounded with a flippant and sassy response.

"What's the matter, sugar?" she drawled as she tossed back her hair. "Not quite *up* to it?"

A roguish grin slid across his lips, giving her the distinct feeling that he saw right through her act. "Oh, I'm plenty *up* for it. But we're doing things *my* way tonight. Do you have a problem with that?"

She almost bristled at his commanding tone until she recalled the sexual promises he'd made to her just a few evenings ago—of how he wanted to take things real slow this time, along with the very thorough way he planned to worship her entire body until she came for him.

That thought alone was enough to make her body quicken with anticipation, lust, and carnal need.

What he was asking for would put him in complete control of her pleasure. It would make him the dominating one and force her to bend to his will, and that was something she rarely did for any man. But he was offering her an invitation she couldn't resist, and just because he was the one calling the shots didn't mean she couldn't find some way to be sure she seduced him in return.

"Take me to your bedroom, Mia."

She didn't hesitate. Slipping her hand into his, she led him down the darkened hallway to her bedroom. Rather than turning on the bright overhead light, she instead switched on the small lamp on the nightstand next to her bed, which cast a soft glow in the room that was far more subtle and romantic. Then she turned to Cameron and waited anxiously for his next request.

"I want you to do something for me. It's a fantasy of mine when it comes to you. One of them anyway," he added with a half-grin as he fingered the chain belt riding low on her hips.

She had no idea what he had in mind, but she'd come this far and she wasn't going to back out now. Besides, she was too intrigued, and she certainly wasn't modest when it came to what felt good to her sexually—no matter if it was his fantasy or her own. "I'll do anything you want."

"Good." He turned away from her and walked across the room. "First, I want you to pretend I'm not here in your bedroom."

It was a bizarre request, but she agreed. "All right."

She had a big, comfortable, cushioned chair in the corner by the window she sometimes curled up on to do her stained-glass drawings or read a book, and he positioned it right at the foot of her bed. Then he sat down, legs spread wide, and his body sprawled lazily.

He continued his instructions. "I want you to get ready for bed like you normally do, as if I wasn't here, then lay down on your bed where I can watch you touch yourself."

She wasn't a prude by any means, but she'd never done anything so intimate with a man *watching*. And to do so with Cameron, she knew she'd be exposing a private part of herself—not only physically, but the hidden secrets to her body and her ultimate satisfaction as well.

She couldn't deny that the thought thrilled her, because

it gave her the opportunity to tempt and tease Cameron in the process. And that was something she always enjoyed. As far as she was concerned, it would be a night of mutual gratification.

Slowly, she rounded the bed to where Cameron was sitting and leaned her backside against the mattress behind her. Tipping her head to the side, she let her gaze drift up from his thighs, along the bulge in his jeans, and all the way up to his face. The man was so gorgeously male, so devastatingly sexual, he literally took her breath away.

She licked her lips. "So . . . you want me to masturbate in front of you?"

"Yeah, I do," he replied huskily and without an ounce of shame. "Watching you pleasure yourself will show me how and where you liked to be touched, what turns you on, and what it takes to make you come." The smile that curved his mouth brimmed with sinful promise. "And then, when you're good and ready, I'm gonna make you do just that."

A smoldering heat surged through her and settled low. Lord, the man had a way with words!

"Mmmm, nice fantasy." She propped her booted foot on the chair, right between his wide-spread legs. Brazenly, she pressed the toe against the fly of his jeans. "Will you help me take my boots off first? They're tight, and it takes a few good tugs to pull them off."

He sat up and stroked his fingers along the four-inch spiked heel. "Ahhh, talk about fantasies."

She raised a brow in surprise. "What? My boots do it for you?"

"In a major way," he admitted as his hand skimmed up her leather-clad calf, almost reverently. "All this soft, supple leather, the snug way it molds to your shapely legs, and then there's these sexy, lace-up ties that put all kinds of wicked thoughts in my head."

He lifted his gaze back to hers, and the lust radiating from him was almost tangible. "If I didn't have other plans for you tonight, I'd insist you keep these boots on."

The vivid images that leapt into her head were downright erotic . . . and exciting enough to make her want to fulfill that fantasy of his someday. "I'll have to remember that."

He helped her remove her boots, first unlacing them, then caressing her exposed skin as he gradually bared her leg. One good tug had them slipping off her foot, which he massaged before giving her other foot the same treatment.

What should have been a simple and quick task, he turned into a sensual, luxurious undertaking that relaxed her entire body. Once he was done, he reclined back in his chair. He didn't say a word. He didn't have to. She knew the next part of the show was all hers, and she intended to give him a performance he'd remember long after their affair was over.

But first, she needed a little eye candy of her own. "Will you take your shirt off for me, so I have something to fantasize about, too?" To her, there was something so incredibly sexy about a shirtless man. Especially *this* shirtless man, with his athletically honed body, a nice, muscular chest, washboard abs, and firm biceps.

Giving into her request, he pulled off his shirt and tossed it aside. "The floor's all yours, sweetheart," he murmured.

She could have stripped naked right in front of Cameron, but she didn't want to give him everything all at once. Rather, she decided to stick to the "less was more" theory and build the awareness and anticipation between them with teasing, provocative glimpses that would have him panting for more.

So she unclipped her gold chain belt and set it on her dresser. Her halter-style dress didn't allow room for a bra, and with her back facing Cameron, she unfastened the neckline and let the outfit drop to the floor, leaving her wearing a skimpy beige G-string that was feminine and lacy in the front and nearly nonexistent in the back. She shimmied that off, too, and grinned to herself when she heard him groan low and deep in his throat.

A shiver of response rippled through her. The last time

they were together she'd ended up only half-dressed. She knew he was waiting for her to turn around so he could look his fill of her completely nude for the first time, but she didn't give him that opportunity. At least not yet.

He'd told her to get ready like usual, as if he wasn't watching her every move. With that in mind, she walked to her adjoining bathroom, put up her hair, and turned on the shower, all part of her nightly routine. When the water was hot and steamy, she stepped inside—making sure Cameron saw nothing more than her naked backside.

But this was where things turned fun and oh-so-naughty. The shower door was lightly frosted, and she took full advantage of the fact that just the silhouette of her body was visible. Turning so he could see her side profile, she soaped up her hands and ran them over her body, taking great care to be sure her breasts, belly, and thighs received a fair amount of attention . . . and fondling. And then she added a few moans and sighs for good measure.

When she'd spent a sufficient amount of time arousing her body for the next phase of the seduction, she turned off the shower and grabbed a towel off the nearby rack. After quickly drying off, she wrapped the towel around her body and finally stepped from the stall, then into her bedroom again.

She glanced in Cameron's direction as she made her way to her dresser and noticed he'd taken off his shoes, socks, and jeans. All he had left on were a pair of white briefs, and there was no mistaking the impressive outline of his thick erection beneath the stretched cotton. It appeared that he wasn't going to give everything up all at once, either, and that just gave her something to look forward to later.

Once again facing away from Cameron, she dropped her towel and opened her lingerie drawer. She pulled out a short, sexy nightgown she'd recently bought, which was made of pink floral lace with a deep V neckline. The sides were held together by small satin bows, and between the flowery print the material was sheer, allowing beguiling glimpses of her skin to peek through. The babydoll nightie was a perfect blend of innocence and temptress, and she slipped it over her head and tugged it into place.

She reached for the matching pair of panties, but before she could step into them, Cameron spoke.

"Leave them off," he ordered in a raspy voice.

Startled by his abrupt command, she glanced over her shoulder and grinned at him. "You're not supposed to be here, remember?"

His eyes smoldered with an intense heat and the desire she'd spent the last half hour inflaming. "Humor me. How can I see the way you touch yourself if you're wearing panties?"

Conceding his point, she left the underwear in the drawer. She pushed the pillows on her bed up against the headboard and then made herself comfortable in the middle of the soft mattress. The hem of her nightie hit her mid-thigh, and she bent her knee at an angle so he couldn't see the most intimate part of her just yet.

Closing her eyes, she inhaled a deep, relaxing breath. Normally, if she was alone, she'd get right down to business, with her ultimate goal her own sexual gratification. But with Cameron as her audience of one, there was no reason to rush the process. She wanted to enjoy the moment, make it last, and push him to the edge of restraint.

She slipped the thin strap of her gown off one shoulder, then the other, and slowly bared both of her breasts to the cool night air . . . and Cameron's gaze. From the foot of the bed, she heard him suck in a sharp breath, and the heady sound emboldened her, made her turn shameless and uninhibited and wanton . . . all for his viewing pleasure.

Her breasts felt tight and achy, and she cupped them in her hands, gently squeezing and kneading the firm, soft flesh before brushing her thumbs across her hard nipples. She thought of Cameron watching her and imagined it was his hands on her body, not her own. She envisioned his warm, damp lips on her breasts, his tongue rasping across the tips, and the wet heat of him sucking her deep inside his mouth.

Her breathing deepened as she slid her palms down her belly, the scrap of lace against her skin building sensation upon sensation. She dipped her hand between her thighs and slid a finger over her slick, wet heat. With a soft, breathy moan, she let her legs finally fall open and slowly, rhythmically stroked the knot of nerves that grew more and more sensitive with each passing caress.

She was so lost in her own private pleasure that she forgot all about Cameron until she felt the mattress dip beneath her. Her lashes fluttered open to find him kneeling between her thighs and his hands skimming her top upward.

"Lift your arms for me," he rasped impatiently. "I want this off."

She did as he asked, and within seconds, the babydoll nightie was gone and she was completely naked. As he was, she noticed, eyeing the upward thrust of his shaft against his belly. Unable to help herself, she automatically reached out to touch him, but he caught her hand before she could wrap her fingers around that hard, masculine flesh.

He shook his head, causing strands of his dark blond hair to fall across his forehead, giving him a bit of a rebel appearance. "This is my fantasy, remember?"

And with that statement, he gradually consumed her stark-naked body with his gaze, from the glistening folds between her thighs, up along her belly, and over her quivering breasts. When he finally reached her face, his eyes seemed lit from within with a hunger so urgent and explicit it shocked her. And thrilled her, too.

He released her hand, placed his palms on either side of her face, and lowered his lips to the side of her neck, near her ear. "No matter what I do to you, keep touching yourself," he said as he nipped at her lobe. "But don't let yourself come just yet."

He'd braced himself above her in a way so only his mouth was touching her skin, along with the occasional brush of his hair and the rasp of the stubble on his jaw. It was the most erotic sensation, knowing just how close the heat of his body was, yet only feeling the warmth of his breath and the damp softness of his lips as they nuzzled her throat.

Lord, how did he expect her to keep caressing herself intimately *and* deal with the drugging magic of having his mouth on her, yet not succumb to the climax that was inevitable from so much sensual stimulation?

"You're a masochist," she complained with a pout.

"No, just selfish." He lifted his head and looked deeply into her eyes, and she found herself mesmerized by the determination in his gaze. "*I* want to be the one to give you that orgasm, not out of macho male pride, but because I want to experience your first time with you."

Her heart squeezed tight in her chest, a distinct warning that she was so dangerously close to falling for Cameron in ways she'd never allowed herself to give to a man. He claimed he was being selfish, but what he wanted to do to her, and for her, was so incredibly generous. And if there *was* a first time, she wanted it to be with Cameron, too.

"I'm all yours," she said and realized too late just how much meaning those words held for her.

But then his mouth dipped down again, scattering her thoughts into the night as he once again trailed his lips along her throat and down to her breasts, where he lavished the plump curves with slow, damp kisses that had a clutch of butterflies fluttering in her stomach.

The words he'd spoken to her a few nights ago came back to her now, adding to the erotic sensations ricocheting through her. *I'd give more attention to these lovely mounds of flesh and take each one into my mouth so I can finally know how you taste. I'd suck on your nipples for a good long time before moving on . . .*

Cameron made good on his promise, using the wet, swirling warmth of his tongue along her breasts, the arousing scrape of his teeth, and finally the deepening suction of his mouth on the beaded tips. She gasped and arched upward as a bolt of white-hot pleasure shot from her breasts to the growing ache between her legs, where the pressure and friction of her fingers threatened to send her spiraling over the edge. She eased back before her climax hit, and she couldn't stop the whimper of need that escaped her throat.

When I finally had my fill of your breasts, I'd kiss your belly and dip my tongue into your navel . . .

And that's exactly what he did. His lips skimmed along her rib cage, and the hot slide of his tongue lapped across her trembling stomach, then delved into her belly button in a wicked, erotic kind of French kiss. She moaned, long and low, and her free hand gripped the covers at her side in a tight fist. It was all she could do to keep herself from coming apart right then and there.

"Cameron," she whispered hoarsely, desperately. "*Please.*"

And then, when you were writhing beneath me and begging for more, I'd go down on you and use my tongue to make you come, no matter how long it took . . .

He shifted between her spread legs and moved lower, settling in so his broad shoulders kept her knees firmly apart. Her body jerked as his mouth touched down on the inside of her thigh. His lips were soft, his breath damp and hot as he slowly, leisurely kissed and licked his way upward until he reached the very core of her.

By then, she was nearly sobbing with need, and still, somehow, someway, she managed to hold back. He tested her restraint even further when he used his tongue to follow the stroke of her fingers along her weeping sex, learning from her own touch and caresses exactly what she liked and what gave her the greatest enjoyment.

He was a quick study, and it didn't take him long to master her rhythm and discover her most intimate secrets. When he was seemingly confident of his ability to take over, he urged her legs up and slipped his arms beneath her raised thighs. He pulled her hand away and laced his fingers with hers at the side of her hips, holding her captive and forcing her to give herself completely over to him.

It was an incredibly easy thing to do, because she trusted him with her body. Maybe even more.

Then that frightening thought fled as the heat of his mouth covered her and his tongue took over where her fingers had left off. Slipping. Sliding. Swirling in and around her soft, swollen flesh before suckling on her clit in the most breath-stealing way. He finessed her body with such utter attention to her pleasure, worshipping her as if she belonged only to him, that she nearly passed out from the glut of sensation he lavished upon her.

He'd told her he'd spend hours if that's what it took to make her come, but within a matter of minutes, she was unraveling from the inside out. She started to pant and then her breath caught on a sob as her climax exploded and she was consumed by a overwhelming rush of pulsing heat. The force and intensity of her release tumbled her into the longest, most powerful orgasm she'd ever experienced.

And then, when you were wet and soft and ready for me, I'd slide deep, deep inside of you . . .

The shudders within her seemed to go on and on, and before the last of the tremors subsided, Cameron was moving up and over her. He covered her body with his own, all hard, lean muscles and barely suppressed hunger. In one long, smooth thrust, he slid into her, and she lifted her knees high against his waist to give him the deepest access possible. Once he was buried to the hilt, he closed his eyes and groaned as her inner muscles clasped him tight.

She knew he had to be aching for his own release, yet he went still, as if relishing the moment, the warmth and softness of being inside her, and the aftermath of the internal contractions still buffeting her body.

I'd make it last so I can savor everything about how you feel, inside and out, and finally, how exquisitely your body feels gripping my cock as I come . . .

As if he'd had a direct link to her thoughts, his lashes drifted back open and his darkened gaze locked with hers. He began to move, rolling his hips hard against hers, then plunging deeply. Again and again. Long, slow, agonizing strokes designed to make the pleasure last—for her, or himself, she didn't know, but it felt wonderful just the same.

He lowered his head and kissed her, the soft, sensual glide of his tongue matching the rhythm of his lazy thrusts. Eventually, the heat and friction and fire caught up to him, finally shattering his control.

She felt the change in him as his pace quickened, his breathing grew ragged, and he pumped harder, faster, toward his own completion. She dug her fingers into the rippling muscles of his damp back, arched high and hard into his thrusts, and felt him stiffen as his climax peaked. He dragged his lips from hers, surged into her a final time, and on a ragged, primitive growl, he spilled himself into her.

Breathing hard, he buried his face against her throat, and she threaded her fingers through his hair, giving him the time he needed to recover. A few minutes passed before he finally lifted his head from the curve of her neck. In the dim light, his features were shadowed, but there was no mistaking the satisfied gleam in his eyes as he stared down at her.

And in that moment, she felt incredibly exposed and vulnerable, because she knew he'd touched her in a way no man ever had—physically *and* emotionally.

"You look quite sated," he murmured as a matching smile curved up the corners of his mouth. "If I don't say so myself."

He was such a typical male, exulting over the fact that he'd just given her a spectacular, unforgettable orgasm. "Quit looking so smug," she said, though it took effort to hold back a grin of her own because he looked so damn adorable. And so incredibly sexy.

"Hey, I have every right to revel in this moment."

Yes, he really did, not that she was going to admit as

much out loud and give him more of a reason to gloat over his sexual expertise. Nor was she ready to deal with the strong, overwhelming feelings directly linked to the orgasm he'd just given her.

Her emotional defenses automatically kicked in, and she instead turned the moment into a light-hearted one by issuing him a playful challenge. "However . . . I do have my doubts that you'll be able to do it again."

Holding her gaze, he slid a hand between their still joined bodies, across her belly, and down to her mound. His thumb pressed against her still-sensitive flesh, and she was shocked to feel her body come alive again. He stroked slowly, wringing a soft gasp from her, his talented touch proving he'd learned her body's responses and needs very well.

He arched a dark blond brow as a shameless liquid heat coated his fingers. Amusement and renewed desire mingled in his smoky green eyes. "Is that a dare?" he asked.

She felt him harden inside her again, felt her own body clutch his shaft, and knew she'd greedily take whatever pleasure this man was willing to give her. Memories to store away when their time together was over.

"I believe it is a dare, sugar." Wrapping her arms around his neck, she brought his mouth down to hers and murmured huskily against his lips. "So what are you going to do about it?"

Over the next few hours, he proceeded to make good on her challenge and gave her a night of erotic, forbidden pleasures that left her limp, spent, and physically fulfilled.

And earned him every right to gloat.

Eight

CAMERON woke up the following morning, momentarily disoriented and confused about where he was, until his sleepy vision and mind cleared and his *feminine* surroundings came into focus—a noticeable contrast to his own masculine domain and a direct reminder that he'd spent an amazingly sensual night in Mia's bed. He could still smell her scent on his skin, taste the sweetness of her body on his lips, and recall the breathy way she'd called his name the last time he'd made her come.

That final recollection made him smile to himself and think of all the different, uninhibited ways they'd made love. He'd always known Mia was a vibrant woman, but last night she'd exceeded his expectations. She had an incredible amount of passion and an abundance of energy when it came to sex, and she was an adventurous lover. There wasn't anything he'd asked for that she'd denied him. No request made her blush. No invitation she refused.

Simply put, she was a man's dream between the sheets.

His dream. *His* fantasy woman come to life. A temptress who knew exactly how to turn him inside out with lust and a need unlike anything he'd ever known. A shameless nymph who wasn't afraid to go after what brought her the greatest pleasure. Physically, they were a match made in heaven.

Emotionally, however, she shook him up inside and left him reeling . . . and trying to decipher exactly what it was about her that affected him so profoundly. Unfortunately, he had no definite answers for that question, but he was coming to realize, and accept, that she was starting to mean more to him than a brief fling. And he had no idea what he was going to do about that, especially when a long-term commitment between the two of them was highly unlikely.

With a low exhale, he turned his head and glanced toward Mia's side of the bed, where she was still fast asleep. Her silky black hair was tousled over her pillow and around her face in a wild disarray, and the sheet was twisted around her naked body. She was on her side in a fetal position, with her arms pulled in tight against her chest and her knees raised up high against her stomach—as if protecting herself in her sleep or maybe to keep anyone from getting too close emotionally.

Even in sleep, she was such a paradox. She'd been confident and assertive last night, but now she looked vulnerable and almost childlike. And while most women wanted to cuddle after sex, once Mia thought he'd fallen asleep, he'd felt her move out of his arms and curl up by herself.

He thought it interesting that she didn't desire the simple human need to be held. He wondered if she felt stifled when she should have felt comforted. Instead, it was as if she preferred to be alone. He wondered if that's how it had always been for her, if being alone was all she'd known. Was she afraid of relying on one particular person too much, even for something as simple as tenderness and a warm, secure embrace? Or was he reading too much in to her actions?

She had three brothers who loved her very much, that

much was obvious to anyone who knew her family. Three brothers and three cousins who took their job of taking care of her, and protecting her, very seriously. So this need to be self-sufficient obviously stemmed from something else that had happened in her life.

As he folded his hands behind his head and continued to watch her sleep, he wondered if he'd ever figure her out and then realized that was such a part of her allure and what intrigued him so much. All those facets and layers showed him that the person she presented to the outside world wasn't necessarily who she was inside.

Finally, nature called and he slid as quietly as he could off the mattress, then headed to the adjoining bathroom. On the way out he found his jeans on the floor and pulled them on, figuring he'd go and make a pot of coffee and watch TV in the living room until Mia finally roused herself from sleep.

But as he fastened the top button to his pants, he caught sight of a drafting table, which wasn't something a woman normally had in her bedroom. Last night the room had been shadowed and dim and his sole focus had been on Mia, but in the morning light, the drafting table piqued his curiosity, especially considering Mia worked as a secretary for her family's tile company. And as far as he knew, her duties didn't require such a large, oversized desk for her to use at home.

He moved closer and glanced at the drawings laid out on the surface, surprised at the talent evident in each one. Some were completed, others only half finished, but all of them were beautifully drawn with eye-catching and vivid details. Some of the pictures were floral designs, others of exotic animals, and some abstract. A few of the sketches were filled in with colored pencils, giving the picture a striking dimension that was sharp and rich looking.

Hearing a rustling sound from the bed, he glanced in that direction and found Mia gradually coming awake. She uncurled her body and stretched with her arms over her head, drawing his eyes to the way the sheet pulled tight across her full breasts and over the curve of her hip. His groin stirred—no big surprise there—and he forced his gaze back up to her face, which was beautifully flushed and glowing with sexual satisfaction.

His heart skipped an odd little beat in his chest, and he grinned at her. "Good morning."

She blinked slumberously, her lashes still weighing heavily with sleep. " 'Morning," she murmured and then sighed blissfully, the sound rife with utter contentment.

A contentment he was solely responsible for.

As if he'd spoken his thoughts out loud, one of her eyes peeped open at him. "There you go again with that smug look," she said, the soft accusation in her tone tempered with humor.

He leaned his backside against the table and crossed his arms over his bare chest. "Can you really blame me?"

"I suppose not," she admitted softly, huskily. "You were pretty amazing last night, and you did manage to prove, numerous times, that you sure do know how to rise to a challenge."

"Believe me, the pleasure was all mine." He winked at her and then swept a hand across the surface of the drafting table. "I was just looking at these drawings. What are they for?"

The light-heartedness between them faded as he watched her expression shut him out and she started to withdraw—from him and the new topic of conversation he'd just introduced. Intrigued, he continued before he completely lost her.

"I didn't mean to snoop or pry," he said, not giving her the chance to shut him out. "I was on my way out of the bathroom and the sketches caught my eye. They're very good. Did you draw them?"

She sat up in bed and reached for the silky robe she'd retrieved from her closet at some point last night. "Yes, I drew those designs," she said, the reluctance to admit as much evident in her tone.

Without an ounce of modesty, she let the sheet unravel

from her body as she stood up, baring her to his gaze for a handful of arousing seconds before she slid into her robe and tied the sash. He swallowed to ease the dryness in his mouth so he could speak again, determined not to let anything distract him from the course of their conversation.

"So you're an artist?"

She rounded the bed to where he was standing and smiled at his surprise, though there was a bit of reserve in the depth of her eyes. "That all depends on who you're asking."

He thought her comment odd but suspected there was a wealth of meaning behind her words and that glimpse of emotion he'd seen in her gaze. "I'm asking *you*." He didn't care about anyone else's opinion.

"I'd like to think I'm an artist," she said as she came up beside him. "It's what I love to do. Drawing. Creating unique designs. Bringing them to life." The brief excitement he'd heard in her voice was suddenly eclipsed by a somber sigh. "My family, however, thinks of this as just a hobby."

"But you want it to be more," he guessed.

She shrugged as she ran a finger along a half-finished sketch that looked like a spotted leopard in the midst of a jungle. "At one time I hoped it would evolve into a career, but I'm beginning to think it wasn't meant to be more than a leisurely pursuit. You know, one of those pipe dreams that's not quite attainable."

"You can't mean that." He couldn't believe that with Mia's drive and determination she'd give up on something she wanted so easily. "There's real talent in these pictures and drawings." And he hated to think such a gift would never be appreciated as more than just a hobby.

"What are these drawings for, anyway?" he asked curiously.

She hesitated for a moment, just long enough to make him think she wasn't going to answer his question. Then she met his gaze and trusted him with something that was obviously very personal for her.

"I create stained-glass art from these designs," she replied as her fingers played with the silk sash tied around her waist. "I even have a degree in 3D glasswork."

He couldn't have been more stunned. "Really?"

She nodded, a wry grin tugging at the corners of her mouth. "Yes, much to my father's dismay. He was hoping for a business degree of some sort, so that was a huge disappointment for him. But I really wanted to give my glass artwork a shot."

"Once you graduated, why didn't you?"

"Oh, I definitely tried," she said and combed a hand through her disheveled hair. "When I came back home after college, my brothers were in need of a secretary, so I took the job, thinking it would be a temporary thing. Except being family, I get paid very well, which makes it very hard to just outright quit and start a new career on my own. Either that, or the inflated pay was a calculated attempt to keep me in the family business."

Cameron highly suspected the latter, that this was her brothers' way of protecting Mia and keeping an eye on her.

"So I decided maybe I could incorporate my stained-glass designs into the business," she went on. "Maybe offer it on the side for customers and companies who were looking for something unique and different to compliment their new tile or restoration work, and let things build from there."

"That's a great idea," he said enthusiastically.

"I thought so, too, but Scott, and even my father, disagreed." A look of tired defeat passed over her features. "They both felt there wasn't a big enough market for my artwork, and that easily, the idea was dismissed."

Cameron absently ran his thumb beneath his lower lip, wondering if her brother and father believed they were making a decision that was in her best interest, a way of protecting her from possible failure. That certainly seemed like the Wilde family way when it came to Mia.

"So now I create the stained-glass artwork and designs

for me, as an outlet and for gifts," she said, seemingly resigned to that fate.

He'd been impressed with her drawings and designs and pictures. Now he wanted to see the completed product. "Do you have any of the stained-glass art that are finished and I can see?"

She rolled her eyes. "Do I ever! I've got dozens I've made and have stored in the closet and beneath the bed, but if you're just being polite about your interest, I'd rather not drag them out."

This last bit was said almost defensively, and her chin had even lifted a notch. But beneath that stubborn act was a woman with real and deep insecurities, along with the inability to believe in herself when it truly mattered.

Reaching out, he touched a finger to her chin and slowly lowered it, telling her without words that she had no reason to put on a tough act with him, because he was beginning to see right through that facade. "My interest is genuine, Mia, or I wouldn't have asked," he said gently. "Can I *please* see your stained-glass art?"

This time, she didn't fight him. "All right."

She turned around and he watched as she got on her hands and knees next to the bed, then reach beneath it, treating him to a spectacular view of her curvaceous backside covered in slippery silk. For a moment, all thoughts of her artwork fled and his *interest* drifted in an entirely wicked direction. Luckily, before he acted on the carnal fantasies heating his blood and making him hard, she stood back up and lifted a large plastic container up onto the mattress.

Exhaling a low, harsh breath, and putting his own desires on the back burner for the time being, he stepped up beside Mia as she tossed aside the lid and withdrew a carefully secured panel of stained-glass art. She removed the bubble wrap, revealing a stunning piece of artwork that exceeded even his own expectations.

He took in the array of colorful orchids that were tied off

with flowing ribbon, all made out of shards of cut glass, and found himself completely in awe of just how gifted Mia truly was. She showed him a celestial design, a fairy with golden blond curls and shimmering wings sitting in a meadow of wildflowers, and an intricately designed dream catcher. All the pieces were breathtakingly beautiful, with rich hues, a vibrant kaleidoscope of colors, and striking jewel tones. Bright. Alive. Passionate.

Just like the woman who'd created them.

He was so impressed with her artistic ability and that she'd managed to keep it hidden from everyone except her family and close friends. "Mia . . . these are incredible."

"Do you really think so?" She bit on her bottom lip.

He nodded sincerely. "Yeah, I really do."

She shifted on her bare feet, and he wondered what was going through that mind of hers. Thankfully, he didn't have to wait long to find out.

She looked up at him, a tentative smile shining through her bout of uncertainty. "There's something else I'd like to show you. Designs no one else has ever seen."

He couldn't imagine anything more sensational than what she'd just shared with him, but he watched quietly as she went to her closet, opened the door, and stepped inside the spacious area. Standing on the tip of her toes, which caused the hem of her robe to ride high on her thighs, she grabbed another container from a top shelf and brought it back to the bed.

Inside was more stained-glass artwork, just as meticulously crafted, lovingly detailed, and exquisite as all the other pieces. She carefully picked up a panel that depicted a peacock with its tail fanned out in full bloom—an intricately designed piece that was created in an array of arresting hues. She held it up to her bedroom window, and the morning sunlight shone through the stained glass, throwing prisms of bold, rich blues, greens, and golds flickering across the walls and ceiling.

Stunned by the dazzling, radiant display, Cameron could only stare in silent amazement.

"What do you see in this design?" Mia asked, her excitement nearly tangible.

He laughed, because it was so obviously a peacock. "Is this a trick question?"

She gave him one of those sassy looks of hers, along with an infectious grin. "Maybe."

Bracing his hands on his hips, he shrugged. "Okay, I see a peacock."

"Very funny, wise guy." She scrunched her pert little nose up at him, though that did nothing to diminish the laughter glimmering in her slate-gray eyes. "Do you see anything else?"

Realizing she was serious, he narrowed his gaze and looked *hard,* studying the cuts of glass and the metal casings around each shard as he tried to figure out what he was missing.

He was about to give up when it *finally* happened. Like one of those 3D magic eye illusions, where if a person stared long enough at a picture a hidden object within the image slowly came into focus, as was the case with this particular piece of Mia's stained-glass artwork.

Then again, he supposed his eyes could be playing tricks on him, because she was insisting that something was there. Still, he went ahead and told her what he *thought* he saw. "Is that an image of a naked woman along the peacock's feathers?"

"You see it?" she asked, the disbelief in her tone mingling with a dose of excitement. "You *really* see it?"

He chuckled, enjoying her girlish exuberance. "Either that, or it was a damn good guess. But what I see, other than the peacock, is right here." He stepped closer to the panel and used his finger to trace the slim silhouette of woman, from her tipped back head and flowing hair, to her high, full breasts, and down her long, lean body.

When he was done, he met Mia's gaze. "Am I right?"

She nodded. "It *is* a naked woman!"

He shook his head, bowled over once again. "And you put that illusion into the design deliberately?"

"Yes. And the best part is, no one has to know about that naked woman unless you want them to."

That was true, because he'd had to search for the image and wait for it to mesh into the vision of a woman. "Show me another one," he said, finding himself caught up in her enthusiasm.

This time she presented him with a Celtic design, a continuation of brightly colored patterns and interlacing scrolls. Again, he stared at the picture, and within seconds a shadowed outline appeared—of a man and a woman face to face, with one of the woman's legs entwined with the man's in a very provocative position.

The images were very sensual and arousing, erotic even—made more so by the fact that they were hidden within a design that appeared innocent at first glance.

He looked back at Mia, and her expression held so much joy—more than he'd seen in her before—and he knew, without a doubt, that this was what she was meant to do.

"Mia, all these stained-glass designs are incredible. You just can't *not* do anything with them."

She shrugged and started wrapping each individual picture to put them away. "Maybe I'll take them to a consignment shop and start there."

He was thinking of something on a grander scale, because he was certain she'd draw a very elite clientele with her unique designs, and especially with the erotic and custom-made stuff that had blown him away. But for the moment, he wanted to bolster Mia's confidence, and he knew the perfect way to do it. And in the process, it would also save him from having to go shopping for a birthday present for his sister.

He picked out a substantial piece, which depicted a

hummingbird sipping from a vine of bright, colorful bougainvillea. There wasn't any hidden images of naked people embracing in this particular design, which was perfect for his older, more sedate sister.

"So if you did sell your designs, what would something like this one go for?" he asked casually.

She thought for a moment as she finished packing the container that went into the closet. "It's one of my larger pieces, so I'd probably sell it for about two hundred and fifty dollars."

He didn't even hesitate. "Consider it sold."

Her gaze jerked to his in startled shock. "What are you talking about?"

"I want to buy it," he said simply and lifted the sealed container and put it back into the closet for her.

She watched him, her arms crossed over her chest and her gaze narrowed almost suspiciously. "*Why?* I really don't think hummingbirds are your thing."

He laughed as he set the stained-glass art he wanted on the drafting table and then slid the other filled container under the bed for her. God, she was so skeptical, as if she suspected he was offering her a pity purchase, which was far from the truth. If her work wasn't top quality, he never would have expressed an interest.

"It's not for me," he said, turning to face her again. "I need a birthday gift for my sister, Claudia, who's turning forty next weekend, and she loves anything with hummingbirds on it. She has a window in her front living room where the sun shines through midday, and that stained-glass picture would look beautiful there."

"Okay," she said and dropped her arms back to her sides, which caused the silky material of her robe to shift enticingly across her breasts. "But I'm not letting you pay for it."

Her nipples puckered, and he slowly dragged his gaze from her chest back up to her face. "Oh, yeah, you most certainly are, because I'm not taking it for free. Consider it your first *real* sale."

She sighed. "Cam—"

He pressed his fingers against her soft, warm lips to stop what was bound to be the beginnings of an argument. "I'm not taking no for an answer, either."

He watched her give in, an acquiescence that was slow in coming, but it was a victory for him, nonetheless.

Grabbing his wrist, she pulled his hand away and gave an exaggerated huff. "And you think *I'm* stubborn."

"Stubborn and talented and sexy." Aiming to distract her, he caught her sash and tugged her closer, and the strip of silk gave way in his hand. Her robe parted down the middle, revealing a line of smooth, soft skin from her chest down to her lovely thighs.

Unable to resist temptation, he brushed his knuckles across the hard nipples straining against the fabric, heard a soft purr escape the back of her throat, and a thick knot of lust tightened his groin.

"I'm thinking maybe I need to give you a deposit of some sort for the design," he murmured huskily. "You know, a show of good faith."

She quickly caught on to the suggestive innuendo in his words and played along, sliding her hands around his waist and down to the back pockets of his jeans, where she began to feel him up. "You've got that kind of cash on you?"

He grinned down at her. "No, something better, and far more pleasurable. Check my front pocket."

With playful amusement dancing in her eyes, she patted him down in front, but not where he needed her touch the most.

"A little more to the left," he directed, and the stroke of her fingers along his thickening cock made him groan. "Ahhh, right *there*."

She cupped his erection and squeezed him tight. "Oh, yes," she breathed seductively. "You do have quite a big, impressive wad right here."

A gust of strangled laughter escaped him. "That was a good one." So good, he couldn't think of a comeback.

He didn't need one because it was apparent they were done teasing. The need and hunger in Mia's silvery gaze glowed hot and bright and urgent as she pushed him back a few steps. The back of his legs hit the bed, and he fell onto the mattress, right where she apparently wanted him. Leaning over his prone form, she unfastened his jeans and stripped them off, then shrugged out of her robe and climbed on top of him until her slender, naked body was straddling his hips.

Without any preliminaries or foreplay, she took him deep inside her in slow, tantalizing increments, surrounding him inch by inch until he was completely enveloped in her tight, wet heat. Once he was buried to the hilt, she arched into him, let her head drop back, and moaned as she rode him like a woman who enjoyed having the upper hand for a change, and control over *his* pleasure.

The thought made him smile as he reached up and caressed her breasts and gently pinched her nipples, then skimmed his fingers along her flat belly. "I always knew you'd have a thing for being on top."

Her lashed drifted open languidly, and she sucked in a quick breath when his thumb delved between her soft, female flesh and found her swollen clit, slippery wet from her own anticipation and desire.

She splayed her hands on his taut stomach and rocked her hips hard against his, taking him deeper still. "I think I just have a thing for *you,*" she admitted huskily.

Cameron liked the sound of that. He liked the sweet, tender look in her eyes even more as she gave herself over to him physically without inhibitions or the slightest reserve. He finessed her with liquid strokes and the silken glide of his fingers, but she was the one who set the pace and seduced him with her soft, erotic sighs and clench and release of her body. She was the one who drove him wild with the overwhelming need to be a part of her, in every way.

And ultimately, she was the one who pushed him over the razor-sharp edge of release and sent him spiraling into an earth-shattering climax that began with him and ended with her.

Nine

MIA glanced down at the current stained-glass design she was working on and smiled to herself, feeling a rush of excitement and satisfaction with the way the image was coming together. After her conversation with Cameron the day before about her artwork, and his positive response to the pieces she'd shown him, she was more inspired than ever. She just wasn't sure how Cameron would feel knowing her latest design immortalized the two of them in a very provocative embrace.

She bit her bottom lip and thought about everything she'd shared with Cameron—not only her artwork, which was personal enough, but even the insecurities and doubts she had about making a living at what she loved to do. Not to mention her family dashing her hopes of integrating her stained-glass designs into the business.

She'd never shared that part of herself with another man before and never meant to enlighten Cameron, either. But he'd seen the sketches, and once he'd started prompting her with questions, it had all spilled out so easily. She had to admit it felt so good to get everything out in the open and to let another person see her more erotic pieces. Cameron's enthusiasm had fed her own, and although she didn't believe putting her regular designs in a consignment shop was going to make her enough money to support herself, it would at least provide her an outlet for all the panels and pieces she'd already created. As for the more intimate stuff, well, those designs were most likely going to be a part of her own private collection.

Including the one of her and Cameron. Just looking at the two images lustfully intertwined made her breasts grow heavy and achy and a familiar tug of desire to curl low. Spending two nights in a row with Cameron had been nothing short of sensory overload, and while she should have been physically satisfied, it seemed she was completely and utterly insatiable when it came to him. Not to mention orgasmic. All because she'd opened up to Cameron, trusted him with her body and more.

By the time they'd finally roused themselves out of her bed yesterday, it had been late Saturday afternoon. With Gina gone for the weekend, they'd ordered in pizza for two and indulged in the meal while discussing the vandalism to her car and the fact that Cameron didn't want her going anywhere alone or without him knowing where until the culprit was caught. Such a strict order would normally go against her independent nature, but knowing he was only concerned for her safety and well-being made the request much easier to accept.

After dinner Mia went to take a shower, and it wasn't long before Cameron joined her. He'd washed her hair for her and scrubbed her back, and she was happy to return the favor. Playful touches and caresses across wet, sleek, soapy skin turned into more sensual strokes and breathy moans of pleasure. They'd barely gotten themselves dried off before they were tumbling back into bed and enjoying another night of fulfilling carnal hungers and sinful, wicked fantasies.

But this morning her idyllic weekend had come to a

disappointing end when a call had come through on Cameron's cell phone from a client that had demanded his immediate attention. He'd given her a kiss and a promise to call her later and then he was gone.

In the wake of his departure, and with Gina still not home from Ray's, Mia had been struck with a sense of loneliness, which she'd tried to shake off by reminding herself that she was used to being alone and usually preferred the solitude. But the quiet felt so oppressive, and she'd picked up the phone to give Carrie a call to see how she was doing. Her friend hadn't been home, so she'd left a message that maybe they could get together for lunch or go shopping one day soon. Then, determined to keep herself busy for the rest of the afternoon, she'd returned to her bedroom and immersed herself in her latest stained glass design.

Now, her stomach growled hungrily, reminding her that she hadn't eaten anything since earlier that morning when she'd had a bowl of cereal. A quick glance at the clock on the nightstand told her it was five-thirty and she needed food.

Heading into the kitchen, she decided on a quick and simple peanut butter and jelly sandwich with a glass of milk to wash it down. She'd just finished her meal when she heard the front door open and quietly close.

"Gina?" Mia called out as she tossed her paper plate in the trash and set her empty glass in the sink.

When she didn't receive an answer, a sense of unease prickled along Mia's spine. She always kept the apartment door locked when she was home alone, and the disturbing thought flitted through her mind that maybe Gina had given Ray a key—or he'd copied one for himself without Gina's knowledge. Mia certainly wouldn't put something so calculating past the distrustful man.

With her heart hammering in her chest, she cautiously walked into the adjoining living room, but no one was there. She moved down the hall to Gina's closed bedroom door and knocked lightly.

Again, nothing.

Her hand dropped to the door knob, and she slowly turned it to the right, finding it unlocked. Silently, she pushed the door open, looked inside, and was incredibly relieved to find Gina standing across the room, putting something away in her dresser drawer.

"Gina?" Mia said softly, not wanting to frighten her friend who obviously hadn't heard her enter the room.

Gina gasped and spun halfway around, her eyes wide and startled. She didn't move or speak, just stared at Mia.

"I'm sorry, I didn't mean to scare you." Mia smiled but couldn't ignore the instinctive feeling that something was very wrong with Gina. Her eyes were puffy, as though she'd been crying, and her entire body seemed stiff and tense. "Hey, is everything okay?"

Gina nodded jerkily. "I'm fine."

Mia didn't believe her. Her friend's tone and body language were too reserved and distant. "Did you have a good weekend?" she asked and slowly took a few steps closer.

"Mmm-hmmm," Gina replied as she deliberately took a step to the side, retreating farther away from Mia's approach. "Look, I'm really tired and I'd like to be left alone."

Halfway across the room, Mia abruptly stopped, a little hurt and confused by Gina's terse brush-off. "All right."

She turned to go and got as far as exiting the room and nearly closing the door when she changed her mind. Mia just couldn't bring herself to walk away and allow Gina to withdraw further emotionally, not when Mia sensed that her friend needed her—even if Gina wasn't in the right frame of mind to admit as much. And that meant being there for her roommate and making sure Gina knew she cared. No matter what.

She swung the door open once again just as Gina turned, completely facing Mia for the first time. Gina's right arm was wrapped in an ace bandage, from her hand all the way to just a few inches below her elbow.

Immediate concern had Mia striding across the room, wondering what the hell Ray had done now. "Gina, what happened?"

Her friend held up her good hand to hold off Mia, but the panic in her eyes spoke volumes. "It's not what you're thinking."

Mia highly doubted that claim, because she knew with absolute certainty that this recent injury, just like all the others, had been caused by Ray. She'd bet every cent she had on her hunch.

Mia crossed her arms over her chest, doing her best to keep her anger in check—along with the overwhelming urge to reach out and shake some sense into her friend. As calm as she could manage, she said, "Then tell me what happened, because I'm not leaving your room until you do."

"Fine." Gina said defensively. "I sprained my wrist."

"How?" Mia asked, wanting, *needing* details.

Gina glared at her, a snap of anger raising her voice to a high pitch. "It doesn't matter!"

"Yes, it does," Mia shot right back, furious now. "Did Ray hurt you?" *Again*.

"He didn't mean it," Gina finally said. "It was my fault. He hit me because I made him angry."

Mia was so stunned by Gina's reply that she felt as though she'd just been slapped, but she quickly recovered. "No man should hit a woman, Gina. *Ever*."

"It's none of your business, all right?" Gina yelled at her as tears welled in her eyes. "Just leave me alone!"

Gina's words felt like a knife in Mia's chest—sharp and cruel. They were also filled with a desperation Mia no longer knew how to deal with. Ray was turning her friend into someone she barely recognized anymore, and all Mia could do was watch helplessly as Gina allowed him to dominate her body, her soul, her entire life.

"It is my business because I care about you," Mia whispered around the tears clogging her own throat. Then she turned and headed back out of the room but stopped before closing the door behind her.

She met Gina's gaze and saw the pain and misery there. "You need to leave him, Gina," she said softly but didn't sugarcoat her words. "Before he does something to *really* hurt you."

On that parting remark, Mia left Gina alone and headed for her own bedroom down the hall. Without a second thought, she picked up her phone and dialed the number for Cameron's cell phone. She needed to tell him to step up the investigation on Ray.

Not for her sake, but for Gina's.

"HERE are a few case files for you to review, along with a new client we're scheduled to meet with first thing tomorrow morning."

Cameron leaned back in his chair and watched his partner, Steve, slide the aforementioned documents across the conference room table to the new guy they'd hired the day before. Wesley Donner was only twenty-five, young by both his and Steve's standards, but surprisingly he'd arrived at his interview with five years of P.I. experience under his belt and an eager, go-get-'em attitude. Steve and Cameron had liked him immediately. Wesley was one of those high-tech computer whiz kids and the first applicant both Cameron and Steve had agreed on, without any reservations, so he'd been the one they'd hired on as an associate.

Now, late Wednesday afternoon, they were in the process of handing out some of the newer cases to Wes for him to take home and review, along with familiarizing him with the business, their list of retainer clients, and how they did things. It was such a relief to have a new guy onboard, and while Cameron's workload still felt overwhelming, he was at least able to hand over a few of his easier cases for Wes to handle and finish up.

In the middle of the meeting, Cameron's cell phone rang, and he glanced at the display to see who the call was from. He had every intention of letting the call forward to voicemail and retrieve it after they were done briefing Wesley, until he recognized the number as Mia's home phone.

He hit the connect button. "Sinclair here."

"Cam, this is Mia. I need to talk to you. Do you have a few minutes?"

The urgency and slight tremor in her voice reminded him of the way she sounded when she'd called him Sunday evening to tell him about her exchange with Gina—and her growing concerns about Ray. And that was enough to make her a top priority for him.

"Of course. Give me a sec."

Cameron glanced at Steve as he pushed away from the table and stood, all too aware of the huge secret he was keeping from his partner. Mainly, Cameron's affair with Mia.

"It's a client." Which wasn't a complete lie, because Cameron *was* handling Mia's case. "I need to take this privately."

"Go on and take the call." Steve waved him away with his hand. "I'll finish up with Wesley. We're just about done here anyway."

"Great." Cameron left the conference room and waited until he was behind closed doors in his own office before he spoke into his cell phone again. "Are you okay?"

"Honestly, no." She laughed, though the strained echo he heard made him realize just how vulnerable she was feeling. "I received more pictures in the mail today. I thought you might like to see them."

He swore beneath his breath, hating that she'd been subjected to yet another assault—and that she had to deal with this latest attack by herself. "Yeah, I want to see the pictures."

Unfortunately, his evening was shit tonight, and he had no idea what time he'd be able to make it over to Mia's place. He had a few interviews lined up for a legal case, and Doug

Shelton had called him earlier to let him know his wife had an "appointment" at seven P.M. and was supposedly working late. Cameron had no idea how long that surveillance would run, but he didn't want to leave Mia home alone, considering her current mental state.

A solution came to mind. "Are you free tonight?" he asked.

"Yes."

Perfect. He glanced at his watch to gauge his time frame. "Tell you what. I'll swing by and pick you up around six fifteen, after I finish up with some interviews I have scheduled. I've got surveillance tonight on another case, but because there's always a lot of waiting time involved, we can use that downtime to talk."

"Okay." She sounded grateful for whatever time he could give her. "I'll be ready when you get here."

"Hang in there, and I'll see you in a while."

He disconnected the call, belatedly remembering he had some very interesting information on both Ray and Mia's neighbor, Will, to share with her in terms of them being suspects in her case. Cameron had been crazy-busy since Monday, and he hadn't seen Mia since leaving her place Sunday morning, so tonight would give him the opportunity to bring her up to date on what he'd discovered so far on both men.

AS usual these days, Cameron was running late. His interviews ran longer than he'd anticipated, and he'd picked up Mia twenty minutes later than scheduled. He was starving to the point of getting a headache, so he'd made a quick stop at a fast-food joint for a burger and soda. Mia had already eaten dinner, so she ordered just a drink.

He'd scarfed down his meal in a few bites as he drove to Trish Shelton's offices, which didn't leave a whole lot of room for conversation with Mia. Luckily, he arrived just as Trish was leaving the building and getting into her car, and he tailed her to the same restaurant she'd gone to the week before. He parked the company's Ford Excursion across the street where it was dark but still afforded him a view of the front entrance of the place.

Cutting the engine, he turned toward Mia, who'd been uncharacteristically quiet since he'd picked her up. Then again, he was certain she had a lot on her mind, which they'd get to just as soon as he made a quick assessment of Trish's after-work meeting.

"I'm going to lock you in the truck while I go inside for a few minutes to find out who this woman is hooking up with," he said, taking the keys out of the ignition. "Stay put until I get back and then we'll talk."

"Don't worry, I'm not going anywhere." She smiled, but he could see she was still very troubled by the pictures she'd received earlier—and he'd yet to get the chance to look at.

He got out of the vehicle, locked her in, and engaged the alarm for good measure. Then he crossed the street and entered the restaurant. Before he could stroll past the hostess stand, the young woman standing behind the podium stopped him.

"Party of one for dinner?" she asked and reached for a menu.

Cameron leaned an arm on the edge of the stand and flashed the hostess a flirtatious grin that usually worked to his advantage. "No, actually I'm meeting a friend for dinner, and I'd like to check to see if he's arrived yet. Do you mind if I take a quick look around?"

She returned his smile with a shy one of her own. "Sure, go right ahead."

Permission granted, he casually scanned the dining area until he caught sight of Trish sitting in a booth—surprisingly, with the same woman she'd met there the week before. They were both into their conversation and the wine that had been delivered to the table, and Cameron couldn't help but wonder what the relationship was between these two women.

Maybe it wasn't another man Doug Shelton had to worry

about, but another woman. Considering what Cam had learned about Mia's neighbor Will earlier that week, this new development with Mrs. Shelton wouldn't shock him at all.

Not wanting either woman to spot him, especially when this case wasn't over yet, he started back out of the restaurant, only to be waylaid by the hostess again.

"Did you find who you were looking for?" she asked, eager to help.

"No." Cameron stopped for a moment so he didn't appear to be in a rush to leave. "Maybe he's running late. I have a few calls to make on my cell phone, so I'll check back in a few minutes."

He exited the establishment and jogged back across the street to the Excursion. He wouldn't be returning inside the restaurant again because he'd already discovered who the focus was of Trish's rendezvous tonight. Last week, he hadn't been concerned about the mystery woman Trish had met with. Now, Cameron had to find out who the other woman was, and if the two of them were possibly involved in an intimate relationship. Something was definitely going on with Trish if she had to lie to her husband to see this other woman.

And just like the last time, he'd stick out this surveillance until they left the restaurant and he could take his pictures and be sure Trish drove home afterward. Despite his suspicions of Trish's relationship with this woman, he needed concrete proof to back his inkling and something more incriminating than the two of them having a private dinner together.

He slid back into the driver's seat and made himself comfortable, because it would be a while before Trish and her date would be leaving the restaurant. So he focused on a different form of business instead.

He glanced across the darkened cab of the truck to Mia, who'd waited patiently for his return. "So let's take a look at those pictures you received today."

Reaching into her purse, she withdrew an envelope and handed it to him. He switched on the overhead light, examined the outside, which looked exactly like the envelope she'd been sent before, without any indication of who the sender was.

As he pulled out the pictures, he noticed that Mia averted her gaze to glance out the passenger window, as if she couldn't bear to look at the photographs again. He flipped through each one, disgusted by the slanderous phrases written across each picture. The photos were just as grainy as last time and seemed to be taken from a distance, but Cameron easily recognized the sexy outfit Mia had worn Friday night, which told him her stalker had been at The Electric Blue that evening.

"Is that how other people really see me?"

Mia's softly spoken question redirected his gaze back to her. Her brows were furrowed, and her expression held a wealth of doubts. She'd obviously had too much time to think about the pictures and the obscene words on them, and she was coming to some pretty unpleasant conclusions.

He felt bad she had to deal with this crap. He wasn't sure how to answer her question, but he was curious to hear her thoughts on the issue. "Is that what *you* think? That this is how other people view you?"

"I don't know." She shrugged, reached for her soda, and took a quick drink. "I'm just trying to make sense of all this, and why someone feels the need to slander me in such a degrading way. They obviously feel, for whatever reason, that I'm a tramp and a slut. It makes me wonder if that's the image I project."

He cast a quick glance at the restaurant and switched off the overhead light so they were sitting in relative darkness once again. The few extra moments gave him time to formulate a response that was truthful but not hurtful.

"You're a very sexy woman, Mia. You dress and act the part, you're flirtatious, and you don't hold back. I suppose someone could feel very threatened by that outward display of sexual confidence."

She set her drink back in the holder as she thought about his reply and then she smoothed her palms down her denim covered thighs. "Do *you* see me that way?"

He turned in his seat toward her, and even in the dim shadows there was no mistaking the insecurities in her gaze. She'd obviously had time to reflect about all this, and he sensed that his reply was very important to her.

Again, he had to tread a fine line so as not to hurt her with his reply, but at the same time he also saw this as an opportunity to make her think about her reckless, brazen behavior and how it might affect a person's perception of her. And he ought to know, because he'd spent years believing she was much wilder than she really was. Only in the past few weeks had he been privy to Mia's softer, more vulnerable side enough to realize that her wild antics were mostly a ruse.

"Do *I* think you're a tramp or a slut? Absolutely not," he said with conviction, knowing without a doubt she wasn't a woman who slept around, despite her flirtatious, teasing nature. "But I do think you deliberately project an outward image of being this hot, tempting party girl as a way of keeping yourself from letting down your guard. You don't want anyone to get too close for fear of getting hurt, and being bold and aggressive does the trick."

A startled look flashed across her features, as if he'd manage to tap into dormant fears, but it was quickly replaced with the defiant lift of her chin. "What makes you say that?"

"I used to think you were this big tease who led guys on only to dump them. That's how it looked, anyway." He stretched his arm along the back of her seat and threaded his fingers through her soft, silky hair. "But you know what? I'm beginning to see a different side to your actions and the motivations behind them. There's so much depth to who you are, so many layers, and I think the outrageous way you sometimes act is your way of hiding something deep and emotional and painful." And he could only hope that in time Mia would trust him with those secrets.

She rolled her eyes—clearly her way of dismissing his too-accurate observation. "Nice psychoanalysis, sugar," she drawled.

The fact that she'd reverted to calling him "sugar" was a sure sign she was feeling emotionally threatened by just how close he was to unearthing the truth.

"You spend enough time with a person and you begin to see who they really are inside. No walls, no pretenses. Just honest actions and real emotions that are gradually revealed." He caressed the pad of his thumb along her jaw and was pleased when she didn't physically pull away from him. "And you, Mia Wilde, are an intriguing, multifaceted woman I find very exciting."

She looked away, breaking the hold of his gaze on hers. "Can we get back to the pictures, please?"

"Sure." He didn't think she'd appreciate him pointing out the fact that *she'd* been the one to veer their conversation off course, not him. But he knew he'd said enough, maybe even gone too far, too soon. But he didn't regret a word. Not if it managed to eventually get her to open up to him and let him past those personal barriers of hers.

"Someone who was at The Electric Blue Friday night took those photos of me," she said as she tucked a stray strand of hair behind her ear. "And neither one of us saw anything."

"You're right." He took one last look at the pictures before putting them back in the envelope, then tucked them inside the middle console so Mia didn't have to see them any longer. "But I don't think it was your neighbor Will."

"Why not?" she asked curiously.

He sat forward again, slid his seat back as far as it would go, and stretched his long legs out in front of him. "Because I came across some interesting information that pretty much rules him out as a potential suspect."

"What did you find out?"

Out of his peripheral vision he saw a couple exiting the

restaurant, and he checked to be sure it wasn't Trish before dropping his bombshell on Mia. "Your neighbor is gay."

Her silver-gray eyes widened in startled shock. "He's *what*!?"

"Not gay as in happy," he said in a light, teasing tone. "But gay as in homosexual. He prefers men."

"I get it. I just can't believe it." She shook her head, still looking stunned. "I never knew."

"No, he certainly doesn't have a flamboyant, look-at-me-I'm-gay personality. I'm guessing he didn't want many people to know about his sexual preferences and tried to keep it a secret."

Her gaze narrowed. "Then how did *you* find out?"

He laughed at her skepticism. "Digging up dirt on people is my job, remember? I ran a check on him for basic information, which is normally a good starting point for an internal investigation, and it came up that he has an exclusive membership to a private gay club called Rainbow V.I.P."

"Oh, wow," she breathed and sank back against her seat. "I guess that explains why I've only seen him with guys and not women. I just thought they were friends of his."

Friends *or* lovers, apparently. "I honestly believe, despite the camera he has, he doesn't have any interest in you, other than as a possible photo subject."

Confusion etched her features. "What makes you say that?"

"He's taking a beginner's photography class, so that's probably why you've seen him taking pictures with his camera. He's strictly an amateur. And as far as I can see, he really has no motive to stalk you or send degrading photos, so for now I'm dismissing him as a possible suspect."

She nodded in understanding. "I agree. So where does that leave us now?"

He'd given that plenty of thought. "Well, your friend Carrie wasn't there Friday night, so that leaves Ray . . . or Gina. Or even someone we haven't even pinpointed yet."

"Gina?" Doubt tinged Mia's voice. "She'd never do something like this."

"I believe that also." As far as he was concerned, Gina wasn't high on his list of potential targets. Staring at the restaurant, he did a quick mental review of last Friday night and the events that took place at The Electric Blue. "You know, there was one point when Ray wasn't with Gina for a good ten minutes Friday night, which would give him the opportunity to vandalize your car. He came back with drinks, but that doesn't mean he'd spent the entire time at the bar." He hadn't followed Ray that night because he was protecting Mia, and he hadn't been about to let her out of his sight.

"Well, I haven't made any secret of the fact that I completely distrust the guy." Her loathing for Ray was unmistakable. "By the way, have you been able to find out anything on him?"

"Not nearly enough." He speared a hand through his hair in frustration. "I've tried to do a basic background check on Ray, and it's as though he doesn't exist before coming to Chicago, which leads me to believe he's taken on a new identity for some reason." And that very real possibility didn't sit well with Cameron, because it meant the guy had something in his past he wanted to hide.

Mia sighed. "So now what do you do?"

"Dig deeper, but it might take some time and work." He planned to pursue Ray until he uncovered his past, no matter how long it took. "I'm going to get to it as fast as I can. We just hired a new guy at the office, so now that Steve and I are passing off a few cases to him to handle, I'll make it a priority. But in the meantime, stay away from him."

"That goes without saying," she said wryly. "I'm just grateful he hasn't been spending much time around the apartment, though I wish Gina would dump him before he does something even worse."

"I know. It's tough seeing someone you care about being

hurt." Reaching across the space separating them, he gave her leg a comforting squeeze. "Just hang in there for a little while longer, until I get some concrete information on Ray. Hopefully I'll be able to find out something that makes Gina change her mind about him."

She nodded gratefully, and they were quiet for a few moments. Cameron took advantage of the break in their conversation to scan the restaurant's parking lot to be sure he hadn't missed Trish's exit. After spotting her car, he glanced at his watch. She'd been in the restaurant for nearly an hour now.

"So this woman you're watching tonight . . . she's cheating on her husband?"

Mia's inquisitive question had him switching his attention back to her. "Supposedly. He believes she's having an extramarital affair, and everything he's told me about her behavior are classics signs of infidelity. So far I haven't been able to gather any solid evidence to verify that she's fooling around on him."

"Do you get this kind of case often?"

"Unfortunately, infidelity cases are common." He exhaled a rough breath. "And they're the cases I hate the most."

"I can understand why," she said quietly. "I mean, why stay together if you're not happy in the relationship and you have to have an affair to make up for whatever is lacking in your marriage? Why not just go your separate ways instead of hurting the other person like that?"

He smiled to himself, because her values reflected his own. Yet another trait about Mia that drew him, way beyond just the physical aspect of their relationship. "I agree, but that's not how everyone thinks or feels."

A large, noisy group of people leaving the restaurant had him glancing back across the street. He scanned the small crowd for a familiar face, but there was still no sign of Trish.

He shifted restlessly in his seat, certain Mia was growing just as impatient with all this downtime. He was used to it, but she wasn't. "I'm sorry about the long wait," he said apologetically. "Surveillance is boring, tedious work, and there's no telling how long this will take."

"I'm in no hurry to go back home, and there's nowhere else I need to be."

Cameron watched in fascination as a slow, seductive smile curved the corners of Mia's full lips and her gaze turned smoky with desire. He knew he was in big trouble when she lifted the console between them, which enabled her to lean in closer and nuzzle the side of his neck with that incredible mouth of hers.

"In fact," she murmured huskily as she tunneled her hand beneath his T-shirt and grazed her fingers across his taut belly, "I can think of a very pleasurable way to pass the time. You game?"

He swallowed back a groan. Hell, he was already rock-hard with wanting her, but for as much as he'd love to fool around with her, he was being paid very well to watch and follow Trish.

"Mia, we can't do this," he forced himself to say before he changed his mind and dragged her to the back of the truck and had his wicked way with her. "I'm working."

"I don't see that as a problem. You work, and I'll play . . . with *you*." Her hand molded to the hard length confined beneath the fly of his jeans, and she nipped playfully at his lobe, sending a shock of arousal straight to his already aching groin. "Keep an eye on the restaurant, and let me blow you."

She followed that provocative comment with a gust of warm, damp air into his ear that made him shudder. God, she knew exactly how to get to him, and it was all he could do to keep from coming right then and there.

"That hardly seems fair to you," he rasped, desperately trying to hang on to the last thin thread of his control.

"I'm not asking for anything in return." She began unfastening his jeans, relieving the pressure against his erection, but creating a stronger, undeniable kind of tension and anticipation instead. "You've done a whole lot for me. I want to do this for you."

Obviously, there was no discouraging her, not when she was so intent on seducing him. Yes, they were in a public place, but they were parked in a darkened, secluded area and no one would see what she was doing unless they walked right up to his window. So when she reached into his briefs and eased his straining dick out into the open, he lost the will to fight what he wanted so badly . . . and she was more than eager to give.

With a sultry smile on her lips, she lowered her head and set out to tease him in the most tantalizing, mind-blowing ways. The soft, wet warmth of her tongue lapped along the underside of his cock, all the way up to the sensitive head, and pure lust slammed through him. Her fingers gripped him tight, and when she finally enveloped him in the moist heat of her mouth and took him all the way to the base of his shaft, a deep, tortured groan rumbled up from his throat.

It was too much . . . yet not enough. Needing to touch Mia, to be connected to her in some small, intimate way, he slid his fingers through her dark, silky hair until his hand was cradling the back of her head. Beneath his palm, he followed the rhythm of her lush mouth sliding up and down his sex. Again. And again. And again.

Even as the building pressure gathered low, he kept his gaze focused on the restaurant across the street, which added to the eroticism of the act—because what they were doing, what Mia was doing to *him,* was certainly forbidden, and incredibly risqué.

The breath-stealing way she slipped and swirled her tongue around his shaft, all the way down, then pulled back up in a long, suctioning pull of her mouth shook his sanity and his restraint. His fingers knotted in her hair, and each time he came close to erupting, she deliberately slowed down, keeping him just on the edge of release and making him a slave to her playful whims.

"Jesus, Mia," he growled in frustration. "You're killing me."

She pulled back, laughing in a way that told him she loved being in control of his climax. "Would you rather I stop?" she asked oh-so-innocently.

"Hell, no," he rasped around a gruff chuckle. "Just remember, turnabout is fair play."

"Mmm." She licked him, her tongue a velvet caress along the length of his cock. "I'm gonna hold you to that promise."

She took him in her mouth once again and settled into a slow and steady rhythm, making the pleasure last for a few more excruciating minutes. Finally, she tightened her grip, adding a slick friction that had his hips instinctively thrusting in tandem with the stroke of her lips and fingers.

Knowing the end was near, he gave her a warning she didn't bother to heed. His cock thickened, and his breath hissed out on a violent shudder as his body clenched in orgasm. She took him all the way, finished him off, and sucked him dry—leaving him dazed, completely wasted, and shaking.

He was still gasping for air when she moved away, a pleased smile on her face as she slowly licked her glistening bottom lip. He groaned, amazed at this woman's ability to turn him inside out with wanting, even after he'd just had an incredibly explosive orgasm.

"That was . . . fun." Mia's amused tone vibrated like a soft purr in the darkened cab of the vehicle. "It's nice to know you *do* have an adventurous side."

When it came to her, he realized he was game for just about anything—and that being adventurous did have its perks. She excited him and added an element of surprise to his life he was coming to enjoy. A whole lot. "Yeah, well, you seem to bring out a reckless, daring side in me."

She tipped her head, causing her hair to slide over her shoulder in a beguiling way. "Is that a bad thing?"

"No. Not at all." Now that his heart rate had slowed and his body was no longer shaking, he readjusted the front of jeans and zipped them back up. "Actually, I kinda like it."

"That's good to hear." Smiling, she glanced out the side window. "Hey, there's two women walking out of the restaurant. Is that who you're waiting for?"

A quick look confirmed it was Trish and the other dark-haired woman who had dinner with her. Swearing beneath his breath, he reached for the camera in the backseat. He'd almost missed her, and how in the hell would he have explained that to Doug Shelton?

I'm sorry, but I was lost in the most incredible blow job of my entire life and didn't see your wife leave the restaurant . . .

Oh, yeah, that would go over real well, he thought wryly.

He took the pictures he needed of Trish and the lady who'd accompanied her and came to the conclusion that bringing Mia on any future surveillance jobs wasn't a good idea. The woman was just too damn tempting and distracting. And resisting her, in any way, was impossible.

Ten

CAMERON'S home office printer spit out the report he'd just typed up, and he tucked the statement of recent events into the Shelton file to courier to Doug on Monday, along with copies of the pictures he'd taken of his wife and the woman he now knew as Margot Talbert, a graphic artist who worked for a reputable firm in Chicago.

Thank God he'd manage to shake the lustful fog after Mia's erotic lip service last Wednesday night enough to remember to get a close-up shot of Margot's car and license plate, which had enabled him to find out her name and home address. Doug didn't know who Margot Talbert was, so it was up to Cameron to discover what the other woman's relationship was to Trish. A casual acquaintance? A business associate? Or something more?

He typed up a few more case reports, answered e-mails, and downloaded some information he needed off the Internet before deciding it was time to call it a night. It was nearly ten P.M., and even though it was Saturday and the weekend, he'd spent the day doing background checks on a few witnesses, tracing a lead on an insurance fraud case, and meeting with Wesley at the office to follow up on the cases he and Steve had given the other man to work on.

So far, Wes was proving to be a huge asset to the company, especially when it came to computers and electronics. The kid could hack into a computer in the blink of an eye, and he knew the ins and outs of surveillance equipment like the back of his hand—including planting bugs and hidden cameras. Wes's knowledge blew Cameron away, and both he and Steve saw this as the perfect opportunity to expand the business to include a security division.

Done for the evening, Cameron shut down his computer and stretched his arms above his head to pull the kinks from the muscles along his back and shoulders. He needed a long, hot shower, and a good night's sleep—but not until after he called Mia for the evening.

It had become a nightly ritual to check in with her. His days were swamped, and she knew he was reachable by cell phone should she need him for anything, but he hadn't had the chance to see her since the night he'd followed Trish. There had been no more incidences with Mia, and despite her contrary nature, fear had her laying low at home per his instructions. He didn't want her out on her own after dark with the possibility of someone watching and stalking her.

They'd skipped going to The Electric Blue this past Friday because Cameron had a meeting with a client. Besides, even though he knew frequenting the popular bar was their best shot at finding the person behind the pictures, he didn't like using Mia as bait or as a plant. Not until he discovered who was harassing and scaring her.

Unearthing the person intimidating Mia wasn't turning out to be an easy process. For one thing, the pictures she'd received weren't traceable, and he only had a few key people as viable suspects—with Ray topping the list. And he was proving to be a very difficult man to track—a man seemingly without a past beyond his life in Chicago.

Releasing a tired sigh, Cameron pushed away from his desk, and from across the room his gaze landed on the hummingbird stained-glass design he'd bought from Mia a week ago for his sister's birthday tomorrow. He'd set the piece up against the window for safekeeping until Claude's party, and in the mornings when the sun shone through the window, the cut glass cast prisms of vibrant, sparkling colors across the walls and ceiling.

Every time the dazzling artwork caught his eye it reminded him of Mia, her talent, and her secret, erotic pieces no one knew about except him. He'd watched her excitement and enthusiasm that night and had known, without a doubt, that this was what she was meant to do.

He wasn't an art collector by any means, but unless he was missing something, he couldn't imagine her artwork not appealing to everyone on different levels. The range of her designs were so broad—from subtle, to striking, to extravagant and even eccentric. She even did custom work, and the erotic stuff . . . man, he knew that once the right people got wind of her specialty and the word spread, she'd be set. If only she had the confidence to take the risk and follow her dreams of making a living with her designs.

She needed to get her designs out there for people to find and buy—and not just in a consignment shop. She needed something bigger, with more exposure and the right clientele. And he had an idea of how she could accomplish exactly that.

With his mind still on Mia and her stained-glass designs, he headed to the master bathroom, stripped off his clothes, and stepped beneath the steamy-hot spray of water to take a shower. He'd purchased the hummingbird piece for Claude because he honestly knew she'd love the design and the way it lit up in the sunlight. But he had to admit he'd had ulterior motives in mind, because his sister's good friend owned an art gallery in the city that showcased everything from paintings to sculptures and anything else that could be interpreted as a rare and one-of-a-kind collectible. He was hoping Claude would see the potential in Mia's creations and possibly put in a good word for Mia and help give her that initial boost she needed to get started.

He shampooed his hair and washed his body, thinking that the introduction and recommendation had to be done in a way that didn't look like an obvious setup. He knew Mia and that stubborn streak of hers well enough to know she'd never accept what she perceived as charity. He needed the idea to be introduced casually and naturally, in a way that didn't come across as planned or contrived.

As he got out of the shower and dried off, he decided the best way to accomplish his goal was to invite Mia to his sister's birthday get-together tomorrow afternoon at his parent's place. When Claude opened her gift, he'd let her know Mia had created the design . . . and then he'd let things play out from there and hope for the best.

He laughed to himself as he thought about his family meeting Mia for the first time, and how they might react to her wearing something as sexy and wild as those lace-up boots of hers. And then there was her outrageous personality that had the ability to shock, and her open sensuality that was evident in the way she walked, talked, and dressed. Outwardly, Mia was the complete opposite of his mother and sisters in just about every way. And he was certain those contrasts were bound to make for an interesting and amusing evening.

FOR the fifth time in the past half hour Mia glanced at the clock on her nightstand to check the time. Like a school girl with a huge crush on a guy, she couldn't wait for Cameron to call. It was silly, really, to feel so excited and eager, but no matter how hard she tried to concentrate on the romance novel she'd curled up in bed with—which was a poor substitute for

Cameron actually being with her—there was no ignoring the anticipation fluttering in her belly.

She hadn't seen him since Wednesday evening, though she spoke to him every night when he called to check in on her and be sure she was doing okay. Now, she looked forward to their easy, and sometimes amusing, conversations.

Funny how she'd spent years trying to break free from her family's protective ways, but with Cameron it was different. He was genuinely concerned about her, but he wasn't overbearing about it and he never made her feel smothered or pressured. And because of that, she found herself relaxing and opening up to him—more than anyone else in her life.

It was a scary prospect, considering their relationship, their affair actually, was a temporary deal that would last only as long as it took to figure out who was stalking her. Then they'd go their separate ways, back to their own individual and vastly different lives, and revert back to casual acquaintances. And because she knew the separation was inevitable, she'd do well to protect her heart and emotions in the meantime.

She was so lost in her thoughts that the ringing of her phone made her jump. Grateful for the interruption, she picked up the cordless receiver, a smile already forming on her lips.

"Hello," she answered, much too breathlessly.

"Hey, there," Cameron said, his deep, sexy voice wrapping around her like soft, warm velvet. "What are you doing?"

Those giddy flutters hatched full-fledge in her belly, like a dozen butterflies being set free. "I'm in bed, reading a book."

"Something good, I hope?"

"Mmmm. It's more entertaining than anything that's on TV right now." Marking her page, she set the novel aside and snuggled beneath the covers. "What would be even better would be having you here. I've been home alone all day, and I'm starting to forget what it's like to socialize with a real person."

His low chuckle traveled through the phone line, and she closed her eyes to savor the husky sound. "Feeling cooped up and restless?" he guessed.

She sighed, not at all surprised he'd accurately pegged her mood. The man had an amazing insight when it came to her. "Yeah, I guess I am."

"Sorry 'bout that," he murmured apologetically. "I know this is tough, but I really don't want you going out by yourself. Especially at night."

"I know, and I'm okay with it." Surprisingly, that was true. "Really."

Something rustled in the background, as though he was trying to get comfortable in his own bed. Mia's imagination took flight, and in her mind's eye she could see him sprawled lazily on his bed with one hand tucked behind his head. He'd be shirtless, his chest bare, with a pair of soft cotton shorts riding low on his lean hips. And under those shorts, he'd be wearing nothing at all . . .

"I was thinking," he said, cutting into her enjoyable fantasy. "How would you like to get out for a few hours tomorrow afternoon?"

"Sure." Not only was she going absolutely stir-crazy, she was also dying to see him again. "What did you have in mind?"

"It's my older sister's birthday, and there's a small get-together for dinner at my parents'," he said, his tone casual. "Why don't you come with me?"

Her heart picked up its beat at his personal invitation and what meeting his family might imply. Then she realized he was just being nice and responding to her need to get out of the apartment.

Still, the situation made her feel uneasy. "I appreciate you asking, but I don't think that would be such a great idea."

"Why not?"

Did he honestly not see how awkward the situation could turn out to be? "It might be a little uncomfortable having me there."

"For whom?"

Frustrated by his persistence, she blew out an upward breath. "Uncomfortable for me. You. Your family. I mean, it's not like we're dating, and I don't want your family getting the wrong idea about the two of us."

"Mia," he said softly, and with way more calm than she was feeling at the moment. "My family doesn't speculate about my relationships, and there's nothing wrong with me bringing a woman friend to a family party."

"Why? Do you do it often?" Her tone was light and teasing, but oh Lord, was that a pang of jealousy clenching her stomach? She feared it was, and she'd never, ever been the jealous type. That it was Cameron who sparked such a telltale emotion wasn't a good sign.

"No, I don't bring women to family gatherings that often at all," he said, and Mia could swear she heard amusement in his voice. "And certainly not lately."

She bit her bottom lip, refusing to read anything deep or meaningful into his words. She felt incredibly torn—wanting to be with Cameron, yet unsure how his family would feel about her. Even as just his *friend*. It surprised her that their opinion mattered, when she normally didn't give a damn what people thought of her.

"I'd really like for you to go with me, for a number of reasons," he said, as if sensing she was on the fence about accepting his invitation. "It'll be good for you to get out for a while and have a good time, with no pressure involved. As for my family, they'll love meeting you. Especially because you're Steve's cousin. And if you say no, I might just have to kidnap you and take you by force."

She laughed at the playful threat, though she wouldn't put it past Cameron to do exactly that—and enjoy every minute of being in control of her and the situation. "All right, all right, I'll go."

"Good." His smug satisfaction was unmistakable, the arrogant man. "I'll pick you up at four, and wear something casual and comfortable."

She smiled. "I'll be ready."

"I'll see you then." His voice dropped to a low, husky pitch. "Good night, sweetheart."

She closed her eyes as his endearment drifted over her like a warm, sensual caress. "Good night, Cameron."

MIA double-checked her appearance in the tall, six-foot-long mirror hanging on the back of her closet door and scrutinized her *final* choice of attire—because Cameron was due to pick her up in just a few minutes and she had no time to change yet again. After spending the past two hours trying on an assortment of skirts, pants, and dresses in her quest to find the perfect, meet-the-parents kind of outfit, she'd finally settled on a pair of white jeans with a pink sleeveless turtleneck top. Accessorized with a pair of pink suede heels and a matching Kate Spade purse, the look was simple yet sophisticated—the exact image she'd been striving for.

There was nothing overtly sexy or flashy about her outfit, and there wasn't any cleavage to be seen. She managed to be comfortable yet look feminine and pretty as well, and she was pleased with the end result.

Due to the negative photos she'd been sent and the revealing conversation she'd had with Cameron the night they'd sat in his truck together, Mia had spent a lot of time thinking about her overall appearance and personality. She didn't like the self-image she'd seen in those derogatory pictures, and it had become a startling eye-opener for her. Not to mention making her more aware of how she chose to dress and the more outlandish ways she sometimes behaved.

She'd come to the conclusion that maybe it was time to

make some changes, to shed a bit of the wild, bad-girl persona and redefine who she was on the outside. That didn't mean she was going to start dressing like a nun. She still enjoyed her sexy clothes, the way they looked and made her feel, and she wasn't ready to give up everything in her wardrobe.

But a part of her felt as though it was time to make some necessary adjustments; let go of the reckless, attention-grabbing girl she'd become after her mother's death so long ago; and embrace a classier, stylish image instead. And tonight would mark the beginning of her new transformation to a subtler, more refined appearance.

The ringing of the doorbell, followed by a brisk knock, jump-started the nerves she'd managed to keep at bay throughout the afternoon. Quickly, she slid a pair of diamond stud earrings into her lobes and put her favorite silver bangle bracelets on her arm. She swiped pink shimmering gloss across her lips and fluffed her hair with her fingers one last time before heading for the foyer just as he knocked again.

Inhaling a deep, calming breath, she opened the door, her delight at seeing Cameron after so many days apart affecting every one of her senses in a heady, overwhelming rush of awareness. That disarming grin curving up the corner of his sensual lips. Those striking green eyes that made her melt inside. Then there was the arousing scent of his cologne that wrapped around her like a seductive spell.

The man was just too gorgeous for his own good. He was wearing casual khaki pants and a collared shirt, and his dark blond hair was slightly mussed, as if he'd combed the strands with his fingers right before he'd knocked on her door. Either that, or he'd driven over to her place with the car windows down to enjoy the balmy afternoon breeze.

"Hi." It was all she could do to keep from throwing herself at him and kissing him liked she'd dreamt about the past four days.

"Hi, yourself," he drawled in a low, intimate tone as his gaze slowly traveled down the length of her, then back up again. "You're dressed very . . . nicely," he said, a stunned expression on his face.

She laughed at his careful choice of description. No doubt he'd expected her to wear one of her normal racy, skin-baring outfits. "Nice and conservative?"

"You could say that." He leaned against the doorjamb but was close enough to reach out and run a finger along the high collar of her turtleneck, making her shiver from his touch. "Don't get me wrong. You look great no matter what, and for as much as I love how sexy you normally dress, you'll fit right into my family wearing a sensible, attractive outfit like this."

The thought of fitting into his family, or rather, *not* fitting in, made her stomach knot with anxiety. She so wanted to make a good impression with his parents and siblings. She wanted them to like her and accept her, and she hated that she was so worried they'd judge her and find her lacking. It was a stupid insecurity, but it was there nonetheless.

And it was too late to back out now, despite her concerns. "Let me grab my purse, and I'll be ready to go."

Once she returned with her handbag, she walked with Cameron out to his car. He'd driven his Porsche today, and she slid into the passenger seat and fastened her belt while Cameron rounded the front of the low-slung vehicle and settled himself behind the wheel. The sports car started on a smooth purr of sound, and with a shift into first gear, they were on their way.

Mia's mind was still on the conversation they'd just had at her apartment door. "So your family is more on the conservative side?" she asked, wanting to know what to expect when they arrived at his parents.

"Pretty much. That's probably why I'm so stuffy, boring, and uptight," he teased and flashed her a quick grin.

She ducked her head sheepishly, because she'd made many references to him being all those things over the year or so of them skirting their attraction—mainly, to provoke him, she had to admit. But she'd learned a lot about Cameron and his personality over the past few weeks of being with him. Although Cameron definitely had this serious, focused side to him, he wasn't nearly as straitlaced as she'd once believed.

Resting her head against the seat, she glanced toward Cameron, admiring his strong, handsome profile. "Give me a quick rundown on your family so I know what to expect."

"Okay," he agreed easily. "There's my mom, Barbara, who works for the school district, and my father, Ed, who's an insurance adjuster. The two of them have been married for more than forty-three years."

She was surprised to learn that his father wasn't connected to the investigative business in any way. "With your father working for an insurance company, how did you become interested in being a private investigator?"

"My first year of college, I took on an apprentice-type job at the local police department as an assistant to a detective doing grunt work." He turned the steering wheel as he spoke, and the car took a swerve in the road with ease. "It started as a part-time job to make some extra cash, but I came to realize that I was incredibly intrigued by the whole investigative process. I've always been one of those kids who loves puzzles and mysteries and solving them, so becoming a P.I. was the perfect career for me."

She had to agree that he was good at his job and seemed to really love what he did. She envied him that. "And your sisters?"

"There's three of them. All older than me. Like you, I'm the youngest."

She hadn't realized they had that in common, both of them being the baby of the family. "Except I'm sure you didn't have to worry about your sisters being overly protective of you, checking out your dates in high school, and threatening them with bodily harm if they dared to touch you."

He grinned, his eyes sparkling with amusement. "No, I suppose it's very different being the only boy, as opposed to being an only girl with older brothers. But trust me," he went on, his tone wry, "I had my own share of headaches having to deal with three hormonal girls in the same house." He shuddered for effect.

She laughed, and because she'd been one of those hormonal teenagers at one time, she could easily imagine what he'd had to deal with—times three. "Are they married?"

"Yep. All three of them. To great guys, too."

There was a sense of pride in his voice, as if he approved of his sisters' choice of husbands. Despite him being the youngest of the family, he still obviously had those strong brotherly instincts her own siblings possessed. It had to be a guy thing, she thought.

"There's Claudia and Phillip," he said, giving her a quick rundown of his sisters and brothers-in-law. "Heather and Ryan. Susan and Ted. And a slew of kids among them all."

She found it interesting that he'd remained unattached while the rest of his siblings were married with kids. "And then there's you, the bachelor of the family. How come you're not married, too?" she asked, voicing her thoughts out loud.

"For the obvious reason." He shrugged. "Because I haven't met the right woman yet. When that happens, I'm all for settling down and having a family. But I only intend on getting married once, and I'm waiting to find someone who shares the same values I do."

She glanced out her window as they entered a residential neighborhood. Undoubtedly, Cameron was searching for a woman who wasn't wild and unpredictable and reckless. No, Cameron was the kind of man who'd choose a wife who was sweet and undemanding and respectable. A woman who didn't enter wet T-shirt contests; wear tight, sexy clothes; and dance on tabletops for fun. Mia certainly didn't have a reputation for being the kind of good girl Cameron would expect to have the same standards and values as he did.

"We're here."

She was so lost in her own thoughts she hadn't realized they'd come to a stop at the curb of a modest, single-story house. A group of kids, ranging from young teenagers to toddlers, were playing out in the front yard, and they all seemed very excited to see their Uncle Cameron.

She inhaled a deep breath and wasn't aware of the fact that her fingers were twisting anxiously in her lap until Cameron grabbed one of her hands to stop her fidgeting.

"Nervous?" he asked.

The warmth of his touch and the concern in his voice calmed her immensely. "Yeah, I guess I am. There's just so many of them," she said, meaning the brood of kids waiting for him to get out of his car.

"But they're a great bunch," he said, brushing his thumb along the back of her hand. "Just be your normal, vibrant self, and you'll do just fine."

As Cameron slid out of the car and then came around to help her out of her seat, she didn't have much time to dwell on being apprehensive because they were instantly surrounded by the most animated, friendly kids—all of whom seemed to idolize their Uncle Cameron. Each one tried to get his attention first, and Mia watched as he managed to dole out hugs to each and every one of them.

"Who's the pretty lady you brought with you, Uncle Cam?" This came from a precocious little boy who had the same dark blond hair and green eyes as his uncle.

Cameron ruffled the boy's hair. "This pretty lady is Mia Wilde, who is a friend of mine."

With that explanation, he proceeded to introduce her to each one of his nieces and nephews. There were nine of them in the bunch, and each welcomed her with friendly smiles and boisterous hellos that had her laughing. By the end of the introductions, she was known as "Miss Mia."

Cameron picked up the youngest member of the group, a four-year-old girl named Lucy, with a cherubic face and brunette ringlets, who was looking up at him in wide-eyed adoration. He tickled her neck with his fingers, making her burst into infectious giggles.

"Now, let's go meet the rest of the family," Cameron said and grabbed Mia's hand with his free one.

He laced their fingers and led the way into the house, uncaring of just how intimate their hand-holding might look to anyone who glanced their way. Once they were inside, he let her hand go and set Lucy down on her feet, and Mia followed him into a large, spacious living room where the adults were hanging out.

Another round of introductions ensued, leaving her feeling overwhelmed and certain she'd never remember everyone's names. Between his parents, sisters, their husbands and kids, his family was huge, but they reminded her of her own large clan. And with her cousins Steve, Eric, and Adrian all married off, and recently two of her brothers, even more chaos was added into the mix.

The Sinclairs were loud, openly affectionate, and obviously all very close to one another. Despite Cameron's claim they were on the conservative side, his family was warm and fun-loving and accepted her as Cameron's "friend" without question or speculation, just as he'd promised. And because of that, she was able to relax and immediately felt comfortable with his family.

Before long, his sisters whisked her off to the kitchen, insisting they needed girl time while the guys did their bonding thing during the final quarter of the Sunday afternoon football game. She accepted a glass of wine his sister Susan poured for her, and then she was put to work spreading garlic butter on the French bread while Susan made the salad and Cameron's mom, Barbara, finished up the spaghetti for dinner.

Because it was Claudia's birthday, she was exempt from helping. So was Heather, because she was eight months pregnant and feeling the strain along her lower back and couldn't stand for long lengths of time because of spasms. The two of them were sitting at the counter across from the large wooden island where Mia, Barbara, and Susan were preparing the evening's meal.

As Mia slathered a pat of seasoned butter on a slice of bread, she glanced in Heather's direction. "So you have the three girls, Lucy, Gwen and Alison, right?" she asked, trying to place the kids she'd met outside with their respective parents.

"Yep, that trio is mine." Heather rubbed her burgeoning belly. "Here's hoping this one's a boy to balance out things a bit."

Claudia grinned at her sister. "You mean so your girls have someone to pick on, like we did with Cameron."

"Oh man, we really did torment him, didn't we?" Susan said as she cut up tomatoes for the salad. "Do you remember when Cameron was about five years old and how we used to put makeup on him, curlers in his hair, and dress him up like a little girl?"

Mia had just taken a sip of her wine and nearly choked on the drink. The image of Cameron as a little boy, being coerced by his three sisters to be their miniature-sized doll to do with as they pleased, was just too funny to imagine.

During the next half hour, as they finished with dinner preparations, Cameron's sisters and mother regaled Mia with more amusing tales that had her in absolute stitches. Each story was more outrageous and hilarious than the last.

Hearing how Cameron had grown up, surrounded by fun-loving girls, made Mia realize just how vastly different *her* life had been with three older brothers watching over her. While the Sinclair sisters had treated Cameron with affection and open candor and acceptance, her own brothers had taken their jobs of protecting her very seriously. Too seriously, she thought, knowing that was part of the reason why she'd rebelled at such an early age.

The kitchen was teeming with feminine giggles and chuckles when Cameron walked in, a playful scowl on his face. "I can hear you girls laughing all the way out in the living room, and I have this sneaking suspicion that I'm the butt of the tales you're sharing with Mia."

"Of course you are," Susan said unapologetically as she grabbed knives and forks from the silverware drawer to set the table for dinner.

From across the wooden island, Mia watched Cameron roll his eyes heavenward. "Did you happen to tell Mia how I had absolutely no privacy in this house and how you'd barge into my room without ever knocking, even while I was changing?"

"Hey, I helped Mom change your diapers when you were a baby," Claudia reminded him with a cheeky grin. "I saw everything there was to see, so it was no big deal."

"Well, it was certainly a big deal to *me,*" he stated with feigned gruffness. "And what about how the three of you hogged the two spare bathrooms for hours on end and used up all the hot water so I had to take cold showers?"

Heather reached out and patted Cameron on the cheek, summoning a sympathetic look. "Awww, poor baby," she said, though it was obvious she was holding in her laughter.

"We were just trying to help prepare you for the future," Claudia piped in as she refilled Mia's empty glass with more wine. "You know, get you used to taking cold showers after your dates."

"Thank you very much." Cameron shook his head ruefully and cast a grin at Mia. "It's amazing that I turned out to be a normal guy without any issues or hang-ups."

"You turned out just fine." Barbara poured the cooked spaghetti into a large bowl and said over her shoulder, "and I have to add that because of your sisters, you learned to treat women with respect. You were a polite boy, and every mother on this street wanted her daughter to end up with someone like you. They knew they could trust you not to take advantage of their daughters."

"Yeah, you were quite the catch during your high school

years." Susan picked up the large platter of heated garlic bread and started for dining room.

It was easy to envision Cameron surrounded by a slew of pretty young girls, all vying for his attention. With his good looks and charm, Mia had no doubts he had the pick of the litter. Probably still did.

Barbara placed a big bowl of steaming, fragrant spaghetti sauce in Cameron's hands. "Now help us set the table so we can eat dinner," she said, treating him no differently from the girls she'd had in terms of domestic tasks—even though he was grown man and no longer lived in the house.

He feigned an exasperated sigh, though he was smiling when he glanced Mia's way. "Some things never change."

Eleven

AFTER dinner and cleanup, the family converged back in the living room with their stomachs filled with a delicious meal and the atmosphere mellowed by good wine. From across the room, Cameron glanced at Mia, who was sitting on the couch next to Heather, while conversing with his family. Thank God his sisters had finally run out of embarrassing stories about him in his youth and had moved on to other topics that no longer centered around him.

Mia laughed at something Susan's husband, Ted, said, the light sound brimming with genuine amusement. Cameron smiled at just how beautiful she looked when she was happy and was glad he'd invited her to come tonight. Not only because he wanted Claudia to meet the woman who'd created her birthday present, but because Mia obviously needed the distraction from the more uncertain issues going on in her life. Even if it was just for a few hours.

She appeared relaxed and very comfortable around his family, which didn't surprise him at all. Despite her initial nervousness, her outgoing personality made it easy for everyone to like her—including his nieces and nephews. The younger ones, especially, seemed drawn to her. And who wouldn't be, considering Mia's warm smile and the way her gray eyes lit up when one of the children came up to her or tried to get her attention—which she always gave them. And that kept them coming back for more.

Three-year-old Marissa, who seemed completely infatuated with Mia, had managed to maneuver her way up onto Mia's lap in that mischievous way of hers no adult could resist. The little girl leaned against Mia's chest, fascinated with the shiny silver bracelets Mia was wearing on her arm and the tinkling sound they made whenever she moved her hand.

"If she's being a bother, just set her down and tell her to go play with the others," Claudia said about her young daughter.

"She's no bother at all," Mia said and gently ran her finger through the little girl's soft curls. "She's just as sweet as can be."

"At the moment, yes," Heather jumped in. As Marissa's aunt, she was very aware of her personality and mood swings, as they all were. "But that's subject to change at a moment's notice."

Marissa, oblivious to the conversation about her, blinked up at Mia, her dark lashes framing her pretty blue eyes. "Bwacelets on my hand?" she asked and pointed to her own wrist.

Mia gave in to the request without hesitation, and Cameron had to swallow a chuckle at what a soft touch she was. "Sure you can wear them, so long as you give them back before I leave, okay?"

"Okay." Marissa beamed happily, and it was clear to everyone in the room that Mia had just been conned by one very sly little girl.

Mia removed the bracelets from her wrist and slipped them onto Marissa's arm. She immediately shook her fist and squealed in delight as the silver trinkets made that musical, jingling sound for her.

"Tank you!" Marissa said and then scooted off Mia's lap and scampered off to show the others what she'd managed to confiscate, the little imp.

Once the laughter in the room subsided, Barbara made an announcement. "It's time for Claudia to open her birthday presents."

Susan helped stack the wrapped gifts on the table in front of Claudia, and his sister spent the next half hour opening each one. She received her favorite perfume from Heather, a luxurious bath and body gift set and certificate to spend the day at the spa for pampering from Susan, a pair of gold and diamond earrings she'd had her eye on from her husband, and a crystal figurine from their mom and dad to add to her growing collection.

"I didn't forget about you, sis," Cameron said once she was done opening those gifts. Standing, he went to retrieve the present he'd left over in the corner for her to open last and handed it to her. "I actually managed to get you something unique and original this year."

"What, no gift card to a department store?" she teased, knowing Cameron had given up long ago trying to figure out what his sisters wanted or needed and had resorted to purchasing gift certificates to their favorite places to shop instead.

"Hey, it's your fortieth birthday," he said as he sat back down in his seat. "I wanted to give you something special to commemorate you being so old."

She narrowed her gaze at him, though laughter sparkled in her eyes. "After that remark, this better be a great present."

As she eagerly ripped off the wrapping paper and opened the box, Cameron glanced at Mia. She was watching Claudia expectantly and biting her lower lip in that adorable way of hers that told him just how anxious she was feeling.

He understood how important it was to Mia that his sister

like the gift, but Cameron already knew she had absolutely nothing to worry about. And moments later, after Claudia had removed her present from the protective bubble wrapping, his sister's gasp of pleasure confirmed what Cam already knew. Claudia *loved* her birthday gift.

"Oh Cameron, this is absolutely stunning!" Claudia said in awe while his other sisters and his mother all *oohed* and *ahhed* in feminine appreciation over the delicate, colorful hummingbird design. "Where did you find such a beautiful stained-glass design?"

Cameron couldn't have hoped for a better opening, and he waved a hand toward the woman sitting across from him. "Mia made it."

All eyes immediately shifted to Mia, whose face flushed pink from all the direct attention. She shrugged as if it was no big deal, and because he was coming to know her well, he could sense the insecurity running beneath the casual gesture.

"It's just a hobby and something I do in my spare time," she said, downplaying her talent because that's what she'd been doing for years.

"A hobby?" Susan exclaimed incredulously. "If the quality of your other work is even close to this piece, you're wasting the kind of artistic ability most of us would kill to possess."

"I couldn't agree with you more," Cameron said, backing up his sister before glancing at Claudia and setting his plan in motion. "In fact, I was wondering if your friend, Amy, might be interested in something like this to add to her gallery? Mia has a dozen or more unique designs that are equally as amazing."

"Oh yeah," Claudia said, nodding enthusiastically. "Amy is always looking for new and different art to sell, and I know this would be right up her alley. I can give her a call on Monday, put in a good word, and you can follow up from there with an appointment to meet with her," she said to Mia. "I'll be sure to give you her name and phone number before you leave."

Mia stared at Claudia in wide-eyed shock, obviously thrown by the shift in conversation that now centered around her and the stained-glass designs she created. "I . . . uh . . . well . . ."

"That would be great," Cam jumped in, because Mia had lost the ability to speak. He caught the uncertainty etching her expression and told himself he was doing the right thing. That this was exactly what Mia needed to give her designs the exposure they deserved.

Whether or not Mia agreed with him remained to be seen.

"TONIGHT went well, don't you think?"

Mia leaned her head against the soft leather seat and glanced Cameron's way as he drove his Porsche away from the curb of his parent's house. It was dark out since night had fallen, but the streetlights they passed enabled her to see the satisfied look on his face.

"Quit looking so smug, Sinclair."

"Smug?" he said, oh-so-innocently. "Why in the world would I be smug?"

"You know damn well why." She was still reeling from his ulterior motives and the flurry of excitement and enthusiasm he'd generated with his family over her art. "You set me up, didn't you?"

"How so?"

He was playing hard to get, but she wasn't going to let him off so easily. "By giving your sister one of my designs as a birthday present."

He brought the car to a stop at a streetlight, which allowed him a free moment to meet her gaze. The honest sincerity in the depths of his eyes made her heart thump hard and fast in her chest.

"First and foremost, I bought the hummingbird design from you and gave it to Claude because I knew she'd love it, and she did. Don't ever doubt that."

She lifted a brow. "And she just happens to have a friend who owns a gallery here in Chicago?"

He shrugged as he shifted into first gear and they started moving again. "Yeah, and?"

"And that was your intention all along, wasn't it?"

He flashed her a nonrepentant grin. "Guilty as charged."

She shook her head and laughed. "If I'd known you were going to make me and my stained-glass art the center of attention with your family, I never would have agreed to come with you tonight."

"Which is exactly why I didn't tell you ahead of time."

She knew she ought to be mad at him for interfering in her life and for giving her that initial push she needed to do something with her designs. But deep down inside she was too appreciative of his support and belief in her to summon any real anger.

Still, her own personal doubts surfaced, and her hands twisted in her lap. "I don't know if I'm ready to do something like this." A consignment shop was one thing. A high-end gallery was another.

His brows lifted in surprise at her confession. "Why not?"

"Because . . ." She drew a deep breath, hating the uncertainty knotting in her stomach. "Because it's just stained-glass art, and I'm sure a gallery owner is looking for something more unique than what I have to offer."

"And you'll give her unique," he said, flashing her a confident grin. "You need to show her your erotic pieces. Those are going to be what sets you apart from any one else who creates stained-glass art."

It was a phenomenal opportunity, so why in the world was she hesitating and so nervous? And then she realized a part of what was holding her back: a healthy does of fear.

If it was just her regular designs, her decision would have been an easy one to make. But she knew it was the more provocative pieces that would intrigue people the most and draw her the most attention. And that's where her fears came into play. Not only would she be putting her art on display for everyone to see, but so many of those erotic designs were like a window into her soul if anyone cared to look deep enough. Those unique creations were filled with her emotions, her hopes, her dreams . . . and everything she secretly wished for in her life but had been too afraid to embrace as her own.

As if sensing her wavering thoughts, he reached across the console, took her hand in his, and intertwined their fingers. "Just go and talk to her, Mia," he urged gently. "What can it hurt? If you find it's something you really don't want to pursue, then you'll have lost nothing but an hour of your time. But if things with Amy work out, it could change your whole life and future."

And that possibility scared her, too. For as much as she sometimes disliked working for the family business and how restricting it could be, the fact remained that it gave her security and stability, whereas the world of art was so unpredictable and uncertain. And very fickle.

Who would have thought she'd be afraid of anything?

"Promise me you'll at least talk to her, okay?" Cameron asked and gave her hand a squeeze.

She forced her doubts and insecurities away, knowing she had to at least meet with Amy or she'd always regret passing up such a prime opportunity. "Okay."

They arrived at her apartment building, and Cameron shut off the car. "Come on, I'll walk you to your place."

Once she was safely inside her apartment, he closed the door behind them. The kitchen and living room were dark and shadowed, indicating that either Gina wasn't home or she'd already gone to bed. So when Cameron turned toward her and slid his hand along her cheek and into her hair and then lowered his mouth to hers, she didn't hesitate to meet him halfway.

Kissing Cameron was not only a sensual experience, but it was magical, too. With just the touch of his lips, he made her entire body come alive. Her skin tingled, her belly tightened, and her nipples hardened into sensitive peaks. No other man had ever had such an immediate effect on her, and she reveled in the pleasure of losing herself in the softness and heat of his mouth on hers.

Gradually, he guided her back a few steps until her bottom came into contact with the nearest wall. He aligned his hard thighs and lean hips against hers, and there was no mistaking the erection straining between them. He placed his hands on her waist and nibbled at the corner of her mouth, used his tongue to trace the lower curve of her lip, and when she sighed he slipped inside and slowly deepened the kiss.

His mouth took hers, hot and soft and with a languid hunger that said how much he wanted her but was in no rush to take this into the bedroom. It had been so long since she'd just made out with a guy, and Cameron was showing her everything she'd been missing . . . the heady buzz of anticipation. The slow, agonizing buildup of sexual tension. The simmer of arousal making her restless and needy.

His hands slipped beneath her top and skimmed upward, stroking her skin all the way up to her sheer, lace bra. She waited for him to cup her in his palm, nearly trembling with the desire to have him touch her there, to drag his fingers across her aching nipples. But instead he merely caressed his thumbs just below her breasts, teasing her and making her moan in frustration.

She felt him smile against her lips just before he slanted his mouth across hers and seduced her with more of his slow, soft, erotic French kisses.

An eternity later he finally lifted his head, and they were both breathing hard. Her lashes fluttered open, and she stared into his hot green eyes, her lips wet and swollen from his generous kisses and her legs as weak as a newborn colt's. Luckily, his solid, male body offered all the support she needed.

Making out with Cameron was like enjoying a piece of Godiva chocolate, she decided dreamily . . . the kind that melted on your tongue, yet the pleasure lasted long after the candy was gone.

"God, that was almost better than sex," she said, amazed at just how much sensual enjoyment this man had given her with just his kisses.

He chuckled. "Mmm, that *was* nice," he agreed huskily, then sighed. "I should go."

"You don't have to," she said, much too anxiously.

He withdrew his hands from beneath her top, and she instantly missed the warmth of his touch. "I know, but I have a long day tomorrow and it starts early."

"All right." She was definitely disappointed, but she understood and she had to work in the morning, too. "Thanks for taking me to your parents' today. I really had a good time. Your family is wonderful." And after meeting everyone, it was easy to see why he was such a great guy.

Smiling, he slid his thumb along her jaw. "They enjoyed having you there, too."

Just as Cameron had promised, there had been no pressure from his siblings and no speculation about their relationship, which had made it easy for her to relax around them. Then she thought about next Saturday, when both she and Cameron would be at her cousin Steve's for his son's one-year birthday party, and wondered how they were going to pull that off with everyone believing they were still adversaries.

She expressed her concerns. "Today was easy enough being your *friend,* but how are we going handle next week with *my* family?"

He leaned his forehead against hers and grinned. "Very, very carefully."

MIA knocked lightly on her brother Scott's office door, then walked inside as Scott and her other brother Alex were discussing an upcoming restoration project they were interested in acquiring.

"Sorry to interrupt," she said as she came to a stop in front of Scott's desk. "Here are those contracts you needed, along with the typed-up estimate for the Franklin Building project that's going to bid tomorrow."

"Great." Scott reached for the stack of paperwork and set it down in front of him to review. "Thanks."

Alex, who was sitting in one of the two chairs in front of the desk, cast a sideways glance at Mia. "I've been meaning to ask you all morning. What's with the button-up suit you're wearing?"

Mia would hardly call her short cutaway jacket, constructed of a soft mint green tweed with braided trim along the lapel, *buttoned up*. Sure, the matching skirt hit her at the knee instead of inches above it, and the jacket only allowed a small glimpse of her cleavage, but the outfit was casual and comfortable. And most importantly, sophisticated and fashionable.

"What, a girl can't wear a suit to work every once in a while?" she asked.

"Well, sure," Scott said cautiously. "But that one you're wearing is just very . . ."

The right word seemed to allude her brother, but not Alex. "Nunlike," he supplied for Scott and laughed. "At least for you, anyway. That's more along the lines of what Dana would wear," he said, referring to his wife of a few months.

Scott leaned back in his seat. "I guess we're both used to your more . . . colorful outfits," he said, and Mia knew "colorful" was his way of softening what should have been termed as *flashy* or *outrageous*. "This nice suit just surprised us both."

She gave the hem of her jacket a tug. "Well don't get used to it, because I'm not changing my entire wardrobe." She'd worn the two-piece designer suit today because she had a meeting with Amy at her gallery and she wanted to look her professional best. She hadn't thought about how her brothers might react to the more reserved look.

"Mia . . ." Scott's tone was tentative, even a little concerned. "Is everything okay?"

"Everything is fine." She went on alert, wondering what, exactly, her brother was getting at. "Why do you ask?"

"I don't know." He shrugged, but he was wearing a slight frown, as if he was trying to figure out what was bothering him so much. "You just seem so much more . . . subdued lately."

"It's called maturity," Alex cut in. "I think our baby sister is finally growing up."

She stiffened. "What's that supposed to mean?"

"Stop bristling," Scott said, smoothing things over between her and Alex before a war could ensue. As the oldest of the family, Scott had always been the peacemaker. "It's not an insult, Mia, but a compliment. We've just noticed some changes in you the past week or so. Good ones. And you seem happy, too."

"I've *always* been happy," she said automatically.

"No, this is different. Your overall mood, your personality . . ." His voice trailed off as he narrowed his gaze on her, as if he couldn't quite put his finger on what had changed. "Is something going on that we don't know about?"

"Or that we *need* to know about?" Alex added, suddenly Mr. Concern.

She immediately recognized the protective glint in her brothers' gazes, and she thought about everything going on in her life that would undoubtedly set them off. Her affair with Cameron. Being stalked by an unknown person. Her appointment today with Amy and the possibility of exposing her very intimate artwork no one but Cameron knew about.

Scott and Alex would come unglued if they had any clue what she was currently dealing with, and she wasn't about to enlighten them. "Look, there is nothing going on you need to worry about. And as for this suit, I bought it because it was a helluva good deal and it looked good on me."

Scott grinned. "Can't argue with you there."

"So stop reading so much into every little thing." Then she deftly changed the subject. "Is there anything else either of you need today?"

Scott thought for a moment and then shook his head. "I think this is all the important stuff I needed."

"I'm good, too," Alex said.

"Great." She turned around and headed for the door. "I'm taking the rest of the afternoon off."

"What?" Scott said in surprise.

"Why?" Alex asked at the same time, equally startled by her unexpected announcement.

She stopped and pivoted back toward her brothers, her chin lifting a fraction. "Because my work is done and I deserve the time off, that's why," she said matter-of-factly.

"I won't argue there," Scott said. "But it's all so last minute."

She stifled an exasperated sigh. Her brothers were so damn nosey, and it was clear they were waiting for more of an explanation. She debated telling them it was none of their business, but she didn't want to rouse their suspicions in any way. And she wasn't ready to tell them about the possibility of her artwork being displayed in a gallery, just in case it didn't work out.

"I'm going to lunch with a friend and then shopping." It wasn't a lie. She was meeting Carrie for lunch and then she wanted to find a new outfit to wear this weekend. She just failed to mention her appointment with Amy. "And I might just buy something shocking to wear to work tomorrow so the two of you will quit spending all your time speculating about everything I do."

Scott shook his head and chuckled. "Okay, now *there's* the Mia we know and love."

Alex nodded his agreement, grinning. "Yep, full of sass and smart-ass comebacks."

"And don't either of you forget it," she said and left the office before she was late for her meeting with Amy.

* * *

MIA was lucky enough to find a parking spot on the street two spaces away from the storefront of the Brennan Gallery. She turned off the engine, closed her eyes, and inhaled a deep calming breath to still her jittery nerves.

She wanted to be sure she arrived early to make a good first impression, so she pushed aside her anxiety and gave herself a quick, bolstering pep talk. Then she grabbed the leather-bound portfolio holding a few of her designs and a photo album of the others she'd left behind and made her way inside the gallery.

She was greeted by a nice-looking young man with short spiked hair and black framed glasses that were very retro in design. He was wearing black slacks and a black silk shirt he'd left untucked, and as he approached her, she noticed a slight sway to his hips that was more feminine than masculine.

She smiled at him. "Hi, I'm here to see Amy."

He looked her up and down and seemingly approved of what he saw. "You must be Mia Wilde."

His soft, slightly lilting voice matched the way he walked, and Mia had the fleeting thought that if things worked out, and this guy was single, she could hook him up with Will. "Yes, I have an appointment at eleven to meet with her. I'm a few minutes early."

"I'll let her know you're here." He went behind the counter, picked up the phone, and spoke in low tones Mia couldn't hear. Then he hung up and said, "She'll be out shortly."

"Thanks."

Actually, Mia was grateful for the extra time alone, which gave her a chance to check the place out and see if it was something that appealed to her. The main area of the gallery was open and spacious, with partitions that gave way to different types of art. The collections included everything from paintings, to sculptures, to collages, and photography. There was jewelry, antiques, and varying degrees of woodwork, all of which spanned pop art, deco, contemporary, eccentric, retro, and everything in between.

There was definitely something for everyone's tastes, but what she didn't find was stained-glass art, which definitely worked to her favor.

"Hi, Mia, I'm Amy Brennan," A female voice said from behind her.

Mia turned around and found herself looking at a tall, slender woman with honey-blond hair styled in a blunt cut that framed her beautiful face. She was wearing a very chic yellow pantsuit, which made Mia infinitely glad she'd chosen her own outfit so carefully.

Switching her portfolio to her left hand, she extended her right hand toward Amy. "It's a pleasure to meet you."

"Likewise." Amy's handshake was firm, like a no-nonsense business woman. "Claudia was pretty insistent that I'd love your work, and I'm not one to pass up the possibility of discovering the next great thing everyone just has to have."

Mia did her best not to feel intimidated or pressured by her comment. She didn't think she had "the next great thing," but hopefully her artwork was original enough for Amy to consider displaying pieces in her gallery.

Amy led her into a private room, expensively decorated and accented with equally expensive-looking art. They sat next to each other on a comfortable black leather couch, and Mia set her portfolio on the glass table in front of them.

"Okay, let's see what you've got," Amy said.

Tamping down the nervous flutters in her belly, Mia withdrew one of her favorite and most challenging pieces—a mermaid perched on a large rock surrounded by the deep blue sea. The mermaid had long flowing hair that covered her lush breasts, and her long, elegant tail fin was designed in rich shades of gold, greens, and blues.

Tilting the panel upward for Amy to view, Mia waited for her response.

Amy studied the design critically. "Hmmm, that is a very beautiful design."

It wasn't the enthusiastic reaction Mia had hoped for. But then again, Amy was only seeing one dimension of the design and not the full scope of what this picture entailed.

"There's more to this piece than just the mermaid," Mia told her.

The other woman tipped her head curiously. "How do you mean?"

Mia glanced around and found a tall marble column braced up against a wall with nothing on the base. There was a spotlight shining down in it, as if someone had recently bought whatever had been displayed there. It was a perfect place to prop up her design and present the more intimate aspects of her stained-glass art to Amy.

"Can I use that marble column over there?" Mia asked.

"Sure, go right ahead."

Standing, Mia crossed the room and set the large panel up on the base and then took a few steps back. The spotlight from above made the colorful shards of glass sparkle and come alive, just as she'd hoped. The mermaid's hair, intertwined with ribbons of seaweed, shimmered in beige tones, and her tail fin became a kaleidoscope of dazzling hues that sparkled like jewels.

"Oh, wow," Amy breathed in awe. She stood and came to Mia's side. "The light on that stained glass makes the picture look absolutely amazing."

"There's something else in this picture I'd like you to see," Mia said, excited by Amy's more positive response. "It's here, in the mermaid's hair."

Just as she'd had to do with Cameron, Mia encouraged Amy to look deeper, to see beyond the original design to the underlying erotic shapes within the original picture. It didn't take Amy long to find the man and woman locked in a sensual, erotic embrace.

Amy gasped and glanced at Mia, her eyes wide in surprise. "How in the hell did you do that?"

Mia laughed. "I incorporate the lovers into the original design as I sketch it, before I do any actual stained-glass work."

Moving up to the marble column, Amy examined the mermaid closer. "Mia, that's incredible. And gorgeous. And so unique." Her voice rose with energy and exhilaration. "I can't believe you haven't done anything with these designs until now!"

Mia shrugged. "I guess the timing wasn't right until now." And it helped to have the right connections, she thought, thinking again of how Cameron had made this possible for her.

Amy casually crossed her arms over her chest, her brow arching in amusement. "You know, Claudia didn't tell me your designs had naked people in them."

"That's because she didn't know," Mia admitted. "Her brother, Cameron, gave her one of my regular designs for her birthday, and I didn't mention the more provocative pieces because I wasn't sure if that was her thing or not."

"Claudia might look and dress like Mrs. Cleaver," Amy drawled with affection, "But she'd appreciate having naked people in her stained-glass design."

"I'll have to remember that for next time," Mia said with a grin.

"So how many of these erotic pieces do you have?" Amy asked, back to business.

"About a dozen, ranging in different sizes and designs. I brought three of them with me to show you, and I have a photo book of all the others I have in the collection, along with just my regular stained-glass designs."

"Perfect," Amy said with a satisfied nod of her head. "Let's go talk numbers."

Mia followed her back to the leather couch, where she showed Amy the other designs she'd brought and they looked through the photo album together and discussed her other work.

Once they were done viewing all the photographs, Amy made her decision. "I want to keep all three of the erotic designs you brought today, and I'll even take a few of your regular pieces, because let's face it, there are some people who might find the provocative ones a bit too shocking," she said with a laugh.

It thrilled Mia that she'd be able to display all of her art. "Sure. I'll drop them by the gallery tomorrow."

"Great." Amy opened a file folder on the table and pulled out a contract to review with Mia. "I work on consignment, a seventy-thirty split, so when the sale is made I automatically take my thirty percent, and at the end of the month I'll cut you a check for your seventy percent."

"Fair enough," Mia said with a nod.

"How would you like to price these designs?" Amy asked, indicating the pieces of art Mia was going to leave with her today.

"I really have no idea." She thought about the amount Cameron had paid her for Claudia's birthday present, but she had no idea if that was a fair price or not. And she certainly didn't want to throw out a price that might make her look presumptuous.

"You know the market better than I do, so I'll leave that up to you."

"All right." Amy thought for a moment. "For the erotic pieces, I don't think we'll have any problem getting you anywhere from fifteen hundred to two thousand dollars, depending on how large and elaborate they are. And if anyone wants a custom-made, one-of-a-kind piece, we could probably get double the amount."

Mia nearly choked on that, certain her stained-glass artwork would never sell at those inflated prices. "You're kidding."

Amy patted her leg, laughing at her naivete. "Trust me.

I've been in this business for a long time, and I know my clientele. You've got something no one else has, and once the word spreads about your art and that unexpected twist you've added, it's going to drive the prices even higher than that. But we need to start low at first, to generate interest and get them sold and in the hands of the right people. And I have a list of clients who love to have bragging rights about this sort of thing."

Mia's head was spinning. She'd only expected pocket cash out of this, play money, not the potential of actually making a living at what she'd considered a hobby for so long. She had no idea if she could keep up with the demand, but she'd worry about that when and if it happened.

Putting her art, and her trust, in Amy's hands, Mia signed the contract that would allow this woman to sell her work. By the time she left the gallery, she was floating on air, and the first thing she did once she was in her car was make a call to Cameron, the one and only person she was ready to share this moment with.

Twelve

AS soon as Mia slid into the chair across from Carrie at the café where they'd agreed to meet for lunch, her friend immediately picked up on Mia's ecstatic mood.

"So what are you so excited about?" Carrie asked once their meals had been ordered and their drinks delivered. "You're actually glowing."

"I'd rather not say just yet," Mia replied, trying to be as gentle as possible with her answer so as not to hurt Carrie's feelings. "I don't want to do anything to jinx what's going on."

"You think I'm a jinx?" Carrie sounded affronted anyway.

"That's not what I meant." Mia sighed and stirred her iced tea with her straw. "I just want to be sure this . . . *thing* pans out before I start talking about it."

"Does it have anything to do with that guy Cameron?" Carrie asked directly. "You know, the one you left The Electric Blue with the night you entered the wet T-shirt contest?"

Mia was surprised Carrie remembered. She was even more shocked that her friend would bring it up now when no one but Gina knew she was seeing Cameron. "No, it doesn't." That much wasn't a lie.

Carrie crossed her arms in front of her on the table. "Are you still going out with him?"

Mia began feeling slightly uncomfortable with the direction of the conversation, along with Carrie's persistent questioning about Cameron and her as a couple. "We're not going out," she insisted. "He's just a friend."

"A friend with benefits?" Carrie smirked.

Before Mia could recover from the shock of that remark, their waiter delivered their lunch, saving her from having to find a reply. Which was a good thing, because she had no idea how to address Carrie's question.

Their server was young and cute and had been flirting with Mia since the moment she'd sat down. Even now he was giving her all the attention at the table, making sure she didn't need any ground pepper on her Caesar salad or a refill on her iced tea. He gave Carrie a cursory glance and asked a quick, polite, "Do you need anything else?" before smiling at Mia again and moving on to the next table.

"God, I hate going places with you," Carrie said as she stabbed her fork into her pasta dish. "It's as if I blend into the woodwork when you're around."

She couldn't tell if Carrie was joking or serious, but she felt bad just the same. As a redhead with a smooth complexion and hazel eyes, Carrie was pretty enough, though she didn't do much to enhance her features or figure. Mia knew she'd be a real knockout if she'd just make the attempt to put more time and effort into her appearance.

"I'm sorry about that," Mia apologized, trying to smooth things over. "I wasn't trying to encourage him."

Carrie waved a hand toward Mia's chest, her lips pursed. "Your breasts alone are enough to encourage any man to flirt with you."

Mia blinked at Carrie. "Excuse me?"

Carrie shook her head, set her fork down on her plate,

and released a long sigh. "Sorry, that was uncalled for."

Mia's first inclination was to agree, but there was no sense in aggravating the situation further. Besides, Carrie's tone held an edge of frustration, and Mia wondered if maybe her friend was just having a bad day.

"Is everything okay?" she asked, genuinely concerned, and also wanting to give Carrie the opportunity to talk about whatever might be bothering her.

Carrie offered up a tight, almost pinched smile. "I'm fine."

Mia went back to eating her salad and didn't push the issue. Carrie had every right to keep things to herself. The thing was, she and Carrie were friends, and had been for more than a year now, but they'd never been close in the way best friends were—the kind who'd push for an answer until the other person finally opened up and spilled her guts.

So instead, Mia changed the subject and made sure Carrie was the focus of the discussion, not her. "So what's going on with you?" She reached for a piece of warm bread from the basket on their table and slathered butter on it. "It's been a while since we've really had a chance to spend some time together and talk. That's why I thought having lunch together would be nice."

"It's the same old thing with me," she said as she pushed her food around on her plate. "My job at the travel agency still sucks. My car's in the shop again. And my mother invited her newest boyfriend to move into our already-cramped apartment. Glad you asked?"

Mia laughed, though there was nothing remotely funny about Carrie's situation—it was just her way of breaking up the tension and negativity surrounding Carrie. Especially when it came to her mother's latest love interest invading their living space.

From snippets of conversation Mia had had with Carrie over time, she'd learned that Carrie's mother's need for the attention of men had been the reason why her parents had divorced when Carrie was just a little girl. Carrie had always claimed her mother had the morals of an alley cat, and she hated the constant parade of men that came through their home, yet even at the age of twenty-seven, Carrie had never made any attempt to move out on her own and seemed to depend on her mother to support her for the most part. All in all, it wasn't a great situation.

Mia kept the rest of their conversation as light as possible as they finished their lunch. She also deliberately kept her interaction with their waiter to a minimum, because she was now self-conscious about his flirting and how it made Carrie feel.

"Do you have time to do a little bit of shopping?" Mia asked after they paid for their bill and walked out of the café, thinking maybe the fun distraction would take Carrie's mind off of her problems for a while. "I have a party to go to this weekend for my nephew, and I'd like to find something new to wear."

"Sure, I'll go with you." Carrie glanced at her wristwatch. "I have about forty-five minutes before I need to be back at the agency to meet with a client."

They were on Michigan Avenue and within walking distance of Bloomingdale's, so they headed toward the department store. It didn't take Mia very long to find an outfit she couldn't resist—a flowing, calf-length gauze skirt and a matching blouse in blues and tans that would go perfectly with the beige lace-up boots she planned to wear. As an added bonus, the ensemble was on sale, which left enough in her budget to splurge on something pretty and ultra-sexy to wear beneath.

In the lingerie section she found a bra and panty set made of sheer stretch lace and embellished with delicately embroidered flowers in blue and beige tones. She imagined Cameron discovering the tantalizing, seductive underwear and how he'd react, and a slow smile eased up the corner of her mouth.

"That lingerie set is kind of trampy, don't you think?" Carrie said from behind Mia.

Mia turned around, startled by Carrie's comment, not to mention the descriptive word she'd used—one she was too familiar with lately. "Trampy?"

Carrie shrugged, though there was nothing in her expression to indicate she knew about the photos Mia had received recently. "It just reminds me of the kind of trashy stuff my mom wears, and it makes it her look like a tramp."

Tramp. Mia told herself Carrie's word choice was a coincidence, that her friend was still feeling raw from the discussion about her mother and her latest boyfriend. Obviously, some of that bitterness was lingering—and she was inadvertently taking her grudge out on Mia.

Besides, Carrie hadn't been at The Electric Blue the second night to take those other photos or to vandalize her car. And that was enough to convince Mia she was overreacting.

"Well, it's not as though the panties are crotchless underwear from Frederick's of Hollywood or anything like that," Mia said, a teasing inflection in her tone.

"It might as well be," Carrie said in disgust. "You can see right through them . . . everywhere."

Mia decided Carrie had to be a simple cotton type of girl and hadn't learned to properly appreciate pretty, intimate undergarments. Or maybe she just hadn't met the right guy to inspire her to be daring and adventurous with her sexuality.

"Well, so long as no one looks under my skirt, I think I'm okay." Mia flashed her a smile.

Done shopping, Mia carried her items to the register, and despite Carrie's disapproving frown, she purchased the panty and bra set, figuring it was Carrie's problem if she didn't like sexy lingerie, not her own.

CAMERON followed Trish's car at a discreet distance, wondering where in the world she was off to on a late Friday afternoon. He'd ruled out the restaurant she'd met Margot at the past few times, because they were heading in the opposite direction. All Cameron could do was sit tight and wait for Trish to arrive at her destination.

His cell phone rang, and he glanced at the hands-free unit in the company truck. Seeing Mia's number, he immediately connected the call.

"Hey there," he said with a smile. "How was your day?"

"Outstanding," she replied, her enthusiastic voice filling the cab of the vehicle. "I just got off the phone with Amy at the gallery, and you'll never believe what she just told me!"

It had been such a long, busy week for Cameron that he hadn't had any spare time to spend with Mia—just phone calls in the evening. And even though he looked forward to those intimate and amusing discussions they inevitably had, he had to admit that he missed seeing her in person and being with her. But hearing her voice, like now, was enough to make his entire day.

"So what did Amy tell you?" he asked.

"You know those erotic pieces I left with her during my meeting with her on Tuesday? Well, she had such a phenomenal response to the stained-glass art, and so many of her clients were interested in purchasing the pieces, that she decided to put them up for auction!"

Her excitement was infectious, and a huge grin spread across his face. "Mia, that's incredible!"

"I know! I'm just stunned. And that's not all," she went on breathlessly. "Amy wants to schedule a gallery show, just for me and my stained-glass artwork. Can you believe that?"

He laughed, resisting the urge to remind her he was the reason her art was on display at the Brennan gallery—because he'd seen the potential in her art, and her mass appeal. "Of course I can believe it."

She grew quiet and then said, "I guess at some point I'm going to have to tell my family about all this, huh?"

He followed Trish into the city, keeping his distance as she started traveling on surface streets. "I think they'd be hurt if you didn't."

"I know." Her soft sigh drifted through the phone. "It's just that they don't know about the erotic pieces, and I have no idea how they'll react to them. I mean, I've done many things over the years to shock my family, but this is just so . . . public. And personal."

Hearing the barest hint of insecurity in her voice, he sought to reassure her. "How can they not be anything but proud of what you've accomplished? A showing is not something every artist gets, so this is a huge testament to just how amazing your work is. And just for the record, I'm *very* happy for you."

"Thanks," she said, and this time he detected a smile in her tone. "Care to celebrate with me tonight?"

God, it had been too long since they'd seen each other. It had been nearly a week since they'd spent the day at his parents, and even longer than that since they'd been together intimately. And he honestly and truly missed being with her, in every way.

Unfortunately, he wasn't going to see her this evening, either.

"I'd love to celebrate with you, but I can't tonight," he said regretfully. "Right now I'm tailing Trish to some unknown destination, and after this surveillance I have to head back to the office to go over some open cases with Wes. Then, I'm meeting with a new client this evening, and I have no idea when I'll be done."

"I understand," she said, but he knew she was disappointed. "I guess I'll see you tomorrow at Steve's."

See, but not touch because their affair was a secret, he thought in frustration. "Just insult me a few times, and everyone will think things are normal between us."

She laughed huskily. "Oh, I plan to do more than just insult you tomorrow, sugar."

That tempting, teasing note to Mia's voice aroused more than Cameron's curiosity. He had no idea what she had in mind, but he wouldn't put anything past her and had no doubt it was something that would include tormenting him in some way.

They said their good-byes and Cameron disconnected the call, though his thoughts remained on Mia and their affair. After spending the past few weeks with Mia and discovering the deep, emotional layers hidden beneath her wild ways and outrageous personality, he already knew he was in over his head with her. Way deeper than he'd ever intended to fall for the sexy, raven-haired vixen. And he was beginning to hate the fact that he couldn't openly date Mia and let everyone know they were a couple and see if they had any chance at a future together.

That thought made his palms sweat and his heart race. He'd never thought of himself and Mia in terms of *the future*. But somewhere along the way, he'd come to realize that the decision to have a hot affair with her to get her out of his system had given way to something far more intimate. For him, it wasn't just about sex anymore. It was about wanting this woman, despite how opposite they were. It was about viewing her as someone he could possibly have a strong and lasting relationship with because she excited him and made him feel things no other woman ever had.

Unfortunately, he knew Mia wasn't ready to take their relationship to an emotional level, and maybe she never would be. He was well aware of her past with men and her inability to sustain anything long term. And for as much as she'd shared with him, and he'd learned about her, there were still a few barriers left for him to scale. He planned to do his damndest to tear every one of those walls down before they were through.

But for now he'd let her believe she was safe with him, that he posed no threat to her heart and emotions. He'd go to the party tomorrow and pretend as though they'd never slept together, that he didn't know how funny she could be, or that she created erotic stained-glass art her family didn't even know about. But once they found out who was stalking her, they were going to have to face what was happening between them—even if it meant forcing her to do so.

He continued to drive a few car lengths behind Trish until she turned her vehicle into the circular drive of the St. Claire Hotel to valet park her car—leading him to believe she had a late-afternoon date with her lover. But *who* was the million-dollar question he'd yet to find the answer for.

Cameron opted for the regular parking lot so he'd be able to see Trish when she left the hotel—hopefully with whomever she was meeting there. He was lucky enough to find an empty space in the first row and took it, though he didn't have enough time to take any pictures of Trish entering the hotel since he needed to stay close behind her. As soon as she disappeared into the lobby, Cameron made his way inside as well, just in time to see her step into one of the elevators with a few other people, effectively putting an end to him following her.

Hands on his hips, he watched in frustration as the elevator stopped on four different floors, making it impossible to figure out what level she'd gotten off on. He swore beneath his breath, seeing yet another dead end to the investigation unless she ended up leaving the hotel with her lover and finally gave him some substantial evidence to report back to her husband.

"Hey, stranger."

The soft, husky female voice was a familiar one, and Cameron turned around to find Ashley St. Claire, now *Wilde*—heiress to the St. Claire Hotel and Scott Wilde's wife—standing behind him. Even though she'd married Scott, she still worked for the family's chain of hotels managing the boutiques. She looked beautiful as always, sophisticated and chic and everything you'd expect from someone of her social stature—but very down to earth despite her wealth and family name.

"Ashley," he said with a smile and then dropped his gaze to the small bump showing beneath her skirt. It had been a while since he'd seen her, and he was surprised to find she was expecting, though that explained her glowing complexion, which he'd seen many times on his own sisters' faces when they'd been pregnant. "Looks like you and Scott have been busy."

Laughing, she placed a hand on her protruding belly. "A honeymoon baby. I'm about five months along. For months I had a nice, flat belly, then about two weeks ago I woke up and nothing in my closet fit because my waist had expanded a few inches. Literally overnight," she said wryly.

"Well you look great. And happy," he said, knowing she and Scott had gone through a lot to be together. But everything had worked out for the two of them in the end, despite their issues. "I'll have to congratulate Scott when I see him at Steve's tomorrow."

"Ah, yes, Cody and Tara's birthday party," she said lightly. "It should be quite a gathering, considering how many family and friends are going to be there."

"Cody *and* Tara?" Cameron was aware of Steve's son's one-year celebration, but hadn't known the party included Eric's daughter as well.

She nodded. "Steve and Eric decided to go ahead and have the kids' parties together this year, because they were born on the same day and the family will all be there. It's like having twins I suppose, even though Cody and Tara are cousins. They'll be sharing the same birthday for a lifetime, and I'm sure as they get older they'll want individual parties."

"No doubt." But at a year old, they didn't know the difference, and it made sense to have their birthday party on the same day.

"So what brings you here?" Ashley asked curiously. "Business or pleasure?"

"Business," he said, remembering Trish's swift getaway. "Which is pretty much over at this point."

Then he had a thought, that maybe Ashley might be able to help him out as far as Trish's visit to the hotel was concerned.

Maybe find out if Trish had been a registered guest for the day, and with whom. At this point, he'd take whatever information he could get.

Except it wasn't a discussion he wanted to have with her in the middle of the hotel lobby. "Can we go somewhere private and talk? I have a favor to ask."

"Sure. Come on over to the boutique." She started in that direction with Cameron following beside her as she said, "I need to relieve my salesgirl for a half-hour break. The shop has been pretty quiet and slow all day, so we can talk there."

Of course slow and quiet wasn't the case once Ashley let her salesgirl leave the boutique for her break. As soon as the young girl was gone, an older woman walked in, wanting to find a new pair of comfortable shoes to wear because the strap on her current sandals had snapped apart. So while Ashley helped her customer, Cameron strolled through the boutique, taking in the expensive items and designer-end accessories on display.

A long thirty minutes later, the woman finally left the shop, happy with her purchases—because of course once she found new shoes she'd needed a new purse to go with them and that had been an ordeal as well.

Ashley came back to Cameron, her expression apologetic. "It figures that would happen, right after I claimed how quiet it was today. I'm so sorry."

"You have nothing to be sorry for," he replied easily. "Business is business, and I completely understand."

"So what kind of favor can I do for you?" she asked with interest.

Knowing he could trust Ashley, Cameron briefly explained his current case, how he'd ended up at the hotel today, and how he needed to find out the name of the person Trish Shelton had met up with.

"If there's anything you can do in terms of finding out if she's a registered guest here for today, or who she hooked up with, I'd appreciate it." Cameron wasn't holding out much hope for that, though, considering her lover had most likely paid for the room.

"Sure. I'll find out what I can and let you know."

"Thanks."

He chatted with Ashley for another fifteen minutes, and just as he turned around to head out of the boutique to wait in his truck for Trish to leave the hotel, he caught sight of her stepping off the elevator—alone.

He cursed beneath his breath. "There she is," he said to Ashley so she could get a good look at Trish as she walked across the lobby. "Have you ever seen her here before?" he asked hopefully.

Ashley shook her heard. "I can't say I have. There are just so many people who come through here on a daily basis. I'm sorry."

It was just his luck, or lack thereof, when it came to this case. He'd just spent an hour and a half tailing Trish, and he had absolutely nothing to show for it.

SHE'D worn those lace-up, fuck-me boots on purpose.

Cameron took a long drink from his bottle of beer, not doubting Mia's wicked intentions for a moment. He'd taken one look at her simple but pretty outfit she was wearing when she'd arrived at Steve's and then saw those sexy leather boots with the ties up the side and had known she meant to torment him today and keep him on the razor-sharp edge of wanting her.

It worked. More than two hours into the celebration and he'd already entertained half a dozen fantasies about Mia in those heeled boots. Even now, as he watched her from across the backyard where she was mingling with her family on the porch and playing with her one-year-old niece and nephew, he was thinking about having her legs wrapped tight around his waist and imagining the feel and friction of that soft, supple leather against his skin. If he wasn't careful, he was going to be sporting a perpetual hard-on for the rest of the day.

She'd already managed to insult him a few times and provoke him with that smart mouth of hers, enough to make her family think everything was normal between them. He went along with the act, issuing a few gibes of his own, though he wanted more than anything to grab her, pull her body flush to his, and kiss her senseless in front of everyone to stake his claim.

Mia stopped to talk to her cousin-in-law Chayse, who'd married her cousin Adrian Wilde a year ago. Just a few weeks ago Chayse had given birth to their first child, a baby boy they'd named Brandon who was currently cradled in his mother's arms. But that didn't last long, because Mia gently scooped him up and cuddled him close to her breast. She spoke to Chayse while looking down at her newest nephew adoringly, the longing on her face so tangible Cameron felt the same emotion deep in his gut.

Then Mia's stepmother, Amelia, joined them to fuss over the baby, too. Recalling the conversation he'd had with Steve about Mia losing her mother at such an early age, Cameron watched with interest at how Mia and Amelia interacted around one another—and learned more than he thought possible.

Though Mia and Amelia conversed easily, something about their body language told him they didn't share the kind of close-knit bond most mother and daughters did. True, they weren't blood related, but it appeared they'd never developed a strong, secure relationship throughout the years. In fact, there was a definite reserve between them—mostly on Mia's part, as if she'd never let those walls of hers down far enough to let her stepmother get close.

"Hey there," Ashley said, approaching the table where he was sitting at out in the backyard. "What are you doing sitting out here all by yourself?"

He shrugged and smiled at her. "Just taking a break. Steve had me flipping hamburgers at the barbecue earlier, and I just want to be sure I'm nowhere near when he needs someone to pull the piñata cord for the kids."

"If you ask me, that sounds like a job for one of the uncles, and there's plenty of them here." She sat down in the chair next to him. "Well, because I finally caught you alone, I thought I'd talk to you about that woman you wanted to get some information on."

"Anything?" he asked and finished off the last of his beer.

She shook her head. "No. I'm really sorry. The front desk had nothing listed under her name."

"It's okay. I honestly wasn't expecting much anyway. I appreciate you trying."

"I'm going to go help Jill and Liz cut the birthday cake." She stood again, her hand automatically coming to rest on the curve of her belly. "Can I interest you in a piece?"

"No, I'm stuffed." He rubbed his own stomach. "I ate two of those hamburgers and way too many servings of all those delicious side dishes you girls made."

She laughed, her green eyes sparkling. "The Wilde gatherings have turned into a huge potluck, which certainly helps since the family seems to be growing by leaps and bounds these days."

Ashley left him alone once again, and Cameron's gaze automatically drifted back to Mia. He was surprised to find she was watching him, too, with a sexy, sinful smile curving her lips. She glanced away again, and as she spoke to her brother Alex and his wife Dana, she lightly touched her fingers to her throat in a way that made him wish he was caressing her there.

She tossed her head back and laughed at something her sister-in-law said, the husky, sensual sound arousing his senses. And when she casually reached down and skimmed up the hem of her long skirt, he wondered what the hell she was up to. She rubbed her fingers along the exposed skin above the top of her leather boot, right where the lace-up ties were.

To anyone else nearby, it appeared Mia was scratching an itch, but Cameron saw right through the pretense. She was flashing those provocative boots his way, tempting him from afar and teasing him with what she knew he wanted but couldn't have.

A low, frustrated growl rumbled up from his throat before he realized he'd let it escape.

"She's getting to you, isn't she?"

Shit. He tried not to wince as Joel appeared from behind him. Cameron had no idea just how long Mia's brother had been watching their exchange or what he'd witnessed. But Cameron wasn't about to admit to anything.

"Who?" he said with an air of nonchalance.

"Don't give me that crap," Joel said, calling his bluff with amusement. He set a fresh bottle of beer in front of Cameron and then took the seat next to him. "You know exactly who I'm talking about. Mia. You've been watching her the entire afternoon, as well as deflecting her remarks, and I'm just waiting for you to snap and jump her already."

Even though Joel's comment surprised Cameron, he managed to maintain a bland expression. "Not likely."

"Want to bet on that?" Joel lifted his own bottle of beer to his lips, a challenge glinting in his gaze.

"Bet on what?" Cameron asked, not completely sure what Joel was getting at. "That I'm going to give into your sister's taunts?"

Joel grinned. "Yeah."

"Not a chance, buddy," Cameron said with a firm shake of his head.

"If you seem so determined to resist her, it should be easy money for you." Joel thought for a moment, glancing from Mia and back to Cam. "Twenty buck says she'll get the best of you before the day is over."

"Yeah, sure. Whatever," Cameron said, agreeing for the sake of putting an end to the issue, especially because Mia was heading their way. "Speaking of which, here comes trouble right now."

Mia stopped at the table, holding a plate with a large piece of birthday cake. "What is this, the singles' table?"

"Yep, the last of a dying breed when it comes to our family," Joel joked. "Care to join us?"

"That all depends," she said with a mischievous twinkle in her slate gray eyes. "Will I look as pathetic as the two of you do?"

Cameron held back a laugh, and instead thought up an appropriate taunt so Joel would think all was normal between him and Mia. "Girls never look pathetic, even when they're old maids."

She set her plate on the table and sat down next to her brother and across from Cameron. "Just for the record, I'm not an old maid, sugar," she drawled sweetly. "I choose to be single, whereas an old maid is a woman who can't get herself a guy at all. I do just fine in that department."

"You know just how to get them to eat out of the palm of your hand, don't you?" Cameron said, sparring right back.

"Only the ones I *want* eating out of my hand." She dropped a small piece of the cake in her palm and held it toward Cameron. "Care for a bite, sugar?"

"Oh man," Joel said on a chuckle. "You are so down for the count, Sinclair."

It took a huge amount of effort for Cameron to resist Mia's outrageous dare, along with the urge to grasp her wrist and nibble and lick the scrap of chocolate cake off her palm until she was squirming and just as hot as she was making him.

When Cameron refused to take the bait, or in this case, the cake, Mia popped the crumb into her mouth and ate it herself. "Can you believe all the babies this family is going to have this year?" she said, glancing at Joel. "Chayse just had Brandon, and Ashley is due in a few months. And Dana and Alex just announced earlier today that they're pregnant, too. God, I hope it's not contagious," she said with an exaggerated shudder.

"What, you don't want to have babies?" Cameron asked before he could censure the question.

Her gaze shot to his, and it was clear he'd startled her. "Well, I haven't given it a whole lot of thought, being an old maid and all."

She was trying to be cute and funny and dismissive, but Cameron was thinking about it now. Having babies. With Mia. "I'd like at least three or four," he said.

She lifted a brow as she dipped her fork into her cake for another bite. "Sounds like you want a wife you can keep barefoot and pregnant."

Cameron grinned. "Yeah, I like that image."

Mia rolled her eyes and licked away a crumb from the corner of her mouth. "And I suppose you'd expect your little woman to stay at home with the kids, keep the house clean and spotless, and be sure you had a hot meal on the table when you walked in after a long day at the office."

"What man wouldn't?" he said, admitting as much. "But only if that's what my wife wanted to do."

"What if she wanted to work?"

Somewhere along the way the conversation had taken an interesting twist, and while Joel probably thought they were arguing, Cameron was fascinated with Mia's questions and answers, which said a whole lot about how she felt about having a family of her own.

"I'd like to consider myself a contemporary kind of guy." He leaned back in his chair as he absently swiped his fingers along the condensation gathering on his bottle. "I'd have no problem if my wife wanted to pursue a career, just so long as the family didn't suffer."

"Ahhh," she said, gaze narrowed and her fork pointed in his direction. "So your wife would have to juggle her job and also be sure everything at home ran smoothly, too?"

"No, my wife and I would find a balance to be sure the

kids didn't suffer because of our dual careers and we had someone we trust to watch the kids when we couldn't. So there would definitely have to be some compromising to make things work."

She stared at him incredulously. "You're willing to help with the cooking and the cleaning and the diaper changing?"

"I cook and clean for myself now, so I can't imagine changing a diaper is that difficult."

"You're a better man than I," Joel said with a shudder. "Diaper changing is so not my thing."

"Spoken like a true macho man," she said and laughed.

"Hey, at least I'm honest." Joel drained the last of the beer in his bottle. "I think I need another drink. This conversation is giving me the hives since I have no intentions of getting married or having any kids. I'm out of here." Standing, he gathered the empty beer bottles and looked at Cameron. "Can you handle being alone with Mia?" he asked, his tone infused with meaning and amusement.

"Don't worry about me," he said, waving Joel away. "I can handle Mia just fine."

As soon as they were alone, a sultry smile curved Mia's full, sensual lips. Lips he was dying to taste and kiss. "So you can handle me, huh?" she murmured as she slowly, oh-so-provocatively ate another bite of her cake.

While Mia's back was facing everyone up on the porch, Cameron was still in full view, which meant he needed to monitor his actions and reactions to Mia's current attempt to seduce him. "I think I've proved a few times just how well I can handle you."

"Mmmm. So you have." Her lashes fell half-mast, and her voice dropped to a soft purr. "I wouldn't mind you manhandling me again. It's been a while, you know."

"You've made me well aware of that." Reclining, he clasped his hands over his stomach. "Especially today, with you wearing those lace-up boots. You wore them deliberately, didn't you?"

"Of course I did," she admitted shamelessly.

Beneath the linen-draped table, the sole of her boot scraped along the inside seam of his jeans and then continued up his thigh until the toe of her shoe was pressing very insistently against his crotch. Heat and lust rushed straight to his groin, and he clenched his jaw to keep a low, tell-tale groan from escaping.

Bracing her elbow on the table, she propped her chin in her hand as she played with the frosting on the cake with her fork, as if she didn't have her booted foot between his legs, rubbing against him in a very arousing way, making him harder and stiffer than he already was.

"If I remember correctly," she said huskily, "You told me they did it for you, in a major way."

"So I did." She was enjoying exploiting that particular weakness of his to her advantage. And because they were surrounded by her family, he had to act blasé, which was one of the most difficult things he'd had to do.

She slowly licked the white, creamy frosting from her fork, a sinful gleam in her eyes. "And judging by the erection you're currently sporting, they're doing it for you, right now, in a major way. Aren't they, sugar?"

He reached down and grabbed her ankle, effectively putting a stop to her foot stroking along his shaft. "You're playing with fire," he warned in a gruff tone. "You have been all afternoon."

"Maybe I'm looking to get burned," she whispered back.

Sitting up straighter in his seat, Cameron leaned toward Mia, using the position to strum his fingers along the sensitive skin at the back of her knee, right where the top of her boot ended. She visibly shivered, offering him a smidgeon of satisfaction that he was able to get under *her* skin in some small way.

His smile was calm for the sake of anyone who might be looking their way. "If you're not careful, sweetheart, you're gonna end up on this table, with your skirt tossed up over your head, and with me having my way with you right here in front of your family."

Undeniable desire darkened her eyes. "How about you meet me in the upstairs bathroom in a few minutes while Cody and Tara are opening their gifts, so no one will miss either one of us, and you can have your way with me there?"

He released her leg, unable to believe what she was suggesting. "You're kidding, right?"

"Actually, I'm absolutely serious. And I'll even keep the boots on just for you." Standing, she licked the last smudge of frosting from her bottom lip, the glimpse of her soft, pink tongue reminding him of how well she could use that mouth of hers. "Don't make me wait long, sugar, or else I'll have to take matters into my own hands."

As he watched her sashay toward the house, he rubbed a hand along his slack jaw, his mind still reeling from her very risqué proposition. God, she was so bold. So daring. And he was beginning to love those things about her, because all that brazenness was directed solely at him.

Oh, yeah, he'd meet with her in the upstairs bathroom. Just as soon as he could walk across the backyard without his erection announcing his intentions.

Thirteen

CAMERON quietly made his way upstairs, making sure no one witnessed his disappearing act. With a soft knock on the bathroom door, Mia let him inside, then twisted the lock, and eagerly pulled him to her. He braced his forearms against the wall on either side of her head, and his blood heated when she tunneled her hands beneath his shirt and skimmed her palms up along his chest, her caresses desperate and needy.

She nipped at his bottom lip and used her tongue to soothe the slight sting. "God, Cameron, it's been too long since we've been together, and I want you so much," she said, her panting breaths telling him just how excited she already was, and he hadn't even touched her yet.

He unbuttoned the front of her top, just enough so one shoulder slid down her arm, exposing a breast covered in pretty, embroidered lace that was sheer and damned sexy. He pulled that stretchy fabric down, cupped her bare breast in his palm, and scraped his thumb across her stiff nipple.

She closed her eyes and moaned softly, her lower body

grinding provocatively against his. "Cameron, please . . ."

"What, exactly, do you want me to do?" he murmured, and exposed her other breast so he could give it equal attention, squeezing and kneading the pliable flesh.

Her lashes drifted back open, her gaze heavy and sensual and just a little bit wicked. Lifting her hand, she threaded her fingers through the hair at the nape of his neck and pulled his head toward hers until her mouth brushed against his ear, her breath damp and warm as she spoke unabashedly. "I want you to go down on me and do what you do so well."

Her sexy, arousing request made him hard as stone and so fucking hot for her. There was something to be said about a woman who spoke her mind and had no qualms about asking for what she wanted sexually. In this, at least, Mia was completely open with him, uninhibited, and his for the taking.

"It would be my pleasure," he murmured huskily, and kissed her, tasting the heat of her anticipation, the depth of her need. She pulled his tongue deeper, suckling him aggressively, greedily, and a low groan rumbled up from his chest.

Knowing her penchant for taking control, he released her mouth before she could take charge, pushed her breasts together, and dipped his head and nuzzled the soft, plump flesh. He laved her straining nipples with his tongue and tugged gently with his teeth until she whimpered and begged him to ease the ache gathering between her thighs.

He dropped to his knees in front of her, pushed her skirt up to her waist, and told her to hold the material out of the way for him. Without hesitating, she did as he asked, giving him a full, unobstructed view of her bare belly, her sheer, barely there panties that matched her bra, her soft, supple thighs . . . and those seductive, lace-up, dominatrix boots she'd worn just for him.

He pushed her legs farther apart, widening her stance, and then slowly stroked his hands up her firm, silky smooth thighs, reveling in her soft sigh of pleasure. Grasping the sides of her panties, he buried his face against her stomach and lavished her belly with soft, damp kisses as he dragged her underwear down her legs and helped her step out of them. Then he sat back and looked his fill of this incredibly sexy, half-dressed woman.

Her voluptuous breasts were bared, and in front of him was the sweetest, softest female flesh imaginable. He reached out and brushed the tips of his fingers over her feminine mound, then skimmed lower, sliding one long finger between those pouty lips to where she was hot and slick with desire.

Her legs trembled. "Stop teasing me," she rasped.

Ignoring her demand, he grinned up at her, deliberately stroking her slower, deeper, heightening the tension building within her. "Remember that night in the truck?" he murmured as he leaned forward, sucked on a patch of skin on the inside of her thigh, and marked her with a love bite before lapping his tongue all the way up to her sex. "You did a whole lot of teasing of your own. Now it's my turn to get even."

She moaned her protest and then inhaled a quick breath when he spread her open with his fingers and finally took her with his mouth. Her back arched against the wall, and her hand twisted in his hair as he slid his tongue along her cleft and delved deep into that hidden pool of honeyed heat, coaxing her into a heady, sexual spell of exquisite wanting.

Three times he brought Mia to the brink of release, teasing her with the promise of an orgasm until she was squirming and writhing and begging him to please, please, *please* let her come.

He would. But not yet. He intended to be buried deep inside her when she climaxed.

With that plan in mind, he stood back up and slanted his mouth across hers in a hot, tongue-tangling kiss. His erection strained against his jeans, full and hot and heavy, pulsing with every heartbeat. Mia's hands dropped to the waistband of his jeans, fumbling anxiously with the snap, then the zipper, until she was holding his thickened shaft in her hand. She squeezed and stroked his hard length, and his entire body jerked when her thumb glided over the sensitive tip.

She broke their kiss, panting. "Cameron, I need you inside me *now*."

God, he needed that, too. Gripping the back of her thighs in his hands, he lifted her, spreading her legs wide to accommodate the fit of his hips while Mia pushed the folds of her skirt out of the way and locked her knees against his waist to give him better leverage. The head of his cock slid along her sex, bathing him in her slick moisture, until he found that perfect fit into her body.

He drove into her, high and hard and deep, the force of his penetrating thrust rattling the pictures on the bathroom wall. He immediately stilled, praying the pictures didn't fall and crash to the floor—and send the Wilde family racing upstairs to find out what the commotion was all about. Mia's eyes grew wide, as if she was thinking the same exact thing, and then she burst into infectious giggles.

He pressed his mouth to hers to quiet her, though he was grinning, too. "I'm thinking doing it up against the wall isn't a good idea." But it wasn't as though they had a bed available.

"As good as it feels, I think you're right." Wrapping her arms around his neck, she arched her lower body, and moaned softly as he surged infinitely deeper. She caught her breath. "How about the counter, behind you?"

He glanced over his shoulder, relieved to see the large, flat surface. "That'll work." He'd *make* it work.

Bracing his hands beneath her bare backside, he turned around and set her on the bathroom counter so her bottom was poised right on the edge. The height was perfect. So was the view of where they were joined.

"Lean back, and keep your legs wrapped around my waist," he said, all too aware of the mirrors surrounding them, which only served to make their tryst more erotic.

She did as he asked, bracing her hands behind her on the counter—a seductive position that ended up being sexy as hell. Her back was arched, and her exposed breasts jutted forward, those taut, rosy nipples so ripe and sweet-looking his mouth watered for another taste. Her tousled hair fell around her face and shoulders like a cloud of midnight silk and then there were the strong, pale thighs gripping his hips and the electrifying scratch of her leather boots against his bare skin.

With his own hands free, he dragged them up the inside of her thighs, until both of his thumbs were touching her intimately, alternately stroking her clit and caressing the petals of flesh that led to the entrance of her body, where his own lust and need had gathered in a throbbing ache.

She whimpered and wriggled against him, and when that didn't get him to move the way she wanted and needed, she clenched her inner muscles around him. The effect was like being sucked into the softest, tightest, hottest of sheaths, and he groaned and instinctively thrust into her. Except once wasn't enough, not when his body was urging him to move harder, deeper, faster, and give into climax simmering just below the surface.

With his fingers still coaxing her higher, he leaned forward and captured one of her pert nipples between his lips. He swirled his tongue over the velvet soft aureole, and grazed his teeth across the pearled tip before doing the same with her other breast. With her hands immobile, she couldn't do anything but let him have his way with her . . . as she'd promised him downstairs.

But as her breathing quickened, escalated, so did the long, smooth pumping of his hips and the friction and pressure of his thumb against her clit. He felt her orgasm building, climbing, and he lifted his head from her breasts so he could watch the slow, dazzling way she came apart just for him.

She was like his every fantasy come to life. So sexy. So intoxicating to every one of his senses. Her beautiful breasts bounced softly with each of his successive thrusts, the muscles in her thighs quivered, and her head fell back as her body convulsed around his and her climax swept her away.

Her lips parted, but before she could let loose a cry of pleasure, he covered her mouth with his own. He kissed her, as hard and deep as their bodies were fused, and groaned right along with her as they both crashed over the edge of a stunning, spine-tingling orgasm.

Long minutes later, her warm sigh drifted along the side of his neck while her hands caressed beneath his shirt and up along his damp back. "You are *so* addicting," she murmured huskily.

So was she. In every way.

Still buried inside Mia's silky heat, Cameron glanced at her face and the content smile on her lips. She looked happy. Sated. And she was glowing like a woman who'd been well pleasured. He wanted to keep her that way . . . forever.

Forever his.

The emotion that swelled in his chest at that moment was raw and possessive and incredibly real. And the more time he spent with Mia, the stronger and deeper it grew, crowding places in his heart that had been empty and just waiting for the right woman to come and along and complete the man he was.

That woman was Mia. He knew it. Accepted it. Just as he knew and accepted she wasn't ready to hear he wanted her to be a more permanent part of his life.

Keeping his thoughts to himself, he smiled at her and smoothed the errant strands of hair from her soft, flushed cheek. "Do you think anyone missed us?" he asked, teasing her.

"Do I look like I care?" she said with her usual abundance of sass.

Cameron laughed, though he knew with certainty that she *would* care if someone came looking for her and found the two of them screwing like rabbits in heat. But he didn't call her on that, either.

Instead, he moved away, cleaned up, and refastened his jeans. "I'll go downstairs first. You can arrive a few minutes later."

Giving her one last quick kiss, he stepped out of the bathroom and started down the hallway and toward the stairs, only to come up short when he saw Mia's brother, Joel, waiting there. He was leaning against the railing, arms crossed over his massive chest, looking way too intimidating in his black T-shirt and black jeans.

Cameron wasn't about to give anything away and tried to act casual, though he had a sinking feeling in his stomach that didn't bode well at all. "What are you doing up here?"

"The downstairs bathroom is occupied." Joel pushed off the railing, but before he could head down the hall, Cameron stepped in front of him, blocking his path.

Shit. The gig was *so* up with this Wilde brother. "You can't go in there."

Joel lifted a dark brow. "Why not?"

Cameron knew Joel wasn't going to make any of this easy on him. Joel *knew,* and now he was going to use every tactical maneuver he'd learned in the military to kick his ass just as soon as Cameron admitted the truth. And then Joel was going to tell his brothers and cousins what was going on, and the entire family was going to castrate him.

Ignoring the twinge in his groin, Cameron 'fessed up, because lying to Joel wasn't an option for him, not if he wanted to earn the man's respect in the end. "Mia is still in there."

Joel smirked. "I didn't realize you needed someone to hold your dick while you took a piss."

Cameron cringed at the sarcasm edging the other man's words, because it was so obvious that Joel was baiting him. Cam kept waiting for a spark of outrage, but Joel remained calm, and that actually worried him more than an outward show of anger.

He'd come this far, so Cameron figured he might as well spill everything. "Mia and I . . . we've been seeing each other privately."

"I can't say I'm surprised."

"You're not mad?" Cameron asked cautiously.

"Why in the hell would I be mad?" Joel looked genuinely perplexed. "It's about damn time the two of you hooked up. We all knew it was bound to happen. Besides, I'd rather see my sister settled with someone like you than some schmuck who can't handle her."

Except Mia wasn't looking to be "settled," and therein lay the rub to their relationship, and the situation.

"By the way," Joel said, an amused grin tugging at the corner of his mouth. "When I made the bet earlier that Mia would get the best of you before the day was over, I didn't mean like *this*. However, a bet is a bet, and the way I see things, you lost."

Cameron wasn't about to argue logistics with Joel. Reaching into his back pocket for his wallet, he pulled out a twenty dollar bill and slapped it into Mia's brother's hand, hoping the payout would work as hush money, as well. "Look, I'd really appreciate it if you didn't say anything to anyone about Mia and me just yet. She's still playing hard to get about all this relationship stuff, and I've learned that she's got to come around in her own good time." Never mind that she was being stalked and he'd yet to find out by whom.

"Fine," Joel said, nodding in understanding as he tucked the cash into his front pocket. "I'll keep this to myself for now. However, if you hurt her in any way, I'll be the first in line to rip your nuts off."

Cameron didn't doubt that for a minute.

LATER that same night, Mia unlocked her apartment door and turned to Cameron, who was standing behind her, his hands tucked into the front pockets of his jeans. Because it was Saturday night and neither one of them had to work to-morrow, she really didn't want to spend the rest of the eve-ning alone. Not after the wonderful day they'd had together at her niece and nephew's birthday party.

"Care to come in for a little bit?" she asked, smiling up at him. "I wouldn't mind having the company. We can watch a movie or just talk," she said, wanting him to know she wasn't inviting him in for the sole purpose of jumping his bones. She honestly, truly, just wanted to be with him tonight, without any ulterior motives in mind.

"Sure, I'd like that," he said and followed her inside the apartment.

She set her purse and keys on the foyer table. "Are you hungry?"

He laughed lightly. "I can't believe I'm saying this after everything I ate today at the party but yeah, I am kinda hungry."

"You're a big boy with a big appetite," she teased, her voice laced with a sexy underlying innuendo. "Come on, let's go see what we can find to fill you up."

She led the way into the kitchen, with Cameron following behind, and was surprised to find that Gina was there. She was standing by the stove making herself a cup of hot tea. As they walked into the kitchen, she cast them a quick, cursory glance.

"Hi guys," she said but didn't turn around as she stirred cream into her tea.

"Hey there." Mia was glad to see Gina was safe at home, instead of at Ray's for the weekend, which had been the norm for the past month. "I didn't realize you were here."

Gina shrugged and lifted the collar of her long-sleeved terry robe so it covered her neck, which immediately tipped off Mia and put her on alert. "I came home from Ray's early," Gina said and finally faced them. "He had some things to do this weekend, and I didn't want to stay at his place by myself."

Mia noticed right away that Gina had been crying. Her eyes were puffy, and her nose was pink. And Mia didn't care for the way she was clutching the thick material of her robe at her throat, as if Gina was trying to cover up something she didn't want them to see. Like new marks or bruises courtesy of Ray.

Gina picked up her mug of tea, and her hand trembled slightly. "I'll just take this into the bedroom so the two of you can be alone."

"You don't need to go," Mia said quickly, hating the thought of Gina sequestering herself in her room when it was obvious something was wrong. "We were just going to make something to eat. Why don't you sit out here with us?"

"It's okay, really." Gina forced a smile. "I'm really tired. I'm going to drink my tea and then go to bed."

Mia watched Gina go, and as soon as she heard her bedroom door close, she released a frustrated sigh. "He's still manipulating and abusing her."

"I agree. All the signs are definitely there." Cameron came up to her, his gaze searching her face. "Do you want me to leave so you can talk to her?"

"No. I've said everything I can, and most of the time she doesn't want to hear what I have to say, anyway." Mia dragged her fingers through her hair. "I'm just grateful she's here at home, where she's safe. I'll spend some time with her tomorrow, just the two of us. Maybe take her to a movie."

"Okay, if you're sure you want me to stay."

"I do." She opened the refrigerator and grabbed the lunch meat, mayo, lettuce, and tomato, and set everything on the counter. "Besides, I just don't trust her excuse that Ray was busy this weekend, and I feel much better having you here. At least for a little while."

"Not a problem, then." He helped her make his sandwich, spreading the mayo on the bread and then layering on the sliced ham and turkey while she rinsed off the crisp lettuce leaves. "If I don't find out something on Ray, and soon, I'm going to have to set up surveillance on the guy."

She cut up a small tomato and added those slices to his sandwich. "I hate for you to have to do that. I know how busy you've been lately."

"It's gotten to the point that I'm determined to find out

who and what he is, and what's in his past that he's trying to hide from."

"I can only imagine." She opened a can of chilled fruit cocktail and poured it into a bowl and then filled two glasses with lemon-lime soda. "Come on, let's take this into my bedroom where we can watch TV and talk while you eat your snack."

In her bedroom, Cameron propped her pillows against her headboard, toed off his shoes, and made himself comfortable on her bed with his sandwich in hand. Mia gave him the remote for the TV so he'd be right at home, and he automatically switched the channel to a cop show. Thinking he was such a typical guy, she grabbed her nightclothes from her dresser drawer and went into the adjoining bathroom to change. Ten minutes later she emerged, wearing a pair of soft cotton drawstring pants and a matching camisole top, both of which were designed more for comfort than seduction.

Still, Cameron's chewing slowed, and his hot, dark gaze raked over her as though she was wearing a provocative teddy instead. After a lengthy and very appreciative perusal, his eyes finally came back up to her freshly scrubbed face, free of any cosmetics.

A warm smile eased up the corners of his mouth. "You look nice without your makeup on."

"Oh please," she drawled, and rolled her eyes as she laid her blouse and skirt over a chair to send to the dry cleaners next week. "We're already having sex, so flattery at this point isn't necessary," she joked.

"I'm being serious." He took a drink of his soda, his expression earnest. "You've got beautiful skin and a great complexion. Even without all that stuff you women wear on your face." Finished with his sandwich, he set his plate on the nightstand.

"Well, thank you." Accepting the compliment, she settled in beside him on the bed, crossed her legs, and picked up the bowl of fruit cocktail. "Judging by pictures I've seen of my mother, I definitely get my looks and complexion from her."

"Thank goodness, because I don't think you'd look very pretty as a female version of Joel."

She laughed as she fed him a slice of peach from her fork. "You know what I mean."

"Yeah, I do." He reclined against the pillows and laced his hands over his now full stomach, content to let her feed him the fruit. "If you get your looks from your mother, she must have been gorgeous."

A warm blush swept across her cheeks, and she picked out a cherry half, her favorite part of fruit cocktail, and popped it into her mouth. "I don't remember much about her, just what I know from photos and from memories that are faded or even imagined at this point since I was only five when she passed away." She felt that familiar pang of sadness that always accompanied thoughts of her mother and the pain of losing her. "I miss her, yet I don't think I ever really knew her, if that makes sense."

"It does," he reassured her and accepted the chunk of pineapple she put to his lips. "What about you and Amelia? The two of you aren't very close, are you?"

His question startled her, and she stiffened defensively before she could catch herself. "What makes you say that?"

"You keep forgetting that my job is to study people, to gauge their actions," he said with a casual shrug. "I find I just do it automatically."

He'd obviously spent way too much time watching her at the party, and that thought made her bristle. "Well, you can stop analyzing *me*."

"I'm not analyzing you," he said, unfazed by her dismissive tone. "I'm just curious about your relationship with Amelia. Did you consider her the wicked stepmother?"

"Of course not!" Amelia had always been nothing but kind to her. If anything, it was Mia who'd been the wicked, difficult one. And that admission, even quietly to herself, evoked a wave of guilt that nearly smothered her.

"Then why do I sense tension between you two?" he asked in that gentle, coaxing way of his. "Not in a bad way, but it's clear the two of you don't have the kind of close relationship a mother and daughter normally would. I was just wondering why not."

Mia knew she had two choices: blow off the conversation and Cameron's personal questions, or tell him what he wanted to know. Her first instinct was to be stubborn and clam up, but she knew that would be the easy way out. She wondered if she shared that private part of her life with Cameron, a part that still caused her grief when she thought about it, that maybe it would help ease the many regrets she harbored about her relationship with Amelia.

The sweetened fruit no longer appealed to her, and she set the bowl aside and then exhaled a deep breath. "I don't even know where to begin," she said truthfully.

"Do you remember when your mother died?" he asked, helping her along.

The answer to that was very complicated, and she attempted to explain the best she could. "The last thing I remember about my mother was her leaving to visit her sister in Florida, and I never saw her again after that. It wasn't until at least a month after she passed away that my father finally told me she'd died in a car accident while visiting her sister."

A slight frown creased his brows. "You didn't go to the funeral?"

"I didn't *know* about the funeral," she said and saw shock register on his face. "I was so upset when she left for Florida, nearly hysterical because I didn't want her to go and we'd never been apart. I remembered kicking and screaming and throwing tantrums every night my mother was gone. I missed her so much."

"That's understandable," he said quietly. "You were just a little girl."

"I was a little heathen, even back then," she admitted with a small laugh. "The first night I threw a fit, my father should have put me over his knee and given me a good spanking, but being the only girl with three older brothers, I don't think he knew what to do with me, or how to handle my tantrums."

Cameron laughed, too, and she knew that was his way of silently agreeing.

"Anyway, my father told me that when my mother died, he didn't think I would be able to handle the news and he made the decision not to tell me about her death right then or take me to the funeral." She swallowed past the growing lump in her throat that always accompanied thoughts of missing her own mother's burial and service. "He said it was his way of protecting me from the pain of losing my mother, and I know he was so engulfed in his own grief that he probably wasn't thinking straight or logically."

Cameron rolled to his side, closer to her, and propped his head against his palm. "He had to tell you eventually."

"And he did, about a month after the fact." Her voice had grown raspy, and the back of her eyes stung. "And of course I didn't believe him, no matter what he or my brothers said. I was in complete denial."

"I'm sorry, Mia," Cameron said, placing his hand on her knee in a show of comfort.

"I know my father did what he thought was best for me at the time, but he made the wrong decision." She couldn't stop the sob that made her voice crack, or the tears that filled her eyes. "Because I never went to my own mother's funeral, there was never any closure for me with her death. I believed for years that she was coming back, that it was all just a bad dream and one day I was going to wake up and my mother was going to be there for me again."

The first drop of moisture trickled down her cheek before she could stop it, and it was Cameron who reached up and tenderly wiped the tear away with the pad of his thumb. She glanced down at him, so grateful for his silent understanding and the warmth of his soothing touch that was like a balm to the pain she'd carried in her heart for so long.

She gathered her composure and continued, because there was a whole lot more to the story to tell. "So now we fast forward three years, when my father has married Amelia and I'm eight years old. I've become this rebellious hellion who is always getting into trouble, mainly for attention, and now I'm feeling as though I've lost my father, too, because he has a new wife."

She drew a shuddering breath to ease the pressure in her chest, but it did no good. "Even worse, I'm this little girl who is afraid Amelia isn't going to love me the same way my mother did, so it just became safer for me to keep up those emotional walls between myself and Amelia. I didn't want to set myself up for the kind of hurt I went through when I lost my mother." Biting on her quivering bottom lip, she met Cameron's gaze. "How horrible is that?"

"It's not horrible at all, Mia. Being a little girl, it was a way of self-preservation for you."

She agreed, but she was also coming to recognize that her actions as a young girl had carried through to her adult years and had affected so many aspects of her life. Including the ability to let anyone get too close emotionally. That had cost her dearly with Amelia.

"It's my fault I never bonded with Amelia," she said, confessing the painful truth. "She tried in so many ways to be a mother to me, but I rebuffed every one of her attempts until she just stopped trying."

"It's never too late to make things right, Mia."

But Mia didn't know *how* to make it right, or how to bridge nearly twenty years of what had been a strained relationship between herself and Amelia. And there was always the possibility Amelia wouldn't forgive her for being the selfish, self-centered stepdaughter she'd been. That thought made her feel so empty deep inside, because she knew she'd missed out on a relationship that could have been priceless and precious.

The realization made her feel so ashamed, and having

just poured her heart out to Cameron, she felt so exposed, so vulnerable, and she tried to cover it up with a light, airy laugh that lacked any real humor. "I bet you're sorry you asked about Amelia, huh?"

"Not at all," he said, his tone as sincere as the matching emotion she saw in his eyes. "It's a part of who you are, Mia, and it's something I wanted to know, or else I wouldn't have asked."

He reached over to the nightstand and turned off the light, so the only illumination came from the TV across the room. As if sensing exactly what she needed, right when she needed it the most, he patted the empty space next to him on the bed.

"Come here," he murmured.

His low, coaxing voice drew her, and the tenderness she witnessed in his gaze made her heart ache for things she'd denied herself for so long. But tonight, she didn't want to refuse the simple luxury of being held, to feel safe and secure in Cameron's embrace, and to know that she wasn't alone as she'd been for years. By choice.

She stretched out by his side, and he gathered her close so her head was resting on the solid warmth of his chest and their legs were entwined. She breathed in his scent and could hear the strong, steady beat of his heart beneath her ear. So rhythmic. So comforting. So real.

Closing her eyes, she relaxed and let the burden of her painful memories drift away as his fingers threaded through her hair and massaged her scalp and his other hand stroked along her side and over her hip. Their embrace was intimate but not sexual, and it was so nice just to be held, without expectations of anything more.

Content and strangely fulfilled with his arms around her, Mia fell into a deep, dreamless sleep. When she woke in the morning, he was gone, and she realized that at some point during the night he'd slid from her bed, tucked her beneath the covers, and left her apartment. After her emotional night, he was giving her space, and while she appreciated his thoughtfulness, she hated more that she'd awakened in a cold, lonely bed without him in it.

Oh, that *so* wasn't good, she thought with a groan, and buried her face in her pillow, wishing the action could make her forget the fact that she'd given Cameron so much of herself last night, a telling glimpse into her painful past. The tears that had showed him just how vulnerable she was beneath her normal I-don't-give-a-damn facade. And the trust she'd never given to any other man she'd dated.

But worse than that, she feared she'd given him something she'd never be able to reclaim as her own—a huge piece of her heart. That notion scared her more than anything she had ever faced, because it set her up for heartache, for loss and failure, and for the kind of pain she'd spent a lifetime making certain she'd never experience again.

Fourteen

MIA headed down the pathway to her apartment after work Tuesday evening, her mind already on the stained-glass design she planned to work on tonight. She realized she'd become somewhat of a homebody, and though she felt her place was too quiet and lonely sometimes, she had to admit she didn't miss going out to bars and nightclubs and the other places she used to frequent in the evenings after work.

Now she had a distinct reason for staying home, and that was to work on her stained-glass art. Amy had scheduled Mia's first showing with the gallery for the end of the month, and Mia wanted to be able to present as many new pieces of the erotic art as possible. Especially because the current silent auction Amy had begun on the pieces she'd left at the gallery had generated not only an amazing amount of bids, but also a flurry of interest in her work. That auction would end the night of the show, and Amy was confident the final bid was going to exceed both of their expectations.

It was an exhilarating feeling, a high that gave her an

incredible boost of energy and excitement that transferred over to her designs and actual artwork. And while a part of her couldn't wait for the gallery show, she had to admit there was one issue she still hadn't yet resolved—how to tell her family about her "unveiling." She knew she'd invite her family, but she didn't think she had the nerve to tell them what to expect beforehand. Scott and her father had rejected her attempt at making something of her normal stained-glass designs, so a huge part of her was nervous and cautious about her family's reaction when they realized that some of her art wasn't as innocent as it seemed.

Working on her designs and artwork every spare minute she found available also kept Mia's mind off of that huge revelation she'd come to about her feelings for Cameron a few mornings ago. She'd at least managed to convince herself that she'd been in a very vulnerable state after telling him about her past, and that had led to her overwhelming and too emotional thoughts.

But now, with a few days between them and that night, she was able to be more objective about the situation—and her affair with Cameron, which didn't allow room for emotional sentiments that would only complicate matters. They made great lovers, and Lord knew she'd grown to care for him beyond anything she could have imagined, but she knew deep in her heart that she wasn't the kind of woman Cameron needed or wanted in his life on a long-term basis. She was also smart enough to recognize her inability to sustain a lasting relationship with any man—her past history had taught her that—and she wasn't about to hurt Cameron in the long run.

With a sigh, she turned the corner toward her apartment and buried those thoughts in the deepest recesses of her heart. Instead, she refocused on the stained-glass design awaiting her tonight. This one was a collage of bright, vibrant butterflies, with an image of an erotically entwined couple silhouetted where the multi-colored wings overlapped. It was an intricate piece and very challenging, but those were the pieces that excited her the most.

She arrived at her place, and just as she lifted her keys to unlock the door, she heard the scuff of footsteps. She glanced over her shoulder and sucked in a quick breath when she found Ray standing directly behind her. His unexpected presence startled her so badly her keys slipped from her fingers and clattered to the ground.

Her guard immediately went up, and she spun around so she didn't have her back to him. She'd been foolish for not paying better attention to her surroundings considering someone was currently stalking her—possibly even this man who'd seemingly snuck up on her when she'd least expected it.

Her stomach clenched in apprehension, and she thought about the keys on the ground, which was her only way to get into the safety of her apartment—but she refused to bend down to pick them up and give him any kind of advantage over her. Instead, she tried to recall every defense tactic her brothers had ever taught her, just in case she needed to use them on Ray. He wasn't a big man, but he was solid and obviously knew how to hurt and dominate women.

"If you're looking for Gina, she's still at work," she said with as much calm and directness as she could manage. "She doesn't get off until seven tonight."

"I'm not here to see Gina. I'm here to see you." He stepped closer, invading her personal space and leaving her no where to retreat. "It seems you've been putting ideas in her head that I don't appreciate."

A chill slithered down her spine, and she recognized the sensation as fear. Refusing to let any kind of weakness show or allow him to intimidate her in any way, she boldly met his gaze. "I have no idea what you're talking about."

The corners of his mouth curved into a smile that was more sinister than pleasant. "She's got it in her head that she needs to leave me, and I'm thinking you put those thoughts there."

Finally, Gina was standing up for herself! Mia felt a rush of relief that Gina was at least trying to get away from Ray. Judging by her boyfriend's ominous expression, though, he wasn't happy about her attempts, and he wasn't about to make it easy on Gina, either.

"Gina's a big girl who can make up her own mind about you and your relationship," she said with a shrug. "And if she wants to break up with you, there's probably a reason for it."

His gaze narrowed on her, and her heart raced in her chest as he clenched his fists at his sides. "Well, I suggest you stay out of it, unless a slut like you would rather take her place. You're putting out for that guy you picked up at The Electric Blue, and I certainly don't mind sharing."

Slut. The familiar word reverberated in her head, a slur that had been scrawled across those pictures someone had sent her. Her mind spun, and she had struggled to keep her thoughts focused on her response to Ray.

"I'm sure Gina *would* mind sharing." *You deranged freak.*

His eyes slid down to the V of her blouse and then back up again, his gaze heating with a depraved kind of lust. "Gina wouldn't have to know."

Her stomach churned. "You're sick," she spat, though she was trembling deep inside.

Finished with the conversation, she tried to move around him but instead found herself trapped between the door and Ray. He braced his hands next to her shoulders, and though he wasn't physically touching her in any way, her skin still crawled. She mentally prepared herself to fight back if that's what it came down to—ready to drive her knee as hard as she could against his balls and slam the heel of her palm against the base of his nose.

"I suggest you back off right now," she said, hating the slight quiver in her voice. "Or I'm calling the police."

"And tell them what?" he sneered, looking ugly and mean. "Nobody has seen me here, I didn't touch you, and as far as I'm concerned, I was never here."

Her heart beat so frantically she feared it would burst from her chest. *"Back off,"* she said angrily, her final warning before she hit him where it hurt the most and crippled him.

As if sensing she meant business, he shoved away from her and then pointed a finger at her. "Keep your nose out of Gina's business," he said and turned and walked away.

Quickly, Mia scooped up her keys, but her fingers were trembling so badly it took her a few tries to get the door unlocked. Once she managed the feat, she bolted into the apartment, secured herself inside, and slumped against the nearest wall.

She forced herself to breathe deeply, to try and calm the racing of her heart and the adrenaline that was making her entire body shake. As soon as she could walk steadily, she went to the phone in the living room and immediately called Cameron's cell number.

As soon as he answered the phone, she didn't waste any time in telling him what had happened. "Ray was just here," she said, her voice raw and raspy.

"With Gina?" he asked, and she heard the confusion in his tone.

She lowered herself to the sofa and swallowed to ease the dryness in her throat. "No. He was alone, and he caught me right outside the apartment by myself. He confronted me about telling Gina to leave him and threatened me to stay out of it." She left the more crude parts of their conversation to herself.

"I'm going to fucking kill the bastard," Cameron growled into the phone, his fury nearly tangible.

As much as she'd enjoy seeing Cameron beat the crap out of Ray, she knew they had to be more level-headed about the situation. "Look, I'm okay physically," she reassured him. "He never touched me, and he didn't hurt me in any way. And if you go after him, chances are he'll take it out on Gina, and I just don't want to take that chance, okay?"

Cameron was breathing hard into the phone, a testament to just how pissed off he was.

"Promise me you won't do anything," she said, practically begging him. Not only for Gina's sake, but for his own welfare, too. "You don't know what Ray is capable of doing, and until you find out more about him, or something you can use against him, we can't risk setting him off."

"Fine," he said tightly, though she knew he wasn't happy about the decision.

She dragged her fingers through her hair, feeling weary and sapped of energy. But there was something she knew she had to do tonight, no matter how unpleasant the task. "I'm going to tell Gina what happened with Ray when she gets home from work."

"Good. She needs to know just what kind of unstable psychopath she's dealing with," he bit out angrily. "Do you want me to be there when you talk to her? I'll leave this surveillance I'm on right now if you want me there."

"No, it's okay." She appreciated the offer, but there was no sense in overwhelming Gina with Cameron's presence. "I can handle it on my own. I'm guessing by what Ray said to me that Gina wants out of the relationship, so hopefully what I have to tell her will prompt her to end it for good."

"We can hope." He exhaled a long, harsh breath, as if that helped to release his pent-up tension and frustration. "Call me if you need anything at all."

"I will." Feeling so much calmer now, she smiled into the phone. "Thanks. I'll talk to you later."

Mia disconnected the phone and then went into her bedroom to change out of her work outfit and into a pair of comfortable drawstring pants and a cotton top. She didn't expect Gina home from her job as a clothing store manager for at least a half an hour, and during that time she welcomed the distraction of working on her latest stained-glass design. Finally, just a few minutes before seven, she heard the front door open and close, and she made her way out to the front of the apartment.

She found Gina in the kitchen, where she was grabbing a small bottle of iced tea from the refrigerator. "Hey, Gina," Mia said in greeting. "Do you have a few minutes to talk?"

Her friend's expression immediately turned wary, but much to Mia's surprise, Gina didn't try to evade the conversation like she would have in the recent past. "Sure. What's up?"

Mia didn't beat around the bush and got right to the point. "Ray came by to see me today."

"You?" Gina's eyes widened in startled surprise. "Why?"

Leaning casually against the counter, Mia crossed her arms over her chest. "Because he said you want to leave him, and he's certain I'm the one who's encouraging it."

"Oh, God, Mia. I'm so sorry." Gina's voice was choked with remorse. "I never meant to drag you into all this."

"First of all, you have absolutely nothing to be sorry for," Mia said, reassuring her friend. "There is nothing I want more than to see you out of your relationship with Ray, and I've never made a secret of that fact."

Gina hung her head as she set her iced tea aside. "I know," she said quietly.

"So is it true what Ray said?" Mia persisted gently, needing answers. "That you want to end things?"

"Yes," Gina nodded and met her gaze. "I finally realized I can't keep going on like this."

"Good for you, Gina." A huge wave of relief swept over Mia. Getting Gina to admit there was a problem was half the battle. The other half came in the form of a very volatile, abusive man.

"You tried to tell me, and I kept denying that anything bad was happening. I made excuses for Ray's actions and behavior because I was blaming myself for making Ray angry." A sense of despair etched her expression. "But Saturday night he started yelling at me because I'd burnt the roast

I'd made for dinner, and I just realized I'd had enough, I wasn't happy, and I knew I never would be. So I tried to break things off, but he went crazy."

Gina's hand fluttered up to her throat, and she swallowed hard, her eyes haunted. "He shoved me up against the wall and put his hand around my neck. And it really, really scared me, to the point that I left his place when he was using the bathroom."

Mia recalled that past Saturday night when she and Cameron had come across Gina in the kitchen, clutching her robe tight and her eyes red and puffy from crying. Now, it all made sense.

Crossing the distance separating her from Gina, Mia grabbed her friend's hands and squeezed them tight. "Honey, you did the right thing. You know that, don't you?"

"Yeah, I do." A smile wavered on her lips. "Of course he's called me since then, telling me how sorry he is, that it would never happen again. But I don't believe him anymore, not when I have so many bruises to show for his abuse."

For the past few weeks Gina had been wearing long-sleeved blouses to work, and as she pushed up the sleeve of her current top, Mia understood why. She'd been covering up bruises on her arms where Ray had obviously grabbed her very roughly. Some of the marks were faded; others were barely beginning to heal.

Gina glanced back up at Mia, her eyes filled with genuine fear. "I'm afraid to be with him, and I'm even more afraid to leave him."

"He's threatened to *really* hurt you if you leave him, hasn't he?"

Gina drew a shuddering breath that was tinged with dread. "Yes."

Fury rose within Mia, immediate and swift. "You're doing the right thing, you know that, don't you?"

"Yes," Gina said, clearly having come to her senses about Ray. "I know I have to end things once and for all. I just can't stay in this emotionally and physically abusive relationship any longer."

"And you shouldn't have to," Mia insisted. "If you want me or Cameron to be there with you when you tell Ray, for backup or support, just say the word."

"No, I need to do this on my own," Gina said with a shake of her head. "It might be the coward's way out, but I'm going to end things with Ray on the phone."

Mia was glad to hear that. "That's not cowardly, Gina. It's smart. He can't hurt you that way, and once that's done you can have a restraining order issued against him so he can't come near you."

"That's what I'd planned to do." She straightened with a determination that made Mia proud. "I'm supposed to see him on Thursday evening, but I'm going to call him instead and tell him we're through. For good. And then because I have Friday, Saturday, and Sunday off, I'm going to go and stay with my sister so I'm not around. That will hopefully give Ray time to cool off."

Mia couldn't have thought of a better arrangement herself, because there was no doubt in her mind Ray would do everything in his power to try and contact or see Gina after she ended the relationship. But that also meant Mia shouldn't be alone this weekend either, because Ray would be looking for any excuse to unleash his wrath on anyone who stood in his way of getting in touch with Gina.

"WHO is Ray Wilkins?"

Cameron glanced from the information on his computer screen he was perusing to Steve, who'd entered his office and was crossing the room to his desk. He'd anticipated something like this would happen at some point, and although Steve seemed only mildly curious at the moment, Cameron didn't expect his friend's calm to last once he explained Ray to him.

"Why do you ask?"

"Wes was doing some trace work on this guy while you were gone earlier," Steve replied. "He said it was for you, but I can't find a case file, so I was curious who he is and if he's a client of ours."

Cameron knew he could tell Steve it was personal and he'd immediately let it go and that would be the end of their discussion. But as partners, and friends, Cameron didn't want lies between himself and Steve. Especially if Steve found out the truth later—that his cousin, Mia, was being stalked and Ray Wilkins was a prime suspect. Even though Cameron had promised Mia he wouldn't involve her family in any way, he trusted Steve to be discreet, and that was what ultimately swayed his decision to tell his partner everything.

Cameron waved a hand toward the chair in front of his desk. "Why don't you sit down. There's something I need to tell you."

Steve lifted a dark brow as he settled his large frame in the seat. "Sounds serious."

"It involves Mia," Cameron said flat out.

"Mia?" Steve looked completely taken aback and then he smirked. "Did you find out she's seeing this guy, and you've got it so bad for her that you're running a background check to scrutinize his credentials?"

Cameron laughed, because it was amusing to think Steve believed he'd be jealous enough to secretly investigate someone Mia might be dating. But there was nothing remotely humorous about the actual situation and the reasons why he was trying to trace Ray and his past. And those answers were about to reveal his own relationship with Mia.

Sighing in resignation, Cameron tossed his pen onto his desk and leaned back in his chair. "Ray is a suspect in a personal case I'm pursuing, which also involves Mia."

Steve's entire demeanor took on a guarded edge. "In what way?"

Cameron explained everything from the beginning, about

the pictures Mia had received by mail, her car being vandalized, and how there was a possibility Ray was behind it all. He also told Steve about Ray's abusive relationship with Mia's roommate, Gina, which was yet another reason to find out who Ray was and what was lurking in the other man's past.

Steve appeared stunned. "I don't get why Mia didn't come to me for help. It's not like the two of you are best buddies or anything . . . or are you?" His tone had turned gruff, and his gaze narrowed with suspicion.

Even from across the expanse of his desk, Cameron felt the heat of his partner's stare. "Mia came to me originally because she feels you guys are way too protective and smothering, and she didn't want you all invading her personal life or space over this. I agreed to help her out, and she made me promise I wouldn't tell you or her brothers what was going on. I figured as long as I was able to keep things under control, and her life wasn't directly threatened in any way, there was no reason to involve anyone else."

"If you haven't noticed, there's a reason why we're all so protective of Mia," Steve said wryly. "Not only is she the only girl and the baby of the family, she tends to be a bit reckless and wild at times."

Cameron had definitely seen that side to Mia, but over the past few weeks he'd also been privy to the woman beneath it all who wanted her family's acceptance more than their protection. "Have you ever thought that with all of you being so overly protective of Mia, it pushes her to be more rebellious just out of spite? You'd be amazed at what she can handle on her own."

A flicker of annoyance passed over Steve's features. "Jesus, when in the hell did you become Mia's protector?" Then, his gaze widened with stark realization. "Holy, shit. Have you and Mia finally hooked up?"

Cameron chose his next words carefully, because he wasn't altogether certain how Steve was going to react to his admission. "Mia and I are seeing one another privately, which is her choice, not mine. It sort of evolved out of me taking on this case." He wasn't about to tell Steve their affair started much earlier, like the night Mia had entered the wet T-shirt contest and tempted him beyond all reason.

"Well I'll be damned," Steve said with a sly grin. "Does anyone else know the two of you are dating?"

Dating. What a novel thought to actually be able to date Mia, out in the open and in public places, Cameron mused. So far, their involvement had all taken place behind closed doors, and that was something Cameron would love to change once the stalker issue with Mia was finally resolved. That is, if Mia allowed their relationship to progress beyond the case.

"Joel knows," Cameron admitted. "He kinda figured things out at your party this weekend." He deliberately left out the more intimate details of Joel's discovery.

"And he didn't kick your ass right then and there?"

"No." Amusement tugged up one corner of Cameron's mouth, along with a good dose of surprise, considering how well Steve was handling the news. "Should he have?"

Steve laughed, a deep, hearty sound. "Naw, he's probably grateful, as I am, Mia is with someone we all know and trust."

Cameron couldn't help but marvel over both Joel's and Steve's similar responses. He'd expected the worst, and instead had come to realize that he'd completely underestimated both of their reactions. They were just looking out for Mia's welfare, and it was nice to know they thought so highly of him.

If only Mia would put as much trust in him as her brother and cousin had, he'd be a happy man.

Realizing how far off track their discussion had gone, Cameron attempted to steer the conversation back to business. "About Ray Wilkins," Cameron said, relieved to have the focus off him and Mia. "I attempted to do a background check on him and came up with a dead end on his current identity, which was why I put Wes on the trace for me." Especially because the guy was such a genius with computers and finding out information through the Internet. "I was hoping he'd find some kind of lead on the guy that maybe I missed."

Steve nodded, and after a thoughtful minute finally replied. "Well, now that I know what's going on, I'll find out what I can on this guy, as well, and make it top priority with Wes."

"Thanks," Cameron said. "I appreciate it."

Determination and a lifetime of being protective of Mia—an emotion Cameron knew was purely instinctual—darkened Steve's features. "Whoever is messing with Mia is going to have hell to pay once we catch up with them."

Cameron had no doubt of that, because he planned to be the one who confronted that person.

THE deed was done. As soon as Gina hung up the phone after ending things with Ray, and cutting him off mid-rage, she and Mia put their agreed-upon plan into action. Mia grabbed her small suitcase, Gina picked up hers, and they left the apartment for the weekend, with Mia heading to Cameron's and Gina to her sister's. The phone began ringing immediately, and because Gina had disengaged her answering machine, at least she wouldn't come back home on Sunday to vicious, nasty messages from Ray.

"That felt good," Gina said, and Mia knew a huge burden had been lifted from her friend's shoulders.

"It was the right thing to do." Mia smiled at Gina, wanting her to believe that without question. Unfortunately, she didn't think this was the end of Ray, despite the restraining order Gina had issued against him before making the final call. "Now you can go to your sisters and enjoy the weekend with her and your nieces."

"Oh, I plan to," she said as they headed down the pathway to the front of the complex. "And what about you? You'll be okay for the weekend?"

"I'll be just fine." Mia withdrew her keys from her purse. "Cameron said I could stay in his guest bedroom."

Gina burst out laughing, and Mia was glad to see glimpses of the old friend she knew and loved. "I'm betting you don't even set foot in that guest bedroom."

"I'll never tell," Mia teased, though she was certain Gina was right. "Hold on. I want to check our mailbox before we leave."

Mia quickly unlocked their box and took out the mail. She handed Gina her bills and correspondences and felt her own stomach drop when she found a larger, padded envelope addressed to her—in the same vein as the two other envelopes she'd received from an anonymous sender.

It appeared her own troubles weren't over yet.

Fifteen

"THIS came in today's mail," Mia said to Cameron once she'd arrived at his place half an hour later. She paced anxiously near the kitchen table, her stomach already in knots over what they'd find inside. "I thought I'd wait and give you the honor of opening the envelope this time."

Cameron picked up the envelope and checked it out, front and back. "No return address, of course," he said calmly. "And it's bigger and bulkier than the others you've been sent with the pictures inside."

And that's what worried her the most, because she was fairly certain her stalker had a different kind of surprise in store for her. "I don't think I want to know what's inside." Dread tightened her chest.

"We don't have a choice." He glanced back at her, his gaze filled with understanding. "I know this is difficult for you, but maybe there's something in here that will help us figure out who is sending you this stuff."

Just like the untraceable pictures she'd received, Mia had

her doubts. Still, there was no avoiding the inevitable, and she wrapped her arms around her middle as if she could protect herself from what was about to come. "Go ahead and open the envelope so we can get this over with."

Cameron hesitated a few seconds, then tore open the seal and pulled out something bright red and silky. He immediately frowned. "What the hell . . ."

For a moment, as Mia stared at the provocative pair of panties, she wondered if she'd recently ordered any lingerie from a catalog, which would explain the risqué underwear dangling from Cameron's fingers. But then she noticed the slashes in the crimson fabric, and worse, the black pen markings on the crotch area where someone had written the word *tramp*.

Oh God. Shock swept through Mia, weakening her knees and making her stomach pitch with apprehension. She didn't want to believe the conclusion she'd just come to, but there was no denying the connection to those panties.

"Goddammit!" Cameron bit out furiously and tossed the underwear back onto the envelope on the table. He was so caught up in his own anger over this latest attack that he wasn't aware of the change in Mia. "Who in the hell would do something deranged like this?"

Mia was certain Cameron still believed Ray was the culprit, but Mia had her own strong suspicions. "Carrie," she said, still stunned by the realization. Didn't Carrie think she'd figure it out? Or maybe she just didn't care any longer.

Cameron's startled gaze jerked to her, and his brows creased in confusion. "What?"

"It's Carrie," she said again and sat down on the nearby barstool before her shaking legs gave out on her. "I'm certain she sent this package, and maybe even the pictures, too."

"Okay." Cameron's tone was cautious, even a little skeptical. But he didn't discount her claim. "Why would you think that?"

She'd never told him about her odd and somewhat strained

lunch with Carrie last week, but she brought it up now. "When I met with Carrie last week, at lunch she made the comment that she hated going places with me, because she felt as though she blended into the woodwork when I was around. And when the waiter paid more attention to me than he did to her, Carrie also made a remark that my breasts were enough to encourage any man to flirt with me."

Cameron leaned against the counter behind him, his expression intent. "It definitely sounds like Carrie is jealous, and even I saw glimpses of that the first night at The Electric Blue, but do you really think she's capable of doing something like this to you? The pictures, your car, and now this?" She waved a hand toward her latest delivery.

"I hate to think she'd be so cruel, but there's more I need to tell you about that day." She gathered her thoughts, remembering, and relayed the events to Cameron. "After lunch we went shopping, and I found a provocative lingerie set I liked and I showed it to Carrie. She wasn't impressed and made the comment that it reminded her of the kind of stuff her mom wore and it made her look like a tramp. Carrie seemed to be having a bad day, so I just wrote off her remark as something that had stemmed directly from the issues she was currently having with her mother and her most recent live-in boyfriend."

"That certainly makes sense," Cameron said.

"But what *doesn't* make sense is, why *me*?" Mia couldn't ever remember doing anything to provoke Carrie into turning on her this way.

"Well, just going on what you told me, I'm thinking that because Carrie can't control her mother's behavior with men and the way her mother acts and dresses, maybe she's trying to control *yours*." As he spoke, he rubbed his thumb absently along his jaw line. "She sees you getting all the attention with men, and it must remind Carrie of her mother in some way. She definitely has emotional issues, and you were an easy target for her."

It amazed Mia how well Cameron could peg people's personalities and motivations. And not for the first time she didn't like what she was hearing about herself within the text of his explanation. It was yet another reminder of how other people perceived her own behavior and actions.

She combed her fingers through her hair and sighed, looking to Cameron for answers. "So what do we do now? Confront her?"

"If we confront her, she's going to deny she did anything. Her involvement is all speculation on our part, and we don't have any solid, irrefutable proof she sent the pictures or this latest package." He sat down on the barstool next to her. "The best thing to do is try and catch her in the act."

"And how do you propose we do that?" Mia asked.

"We start by going back to The Electric Blue. Let her know you'll be there this weekend, like this Saturday. And then we wait and see if she shows up to take more pictures." He placed his large, warm hands on her legs and gave them an encouraging squeeze. "Now that we're certain it's her, I'll keep my eye on her at all times until I see her do something and we can nail her for it."

Spending another evening at The Electric Blue didn't appeal to Mia as it once would have. She'd rather stay at home and work on a few new stained-glass designs, but to end the insanity that Carrie was putting her through, she knew it was necessary. Maybe, then, her life would get back to normal. If she even knew what that was anymore.

"Okay," she said in resignation. "We'll do it."

THE following afternoon, on Friday, Cameron was heading home after work when his cell phone rang. He didn't recognize the number on the display, but he answered the call anyway just in case it was a client.

"Hello, Sinclair here."

"Hi, Cameron," a familiar female voice replied. "It's Ashley."

It took him an extra moment to realize it was Ashley Wilde—on the line. "Hey, how's it going?" he asked, surprised to hear from her.

"Everything's good," she said, though there was an energized lift to her voice. "You'll never believe what happened today while I was working at the boutique. You know that woman you pointed out to me last week at the hotel?"

"You mean Trish Shelton?" he asked, his interest piqued.

"That's the one. She was here again today in the early afternoon. I just happened to glance out in the lobby as she was walking in and I recognized her. And this time, I followed her into the elevator to find out where she was heading. You'll never guess what she was at the St. Claire Hotel for."

He'd believed she was having an affair, just as her husband had stated, but he had a distinct feeling Ashley was about to shatter that notion. And Cameron was curious to discover what she'd learned about Trish Shelton. "Don't tell me she was there for a spa treatment," he joked, wondering if he'd misjudged her original visit to the hotel.

Ashley laughed. "No, it wasn't for a spa treatment," she said and then went on to tell him the real reason why Trish Shelton had been frequenting the hotel.

By the time Cameron disconnected the call, he was blown away by the facts Ashley had relayed to him, which put the Shelton case to rest and also explained Trish's meeting with Margot. All that was left for Cameron to do was to put together a final report for Doug and then contact him with the details and explanation for his wife's behavior, secrecy, and clandestine meetings. Mia knew about this case, too, and he couldn't wait to tell her how it had ended.

He arrived at home, parked his car in the garage, and stepped inside the house. Rich, redolent scents greeted him, and he followed the delicious smells into the kitchen where he found Mia standing in front of the stove cooking dinner. She was wearing a sexy pair of jean shorts and a pink ribbed tank top, and he had the fleeting thought that if this is what it was like to come home to Mia every night, it was something he could definitely get used to.

"I didn't know you could cook," he teased as he sauntered more fully into the kitchen.

She glanced over her shoulder and smiled, her soft gray eyes sparkling with pleasure at seeing him. "I'll have you know I'm *great* in the kitchen."

He came up behind her, slid his hands around her waist so his fingers were splayed on her belly, and nuzzled her neck. "I have no doubt you're *phenomenal* in the kitchen," he murmured in her ear, his voice rumbling with sexy innuendo. "And in the bedroom, and the bathroom . . ."

She turned around in his arms and gave his stomach a playful punch. "I meant *cooking,*" she chided him, her face alight with amusement.

"Yeah, that, too." He grinned down at her.

She rolled her eyes, though she was laughing. "You've become completely incorrigible."

"It must be your doing," he said, casting the blame her way. "I've always been an upstanding, moral kind of guy . . . until you."

"True." The corners of her mouth curled upward as she smoothed her fingers over the collar of his shirt. "You're not quite as uptight and stuffy as you once were."

The timer on the counter rang, indicating that something was done. She returned her attention to the meal she was preparing. There were a few pots and pans on the stove top, all of them covered, and she lifted the lid on one of them and stirred the thick, bubbling sauce inside.

"You didn't have to make dinner," he said and leaned a hip against the counter next to her. Whatever she was making smelled heavenly, but he didn't want her to think he expected anything from her because she was staying at his place for the weekend. "We could have ordered in pizza."

She wrinkled her nose at him at that suggestion. "You're truly a bachelor, aren't you? Why have pizza when you can have chicken Parmesan, spaghetti, and a fresh salad?" Scooping up a small spoonful of the sauce, she lifted it up to his lips. "Taste this."

He did and was impressed with the savory flavors that filled his mouth—tomato sauce, basil, and garlic. It reminded of his mother's cooking, meals made from scratch, which he missed because he never took the time and effort to make anything elaborate for himself. It was so much easier to grab something on the run or pop a frozen dinner into the microwave.

This was a welcome change of pace. "If you keep this up, I'm not going to let you go back home."

She went back to checking the entrées on the stove. "You like playing house, hmmm?" she said in that light, frivolous way of hers.

Oh yeah, he liked coming home to Mia, enjoyed seeing her cooking barefoot in his kitchen, and loved having her in his bed all night long. It was a temporary arrangement he wanted to make much more permanent.

"Here, could you put this on the table for me, please?" she asked and handed him a platter of fried, Parmesan-encrusted chicken.

Between the two of them they put everything out on the table and then sat down across from one anther to eat. Cameron heaped his plate with spaghetti and a slice of chicken and smothered both in the sauce. Then he added a side of salad with Italian dressing.

"How did your meeting with Amy go today?" he asked, remembering that Mia had an afternoon appointment at the gallery.

"It went well." She took a sip of her drink. "Only a few more weeks until the show. Invitations go out next week, and

I have a couple designs I want to finish up before the date. It's all happening so fast."

He noticed she hadn't mentioned her family at all or how she felt about them attending the show. He thought about asking but then decided not to. This was a huge step for Mia, possibly even a break from the family business, and she needed to play it out *her* way.

She looked both nervous and excited about the gallery show, but he knew in the end she would be just fine. She was a woman who persevered in the face of a challenge—just so long as it was a situation she *wanted* to take on.

He let that thought go and recalled his earlier conversation with Ashley. "I finally discovered what Trish Shelton has been up to," he said and took a bite of the delicious, tender chicken.

"Oh?" She glanced across the table at him as she spun spaghetti around her fork. "Was it an affair like her husband thought?"

"Thankfully, no," he said, and that was rare in cases where a spouse was suspected of infidelity. Usually, Cameron presented his client with a guilty verdict and evidence, but not this time, and he could only hope Trish's husband appreciated his wife more than ever after this case. "All the signs were definitely there, and Doug Shelton automatically thought the worst, but he needs to have some faith in his wife."

"Why?" Mia's gaze was bright with curiosity. "What was she really doing?"

"Thanks to Ashley, I now know Trish has spent the past few months planning a very big and lavish surprise party for her husband's fiftieth birthday. It's taking place tomorrow evening in one of the ballrooms of the St. Claire Hotel. Trish was there today to firm up the final details with the banquet manager."

"Wow, all that surveillance and there was no affair after all," she said as she cut her chicken into small pieces. "So how does that other lady Trish was with at the restaurant fit into all this?" Mia asked.

"Margot? She's a graphic design artist, and when I asked Ashley if she was familiar with the name, she said Margot Dalton was working with the banquet manager on some graphic art work for the party. Probably for the invitations or the favors." Finished with his first serving of dinner, Cameron piled more chicken and spaghetti on his plate.

"What are you going to tell Doug Shelton?" she asked as she absently pushed her salad around in her bowl. "Are you just going to let him go to the party and be surprised and then give him your final report afterward?"

Cameron was tempted to do that, but his job as a P.I. dictated that he report the facts as he received them, even if it meant spoiling a surprise. Unfortunately, that was the man's problem, not his, and Doug was going to have to put on a convincing "surprise" act if he didn't want to rouse his wife's suspicions in return.

"I have to tell him what I know," Cameron told her. "According to the contract he signed with the firm, I'm bound to reveal any information I come across during the investigative process. That's what he's paying me for."

He met Mia's gaze from across the table, wanting her to really think about what he was going to say next. "I might investigate these cases more often than I'd like, but there comes a point when you have to know and trust the relationship you're in. In this case, Doug and Trish had a good relationship. He was just being an idiot."

He ate a bite of spaghetti and chased it down with a long, cool drink. "Quite honestly, maybe this will teach Doug to believe in his wife a little more instead of jumping to wrong conclusions. It's all about unconditional trust between a couple. A marriage or relationship can't survive without it."

And in the worst way, Cameron wanted Mia to trust him, unconditionally. To believe in him. To let him into the deepest recesses of her soul where she'd never, ever, let any other man before. He wanted to be the first to claim that wild, untamed heart of hers, and the very last.

As if she could read his thoughts in his eyes, she glanced back down at her plate and started making small talk about her day at work with Scott and Alex, and how she was feeling restless in her job as their secretary. That didn't surprise Cameron at all, now that he knew what her real passion was.

He could only wonder if she'd come to realize that she was meant to embrace her stained-glass art and make a career of it, or if she'd just continue on with the family business for the rest of her life because of deep-rooted fears and insecurities.

It appeared Mia was going to be facing some very difficult choices and decisions in the upcoming days and weeks. Cameron could only hope he would part of whatever future she chose.

"I don't think Carrie is going to show," Mia said over the loud music playing at The Electric Blue the following night. After two hours of waiting and mingling and dancing, she was starting to think their plan to catch Carrie in the act had been pointless.

"I wouldn't be so sure about that," Cameron replied, his sharp, assessing gaze focused on the entrance to the bar. "I think I saw her come in a few minutes ago, but if it was her, she's doing a good job of laying low and keeping herself inconspicuous."

That behavior matched what Cameron had told Mia earlier, when she'd asked how Carrie could have taken those second set of pictures and written all over her car when she hadn't been at The Electric Blue that night. He'd explained that because Carrie knew Mia would be at the bar, she'd most likely saw it as an opportunity to vandalize Mia's vehicle and take more pictures without Mia ever suspecting her as the culprit. Her plan had worked . . . until her latest package had given Carrie away.

It appeared Carrie might be operating on the same assumption this evening.

"Why don't you and Rick go on up to the stage and dance," Cameron suggested, because they'd invited his friend Rick along tonight for that purpose—to use him as a diversion so Cameron could blend into the crowd and watch Carrie without her knowledge.

"Ahh, I finally get to dance with Mia," Rick said and rubbed his hands together in anticipation. "This is what I've been waiting for. Let's go give Carrie a reason to take some more pictures of you." He waggled his brows at Mia in a playful, teasing manner.

Mia laughed and stood and then gave her sexy, body-hugging sheath of a dress an adjusting tug. "This is going to be fun."

"Just keep your hands to yourself," Cameron warned Rick in a gruff tone and then drained the last of his beer. "Nothing below the neck and nothing above the knee."

Rick held up his palms. "These hands won't touch anything they're not supposed to."

"Oh, come on," Mia said and grabbed Rick's hand, amused by Cameron's show of possessiveness. "Let's go do some dirty dancing."

Cameron scowled after them, wondering when in the hell he'd become such a jealous man. Oh yeah . . . since Mia. But ultimately he trusted Rick and knew the man wouldn't do anything inappropriate. Cameron understood that the two of them had to make it look real and convincing to prompt Carrie to take her pictures, and that would mean more *touching* than Cameron would have preferred.

Cameron's only consolation was that Mia would be going home with *him* tonight, and he planned to do more than just touch her body. Before he was done with her, he was going to entrench himself into her heart, her soul, her emotions.

He was going to make her completely his, and be sure she knew it.

With Mia and Rick up onstage dancing, Cameron skirted the edge of the room, staying in the shadows and working his way to the front of the establishment in search of the woman who'd walked in about ten minutes ago and resembled Carrie. He scanned the area and finally saw a redheaded woman making her way through the crowd on the main floor, toward the stage area.

Certain it was Carrie, he followed from a distance, watching her every move. She kept to herself, and it was as though she was drawn to the dance floor—specifically, to Mia and Rick, who were putting on a convincing act with their bold, uninhibited dance moves.

But then, Mia was so naturally sensual, her movements so inherently provocative no matter what she was doing. Men naturally stared at her, watched her, lusted after her. Tonight, though, Cameron noticed a big difference in Mia. She was laughing and dancing and having fun with Rick, but it wasn't a deliberate attempt to draw attention to herself as it had been in the past. Rather, it was an act to catch Carrie, and Mia no longer felt the need to be wild and reckless for the sake of shocking everyone.

It was an amazing change, a maturity he hoped would carry over to their relationship. Especially after tonight, which marked the end to their agreed-upon affair but could be the beginning of something much bigger and better. *If* she allowed it to happen.

With his gaze still on Carrie, he watched her lift something up to her face and realized it was a small, disposable camera—which made perfect sense considering all the photographs Mia had received in the mail had been grainy and taken from a distance. She took a few pictures, and the strobe lights overhead camouflaged the camera's flash. When the current song ended, Carrie wended her way through the crush of people and down the corridor leading to the restrooms.

Before the next song could begin, Cameron flipped open his cell phone and called Rick. He'd specifically told him to put his phone on vibrate, and he knew the exact moment his call had gone through. Rick jerked in startled surprise and then grinned wryly as he pulled his phone from his jean's front pocket.

As soon as he answered, Cameron said, "Carrie is here with a camera. Meet me at the bottom of the stairs to the dance floor."

Rick disconnected the call, said something to Mia, and then grabbed her hand and they both headed toward the stairs. Cameron arrived just as they did.

"Change of plans," he said to Mia. "She just went into the women's restroom. Why don't you go in there and act surprised to see her. That way she can't try and sneak out of here without being seen like she did the last time. I'll wait just outside the restroom, just in case you end up needing me for anything."

She exhaled a deep breath. "I'm sure I'll be fine."

As Mia headed down the hallway to the restrooms, she hoped her words proved to be true, that she *would* be okay by the end of all this. Even though she knew Carrie was responsible for everything, she wasn't looking forward to the confrontation that would undoubtedly occur.

She pushed open the door to the ladies room and stepped into the spacious women's lounge. The room was occupied by at least a dozen women sitting on the couches and chairs as they chatted and freshened their makeup. Carrie wasn't there, so Mia continued on to the bathrooms, and as soon as she entered the area she saw Carrie jerk away from the large mirror above the row of sinks and then quickly stuff something into her purse.

"Mia!" she exclaimed, her eyes wide and startled. "I've been looking for you!"

The lie hurt, especially when Mia knew exactly what Carrie was up to. She also knew that if Carrie hadn't been caught right now she most likely would have left The Electric Blue without contacting Mia at all.

"I was on the dance floor," Mia replied and refused to let Carrie off easy. "Why didn't you tell me you were coming tonight?"

"Oh, it was a last-minute thing. I wasn't going to come, then changed my mind, and because it was all so spur of the moment, I figured I'd find you here," she said, speaking in a fast, nervous rush. "Come on, let's go back out and get a drink." She stepped toward Mia in an attempt to usher her out of the bathroom.

Mia turned to go, but something on the mirror caught her eye. At first she thought it was a reflection of something in the bathroom, but when she stepped back to get a better look, she realized someone had written on the mirror itself—in what appeared to be bright red lipstick.

Mia Wilde is a slut.

The slur, coming from someone she'd once believed was a friend, hurt. Badly. She glanced back at Carrie, who now looked panicked because she knew she'd been caught red-handed.

And the only thing Mia could think of to ask in that moment was, "*Why?* Why write this about me? Why the pictures? The stuff you did to my car? The panties you sent? *Why,* Carrie?"

Mia expected Carrie to initially deny everything, but instead she lifted her chin scornfully. "Because I wanted *you* to see the way you act around men. The trampy way you dress. You want attention? Well, I made sure you got it."

A woman walked into the bathroom area, and Mia ignored her, knowing she couldn't let Carrie walk away now. "God, Carrie, what did I ever do to you?"

"You're a tramp," she said, as if that explained everything.

Mia thought back to her conversation with Cameron and his own explanation for Carrie's possible behavior. "Is this because of your mother?"

Carrie stiffened defensively. "Of course not. It's all about *you*. You're like a bitch in heat around men."

Mia tried not to flinch at Carrie's cruel words, though she couldn't deny they did sting. "I think this does have to do with your mother, whether you realize it or not," she said with more calm than she felt. "You can't control your mother's actions when it comes to the men who come and go from her life and the way she acts around them. And you blame your mother for your parents' divorce, so you've focused all that anger my way."

"My mother is, and always will be, a whore," Carrie said bitterly. "Just like you."

Although Mia was still hurt and angry, she could no longer take it as personally as she once had. She could only feel sorry for Carrie, that she was so wrapped up in her mother's life that somewhere along the way she'd lost control of her own. And until she disengaged herself from her mother and the situation at home, it would always continue.

But before she let Carrie go, she wanted her to know one thing. "In a lot of ways, you did me a huge favor. Those pictures you sent *did* make me see how my actions and behavior made me appear to other people. It made me think and change certain things, like how I dress and act. So if that was your intent, it worked."

The corner of Carrie's mouth curled in a malicious smile. "Just remember, once a tramp, always a tramp."

Carrie pushed around her, and Mia let her go. There was nothing left to say, and this was one friendship Mia didn't care to salvage. With a tired sigh, Mia followed her out of the lounge just in time to see Cameron catch Carrie by the arm and stop her mid-stride.

"Can I have the camera, please?" he asked politely and held out his free hand to confiscate the item.

Carrie yanked her arm from Cameron's grasp and narrowed her gaze at him. "I don't know what you're talking about."

"Oh, I think you do." He smiled, though the look in his eyes spoke volumes and told Carrie just how serious he was.

"I saw you taking pictures of Mia while she was dancing with Rick, and unless you want Mia to press charges against you for all the other crap you've pulled, then I suggest you hand over that disposable camera you used tonight."

"Fine," she huffed. She dug through her purse, found the disposable camera, and shoved it into his hand. "You don't need pictures to know she's a slut."

Cameron's jaw clenched in anger, but he maintained a cool composure when he replied to Carrie's rude comment. "If you ever use the word *slut, whore,* or *tramp* in the same sentence as Mia again, I can guarantee you'll be slapped with a lawsuit for slander so fast your head will spin."

Carrie stormed off, and Mia glanced at Cameron. "Thanks for that."

"Of course." His fingers flexed around the camera he still held in his hand as if he had to resist the urge to crush it into tiny pieces right then and there. "Are you okay?"

"Yeah, I'm good." She offered him a smile, because she was so grateful she no longer had to worry about when the next assault was going to happen. "It's finally over. Let's go home."

Her case was over. And after tonight, they would be, too.

Sixteen

AS soon as they arrived back at his place, Cameron noticed an immediate change in Mia, as if she were already withdrawing emotionally from him because she sensed the end for them was near. By the time they reached his bedroom, he was determined to break through that reserve of hers and make Mia his in every way that mattered—heart, body, and soul. Tonight, he wanted it all and would give no less to her in return.

But before he could make the first move, she slid her arms around his neck, pulled his mouth to hers, and initiated a hot, deep, take-charge kiss. The kind that tasted like sex and sin and desire, and promised erotic, anything-goes pleasure. The kind that could drive a man crazy with the need to get inside of her as soon as possible.

His body responded to the soft warmth of her breasts pressed against his chest and the seductive way she rolled her hips against his. But for as much as she aroused him, he recognized her assertive approach as an attempt to be in control of tonight's encounter, and to keep a wealth of fears and insecurities at bay . . . to keep what they were about to do within the confines of pure, mindless, fuck-me sex so she didn't have to think or feel about anything beyond the moment of self-indulgence and physical satisfaction.

Her hands tugged the hem of his shirt from the waistband of his jeans in an attempt to get him naked. Complying, he raised his arms so she could strip off the shirt, but when her fingers dropped eagerly to the button fly securing the front of his pants, he grasped her wrists and pulled her hands away. He knew, just as she obviously did, that he couldn't think straight when she touched him intimately. He had no doubt she'd been counting on exactly that, but he wasn't about to let go that way . . . not until his fingers were on her, not until his cock was buried deep inside her, not until he felt her come.

He broke their kiss, and before she could issue a protest, he turned her around so she was facing his dresser mirror and he stood behind her. In the reflection, their gazes met, hers a dark shade of smoky gray as he lowered the zipper of her dress down her back. His fingers touched the soft, smooth skin he exposed, and he felt her shiver from his caress.

A slow, sensual smile curved her lips. "I didn't realize you liked to watch," she murmured.

He pushed the sleeves of her dress off her shoulders and down her arms, then skimmed the body-hugging material over the curve of her hips until it finally dropped to the floor. His mouth went dry as he took in her provocative, black, sheer lace bra and matching G-string panties that made her look as though she'd just stepped from the centerfold of a men's magazine. Except she was all *his*. His fantasy. His desire. His future.

He unfastened her bra and tossed it aside as well. Her breasts spilled forward, full and voluptuous and perfectly proportioned to her slender waist and the swell of her hips. "Watching adds an element of excitement, don't you think?" he whispered in her ear.

She dampened her bottom lip with her tongue. "I don't need a mirror to make me hot for you."

Cameron suspected she didn't care for the mirror because it forced her to see beyond the sexually confident temptress standing in front of him to the vulnerable woman beneath. That's exactly what he wanted her to see, and face, and come to terms with. That she was a woman with needs and emotions and she didn't need to hide anything from him.

"Indulge me," he said and brushed his lips along the side of her neck. "And if you don't want to watch, you can always close your eyes."

He'd infused just enough of a challenge in his tone to get the reaction he wanted from her. It was subtle, but enough to assure him she wouldn't look away from what he was about to do.

He started with her bare breasts. Cupping the heavy weight in his palms, he kneaded the firm, soft flesh and then scraped his thumbs across her nipples. They instantly grew tight, hardening beneath his touch, just as his cock lengthened and thickened against the confinement of his jeans, which pressed against her bottom.

Her breathing deepened as he continued to stroke and caress and tease, and he could feel her fighting against the need to just let go and enjoy. She was holding back, emotionally and physically, which only made him more driven to shatter every one of those barriers she'd put between them tonight.

Wrapping an arm around her waist, he skimmed his other hand down her stomach and beneath the black scrap of fabric covering her mound. His fingers stroked her intimately, deeply, where she was all velvet softness and slick, wet heat. Her head fell back against his chest, and a low moan escaped her throat.

The view of the two of them in the mirror was highly erotic, with one of his tanned hands splayed on her belly and his other concealed beneath black silk—the color of rich decadence and forbidden desire. He watched the flutter of her thick lashes, the rise and fall of her breasts, and the flush sweeping across her cheeks. Even his own eyes were hot and hungry, his features taut with carnal need—a need he swore he'd deny himself until she gave him want he ultimately wanted . . . her orgasm. The one she was holding back from him.

Frustrated but still determined, he lowered his head and nuzzled her neck and then gave her a gentle love bite on her shoulder that made her gasp in shock. "God, I want you." His voice rumbled with intensity and raw emotion, more than he'd ever intended to reveal in that moment.

His hold on her had loosened just enough for her to slip from his embrace, and she did so before he could stop her. She climbed up onto his bed and settled onto her knees, with her back to him, showing off the sexy slope of her spine and her bare, heart-shaped bottom. She was still wearing her G-string panties, and attached to the top elastic band spanning her hips were three pink butterfly appliqués that made Mia look sweet and innocent, but he knew better.

She glanced over her shoulder at him, a come-hither look in her eyes, and then rose up on her hands and knees. "If you want me, come and get me." A dare. A challenge of her own. A way for her to take control once again. To be the one calling the shots.

She was in for a big surprise.

Hastily, he toed off his shoes and pulled off his socks, then shucked his jeans and briefs. Her gaze dropped to his jutting erection, and she licked her lips in anticipation, fueling the fire already burning within him. He moved up onto the mattress, right up behind Mia, and with his hand splayed in the middle of her back, he gently pushed her upper body down onto the bed until her head was resting on a pillow but her bottom was still raised.

Hooking his fingers in the side straps of her panties, he drew them down her thighs until they pooled around her knees. Then he leaned over her, kissed the base of her spine, then skimmed his lips higher, until he was completely covering her from behind and his face was buried in the fragrant curve of her neck. She was already panting in anticipation, wanting this. Wanting him.

Hips perfectly aligned, he slid his cock between her thighs to the silky soft lips of her sex. The head of his shaft found her opening, and with a long, driving thrust, he was exactly where he ached to be. Her fingers gripped the comforter, and she moaned and arched and pushed against him, drawing him deeper into her body, threatening his sanity and his restraint.

Refusing to give into the orgasm rising to the surface, he denied the demands of his body—not until Mia was right there with him. Reaching a hand beneath her, he stroked her in the same slow, heated rhythm as his pumping hips. Over the past few weeks he'd learned her body well. Knew just how to touch and caress her to make her unravel. Knew what she liked, what turned her on, and what made her come.

And still, she denied him.

A spark of anger flared within him. In that moment, he decided Mia could try and withhold her feelings for him and deny what was in her heart, but there was no way in hell he was going to allow her to take *this* away from him. He wanted her orgasm, and he wouldn't be satisfied until she finally gave herself over to him that way.

Abruptly, he pulled out of her, shocking her with the unexpected move. "I gave you what you wanted," he said with rough impatience and sat back on his heels. "Now I want you to lay down on your back for me."

She did as he asked and turned over, eyeing him warily. "You didn't come," she said, glancing down at the upward thrust of his erection.

Oh, but how he'd wanted to. He was so fucking hard he was about to burst. But he wasn't going to let her win this round tonight. She was trying to shut him out, make this impersonal when it was anything but. "I will when you do."

That said, he striped off her panties, pushed her legs wide apart, settled in between, and put his mouth on her. She sucked in a sharp, startled breath and tried to rise up, but he pressed a strong hand to her belly to hold her down. He heard her call his name in a trembling panic, felt her fingers knot in his hair to pull him away, and ignored every attempt she made to stop him.

He was relentless in his pursuit. Persistent and tireless as he licked and lapped at her, then swirled and dragged his tongue over her sensitive cleft. Again and again, until she was thrashing beneath his unyielding assault and moaning softly. Minutes could have passed, or an hour. It didn't matter and he didn't care, because he wasn't letting her go, wouldn't stop until she gave herself over to him completely.

He thrust two long fingers deep inside of her, giving her that extra, insistent, ruthless push of sensual pleasure, and it was finally enough to send her over the edge. Beneath the hand still splayed on her belly, he felt her tense. Her inner muscles clenched around his fingers, and her nails dug into his shoulders in a last attempt to resist. Then the wave broke, and she sobbed as her body convulsed with the beginning tremors of a powerful, undeniable climax.

He reared up over her, replaced his fingers with his cock, and drove deep, deep inside of her as her orgasm crested, squeezing his shaft, milking him, enveloping every hard inch of him like a tight, hot, velvet glove. With an unraveling groan, he slid his arm beneath the arch of her back and pulled her hips tighter against his. Then he slanted his mouth across hers in a fierce, devouring kiss and rode her hard and fast. It didn't take long before his own violent spasms jerked and shuddered through him.

He collapsed on top of her, his breathing ragged, his entire body spent. Beneath him, Mia didn't move, though he could feel her thundering heartbeat against his chest. Lifting his head from the damp curve of her neck, he glanced down at her, and his stomach clenched at what he saw. She'd turned her face to the side and her eyes were closed, but there was no mistaking the moisture on her cheeks.

"Don't shut me out, Mia," he said and recognized the desperation in his voice. But he feared it might be too late, and there wasn't a damned thing he could do about it.

So instead, he gathered her in his arms, gently wiped away her tears, and said nothing more because at this point, there was nothing left to say. He'd just given her everything he had, and he could only hope that in the morning light it would be enough for her to stick around and give the two of them a chance at a future together.

MIA had avoidance and denial down to an art form, Cameron thought as he closed the case file he'd been working on the following Sunday afternoon. Pushing away from his desk, he went to the large window in his home office, from which he had an unobstructed view, and glanced out toward the back patio.

Mia was still sitting out on a chaise lounge in a pair of shorts, with her bare, slender legs soaking up the warm sunshine. A few hours ago when he'd told her he had some things to do in his office, she'd taken her sketch pad outside and had been there ever since. Currently, she was drawing something on the paper that had captured her complete attention, and he assumed it was a new stained-glass design.

He released a long breath, knowing the time had come to talk to Mia about the two of them. He was going to have to initiate the conversation, because it was obvious Mia had no desire to talk about what had transpired between them last night, or discuss where their relationship was headed now that her case was over.

After keeping Mia secure in his embrace for most of the night—a huge feat considering she was so used to curling up on her own to sleep—he'd woken up alone in bed this morning and immediately thought she'd called a cab and headed home sometime in the early hours of dawn. That wouldn't have shocked him at all since he'd come to learn Mia was used to running and hiding from her feelings instead of facing them, and there was a helluva lot of emotions for the two of them to deal with after last night.

Mia hadn't run, which he'd initially seen as a positive sign, but when he'd walked into the kitchen to find her making French toast for breakfast, she'd acted as though nothing had changed. She'd been bright and cheerful and chatty as they ate, talking about everything from Carrie, to her gallery show, to inconsequential things that didn't really matter. Not when their entire relationship was at stake.

Cameron recognized her forced, light-hearted attempt at conversation for the diversion it was and decided he'd give her a bit of time and space to come to terms with her feelings for him. He'd hoped that at some point during the day she'd come to him, but it was becoming increasingly clear that if he left it up to Mia, they would never resolve the one big issue still standing between them.

Where did they go from here?

He knew what direction *he* wanted to go, but he had no idea if he'd be traveling down that road with Mia or on his own. And it was time he found out.

He headed through the house and out to the back porch. As soon as he closed the sliding screen door behind him, she glanced up from her sketch pad and smiled at him. Unfortunately, since he'd come to know her so well, he could see right through her welcome pretense to the guarded reserve glimmering in the depths of her eyes.

"Hey there," he said, striving for a casual tone when he was feeling anything but.

"Hey yourself," she replied, her gaze searching his features—most likely to gauge his mood. "Is your work all done?"

"Most of it. The rest can wait." What he had to say to her couldn't. Not any longer. He dragged a chair over to where she was lounging, parked it close to the chaise, and took a seat. "You and I need to talk."

She eyed him warily, just as he'd expected. "About?"

"Our relationship," he said, getting right to the point. "Especially now that your case is over. One has ended, but the other doesn't have to."

The change in her was immediate. She set her sketch pad aside, drew her knees up, and wrapped her arms around her legs, as if to safeguard her heart and emotions from what was about to happen. "I knew this was coming, and I've thought a lot about you and I and where we go from here."

"And?" He was curious to hear what conclusions she'd drawn about them.

She exhaled a deep breath. "And I think this is it for us," she said, trying to put on a brave front.

"This is it," he repeated flatly, unable to believe she could dismiss the past few weeks they'd spent together so frivously.

"We agreed on a *temporary* affair for a reason, Cameron," she said, much too pragmatically. "While the sex between us is fantastic and amazing, when it comes down to you and me on a long-term one-on-one basis, we're two very different, incompatible people."

Leaning forward in his chair, he clasped his hands between his knees and pinned her with a direct and unwavering look. One she couldn't escape. "Different and incompatible how?"

Her lips pursed with impatience. "You're going to make me spell it all out, aren't you?"

"Yeah, I guess I am," he persisted, refusing to let her out of this discussion so easily.

With an irritable sigh, she stood up and paced across the patio, putting a decent amount of physical distance between them before she turned around and spoke. "There's a good reason why we never hooked up before I came to you for help a few weeks ago, and that reason hasn't changed just because we've slept together. I'm stubborn, unpredictable, and too reckless, remember? And you're Mr. Cool, Calm, and Collected. The two just don't mix."

Luckily, that was an argument he'd anticipated. "Seems to me we'd balance each other out pretty damn well. I'd keep you level-headed, and you'd make sure I didn't revert to being uptight and stuffy." He said the last part jokingly, but she didn't seem in a humorous mood.

Instead, she crossed her arms over her chest. "I distinctly remember you saying that I was all wrong for you, and in a lot of ways, we both know that's true."

"That was before I really got to know you, *inside*." He stood and approached her but still gave her the space she seemed to need. "During our time together I changed my mind. *You* changed my mind."

"For the moment, yes," she said, her exasperated attitude disguising deeper insecurities she refused to face. "But in the long run, we'd drive each other crazy. We spent the past two years annoying the hell out of one another, and once this 'new relationship' glow fades and the thrill is gone, all those annoyances are going to creep right back up and be glaring issues between us."

Her expression turned imploring, as if she was silently pleading with him to understand. "It's happened to me before, in other relationships, Cameron. You're going to want me to change. Be something or someone I'm not. And I just don't know if I can be the kind of woman you need in your life. Someone stable and grounded and refined. And in the end, you'll come to resent me and the relationship."

He heard the catch in her voice and saw those familiar, lifetime fears she was desperately fighting against. What she didn't realize, or wasn't ready to admit or deal with, was that she'd already changed in the course of their short relationship—all in good, positive ways that made her a stronger, better person. But she had to come to see and accept those changes in herself.

He formed his response carefully but firmly. "If you

honestly think I'd ever resent who and what you are, then you don't know me very well at all."

She shook her head in frustration, causing her silky black hair to swirl around her shoulders. "Come on, Cameron, let's at least be honest with each other about all this, okay?"

His jaw clenched, because his own patience was quickly reaching its limit. She wanted honest? Well, she was about to get more than she'd bargained for, because he was going to lay everything on the line. He figured he had nothing left to lose at this point.

"Listen up, sweetheart, because I'm about to prove to you just how well I know *you,*" he said and started toward her slowly but purposefully.

Apparently, he was getting too close for her comfort zone, physically and emotionally, and when she attempted to dodge around him, he was faster. He stepped to the side, trapping her up against the side of the house. Before she could bolt again, he flattened his palms on either side of her shoulders, keeping her within the confines of his arms.

"Dammit, quit running from me," he growled furiously. "From *us*."

Her chin jutted out mutinously, but her gray eyes were wider than normal. "I'm not running from anything," she shot back.

"That's bullshit, and we both know it." He hoped like hell she was able to handle the honesty he was about to dish out in abundance. "You've spent your adult life avoiding intimacy with a man, especially when you start feeling threatened emotionally, and that's exactly where you are with me. *I* threaten you emotionally, and that scares the crap out of you. You don't want to deal with those feelings, and so it's easier for you to cut loose and run than risk being hurt. The same kind of hurt and pain you've lived with since your mother's death."

She rolled her eyes at him in an attempt to dismiss his words, no matter how true they were. "There you go again, sugar," she drawled. "Psychoanalyzing me."

"It's what I do best." And there was a helluva lot more where that came from. "I know just how vulnerable you are, even though you want everyone to believe you're tough and strong and don't need anyone at all," he went on ruthlessly. "I know you hate the way your brothers and cousins smother and protect you, even though you know they do it because they love and care about you. I know how badly you crave your family's approval, of who you are and what you do. And I know just how talented you are and how those erotic pictures you create in your stained-glass designs are all a part of the sensual woman you are, inside and out. A woman with a romantic soul who is searching for an unconditional kind of love and acceptance."

She drew a trembling breath, and her eyes shone with telltale moisture. "You have no idea what you're talking about," she whispered hoarsely, desperation evident in her tone.

He pressed two fingers to her soft, damp lips to keep her quiet. Lips he ached to kiss in the worst way. "Oh, I know exactly what I'm talking about, and I'm not done yet," he said, locking his gaze with hers. "I agree that our affair started out as all about sex and getting you out of my system after wanting you for two years. And what we shared sexually has been hotter and more erotic than anything I've ever had with another woman."

He let his hand fall away. "But I'm a man who sees more than just what's on the outside, and over the past few weeks I've discovered a side to you I don't think any other man has ever taken the time to learn or know. And for you to let me in so intimately, you have to feel something for me, too."

She closed her eyes and tried to turn her face away, but he gently touched her jaw and waited until she was looking at him again. But this time, when her lashes fluttered back open, there were tears in her eyes. And a wealth of feeling. Her entire body trembled with the emotion she was trying so hard to suppress, and he suspected that was a very instinctual reaction for her.

"You can hide behind your erotic stained-glass art and your wild and outrageous personality, but I know who you really are, Mia," he said softly. "Deep inside where it counts. In your heart. In your beautiful, lost soul. And that's the woman I fell for. The woman no one else knows as well as I do."

She blinked, and a big, fat tear fell down her cheek. "God, how can you want a woman with so many hang-ups and issues?"

"Because I love you," he said simply.

A panicked sob caught in her throat, and she shook her head in denial. "You can't!"

"I can, and I do. It certainly wasn't something I'd planned on, but it happened. I want to love you, Mia, like you've never been loved before." He gently wiped away yet another tear with the pad of his thumb. "You trusted me with your body, and I gave you nothing but pleasure. You trusted me with your past and secrets, now trust me with your heart, and I swear I'll keep it safe from the kind of hurt and pain you're so afraid of."

"You can't make those kinds of promises, Cameron. No one can. I know you believe in this moment you can give me those things, that the two of us can make it work, but I can't handle a broken heart if it doesn't. I know what that feels like, and the emotional pain of losing someone is something I can't bear to go through ever again."

He knew she was referring to her mother's death, which had scarred her deeply and affected so many relationships throughout her life. Men, definitely, but shutting people out of her heart had all started with her stepmother, Amelia. And that was a situation Cameron couldn't repair for Mia, even though he suspected that scarred relationship was the crux of most of her emotional issues.

"I'm sorry," she whispered.

Cameron understood that she was frightened of what she was feeling for him, but he'd hoped that during the course of their conversation today she'd face those fears and take a chance on something genuine and real. Him. Them. Together.

He'd been sorely mistaken. Her rejection felt like a knife through his heart.

Admitting defeat, he pushed away from Mia, letting her go. There was nothing left for him to do. Nothing left for him to say. She'd made it very clear that it was over, and he wasn't going to beg and plead.

"Come on," he said with a heavy sigh. "I'll take you home."

Seventeen

CAMERON skimmed through the rap sheet on Ray Wilkins, a.k.a. Billy Dearborn, that Wesley had just handed to him, not at all surprised to discover that the man had a list of transgressions attached to his *real* name. The guy had a criminal record that spanned everything from physical to sexual assault, varying degrees of theft, vandalism, drug use, carrying a concealed weapon, and even a few felony violations he'd done prison time for.

"Jesus," Cameron said in disgust and was damn grateful Gina had finally come to her senses and ended her relationship with the guy. Not to mention issuing a restraining order against him. Dearborn was a hot-headed, dangerous criminal without a conscience, and it looked as though Gina needed whatever protection she could get against him.

Jaw clenched, Cameron glanced back up at Wesley, who was standing on the other side of his desk. "How in the hell did you finally nail this guy?"

"Billy Dearborn changed his name, but not his Social

Security number or birth date," Wes replied wryly. "As soon as I started tracing his Social Security number through public records, one thing led to another until I tracked him down to the last place he'd lived before moving to Chicago, and that was Florida."

Cameron shuffled through the other paperwork and printouts Wesley had given him. "Do you know what sent him packing?"

"Actually, I do, and I came across more than one reason why he left the state. I have a few P.I. contacts in Florida I've kept in touch with from the last firm I worked for, and I put a call in to someone I know and trust." Wesley's lips flattened into a grim line. "It appears that Billy Dearborn was involved in a drug-smuggling ring, and about six months ago he pocketed a cool twenty grand that belonged to the organization he was working for. They found out about the theft, beat the crap out of Billy, and gave him a week to pay back the money, but Billy changed his identity and moved here to Chicago."

"They didn't try very hard to find him," Cameron muttered irritably, wishing they'd tracked down Dearborn *before* he'd hooked up with Gina.

"Unfortunately, I'm sure they have bigger fish to fry in their line of business," Wesley told him. "Billy was small shrimp in comparison, though I'm betting if they knew where he was they wouldn't hesitate to try and get their money back from him any way they could. Even in blood."

That thought gave Cameron a semblance of satisfaction.

"But that's not all," Wesley said. "This guy has a warrant out for his arrest for sexually assaulting a woman."

Cameron swore beneath his breath. "Well, it looks like Gina is going to be the last woman he assaults for a very long time, because I'm turning his ass in." There was no way Cameron was going to let this bastard hurt another woman again. "And while I'm at it, I'm going to scare the shit out of him with the information we have about the twenty grand he stole to keep him away from Mia and Gina for good."

Standing, Cameron gathered up the paperwork on Dearborn. "Can you give me the entire file on this guy so I have everything you've covered?"

"You got it." Wesley gave him an affirmative nod.

"I'm also going to share it with Gina and Mia so they know exactly what kind of guy they're dealing with."

Once Wesley left Cameron's office, he picked up the phone and dialed Mia's home number. When the answering machine picked up, he looked up the number Mia had given him for Gina's phone and dialed that. Gina picked up after a few rings, and Cameron let her know he was coming by to talk to her. Cameron figured Gina could relay the information to Mia, which was probably for the best considering Cameron hadn't talked to Mia since they'd parted ways four long, miserable days ago. She hadn't made any attempt to contact him, and the ball was squarely in her court if she was at all interested in salvaging their relationship.

So far, it appeared she was not.

Cameron glanced at his watch. It was after six in the evening. Steve had already left work a few hours earlier to spend some quality time with his wife and son. Ironically, now that Wesley was picking up so much extra work, everyone's schedule had been freed up. Except Mia was out of Cameron's life, and that gave him too much time to think about things better left alone.

Within fifteen minutes Cameron was on the road, heading toward Mia and Gina's place. Once he arrived, he made his way to the apartment, file folder in hand, and as he neared the door he noticed that it was cracked open a few inches. He frowned, prepared to berate Gina for being so careless when he heard a loud, jarring thud coming from inside, along with something crashing to the floor and a woman's muffled screams.

Adrenaline rushed through Cameron's veins as he pushed the door open and moved cautiously inside, keeping as quiet as possible until he could assess the situation. He found Ray pinning Gina up against the wall in the living room, one of his hands pressed tight against her throat and the other holding her arm to the side at an awkward angle. Gina had a big long gash above her eye that was trickling blood down the side of her face, and while that was the only injury Cameron could visibly see, he feared she was going to end up with even more bruises from Ray's rough handling.

"Bitch," Ray sneered, so focused on dominating Gina he was completely oblivious to the fact that anyone had entered the apartment. "There's not a chance in hell I'm going to let you leave me, and no restraining order will keep me away. Got that?"

Gina nodded jerkily, her entire body trembling in fear. While Ray spoke Cameron made his way quietly closer. For as much as he wanted to kick the shit out of Ray right then and there, he had to get Gina out of his grasp and away from Ray first so the other man didn't use her as pawn between them.

"You try and leave, and I'll hunt you down and break every bone in your body . . . just . . . like . . . this," Ray said maliciously, and twisted her arm until she started crying out in pain and tears rolled down her cheeks.

Fury ripped through Cameron. "You're a sick, pathetic bastard," he said, finally announcing his presence.

Startled, Ray immediately released Gina and spun around to face Cameron. His eyes narrowed, and his hands curled into fists at his sides. Thankfully, Gina took the opportunity to scramble away and put the couch between herself and Ray.

With Gina out of the way, Cameron took another step toward Ray, watching his body language and anticipating his next move. Ray wasn't a big guy at all, which was probably why he preyed on the weaker sex—to make him feel manly when he was anything but. Cameron estimated that he outweighed Ray by a good twenty pounds of solid muscle, and he intended to use that to his advantage.

"Billy Dearborn, isn't it?" Cameron taunted and watched the man's eyes fill with disbelief and even a flicker of apprehension.

Then Ray straightened, his expression menacing. "Fuck you," he said and swung his fist toward Cameron's face.

Cameron jerked his head back out of the way but caught Ray's punch before it could connect with his jaw. With his fingers encircling the other man's wrist, he twisted his arm, spun him around, and shoved him up against the wall. Ruthlessly, Cameron wedged his knee between Ray's to keep him pinned in place and jammed his contorted arm higher up his back until Ray cried out in agony. Then, for good measure, Cameron jammed it even higher, harder, increasing the pain.

"Do you like the way that feels, you worthless piece of shit?" Cameron asked.

Ray muttered another crude expletive at Cameron and struggled for freedom, his mouth spewing all kinds of vicious words. Ray hadn't learned his lesson the first time, so Cameron rammed his knee up between Ray's legs, crushing his balls, and the other man's legs buckled as he screamed out in raw anguish. Ray dropped to the floor, writhing in excruciating pain, and Cameron kept the other man shoved face down on his belly with his arm still bent behind his back.

"The pain you just felt is nothing compared to what I'd really like to do to you, you miserable weasel," Cameron bit out gruffly. "So just go ahead and give me a reason to snap your arm in two."

"Cameron," Gina said in a quivering voice. "I called the police."

He glanced up, noticing that Gina was clutching the portable phone to her chest, her eyes still wide with fear. He was surprised she'd been thinking clearly enough to call the cops. "Good girl," he said. That gave him a few minutes to have a chat with Ray before law enforcement arrived.

"Listen up, Dearborn, because I'm only going to tell you this once," Cameron said to the man on the floor. "I know all about who you are, where you're from, and why you changed your name. First, you have a warrant still out for your arrest. Second, it seems your sticky fingers lifted twenty grand that wasn't yours, and there are some guys looking for you and that money. From what I hear, they'd be happy to cut you up into little pieces and feed you to the sharks."

Ray stopped squirming and started listening intently to Cameron. His breathing was labored, and his body had grown tense.

"So I'm going to issue you a friendly warning. I'm sending your ass to jail, but if I ever see your face again, or if you harass Gina or Mia, all it will take is one phone call to ensure you're dead meat. That is, after *I've* had my turn with you. Got that?"

Ray stubbornly, and stupidly, refused to agree.

Cameron took great pleasure in giving his arm another forceful twist and added a sharp, digging pressure against Ray's shoulder blades with his knee. "Got that?" he repeated, harsher this time.

Finally, the other man complied with a fierce, yell. "Yes, I got it!"

Cameron smiled grimly. "Good, I just wanted to be sure we understood one another."

MIA came home to chaos, with the police and the paramedics walking in and out of her apartment and a handcuffed Ray being escorted out the door by a uniformed cop. She immediately panicked, and fearing the worst, she rushed inside and found Gina sitting on the living room couch with a female medic putting a butterfly bandage on her roommate's forehead and another checking her blood pressure.

Stunned, Mia glanced around, seeing the lamp that had fallen to the floor and shattered. Her stomach cramped at the thought of what had happened while she'd gone by the gallery for a few minutes to drop off some new designs for Amy to display. If only Mia had come home right after work, maybe she could have stopped whatever had happened.

Out of the corner of her eye she saw someone heading her way. Shaking herself out of her stupor, she looked in that direction and found Cameron approaching her.

"Cameron?" she said, confused now. What was he doing here? Had he stopped by to see her? Her traitorous heart picked up its beat at that thought, forcing her to realize just how much she'd missed him the past week. "What happened?"

"I found out some information on Ray. Actually, his real name is Billy Dearborn. I came by to tell you and Gina what I'd discovered about him." His tone was all business, though his eyes seemed to drink up the sight of her. "Instead, I found Ray in the apartment, roughing up Gina."

He went on to tell her how he'd handled the situation, and Mia shivered at the replay of events. "Oh, God," she said and peered around Cameron to look at Gina again. "Is she okay?"

"Ray gave Gina a pretty nasty cut above her eye, and she'll probably bruise pretty badly, but at least that will be the last time." Cameron pushed his hands into the front pockets of his jeans, as if to keep from reaching out and touching her. "She's pretty shaken up right now, but she'll be okay, especially because I highly doubt she'll ever have to deal with Ray ever again."

"Really?" Mia asked hopefully.

He nodded. "Not only does Ray have a warrant out for his arrest, but he has a past he doesn't want to catch up to him. He and I came to an understanding of sorts." Cameron gave her a rundown of Ray's past transgressions, and the threat still looming over him, and how Cameron had no qualms using that information if Ray ever contacted Gina again. "Trust me, between jail time and his theft, he's gone for good."

She trusted Cameron unconditionally. The guy was solid as a rock and as good as his word. Her own thoughts startled her, but before she could reflect on her realization, Cameron spoke again.

"Gina has already given a statement to the police, and so have I," he said and nodded his dark blond head toward Mia's roommate. "Why don't you go over there and let her know you're home."

Mia suddenly didn't want to leave Cameron, even to cross the room to Gina, but her friend undoubtedly needed her comfort and support, and that was more important at the moment.

A cop came up to talk to Cameron again, and Mia took that opportunity to walk over to where Gina was sitting on the couch. She settled in next to Gina and wrapped an arm around her shoulder.

"I'm so sorry you had to go through all this alone," Mia said, wincing at the large band-aid the medic had put on her forehead, certain it hid a sizeable wound. "But I'm so glad you're okay."

"Because of Cameron," Gina said gratefully. "I don't want to think about what could have happened if he hadn't showed up when he did." She shivered.

"The guy is a regular white knight," Mia joked, and that comment earned her a smile from Gina.

After a moment, Gina's expression grew serious. "Mia, there's something I need to tell you."

Mia tipped her head. "What is it?

"Even before today with Ray, or Billy, or whatever his name is," she said with a frown, "I'd already made the decision to move back near my sister. Spending last weekend with her and my nieces made me realize how much I miss being close to my family. And right now, I think that's where I need to be."

As much as Mia would miss Gina as a roommate and friend, Mia understood. As the medic asked Gina a few last questions about how she was feeling, Mia glanced to where she'd left Cameron, but he was gone from the apartment.

Just as he was gone from her life.

THE turnout for Mia's stained-glass art show at the Brennan gallery was a huge success, more than anything Mia ever could have anticipated. When Amy had told her she was sending invitations to more than one hundred of her best clients, Mia had been skeptical and figured she'd be lucky if a fourth of that number showed up. But now, as she glanced around the crowded gallery, she found herself overwhelmed by the number of people milling about and perusing her artwork—even if a good two dozen of those guests were her immediate family.

Even Cameron's sisters had shown up with their husbands, and it was so nice to see all of them again. But their presence made her all too aware of the fact that Cameron had obviously opted *not* to come to the showing. It was a good twenty minutes into the event, and although a part of her understood why Cameron might want to stay away, another part of her had secretly hoped he'd attend. After all, he was the reason why she was having the show in the first place.

Sighing, she accepted a flute of champagne from a passing tray and took a sip of the bubbly liquid as she watched Scott and Alex and their wives, Ashley and Dana, disappear into the far room where Amy had displayed her erotic stained-glass pieces. Mia's stomach dipped nervously, because while her family had been surprised to learn that she'd put her stained-glass designs into an art gallery, they still didn't know just how provocative some of her art was. But they were about to find out, and she could only imagine and anticipate their shocked reactions.

However, no matter what they thought, she'd decided

their approval no longer mattered. This was who she was, and there was a piece of her in every design and picture. If her family didn't learn to appreciate her art, she knew many others who would.

She'd spent every spare moment of the past few weeks making as many designs as she could for the show—most of them the erotic pieces, because that's what had captured everyone's interest the most. She'd been grateful for the distraction because it left her little time to think about Cameron and her aching heart, or just how empty and lonely the apartment was now that Gina had moved out. But after tonight, she was going to have a whole lot of time to think about things she'd put out of her mind for weeks. And she wasn't looking forward to dealing with herself, for fear of what she might uncover.

The next hour whirled by in a quick blur. Between being introduced to dozens of Amy's clients, to doing a quick interview for the local newspaper for a piece they planned to write up about her and the show for an upcoming article, Mia was swept up into the excitement and satisfaction of a successful event. It wasn't until she saw Scott and Ashley heading her way that she realized she'd yet to talk to her family about the erotic aspect of her artwork.

"Wow, this is quite an event," Scott said, seemingly awed by all the people and the flurry of activity around him. "And I have to tell you, none of us had any idea you were putting naked pictures into your designs."

Mia couldn't tell if Scott approved or not. "I just put those into some of the artwork. There's plenty of stained-glass designs without naked people in them," she said, waving her hand toward a collection of floral pieces that were very G rated.

"Those erotic designs are beautiful, and very impressive." Ashley looped her arm through her husband's and smiled up at him adoringly. "Scott bought me the mermaid one."

Mia stared in shock at her brother. "You did?" She

couldn't believe he'd spent that kind of money on one of her stained-glass designs.

He shrugged. "It's a very unique piece, and we both liked it. Besides, I want to be sure I get one of your first, original designs. That way when you become this famous artist, it'll be worth a whole lot more." Scott winked at her.

Now Mia just outright gaped at him. "Is this my brother Scott talking? The guy who turned down my idea of incorporating my stained-glass designs into the family business?"

Scott frowned at her. "What's that supposed to mean?"

"I'm just surprised, is all," she said with a shake of her head. "You crushed my hopes and dreams when I came home from college, and now you're suddenly one of my biggest supporters."

"Of course I am. God, Mia, Dad and I had no idea we were crushing a dream of yours, or else we never would have said no." A wealth of regrets deepened the blue of Scott's eyes. "I guess we didn't realize just how serious you were about your stained-glass art. And if we'd really known and understood how important your art was to you, we never would have deliberately held you back."

Mia paused in thought, surprised by her brother's reaction. She'd been so insecure back then, that at the first sign of rejection she'd automatically pulled back and kept her artwork to herself instead of putting up an argument. How unlike her, a woman who was so aggressive in all other areas of her life, she thought wryly.

Then, through the years, she'd kept her erotic pieces hidden, until she'd shared them with Cameron and he'd given her the confidence to pursue her greatest passion. She knew in her heart that her family loved her despite their overprotective ways, but it was Cameron who knew her better than any of them.

"I suppose now that you've made it on your own, very successfully I might add, that Alex and I should start looking for a replacement secretary?" Scott teased.

Her brother might have been joking, but Mia had given that a lot of thought the past few weeks. She'd come to the conclusion that if she wanted to make this her career, she had to give her stained-glass art one hundred percent of herself.

"This is what I love, Scott, and I can't see myself doing anything else," she told her brother. "So I guess you can consider this my two weeks notice."

Scott's mouth gaped open, and Mia tried not to laugh. She'd definitely shocked Scott with her announcement, but before he could reply, Alex and Dana joined them and then Steve and Liz. Soon, she was surrounded by the entire Wilde clan as they complimented and congratulated her on her designs and the phenomenal success of her first show.

Mia approached her stepmother, Amelia, who she'd yet to get a moment alone with tonight. She was standing next to Mia's father, and it struck Mia in that moment just how in love the two of them were. Her father deserved that, and Amelia deserved so much more than Mia had ever given her. Like her affection. Her love. A real mother-daughter relationship.

Mia's throat grew tight with the realization, and she swallowed back the knot and smiled at her father and Amelia. "Thank you both for coming tonight," she said and kissed her father on the cheek, then Amelia's. "It means so much to me to have the entire family here."

"We wouldn't miss something as important as this, Mia." Amelia grasped Mia's hands and gave them a warm squeeze that spoke volumes. "Your father and I are *very* proud of you."

The truth of Amelia's words reflected in her eyes, and another swell of emotion rose within Mia. For so many years Mia had been so caught up in her own personal pain and rebellion that she'd denied Amelia any real emotion. And it was so obvious just by looking into the other woman's eyes that she was *still* hoping it would happen one day.

God, Mia'd been so incredibly selfish!

"Mia," Amy called out from across the gallery where she was standing with a middle-aged couple. "Would you mind coming over here, please? I have someone interested in talking to you about having a custom piece designed."

Mia hated letting this moment between her and Amelia pass without saying more, but she had no choice. "Excuse me," she said and went to discuss business with the couple.

Once again, the business end of her new career took precedence. One custom order led to another, and in between were the stained-glass purchases the guests were making so they could take their art home with them tonight. Finally, the last call was made for anyone who was interested in placing a bid on the silent auction items.

Needing a break and a moment alone to catch her breath, Mia slipped into the back room where the erotic pieces were displayed while everyone else was congregated in the front area of the gallery. She took a drink of her second glass of champagne as she glanced at one of her designs with a SOLD tag attached to it, feeling both giddy and amazed at how much the piece had gone for—almost enough to pay her rent for the next month. Amy had told her everything was going so well that Mia could easily expect a five-figure check before the night was through.

Her success was definitely heady, but one thing was undeniably missing from tonight's festivities: the one man who'd made it all possible. *Cameron.* She felt that loss in a soul-deep way. Even though she'd accomplished so much tonight, she had no one to share it all with.

"You look absolutely beautiful tonight."

The deep, sexy voice belonged to only one man she knew. Mia was certain she was dreaming, or hallucinating, until she spun around and found Cameron standing directly behind her. He looked so good, with his tousled dark blond hair, a collared shirt that showed off his wide shoulders and chest, and a pair of khaki trousers that fit him to perfection. Although his demeanor seemed reserved and guarded, his gorgeous green eyes told Mia just how much he wanted her. *Still.*

She was so elated to see him, she nearly jumped right into his arms. Instead, she exclaimed breathlessly, "You came!"

Disappointment, and even a hint of sadness, passed over his features. "You didn't think I would?"

Her fingers curled tight around her champagne flute. "Honestly, I wasn't sure."

"You still haven't learned to believe in me, have you?" It was a simple question that didn't require an answer, and he didn't wait for one. "I've been here for a while. An hour at least. I've been watching you bask in your well-earned success."

She laughed and shook her head. "Amazing, isn't it?"

"Not considering the talent in all these designs," he said with a smile that went straight to her senses. "I had no doubt you could do it."

"I owe you a huge thanks," she said, the words feeling so inadequate when they'd shared so much.

"It's not your gratitude I want, Mia." There was a bite to his tone, and he glanced away for a moment as if to compose himself before looking at her again.

"I came in here to tell you that I know how difficult this was for you, to let your family see this side to you, but everyone I've talked to is very happy for you, Mia." His voice was gentle this time, as were the fingers he tenderly brushed across her cheek. "Now that you've put yourself out there, don't hide who you are inside. Be true to yourself, your feelings, and what you want out of life. And if this is it," he said, gesturing toward her work, "then embrace it with everything you have and everything you are."

He turned and left before she could reply, but his words remained with her long after he was gone. Could she be true to herself and what she wanted? With her stained-glass art, yes, she'd finally taken that step. But with Cameron . . . that loose end haunted her long after the guests had left for the evening.

By the end of the night, her career as a stained-glass artist had taken off. Her personal life, however, had crashed and burned.

Eighteen

MIA had known since the night of the gallery show that she and Amelia needed to talk, and it was a conversation long time in coming. She chose Sunday morning to pay a visit to Amelia, because she knew her father would be out fishing with his buddies and her stepmother would be home alone.

Mia pulled up to the house she'd grown up in and found Amelia out front on her knees as she planted new flowers along the walkway. Gardening was Amelia's passion, and Mia experienced a pang of regret for all the times her stepmother had tried to share her love of plants and flowers with Mia, only to have Mia rebuff her attempts.

Releasing a breath to ease her anxiety, Mia slid from the car and made her way toward Amelia, wondering if her stepmother would ever forgive her for being so self-centered and such a spoiled brat as a child. For rejecting the love and affection Amelia had tried so hard to offer her, until finally her stepmother stopped making the effort.

The clicking of her sandals on the walkway alerted her

stepmother of Mia's presence, and Amelia glanced up at her in startled surprise. She was wearing a wide-brimmed hat to shield her face from the sun, but the warmth Mia saw in her stepmother's eyes was from a different source entirely. It came directly from Amelia's generous heart, and this time Mia basked in that warmth and kindness like one of the flowers Amelia was planting.

Amelia smiled up at her. "Hi, Mia. Your father isn't home," she said automatically.

"I know." Mia shifted on her feet and swiped her palms down the sides of her jean skirt. "I stopped by to talk to you."

"Oh." That announcement took Amelia off guard, and she stood, tugging off her gardening gloves. "In that case, let's go inside. I could use a cool drink, and I just made some fresh lemonade this morning."

Mia followed Amelia into the kitchen, and when she tried to help with the drinks, Amelia gently shooed her away. So Mia sat down at the table, and a few minutes later Amelia set a glass of lemonade in front of her, along with an empty plate and a big basket of fresh baked muffins.

Mia picked one of her favorites from the abundance of baked goods—a French apple streusel muffin—and smiled at Amelia. There were enough muffins in the basket to feed a small army. "Were you expecting company?" she asked, a teasing inflection in her voice.

"Actually, no." Amelia laughed and selected a blueberry muffin for herself. "Somtimes I forget that it's just your father and I. I prepared such large meals for so many years to feed all you kids, the boys especially, and sometimes I slip back into old habits."

Mia sliced open her muffin and slathered butter on one side. "You took very good care of us, you know that, don't you?"

"I certainly tried." Amelia tipped her head toward Mia, her expression curious. "Where did that comment come from?"

"My heart," Mia said without hesitation, and because it was the truth. "I came by today because there's a whole lot of things I need to share with you. Things I should have said and done years ago."

Worry replaced Amelia's initial speculation. "Is everything okay?"

"I'm hoping it will be, after today." Mia took a bite of her muffin, taking the moment to gather her thoughts. "First, I want to apologize for the way I've treated you, and for not letting you be a part of my life."

"Mia," Amelia began softly, and Mia was certain her stepmother was about to smooth things over and tell her it was okay.

But her past behavior *wasn't* okay, and Mia held up a hand to stop Amelia from speaking. "I *need* to tell you this."

Amelia sat back in her chair, her gaze reflecting a deep understanding. "Okay."

Mia pushed her half-eaten muffin aside, her appetite gone for the moment. "When my real mother died I was only five, and because my father waited a month to tell me she'd passed away, and I didn't go to the funeral, I honestly believed my real mother was going to come back home someday. Then a few years later he married you, and I was in such denial I didn't want to accept you as my new mother. I resented your presence and what you stood for, and I rebelled and took it out on you. I'd lost my mother, and in my mind I felt as though I'd lost my father now, too."

Reaching across the table, Amelia placed her hand over Mia's. "Oh, honey, I never meant to make you feel that way."

"The thing is, you never did. It was all me." Accepting the blame that was her burden to bear, Mia curled her fingers over Amelia's hand and gave it a reassuring squeeze. "Then, as the years passed and I realized you weren't the wicked stepmother I'd imagined you to be, by then I was so certain you wouldn't love me because I'd been such an awful, disruptive child. I certainly didn't give you any reason to love me."

Mia's voice cracked with emotion, and she exhaled a trembling breath before continuing. "So it became easier and safer for me to keep my distance from you emotionally, than risking the kind of hurt and pain I'd gone through when I lost my mother. That was something I never wanted to experience again."

Amelia waved her hand between them. "First of all, I've always loved you and your brothers as if you all were my own. Even when you were an awful, disruptive child," she said with a gentle, maternal grin. Then she grew serious. "Your father and I decided not to have any children together because I was perfectly content with the four of you. But I'd be lying if I said I didn't miss not having a close mother-daughter type of relationship with you. Then again, I never wanted you to think I was trying to take your mother's place, so I took my cues from you."

And they'd been angry, selfish cues, Mia knew. "We've both missed out on so much. Is it too late to ask for your forgiveness, with the hope that maybe we can start out fresh and new from this point on?" This time, there were no fears or insecurities about opening herself up emotionally to Amelia. Mia was coming to realize that without risk, there was no gain.

"I'd like that very much." Moisture dampened Amelia's eyes—tears based in pure joy. She leaned toward Mia and wrapped her in a warm, tight hug. "All I ever wanted was for you to be happy, Mia."

Closing her eyes, Mia absorbed Amelia's embrace. Such a simple gesture that meant so much. Finally, they pulled apart and a smile played at the corners of Mia's mouth when she thought of how far she'd come in the past few weeks—and where she was headed. The confidence she felt was amazing and exhilarating. So was the inner peace filling her as a result of her visit with Amelia today.

"For the first time in my life, I'm *very* happy," Mia said and knew she meant every word.

Amelia's soft brown gaze searched Mia's expression. "Does it have anything to do with Cameron?"

Unsure where Amelia's question had stemmed from, Mia treaded cautiously, not quiet sure what she willing to reveal just yet. "What makes you ask that?"

"The night of the gallery show Joel made mention that he hoped things worked out between the two of you," Amelia said as she folded her arms on the table.

Mia was shocked to learn that Joel knew about her relationship with Cameron. She was even more stunned that her sometimes-overbearing brother hadn't said anything directly to her about it. Maybe, hopefully, her brothers were learning that she needed to stand on her own two feet and no longer needed them to shelter and protect her.

"I have to say, I agree with Joel," Amelia went on. "Cameron is a good man, and I could see by the way he watched you from afar that night that he cares for you very much."

Actually, Cameron *loved* her, Mia thought, reveling in the knowledge that such an incredible man wanted *her*. And there was no doubt in Mia's mind that she loved him as well. It had just taken her a little bit longer to embrace the emotion, to believe in it, to know it was lasting and true.

"Well, I'm finally in the right place, mentally and emotionally, to give my all to a relationship with Cameron," Mia said, thinking just how far she'd come in just a few short weeks. "There were some things I needed to take care of and do on my own first." Like going public with her stained-glass art and mending her relationship with Amelia. "And now, I'm ready to be the kind of woman Cameron needs in his life."

"So what are you waiting for?" Amelia encouraged her, as only a *mother* could do. "Go and tell him how you feel."

Mia planned to. Because she'd learned just how precious an emotion like love was, and she wouldn't take it, or Cameron, for granted ever again.

* * *

THE last person Cameron expected to find when he opened his front door was Mia. But there she was, looking like she'd just stepped from the dreams that consumed him on a nightly basis. Dreams of Mia, and what could have been.

She looked like a vision with her silky black hair tousled around her beautiful face and her soft gray eyes staring at him expectantly. *Hopefully.* She didn't try to hide the emotions in her gaze, the open vulnerability. But he also saw something else in her anxious expression. Real and candid feelings he dared to believe were meant for him.

A tremulous smile eased up the corners of her mouth. "Can I come in?"

He shook his head to clear it. To be sure she wasn't some kind of apparition. When she didn't disappear, he stepped back to let her enter. "Uh, yeah, sure."

He led the way into the living room and then turned to face her. "So what brings you by?"

"This, for starters." She stepped toward him and held out a long, flat package wrapped in dark blue paper. "It's for you."

If a part of him had been secretly hoping for an undying declaration of love, he'd been sorely mistaken. He glanced from the gift back up to Mia's face. She was biting her bottom lip, looking so endearing and tempting he ached to slide his fingers into her hair, pull her sweet mouth to his, and kiss her senseless.

He reined in the urge, because he'd yet to figure out her motives for visiting and the present she'd brought with her. Was it a parting gift or a token of her affection? "I don't remember it being my birthday."

"It doesn't need to be," she said and pushed it into his hands so he was forced to take the package from her. "Not for this. Open it, and you'll see."

His curiosity was definitely peaked. Sitting down on the couch, he tore the paper off the box and then lifted the lid. Because of the size of the package he had a good idea of what might be inside, and as he peeled back layers of tissue paper he discovered his assumption was correct. She'd given him one of her stained-glass designs. It was a piece he hadn't seen at her gallery show.

At first glance, he saw a striking, abstract pattern, one that was complex and intense, with vivid, brilliant colors that seemed to shimmer and glow with a life of its own. But it didn't take him long to see beyond that initial design, to the erotic image of a man and woman in a sensual, carnal embrace. The passion and emotion between the couple was nearly tangible, more so than he'd ever seen in any of her other stained-glass designs.

"I sketched that design after our first night together," she told him.

Which explained the chemistry and sexual tension radiating from the couple. While he understood that the man and woman in the picture represented the two of them, Cameron still had no idea why she'd given it to him. So he took a guess. "What is this? A souvenir of our time together?"

She was standing a few feet away, and she shifted on her sandaled feet, suddenly looking nervous and uncertain. "No, that picture is how I see our future. You and me, together."

His heart started pounding in his chest, but he wasn't about to assume anything. "You want an affair?"

She laughed lightly and shook her head. "I was thinking more along the lines of a *real* relationship. Going on real dates. No sneaking around my family or yours. Hand-holding in public."

Oh, he definitely liked the way that sounded, but her enthusiasm and turnaround seemed almost too good to be true. Especially after how they'd parted ways.

"Why?" he asked, needing to hear solid, concrete reasons. "What changed your mind? It's not like all those issues you brought up have gone away."

"No, they haven't gone away," she agreed. "And chances are it will take me some time to work through some of those issues. But as to what changed my mind? The answer is simple. I trust you, and more importantly, I love you, Cameron Sinclair. And I know you'll be there for me whenever I need you, to help me through those insecurities and fears that will creep up from time to time."

Cameron sucked in a sharp breath as the words *I love you* reverberated in his head. *Mia loved him.* He was afraid to speak for fear he'd shatter this incredible moment.

"But there's so much more I need to tell you," she said and paced across the living room as if to walk off some restless energy. "One of my biggest concerns, as you know, is that the differences between us will eventually drive us apart. You tried to reassure me, but at the time I wasn't willing to listen. I had this huge emotional barrier up where you were concerned because I honestly didn't believe that you could want a woman like me. Not for a lifetime."

"A woman like you?" he asked, interested in hearing how she viewed herself.

"Brazen. Reckless. Unpredictable." She smiled sheepishly. "Every one of those traits go against the upstanding, ethical kind of guy you are. And I always swore to myself that I wouldn't change for anyone."

Standing, he crossed the room to her, so close, but not as close as he wanted to be. "I'll admit you can drive me crazy with your wild antics sometimes, but I don't want to change anything about you, Mia. All I want is for you to let me love you."

"I know." Her gaze softened with adoration. "But I *have* changed, hopefully for the best. Walking away from you was one of the most painful things I've ever done, but it was necessary, because it made me sit back and reevaluate what's important to me and forced me to analyze my life. My past. Where I am today and what I want in my future. And with those realizations I've embraced my erotic stained-glass art as a part of who and what I am. I've made amends with Amelia, and I gave my brother Scott my two weeks notice at work so I can devote all my time to my stained-glass art."

Cameron was so proud of her. In just the past month she'd grown so much. Matured. Evolved in so many ways. All on her own.

He finally touched her, skimming his thumb along the silky soft line of her jaw, and saw his future in her eyes. "You are *so* amazing."

She gave him a cheeky grin. "You're not too bad yourself, sugar." She placed a hand on his chest, right over his rapidly beating heart. A heart that loved her unconditionally.

She tipped her head thoughtfully. "You know, I owe Carrie a big thanks. Because if it wasn't for those photographs she sent to me, I never would have come to you for help, and we'd probably still be provoking one another with smart-ass comments and skirting our attraction."

He couldn't contain a deep chuckle, but her words held a wealth of truth. "You're probably right."

"And those picture also made me realize that I don't want to be that attention-seeking woman any longer, not out in public, and not when I have you." Her features took on a serious cast. "But despite all my changes, I haven't turned into this neat little package you can peg, and I'm certain I never will be. I'm just not the sweet and docile type."

He smoothed a finger over her furrowed brow. "And I don't expect you to be, Mia."

That stubborn chin of hers lifted high. "That's good, because I know there will be times when I do things without thinking, and I'm sure I'll test your patience a time or two."

He groaned, knowing this woman would keep him on his toes and his life exciting. "You really are too wild to tame, aren't you?" he said, thinking back to the T-shirt she'd worn at The Electric Blue that first night.

"Come on, admit it," she murmured seductively and slid her arms around his neck. "You like that wild and daring side to me. And you like the fact that you've become more adventurous, too." She poised her mouth inches below his, tempting and teasing him with the promise of a kiss.

"I'll give you adventurous," he growled playfully. Done talking, he smoothed his hands beneath her skirt, cupped her bottom in his large palms, and lifted her against his body.

Her feet came off the floor, and she squealed and wrapped her legs around his waist to hold on while he made his way down the hall to the bedroom. There, he tossed her onto the mattress, and she laughed and came up on her elbows, watching as he quickly stripped off all his clothes. Then he grabbed her ankle and pulled her all the way down to the bottom of the bed where he proceeded to get her naked as fast as possible, too.

By the time he was done she was breathing hard, her breasts firm and full and her nipples tight. Her smoky gray eyes, filled with heat and desire, begged him to have his way with her. Her legs were splayed, and her sex glistened, beckoning to him in the sweetest kind of way.

He didn't waste time with foreplay. None was necessary, not when they were both so eager for a fast, hot, hard joining. Still standing at the foot of the bed, he lifted her legs so her ankles came to rest on his shoulders in a very erotic position that gave him complete control.

Her body accepted his deep driving thrust and the rhythmic pumping of his hips. She moaned and arched against him, taking him deeper, needing *more*. Flattening his hand on her stomach, he slowly drew it downward, until his thumb slipped between petal-soft folds of flesh and he was right where she needed his touch to be. He stroked her intimately, building the tension within her, and when she gave herself over to him in hot, liquid release and cried out his name, he sank into her one last time, let go, and came in a rush of intoxicating sensation.

He groaned like a dying man . . . and that's exactly what he felt like. As though he'd died and gone to the sweetest kind of heaven and ended up with an angel in his arms.

Once they both recovered, they scooted up on the bed and she automatically cuddled up to his side. He turned toward her, tipped her chin up, and kissed her—nice and slow and deep. He ran his hands slowly up and down the length of her body, loving the feel of her bare skin beneath his fingers. Loving everything about her.

"God, I missed you," he said after long, sensual minutes had passed.

She looked up at him, her eyes bright and vibrant. "I missed you, too. Badly." Her hand wandered down his chest, and that easily, that quickly, he felt his body stir again.

"You know, I'm afraid if we continue on like this your brothers are going to come after me with a shotgun," he teased and squeezed her bottom.

"So you'll be forced to make an honorable woman out of me?" She rolled her eyes, though it did sound like something her brothers would do. "No one is going to force you to marry me. It's the twenty-first century. Living in sin is pretty much acceptable these days."

He wondered if living in sin was *preferable* to her, and knew he wanted, needed, more than that. "So what would it take to convince you to marry me?"

Her eyes widened in startled surprise, which was quickly replaced with uncertainty. "A proposal?" she said cautiously, as if he'd just asked her a trick question. As if she couldn't believe he'd want to make her his wife.

Rolling to his side, he lifted up on his arm and stared down at her. A proposal was something he could easily handle. "Mia Wilde, I love you. Will you marry me? Will you be my lover, my best friend, my wife, and the mother of our children?"

Tears gathered in her eyes, tears of disbelief and joy and wonder. "Oh, wow," she breathed.

She was making him wait. Killing him with her silence.

Then she smiled, and he'd never seen her look so beautiful. So confident. So utterly unafraid. "Yes," she whispered. "Yes, I'll marry you."

"Thank God," he said in relief because he didn't want to have to go another day without her in it.

He kissed her again, and this time she pushed him onto his back and took charge. As she set out to seduce him, Cameron knew without a doubt that life with this particular Wilde woman would never be boring.

And he wouldn't want it any other way.